ACCLAIM F̶̶̶̶̶̶̶̶ OUTSTANDING NOVELS OF UNFLINCHING HORROR

'One of the best contemporary British horror writers
... Watch this man climb to Horror Heaven!'
Deathrealm

'Not since I discovered Clive Barker have I enjoyed
horror so much'
Nightfall

'A superb new horror writer'
Manchester Evening News

'Simon Clark is one of the most exciting British horror
writers around'
SFX

'*Vampyrrhic* is a dark and powerful novel which starts
slowly and innocently and builds to a crescendo of
violence and fear. Be prepared to sleep with the light
on until the memories of the horror dim'
Peterborough Evening Telegraph

'To say that Simon Clark is the best novelist to emerge
this decade is self-evident. Simon has simply out-
grown genre restrictions'
Andrew Darlington

'The hottest new purveyor of horrific thrills currently
working on these shores'
Big Issue

About the author

Born in 1958, Simon Clark lives in Doncaster, South York-shire. His short stories have appeared in several magazines and anthologies, including *Darklands 2*, *Dark Voices 5* and *The Year's Best Horror Stories* (four times). He has pub-lished a collection of short stories, *Blood and Grit*, and five earlier novels, *Nailed by the Heart*, *Blood Crazy*, *Darker*, *King Blood* and *Vampyrrhic*. His work has been broadcast on BBC Radio 4 and he has also written prose material for the internationally famous rock band U2.

You are welcome to visit the Simon Clark Web Page at:
www.bbr-online.com/nailed

The Fall

Simon Clark

NEW ENGLISH LIBRARY
Hodder & Stoughton

Copyright © 1998 by Simon Clark

First published in Great Britain in 1998
by Hodder and Stoughton
A division of Hodder Headline PLC
First published in paperback in 1999
by Hodder and Stoughton
A New English Library Paperback

A CIP catalogue record for this title
is available from the British Library.

ISBN 0 340 69611 7

Printed and bound in Great Britain by
Mackays of Chatham PLC, Chatham, Kent

Hodder and Stoughton
A division of Hodder Headline PLC
338 Euston Road
London NW1 3BH

This one's for Janet for having the patience
of at least half a dozen saints.

It's also for a number of mould-breaking individuals from
times past who influenced the writing of this book:-

Roger Rolle (1300–1349)
Arthur Machen (1863–1947)
James Marshall Hendrix (1942–1970)

INTRODUCTION:
SOME TRUE STORIES

This book is about time.

And time is a peculiar thing. Professor John Wheeler of Princeton University described time as 'nature's way to keep everything from happening all at once.' And although scientists have difficulty in agreeing a universal definition of time, most would agree that it is a one-way street: there's no going back.

But have you ever wished you could change history? Think of those big events such as wars, shipwrecks and aeroplane crashes where a quick trip back through time could save hundreds, thousands, if not millions of lives.

For instance, imagine you found yourself in Southampton on that fateful 10th April in 1912, just before the *Titanic* set sail for New York. Would you warn those about to board that it would sink? Like many people, I've slipped into the shoes of an imaginary time traveller and wondered what would have happened if I'd run along the queue of passengers telling them that an iceberg would open up the ship like a sardine can.

Probably like you, I reached the conclusion that in a very short time men in white coats would have come and taken me away to the place with padded walls where you eat dinner with a wooden spoon.

But I imagine, when all's said and done, that many people would prefer to change something that happened in their own personal past. How many times have we wished we could turn back the clock and warn ourselves not to set out on *that particular car journey?* Or wished we'd never bought *those particular shares.* Or that house, or that holiday. Or even married *that particular person* . . .

If there was a turnstile that led to the past I imagine it would be pretty much clogged by now with men and women trying to rush back into history. They might not have been going back with the intention of assassinating Hitler, or telling James Dean to keep the speed down, or suggesting to Buddy Holly that a plane ride on a certain night in 1959 is a definite no-no. But they might be keen to go back in time to avert some more personal disaster.

In fact, if you look back at your own life you realize there are a few such crucial moments when the course of action you chose changed your life. A job interview, a marriage proposal, or simply believing you could lean just that bit further out of your bedroom window to wipe away a speck of dirt from the glass . . . those life-changing moments seem to teeter on a knife's edge. So easily they can go one way or the other and the course of your life changes forever.

Now. Although the current consensus of opinion is that it's impossible, at present, to turn back the clock, many eminent scientists are confident that time travel might be possible in the next two hundred years. They speak of wormholes, black holes and quantum-mechanical tunnelling where particles have been shown to do the impossible: namely, to travel faster than the speed of light.

It makes you think, though, doesn't it? Wouldn't it be something if we were given just one opportunity to turn back the clock and prevent some godawful calamity in our lives? Which one would it be? I'm writing this introduction in the spring of 1998. It's almost a year to the day since my seven-year-old daughter jumped off a park bench and broke her arm. A bad break that *might* need surgery and *might* be permanently disabling, said the doctor. Fortunately, his original dark prognosis was wrong on both counts.

Although for weeks after I'd berate myself: 'Why did I have to watch the end of that stupid film? If only I'd gone and collected her from the park ten minutes earlier . . .' Luckily it wasn't a huge tragedy, harrowing though it was at the time. Still, if some time traveller just happened to be passing through 1998 I'd be tempted to hitch a ride back twelve months. Then I'd dash across to the park before Helen decided it would be the coolest thing to launch herself off the park bench.

Of course, I know I can't. Much as I long to. That nubby lump above my daughter's elbow where her bone snapped like a stick of celery is still there. It will always be there.

But time is a peculiar thing. Einstein states that the faster you travel the slower time passes. In the Seventies a pair of scientists loaded an atomic clock onto a Jumbo jet and proved just that.

And don't forget, a number of scientists are saying that their successors will be cranking up those first time machines in less than two hundred years.

Keep that in mind as we now move into stranger territories. On my bookshelves are a couple of leather-bound books that are more than two hundred years old. They belonged to my late grandmother, Ethel Skilton. I first saw them as I rummaged inquisitively through an ancient tin trunk when I was a child (which seems next to no time at all ago; again, time plays tricks on the mind as well as on reality). As I typed these opening pages an idea struck me: a strange and thought-provoking one at that. It occurred to me that if I can leaf through those two-hundred-year-old books today, isn't there every reason to suppose that someone two hundred years from now, say in the year AD 2200, just might possibly be reading this introduction to *The Fall*?

I know I'm fast-forwarding towards the pit of total whimsicality here, but consider this: there's also every chance that in the year 2200 time travel will be a reality. That men and women will be able to flit backwards and forwards through time like we today make those weekly runs to and from the supermarket. (Come to think of it, dear reader of 2200, do you have supermarkets? Perhaps you do, and perhaps that trolley with a wonky wheel is as enduring as Christmas and true love.) Well, here's my point: this introduction can serve as a message transmitted from here, 1998, into the future. If you're reading this long after I've gone, if the spine of the book is cracked, its pages falling out, and if you have access to that time machine, here's an invitation to call on me on Saturday, 11th April, 1998 in the little village of Hampole, South Yorkshire. There, at that time, I parked my red car near the spring that still gushes cold, pure water and waited from two p.m. BST until around ten past the hour. Why this particular location? That's easy. Until now the characters in my books have always been fictional. This one, however, features the real-life – and exceedingly astonishing – Roger Rolle who lived in Hampole from around AD 1340 to AD 1350. Teenage rebel, hermit, mystic and writer, he devoted most of his time, I think it's fairly safe to say, to 'boldly going where no man has gone before'. Reading his accounts of his transcendental voyages into his psyche still well and truly boggles the mind even today.

Anyway, dear reader of 2200, if you can make it to Hampole on that blustery April day in 1998, you can't miss me. I'm above average height, my head is shaved down to the wood (as one contemporary saying goes) and I'm wearing a wax jacket and black jeans. After pottering around the spring and taking a look at the rather dingy-looking monument to Mr Rolle I returned home for coffee where I chatted to my wife Janet about my time-travel experiment and about what happened during that short vigil.

If you don't have your own time machine, however, you're more than welcome to visit me in cyberspace. My URL address is:-

www.bbr-online.com/nailed

Well, I've talked about the nature of time for longer than I intended, and I've said nothing at all yet about *The Fall*. Like all of my novels the story surprised me as much as anyone. So, as always, I wonder deep down if the story somehow already exists in some other place – or time – and I just happen to be the one who sets it all down on paper.

About twelve months ago the book's characters came one by one into my life where they became so real they vied with my family for my time and, on occasion, managed to take over my waking hours completely.

In closing, I'd like to thank you for giving me the most precious commodity of all: *Your time*. And to invite you to turn to the first page of a strange tale that fascinated and sometimes frightened me as it either unspooled itself from some dark recess of my mind – or simply used me as a flesh-and-bone antenna. Well, either way, ladies and gentleman, the story is just about to start and that first page lies but a moment away . . .

Simon Clark
Doncaster, Yorkshire, 1998

Chapter One

One

Thursday was an amazing day. One to remember by anyone's standards.

A day of secrets shared.

Mysteries revealed.

New experiences.

Tobacco.

Jack Daniel's Tennessee sippin' whiskey.

Playboy magazine.

An entire cooked chicken.

Mayonnaise (for dunking).

Chocolate fudge cake, a whole quart of fresh cream.

Tony Urtz finally buying ammo for his rifle.

A crisp $50 bill.

Which was probably the catalyst for such a day as this, anyway. And the Vermont sun shone down, basting the whole damn' scene in hot, brilliant sunshine.

The three twelve-year-olds sat high in the pear tree upon a platform of good seasoned timber. The three were Sam Baker, a New Yorker, and Vermonters Jools McMahon and Tony Urtz. The Vermonters were home-grown natives of a fly-speck that sat an easy stone's-throw from Route 91, complete with a homely white-spired church and a village green.

Tony Urtz, barefoot and carefree, wore a red checked

shirt complemented by a straw hat frayed to whispy strands around the rim. He smoked a corn-cob pipe while caressing the barrel of the rifle that lay across his knees. The fact that he looked a lot like a popular image of Huckleberry Finn wasn't lost on Sam Baker.

In contrast to Tony's countrified look was Jools McMahon's image of urban chic with Levis, a 'Just Tokin' Dope' T-shirt, sunglasses and old trainers that looked sassy rather than scruffy.

Sam Baker, as always, felt awkward in the clothes his mother had chosen for him. As if he'd borrowed them from someone else. Even at twelve years old he knew clothes should fit you psychologically as much as physically. These yellow chinos and jungle-pattern shirt made him feel overlarge, gangling and anything but cool.

Nevertheless, he sat there with his back to the tree trunk, legs stretched out in front of him, with as much nonchalance as he could muster. All three sat, or lay, on the boards of the platform, which rested on the branches of the pear tree some twenty feet above the soft green grass of the orchard. Arranged around them on the platform were the goodies they'd bought with a crisp, sweet-smelling fifty-dollar bill that providence had brought their way. The chicken, now picked down to its bones, attracted a softly buzzing fly or two; there were cartons of rifle shells and cigarettes; the magazine opened at the centrefold and the rest of the finger-lickin' stuff.

This is good living, Sam thought contentedly, taking his turn at the whiskey bottle (wetting his lips only, not drinking: he didn't want to barf back the chicken, cake and cream). After passing the bottle to Tony, he pulled lazily on the cigarette, all the time savouring the illicit, buzz-in-your veins thrill of it all.

Especially he liked the comradeship of his two new friends. And he loved to sit with them doing a whole lot of nothing in particular: chatting about this and that, sipping whiskey, allowing his eyes to contentedly rest on the beautiful scenery that comprised a dozen or so acres of apple and pear trees, heavy with fruit and set on a slope running gently downhill in the direction of the Connecticut River that shone like a highway of liquid silver beneath the noonday sun. In the sky a single cloud radiated black arms like the ghost of some spiral galaxy. But for the moment the sun shone clear and free.

'Boys. Reckon it might rain some?' Tony Urtz spoke slowly in his best old-man-a-rockin'-on-his-porch style.

'Yup,' Jools and Sam agreed.

'Best make the most of this sunshine then, boys.' Tony sucked thoughtfully on the corn-cob pipe while watching Sam light another cigarette. 'This the first time you smoked cigarettes, young feller?' He pronounced cigar-ettes 'see-gar-rettes'.

'Nope,' Sam said, imitating the lazy Southern drawl. 'Been smoking since I was knee high to Jimminy Cricket.'

'You know, once that nicotine works its way into your blood? Gets ya like hookworm. Yah'll never get it out. Devil old nicotine we call it round abouts here.' Tony pronounced nicotine as 'nick . . . oh . . . teen', stretching out the vowel sounds by about a mile or so into that easy drawl which was nothing like his own New England accent.

'And don't forget the liquor, y'all? She gets in your system, nothing gonna get that bitch out no way, no how,' Jools added in a mock Southern style that veered more to cotton-pickin' Uncle Tom than any genuine patois. 'Ashes to ashes, dust to dust, if the liquor don't get yer, the women must.' They laughed. Tony let his leg swing over the edge of the platform. Again he looked the image of Huckleberry Finn: for all the world he could have been smoking his corn-cob pipe on a raft while allowing his bare toes to be caressed by the waters of the muddy Mississippi.

Sam Baker knew this was the day he could be honest about himself, tell any kind of secret, confess anything, and it would be heard by the other two with mature under-standing. *Perhaps this is what it's like to be an adult,* he thought. If it was then growing old was just fine with him.

So, on impulse, he switched the cigarette from his right hand to his left. Then he held up his right hand, fingers splayed.

Tony drawled lazily. 'Burn yourself on your cigarette there, young feller?'

'Want to see something gross?' Sam asked, dropping the Southern drawl.

'I see your hand, boy. I see nothing gross.' Tony pushed back the rim of his hat with his finger.

'Don't you see anything? Anything strange?'

'Only friction burns from excessive personal abuse.' Tony and Jools dissolved into boozy giggles. Their laughter was enough to shake the platform, toppling an empty coke can that rolled over into fresh air and dropped down onto the turf twenty feet below.

'No.' Sam grinned. 'My hand. What's wrong with it?'

'Give us a clue.'

'Look, I've got five fingers.'

They both giggled again. Tony took off his hat and fanned his face with it. 'We've all got five fingers, boy. Hadn't you better lay off of that darn booze for a while?'

'No, you haven't.' Sam's grin broadened. 'You've got four fingers and a thumb. Look. I've got five fingers.'

'Jesus. Let's have a look,' Tony said as both he and Jools quickly kneeled up on the platform to grab a closer look.

'How the hell did that happen?' Jools asked, so impressed he had to slip off his sunglasses to examine Sam's fingers.

'I was born with five fingers and a thumb on each hand. That's a grand total of twelve digits.'

'What happened to the thumbs?'

'I had an operation to remove them. My parents didn't want me to grow up looking like a mutant.'

'Cool.'

'Is that the scar where they chopped off the thumb?' Tony asked, pointing to an oval-shaped mark near one of Sam's wrists.

'That's the one. You can still feel the nub of bone beneath the skin. Here, feel.' Each solemnly touched the scar tissue that covered the nubby bump of bone. 'The joint's still there. Feel it going up and down? I can still wiggle the stump under the skin.'

'Uh! Now that *is* gross!' Jools exclaimed with a delighted grin. 'C'mere, let me have a look at your thumb again.'

All three studied Sam's left hand. 'There, you can tell now, can't you? Fingers have two joints, thumbs have one. That there digit on my hand is in the same place as the thumb but it's got two joints.'

'Ergo a finger,' Tony said, dropping his Southern drawl at long last. 'Didn't they let you keep the thumbs in a jar of formaldehyde or something?'

'No. Like I said, I was a baby when they chopped them.'

Jools replaced his sunglasses on the bridge of his nose, then solemnly raised the bottle of Jack Daniel's. 'We should toast the guy with five fingers per hand. All hail the mutant.'

'All hail the mutant,' Tony echoed and reached out for his turn from the bottle.

After that, they toasted the girls in the magazine, then the pears on the tree, then whatever they could muster.

'All hail the black cloud,' Tony raised the bottle to the cloud that spiralled slowly above them. 'May it never piss on our parade.'

'May it never piss on our parade,' they all echoed. As Jools took his slug of whiskey he suddenly thought of something. 'Hey, we forgot to buy peppermints. My Dad's sure to smell the whiskey on my breath.'

'No, he won't,' Tony said with a wry smile.

'Why not?'

'The cigarettes'll mask the smell.'

'Oh yeah, he'll tear me a new corn chute for these, too.' He held up the cigarette, gave it an accusing glare, then, shrugging, put it into his mouth again. 'What the hell. I'll brush my teeth when I get in. Say,' he sat up, remembering. 'You all going to the fair on Saturday?'

Tony clasped the pipe between his teeth. 'Count me in, boy.'

'Sam?'

'Sure. If I can get . . . oh, hell, no. I can't.'

'Why not? Damned fine rides there.'

Sam felt disappointment weigh down in his stomach like a stone. 'I'm going home Saturday. Shit. I forgot all about that.'

'Back to New York?' Tony asked, dismayed. 'You can't. School isn't for another fortnight yet.'

'I know, but my dad's flying in from Miami and I arranged to spend that last fortnight with him. Oh, shit.'

'Well, you'll be relieved to get away from this hicksville.' Tony took a slug from the bottle. 'Back to the Big Apple. I bet it's pretty cool roaming those mean streets, isn't it?'

'Yeah,' Sam said with no enthusiasm whatsoever. 'It's OK.'

The truth was he didn't roam any mean streets. New York was a God Almighty prison for most kids. If you weren't at school you stayed home with the door of the apartment locked and bolted. In his neighbourhood you certainly didn't go out after dark. Night-time was the personal territory of street gangs, pimps, drug dealers and any demented asshole with a gun.

No and damned no. Shit to it. Shit with bells and whistles stuck into the whole steaming heap. He wanted to stay here among the hills, fields and forests of Vermont. He wanted to stay with his friends who were open, honest and easygoing. Through the branches of the tree, dangling pears in crazy profusion, he could see the white timber house where he was staying with his aunt and uncle. Here you could leave your windows open to the fresh air. There was no need for deadlocks, security shutters and electronic surveillance systems designed to stop some smackhead razoring your throat open as you slept. You didn't live with the perma-hum of the air-conditioner. You didn't breathe that Big Apple air of car fumes and fear. Shit, this was a good place. He liked it.

'Uh-oh.' Tony cocked an eye at the sky. 'Looks as if black Bertha's gonna piss on our parade after all.'

A single raindrop fell onto the magazine, splashing wetly on the bare stomach of Gina La Touche, the blonde bombshell from Arkansas. (Only the cuffs didn't match the collar, as Tony Urtz sagely observed.)

'You save the ladies, Jools,' Tony said, closing the magazine. 'I'll grab the booze. Sammy boy, you take the cigarettes. Got anywhere you can stash them at your aunt's place?'

'No problem,' Sam said as another raindrop splashed onto a carton of rifle shells.

'Can't let these babies get wet,' Tony said, taking off his hat. Quickly, he popped the cartons of ammunition into it and then covered it with a plastic carrier bag. 'Righty-ho, boys, where do we go from here?'

Sam opened his mouth to speak. He wasn't ever sure if he did manage to get the reply past his lips. Nor was he ever sure exactly what did happen in the next two to three minutes. Because that was when his universe – space and time and the whole of creation – was turned inside out in one searing flash of bluish-white light.

Two

The cloud had been drifting north, pushed by warm, sticky air from the Gulf of Mexico. It had begun life as a tropical storm, shredding palm trees, flattening tobacco plants, tearing the corrugated-iron roofs off houses from Jamaica to Cuba. Its passing there would jack up the price of bananas in supermarkets nationwide six months from now; already farmers were burning ruined crops while turning their minds to the task of lobbying governments for disaster relief.

But all that was a long way from the orchard in Vermont.

Now the cloud was slowly dying. In an hour or two it would dissipate in the cool, clear air above the pine-clad mountains of the American-Canadian border. But at a little after one on that Thursday afternoon it decided on one final act of violence (if you choose to anthropomorphize a billion or so water droplets that have become electrically charged): whatever – it discharged a hundred million volts in the form of a lightning bolt to the ground.

The nearest thing to it that could be described as an 'earth' was the pear tree in which the three twelve-year-olds sat.

Three

Sam Baker's recollection of the lightning strike made no sense to him for years afterward. He recalled a series of images so vivid they seemed to have been burned deep into his very brain tissue. But even though he tried his hardest he could not order them into their proper sequence.

He remembered standing beneath the pear tree. The grass was a stunning green: a far brighter green than it should have been. (Grass stalks had been boiled in their own juices by the lightning flash, so his uncle later told him.) The pear tree had become a blackened skeleton. Pears, cooked first on the branch, steamed on the ground, the pulpy flesh bursting from the skins. While hanging thickly in the air was the sweet aroma of the fruit's roasted flesh. And Sam remembered being suspended in space, floating as weightlessly as an astronaut. For some reason he was convinced he was floating upward into what appeared a snowstorm of swirling flakes. Only these flakes were a violent electric blue that swirled around him in a dazzling shower of sparks.

And he remembered a great silence.

A complete and utter silence that, as he later reasoned, must have been impossible because the lightning flash would have been accompanied by an almost simultaneous explosive roar of thunder.

Whether these images or hallucinations – tag on any label you want – came before or after his memory of standing beneath the tree, blasted black by lightning, he couldn't tell. (And the doctor at the hospital did indeed stress that shock –

both physical and mental – would scramble all memories until they were a cock-eyed mess of fragmented pictures).

He recalled, too, clumps of clothing lying on the ground, gently smouldering. What he took at first to be red buttons on a shirt were little spots of flame. He saw the sun-glasses worn by Jools lying on the ground with one lens knocked out. He saw the burning stock of the rifle, the steel barrel bent into a question-mark shape. A symbol for this singular experience? Most wonderful of all was that an angel lay on its back on the grass, asleep. It was an angel, he decided, because the face was made out of gold. He saw the nose, the chin, the forehead, the closed eyes all covered with a golden skin. It was only months later that he realized that what he had actually seen was the dead body of Tony Urtz. The brass cases of the rifle ammunition had melted in the lighting blast and sprayed into his face like an aerosol. Doctors, police, friends, relatives – all assured Sam that Tony Urtz wouldn't have felt a thing. That he must have been dead by the time the molten metal splashed his skin.

No one survives a lightning strike like that.

But then why did I? Sam would ask himself this for years to come. *How come I stood there in the centre of that electric furnace and survived?* Physically suffering nothing more serious than singed eyebrows and a bruised shoulder from the fall out of the tree.

In the hospital the Sheriff had stood by Sam's bed, turning his hat round and round through his fingers, and tried to answer that one.

'Lightning strikes are strange things, Sam. Why, I've seen where they've hit a group of golfers on the green. It takes one and spares another even though they might be closer to one another than you and I are now. I know losing your two friends like that's going to be hard. Not much takes the pain out of it. That is, unless you have religious convictions?'

Sam had shaken his head, then closed his eyes.

And all the time the memories were there inside his head. They were painted in vivid, jangling colours as bright and as unreal as when you fool around with the colour control on your TV. He remembered standing there. In the ruins of the scorched tree. The bodies of his friends burning at his feet. Tony Urtz in his mask of brass. A bumble-bee had walked down across the burnished forehead to the tip of the shining nose. The smell of roasting pears with their sweet-as-syrup aroma. The grass that was a brilliant day-glo green. And there, nesting among the grass stalks, was a pocketful of nickels and dimes fused into a single lump; white butterflies the size of paperback books flitted to and fro.

And there were images that came right out of left field, too. Jumbled with what must have been genuine memories were rogue images of a man hanging on this huge wooden cross. He had jet black hair and wore peculiarly vivid red shoes. A ghost girl sat beside him singing in a soft, husky voice, 'Buffalo girls gonna come out tonight, gonna come out tonight . . .'

The face of a bearded man with his eyes as lightly closed as a sleeper's suddenly loomed before Sam. The man opened his eyes. And the moment the eyelid unsealed itself from the skin beneath the eye something darted from the eye socket to strike Sam on the lip, pricking it so sharply it felt as if he'd been stabbed with a pin.

Sam rocked back on his heels in surprise.

And all the time, the girl sang under her breath:-

> 'Buffalo girls gonna come out tonight,
> Gonna come out tonight . . .'

Of course, those were just dreams, he told himself. *Do you hear, Sam Baker?* Nothing more than bizarre hallucinations triggered by what was, after all, one hell of a shock.

What really happened immediately after the lightning strike was that his aunt had found them.

He remembered she'd run back to the house and returned with a wet flannel with which she'd washed his face as he stood there, still as a statue. Weird. Why she washed his face he didn't really know, nor had she ever explained the reasons since. Only she must have decided it was vitally important, and that it seemed the right thing to do. To vigorously rub away the sooty smears and scorched remains of his eyebrows with the wet flannel while his friends lay at his feet roasted to their very hearts.

Later, back home in New York, he'd sit up late at night with his electric guitar across his knee, his fingers probing the fretboard for notes, even for sounds that would say how it feels to stand there eyeball to eyeball with death. He was going to compose a song about it.

Only he never did find the sounds. He could never even find a title. Meanwhile, outside, the city's traffic played its own melancholy heart-song that, in its own way, sounded like the rumble of distant thunder.

And he'd fall asleep thinking back to that holiday in Vermont when he was twelve years old. It was the first time he'd smoked a cigarette, drunk whiskey, fired a rifle. Oh, boy . . . that Thursday should have been an amazing day.

Chapter Two

Fourteen years after the lightning strike that had knocked Sam Baker out of the pear tree and killed his two friends, he kicked open the TV studio's gallery control room and headed for the staff lounge, where he poured himself a well-earned coffee.

After sitting in the director's chair, mixing four hours of football that was being beamed out live across the whole of the blessed United States, he was more than ready to remove his head and leave it in a refrigerator to chill for a while. His brain sizzled like a hot roast inside his skull. At least, that was what it felt like. It had been a hell of an evening. Two cameras at the stadium had gone on the fritz. The commentator had forgotten the players' names and had um'd and ah'd his way through the first match. Thunderstorms cavorting over New York had played havoc with the microwave link-ups.

Now Sam lusted after a few beers – a few very cold beers – in the Irish bar across the street. Then he wanted to go home to bed where a few hours' sleep might soothe his frazzled brain.

Hell, whoever said TV work was glamorous needed their own head tested for brain-tissue content. Or lack thereof.

As the sign over the coffee machine so rightly said, *You don't have to be mad to work here – but it helps.*

Sam folded himself down into one of the low armchairs, closed his sore, tired eyes and sipped the coffee.

'My God, Mr Baker, how people would envy you! Paid good money to sit with your eyes closed and drink free coffee.'

The voice felt like a slap against his jangling head. Nevertheless, Sam smiled and gave a mock salute. 'I'm not sleeping, I'm just regaining my will to live.'

A man of around fifty with flyaway white hair and a pink bow tie stubbed his cigar out into a potted plant on the window-sill before helping himself to coffee. Joe Kane was one of the indestructibly cheerful sort. Even after a ten-hour shift as deputy station manager. Grinning, he sipped his coffee with a grateful 'Ah . . . that hits the spot. You're not finding that director's chair a might too big, eh, Sam? Too wild and woolly?'

'What, me? Sam the Wonderkid? Hell, no.' He smiled. 'Give me six hours' sleep and I'll be ready for the noon shift tomorrow.'

'Oh, you're on *Football Shots* at twelve?'

'Sure am.'

'I see.' Joe Kane looked down at his reflection in the coffee cup, his forehead wrinkling as he worked through a problem. 'I'll have to ask Katie to sit in the director's hot seat, then.'

Jesus Christ, I'm being fired! were the words that snapped through Sam's head. He sat up straight, suddenly wide awake. 'What's happening, Joe? I've been directing *Football Shots* for the last six months; I've been keeping it fresh, haven't I?'

'Fresh as a daisy, Sam.'

'But it sounds from where I'm sitting as if I'm being shown the exit.'

'Fired?' Joe raised his white eyebrows in surprise. 'No, you're not being fired, Sam. Far from it. With all those director's awards cluttering up your mantelpiece you're obviously far too brilliant for your own good.'

'I take it this is where you give me the choice of whether to hear the bad news or the good news first. Am I right?'

'Something like that, Sam.'

'OK, shoot.'

Joe took a seat opposite Sam and looked round the lounge to make sure that they were alone. Then he leaned forward in a way that suggested he was going to share a secret. 'The lady up-stairs,' he began in a low voice, 'needs someone to plug a hole in our ranks . . . our directorial ranks, that is.'

Sam leaned forward, head tilted slightly, listening hard, trying to detect any sign he was being sidelined, or demoted into directing weather bulletins or some other low-grade programming.

Joe continued in the low voice, not wanting to be overheard by station staff passing by in the corridor, 'Danny Trepinski's taking a little vacation.'

'Danny? He never goes on vacation. Why, his butt might be nailed to the director's chair for all the times he leaves it.'

'Ah, well, there was a melodramatic scene in the station manager's office this morning. Danny Trepinski was called to the office just before lunch to find not only the lady upstairs herself there but also his wife and sister. Can you believe that?'

'I think I'm starting to get the picture.' Sam mimed drinking from a bottle. 'Glug, glug?'

'Spot on, Sam. The management and his own family ganged up on Danny and forced him to go dry out at Tranquillity Meadows or whatever crapola name they call it. They got him into a hospital car so fast he didn't even have time to collect his jacket. In short, he's got three weeks to kiss the vodka bottle goodbye or he's out of here on his bony ass.'

Sam nodded, half guilty, half relieved that the bad news didn't involve him. 'Poor Danny. There but for the grace of God . . .'

Joe pointed a finger at Sam's coffee. 'So, you stick to that stuff . . . you'll be all right. Savvy?'

'Aye, aye, captain. But where does that leave me? Danny Trepinski doesn't cover sports. He's strictly light entertainment.'

'Well, here comes the good news, Sam. You've been promoted. And your first assignment is for something your colleagues here would kill for.'

Again, Sam felt a surge of suspicion. 'And that assignment is?'

'You're going to direct a live rock concert!'

'A rock concert? Be serious, Joe, I've never handled anything like that before. What if I make a hash of it?'

'You won't. The lady upstairs has every confidence in you.'

'But Joe—'

'But Joe nothing. It's outside-broadcast work just like football or athletics or baseball. You can sleepwalk through it.' Joe's smile faded. 'You're not going to walk away from an opportunity like this, are you, Sam?'

Sam shook his head and smiled. The only way he could walk away from this assignment was to walk away from the building and never come back. 'No way,' he said, injecting a note of confidence into his voice. 'As you say, it's a great opportunity. When is it?'

'A week on Thursday. Some big stars, Sam. Pull this off and you can write your own ticket. Any questions?'

'Only one: where is it? Carnegie Hall?'

'Out of town.'

'Boston?'

'A little further east than that.' He paused, enjoying keeping Sam in suspense. 'England.'

'England?'

'Sure, a little island across the Atlantic. You can find it in any atlas. And don't worry, you can drink the water and they speak the same language – more or less, anyway.' Chuckling at Sam's wide-eyed expression, he climbed to his feet and dumped his cup in the bin. 'Oh, you best move quickly. You're booked on a flight that goes in precisely . . .' He looked at his watch. '. . . Precisely thirteen hours. Bon voyage. And don't forget to send us all a postcard and a beefeater doll or two.'

Outside, thunder rumbled like the stirring of ancient gods.

Chapter Three

Ben Middleton made his last check of the evening. He strolled round the kennels, murmuring gently to the dogs that were his paying guests, reassuring them that their owners still loved them and that they would soon return from holiday to take them home.

Ben was sixty years old, short, stocky, with a full head of baby-fine blond hair and with big, baby-blue eyes to match. He was a kindly man, well liked by his staff.

He ambled slowly along the gravel paths that linked the kennel buildings. The dusk air was warm, still. Swarms of midges hovered above the lawns. The fifty or so dogs were settling down for the night, making barely a sound as they turned round and around on their beds as their ancestors had done for the past twenty million years before them.

Ben paused to gaze back at the house of honey-coloured stone. It looked warm and comfortable in the last lingering rays of sunlight and he found himself relishing the prospect of sitting in front of the television with a glass of wine and his own dogs sleeping at his feet.

Already the light sensors had tripped the power on the big sign on the gable end wall. Bold letters spelt out the name of the business to which he, Ben Middleton, had devoted his life:-

PERSEVERANCE FARM BOARDING KENNELS
TEL. CASTERTON 334499
(ESTAB. BY HAROLD MIDDLETON, 1902)

For a moment or so, he dead-headed flowers in the hanging baskets that hung on the wall of what had once been the old barn.

Two years ago he had had the barn's hayloft converted to a records office but Mrs Newton, whom he employed as a secretary, flatly refused to use it. Perhaps he should have seen something like it coming because Mrs Newton moonlighted as a clairvoyant, holding 'readings' at her home in Casterton.

'What's wrong with the office, Mrs Newton?' he'd asked her politely. 'Is it the stairs?'

'What do you take me for, Ben Middleton? A geriatric? No, of course it isn't the stairs.'

'But the—'

'I could manage twice as many stairs as that, thank you very much.'

'But it seems such a comfortable-looking—'

'No . . . well, you see, Ben, the building has bad vibes.'

'Bad vibes?'

'Yes, something happened there that wasn't quite right.'

'Oh, a death?' Ben Middleton knew of her part-time clairvoyant work. He nodded good-naturedly. He'd seen enough of a dog's sixth sense not to disbelieve in the paranormal entirely.

'Oh, no.' Mrs Newton had looked the old barn over with wide, knowing eyes. 'Not a death. But when I'm alone in the office, especially when it's getting dark on winter's afternoons, I can hear noises.'

'Noises?'

'Yes, banging, sawing, hammering, shouting as if a whole army of people is working.'

'Well, this was a working farm once, so I imagine farmhands and the like would have worked in the barn to repair ploughshares and—'

'Oh no, it's nothing like that. These people are working because their lives depend on it. Oh, I get so cold, Ben, when I hear it. It's like an icy hand just gets a-hold of me. I can

22

hardly breathe, I shiver from head to foot, and do you know why?'

'No. Why, Mrs Newton?'

'Fear. Pure fear. Not mine, but theirs. The people who are working in the barn are terrified for their lives. Something horrible has happened to them and they're working, working, working. Because they know if they don't finish whatever it is they're doing they'll be . . . well . . .' She took a breath. 'They'll suffer in a way that doesn't bear mentioning.'

'Perseverance is a very old farm. I understand it was occupied by Cromwell's forces after the battle of—'

'No, I don't see that, Ben.'

'What do you see, Mrs Newton?'

'That's what's so strange. It's all so confused. I see people dressed in old-fashioned clothes, oh, Victorian, I suppose, and they're shouting, *shouting*; it's not anger, it's through fear and urgency. Hurry, hurry, hurry! And I hear this hammering sound going on and on. You know, Ben, I think that—'

'Now, now, Mrs Newton, don't go upsetting yourself. Why don't we move the records office back into the annexe? I know it's a little on the small—'

'Oh, will you, Ben? Thank you. You know, that's such a weight off my mind.'

'Ah, we must keep our staff happy, Mrs Newton. You know the dogs react to our emotions. If we're unhappy or ill at ease then it's so easy for them to go off their food and begin to pine.'

And that's how the conversation went. Mrs Newton got what she wanted.

Ben Middleton moved the furniture back to the annexe. After the third trip up to the hayloft he murmured to himself, 'Bad vibes, my foot. It's the stairs, after all.'

But then the barn was a peculiar place. When he'd been clearing the accumulated dirt from the stone floor last year he'd found a coin. It had been buried under a thick concrete-like mud. Delighted, he'd hurried away to clean it, wondering if it might be a Victorian sovereign or some such treasure. After carefully soaping it with washing-up liquid and rinsing it under the tap, he'd dabbed it dry with kitchen roll.

The coin was blackened with age. He began to speculate that it might be part of some highwayman's horde from centuries ago.

Moments later he'd held the coin under the kitchen light and scrutinized it closely. Forehead wrinkling, he managed to make out the date. At first he'd read it as 1897 . . . then 1797.

'Oh?' he'd said, surprised, as he used his thumbnail to scrape away a spot of dirt. '1997?' The coin was nothing more than a ten-pence piece minted a couple of years ago. All that work, too. He blew out his cheeks. Why, it looked as if the thing had been buried there a century, never mind a few months. Surmising that the mud in the barn possessed powerful aging properties he'd dropped the coin into the PDSA collection box and thought nothing more about it.

With it all but dark now Ben walked back to the house. Once inside he locked the doors, then checked that the CCTV monitors were working.

He fully appreciated that the people who boarded their dogs here at Perseverance Farm wanted to know their animals would be safe as well as having heated kennels, individual outdoor runs and the like. Ben was happy to reassure them. His establishment boasted closed-circuit television surveillance which he could monitor from a bank of screens in his living room in the farmhouse.

He poured a glass of wine, then stood with a black Labrador pup under one arm and watched the four TV screens for a moment. Three showed high-level views of the kennel buildings, the fourth covered the area just outside the front door at eye level.

'All shipshape and Bristol fashion,' Ben announced.

From there he went to the sofa. His other three dogs had already claimed the hearthrug.

For an hour he watched television. The Labrador pup curled up in his lap slept soundly.

Ben wasn't particularly interested in what the television had to offer. Tonight it just happened to be a crusty detective with a permanently sour expression who was on the trail of a murderer in San Francisco. If anything, Ben simply enjoyed being part of his pack at rest. He sensed some kind of mystic link between himself and the dogs. They – and he included himself – weren't individuals as such, but each was part of a whole. If one dog was disturbed by a noise, all would lift their heads, Ben included, look round for a moment, then, when all were satisfied nothing was amiss, they'd relax once more.

He sipped his wine.

The TV detective ate doughnuts in a seedy diner while claiming that although his methods weren't orthodox they got results.

Ben's attention wandered to the framed photograph of his great-grandfather on the wall. Harry Middleton had battled childhood illness to become a successful solicitor, justice of the peace and alderman. Unusually, for a product of the Victorian age, Harry Middleton had despised any kind of cruelty to animals. More than once he'd torn the whips from horsemen who had been beating their animals and broken the instruments of brutality over his knee. Later in life, he'd retired from the legal profession to set up a stud farm and dog-breeding business. Gradually, over the years, it had evolved into what it was today, a thriving boarding kennel.

For Ben Middleton no saint stood nearer to the Almighty than his great-grandfather Harry Middleton.

Ben allowed his eyelids to droop. His drowsy breathing synchronized with that of the dogs.

At a little after eleven he suddenly snapped awake. The dogs had lifted their heads and were looking round, eyes bright. Even though he'd slept, by some miracle the glass still stayed upright in his hand.

For a moment Ben wondered what had disturbed the dogs.

He couldn't hear anything. The dogs in the kennels weren't barking.

He looked round the room. Everything was in its place.

Then he turned to the curtained window. A brilliant white light shone through it.

Something had triggered the security lighting.

Placing the glass on the table, but still carrying the puppy, he walked quickly to the CCTV monitors. He had a sneaking suspicion what he would see. Often he'd watch the monitors and see a fox slinking along the paths between the kennels. Of course, the dogs couldn't get out and the fox couldn't get in. Still, there would be pandemonium as all those domestic pets scented for the first time in their lives an animal from the wild. Ben thought there must be something exciting and provocative about that scent because the dogs would bark like mad.

Ben screwed up his eyes at each colour monitor in turn.

Beneath the brilliant lights the paths gleamed whitely. Moths attracted to the lamps darted in and out like specks of fire.

But there was no sly old fox.

Occasionally, however, there would be a dog owner returning home late from the airport who'd decide to call in en route. Strictly speaking, clients had to collect animals during office hours, but Ben appreciated that some people missed their pets so much they just couldn't wait. Ben understood the emotion well enough. The idea of being away from his own dogs for two days – never mind two whole weeks – was nothing less than nightmarish to him.

He turned his attention to the monitor that showed the area around the front door.

Again it revealed nothing more than flitting moths, ornamental shrubs and the low hedge that bordered the front garden.

He thumbed the button that activated the intercom.

'Hello? he said. The speaker beside the front door would carry his voice into the front garden.

He listened for an apologetic, 'We're sorry to trouble you so late but we wondered if we could collect . . .' The sentence would be rounded off with a dog's name.

But there was no answering voice.

'Hello?' he repeated. 'Can I help you?'

He listened for the sound of a voice, or at least footsteps on the gravel path.

Nothing.

But he had begun to hear barking coming from the kennels. Already, his own dogs were standing, ears pointing, muscles tense.

'Now, now, now, what's all this, then?'

He studied the front-door monitor, thinking he'd caught a faint sound.

He cocked his head to one side in unconscious imitation of his dogs.

At first he thought static had affected the speaker.

He could hear a faint sizzling. It was almost the same sound as sand being drizzled onto paper.

Strange.

The speaker had never done that before.

Maybe there was going to be a thunderstorm?

But, come to think of it, it was more of a hiss than a sizzle. *Wait* . . .

He glimpsed a shadow on the path. Expectantly, he waited for a figure to appear, but the shadow receded again, almost as if whoever had cast it had retreated into the bushes.

Now this is odd, he told himself. *Most odd indeed*.

He still cocked his head to one side as that sizzling (or hissing) sound receded.

Wait a minute, he told himself. Now he did see a shape at the edge of the monitor screen that hadn't been there before. Perhaps he was seeing a shoulder or part of a head in extreme close-up. Certainly an indistinct bulk.

He scratched his head. 'Hello. This is Perseverance Farm Boarding Kennels. Can I help you at all, please?'

He leaned forward, holding the puppy close to his chest. Carefully, he studied the screen from a distance of a few inches.

Then a bizarre thing happened.

Shocked, he recoiled from the screen as an image suddenly filled it.

For a moment he stared at it. It didn't make sense.

He blinked. He was looking at what appeared to be a nest full of blackbird chicks. He saw the open beaks, the fluffy bodies. All were chirping noisily as if agitated.

'The cruel devils,' Ben said at last, shocked. Not only cruel but deeply perverse.

He realized now what was happening. Someone had taken a bird's nest that was full of chicks and had held it just inches from the security camera lens by the front door.

What on earth were they playing at? The chicks would die within an hour or so of being disturbed like that.

Ben didn't hesitate now. Still clutching the puppy, he hurried out of the living room, closing the door behind him; then he scuttled along the hallway to the front door.

'Monstrous, monstrous,' he muttered to himself, sweeping back the bolts.

As he turned the key he suddenly paused. He realized what else he'd seen on the monitor screen. Now that didn't make sense at all. The clutch of chicks had filled the screen. But there had been something else. He fancied he'd seen a pair of eyes, too.

But these had been human eyes. As if they'd peered into the camera through holes in the nest.

But then another thought struck him, one that was quite macabre.

Or had a pair of eyes been put into the nest that had then been held up to the camera lens?

The puppy whimpered.

'There, there, Toby. We'll put a stop to all this.'

He swung open the door.

The security lamp's brilliant light washed through the garden. He screwed up his eyes against the glare.

There was no one there now.

But perhaps they'd dropped the nest full of chicks somewhere close by? He couldn't leave them to die.

The sound of barking dogs echoed across the garden.

He stepped onto the path. There, a peculiar smell reached his nostrils. He sniffed the air. *Now that's peculiar*, he told himself. Riding roughshod over the delicate perfume of the night-scented stock in the flower beds was the pungent odour of wet wool. The same kind of smell an old pullover left in the rain would make. Frowning, he peered into the bushes.

At that moment he heard the sizzling sound again. It was surprisingly loud. As if a whole stream of sand was cascading onto newspaper.

Suddenly the dogs' barking became frenzied. Ben Middleton recognized the warning note that sharpened the sound, and that sent a whole wave of shivers running through his body.

To his left the bushes parted.

He turned in shock to look; his muscles snapped taut, making the puppy yelp in his arms.

And then, when Ben Middleton saw what would take his life, he screamed.

Chapter Four

One

Within forty-eight hours of flying out of New York, Sam Baker found himself standing in a field somewhere in a northern part of England. The sun shone brilliantly.

He'd heard of Yorkshire pudding. Eaten it plenty, usually with roast beef, occasionally with syrup and smothered with cream aerosolled fresh from a can. (Who says that by the age of twenty-six bachelors haven't already developed perverse eating habits?) Only he'd never realized there was an actual place called Yorkshire. This, then, his on-site PA had told him, was the biggest county in England. A population of four million, encompassing an area that comprised more acres than there were words in the Bible. He stood in the middle of green rolling pastures that went on rolling all the way down to a big, wide river.

In the middle of those pastures lay an old Roman amphitheatre – scooped from the living rock, no doubt, by the sweat of well-whipped slaves. And he, Sam Baker, had been assigned the job of televising, live, a midsummer rock concert and beaming it back to the States via satellite.

He'd done this a lot from sports stadiums. Well, filming sports events, anyway. The only problem was that, unlike the stadiums that were carefully designed and built with camera emplacements, commentators' studios, microphones already embedded in pitches and the whole caboodle cabled up to satellite dishes, here in this green Yorkshire field that abutted a wide shining river on which ducks swam and boats bobbed, what he got was what he saw: turf and rock and water – and not so much as a single power point.

He'd have seven days to bring in what he needed. Sure, a local TV company was providing the outside-broadcast hardware – generators, cameras, mixing consoles, trailers and the like – but he'd have all the fun of making sure everything went in the right place and that the crew knew what they were doing. All to ensure that he'd be sitting in the director's chair in the OB control vehicle (ubiquitously referred to as 'The Scanner' by TV folk) when the red light went on, calmly telling his assistant sitting at the console beside him, 'Run credits, go to camera one, go to camera two. Run VT.' And so on, and so on, for the three hours they were going to be on air.

He turned to his PA who was diligently annotating a plan he'd sketched that morning. She was probably a little younger than him, with long auburn hair woven into a plait that looked as strong and as thick as a ship's cable. When she turned her head quickly (which was often: she crackled with energy) the plait slashed from side to side like a whip. Her eyes were a dark, solid brown that made him think of fresh chestnuts. She went by the name of Zita and made a formidable PA. Her tiger-skin leggings and raunchy studded tongue only added to her aura of barely contained energy (and he didn't doubt she could be a ferocious wildcat, too, if riled).

He worked hard to keep up the air of directorial authority. 'I thing we've got this licked,' he called across to her. 'The site's only running a slight incline down to the river. Ground's solid. Weather's perfect.'

'I wouldn't count on it.' She pushed the pencil into her thick hair, using it as a pen holder. 'The weather's unpredictable here. It might be raining cats and dogs by tonight, then this ground will be a mudbath. The OB trailers will bog down.'

'Best ring round the local farmers, then. Have them on

standby with their tractors just in case we need pulling out of the poop.'

'They'll want paying. And probably in whisky, not cash.'

'Another quaint local custom?'

'No. Tax evasion, pure and simple'

'Don't worry.' He flashed her a smile. 'I made sure I came away from the States with a copy of the budget in my pocket. There's a sizeable amount included for contingencies. Shall we take a look at the amphitheatre?'

They walked side by side, talking as they went.

'The amphitheatre itself is protected by law as an archaeological site,' she explained. 'We can't touch that, so no heavy equipment can be brought onto it: no scaffolding, not so much as a single tent peg.'

'We'll need to run cables across it,' he said. 'Either that or put the OB trailers and satellite dish behind the stage, but then that's going to obscure the view of the river behind it.'

'We could use radio links?'

'No way. A thunderstorm thirty miles from here would leave viewers across the Atlantic with a screen full of snow flakes. We use cable.'

'Cable,' Zita echoed (doubtfully, he thought) as she jotted the word down on the equipment schedule.

'How old is this, then?' he asked.

'The amphitheatre? Getting on for two thousand years.'

'You don't say? So this is where they fed the Christians to the lions?'

'No, I think it was only Rome itself where they did that. This was probably a theatre for plays and the like.'

'So you live round here?'

'No. But you wouldn't recognize my accent. I'm from Wales.'

'Which part of England's that, then?'

'Don't let the Welsh hear you say that. It's not part of England, it's a country in its own right.' Suddenly she stopped and smiled. 'You're pulling my leg, aren't you? You're playing the dumb Yank act?'

32

He smiled. 'Guilty. I was just trying to break the ice. So call me Sam, not Mr Baker, do you hear? Or I'll start wearing loud checked shorts and demand to be taken to McDonald's at the top of my voice.'

She laughed, sounding genuinely friendly for the first time since he'd met her. 'OK, OK. Sam.'

'OK, Zita. Once we've finished up here what do you say to me buying the two of us some lunch?'

'Fine, you're on.'

'What's good to eat around here?'

'Fish and chips.'

'Posh?'

'Extremely.'

'Do I need to reserve a table?'

'I think we'll be OK today.'

'Hey, looks as if the cavalry's arrived.' A coach rumbled by on the road that led to the amphitheatre. It swung into the car park and pulled up by a line of half a dozen or so cars. At the far side of the car park was a timber-built visitors' centre with racks of postcards, travel guides and imitation bronze busts of Roman emperors. Not far from that, an ice-cream van did a brisk trade refreshing thirsty tourists. Sam shielded his eyes from the brilliant sun. 'From the look of those shorts and hats it looks as if this part of Yorkshire's managing to pull in the mighty dollar. Come on, let's get a proper look at the amphitheatre; after that we'll fax these equipment schedules off to your boss.'

In the otherwise perfect blue sky hung a single dark cloud. The man in the ice-cream van leant out to look up at the cloud and said a single word: 'Thunderhead.'

Two

It took barely three minutes to walk to the car park which was a little behind the amphitheatre. It also stood on slightly higher ground, allowing Sam to look down into the arena that antiquity had bequeathed them.

33

It sat on a slope running down to the river that was perhaps two hundred yards away. The amphitheatre itself was, as he'd seen earlier, cut from the bedrock to form that classic bowl shape, a good fifty yards in diameter and maybe twenty deep, with shallow concave sides. Sam noticed that, unlike most amphitheatres he'd seen before in photographs, the sides were smooth and the seating, like the steps down to the centre of the stage area, was constructed from timber rather than cut into the stone itself. He guessed the wooden seats were a modern addition. The original Roman seating must have long since rotted down to a mulch and been blown away by the cold winds of the Dark Ages.

The back of the amphitheatre had been cut away in the dim and distant past so that someone sitting in the bleachers could have seen the actors on stage (or Christians being shish kebabed, Sam thought with relish) with the river as a backdrop.

'Want one?' Zita offered him a cigarette pulled partway from its carton. He noticed her fingernails were painted red. The colour of danger, he thought with an inward smile.

'No, thanks. The last time I smoked one of those I got struck by lightning.'

She laughed and put her hand to her mouth. A moment later the laugh died as she looked at him more closely. 'My God. You're not joking, are you?'

He shook his head. 'Perfect aversion therapy. Never touched one since.'

'Were you badly hurt?' She looked at him, eyes wide, scanning his face as if expecting to see some *Phantom of the Opera*-type scars cleverly concealed beneath make-up.

He smiled. 'No. But I wouldn't want to repeat the experience.' He saw her ease the cigarette pack back into her bag as if she'd unwittingly flashed a pack of condoms at a nun. 'No, go ahead, smoke if you want to. It was a long time ago. I won't run screaming. Anyway, it's not as though I belong to an elite band, either. More than a thousand people are struck by lightning in America every year, and eight hundred of those will survive the experience. Now . . .' He folded his arms and looked down into the amphitheatre. 'I'm going to put camera one here, on the rim of the amphitheatre. Then we'll get a clear view of the stage, dead centre. This will form the base shot which we can keep returning to, particularly between bands. Camera two will go down on the floor level, directly below us here. I noticed a church about five minutes' walk back thataway. I want to mount a remote camera on top of the tower. That'll give us some lovely bird's-eye shots of the crowds arriving, and wide-angle shots of the amphitheatre and surrounding fields. Oh, and there's some moorings down there at the water's edge. See those boats to the left of us? They're all right. They won't be in shot. But we don't want any moored directly behind the stage on the night. When Eric Clapton stands there, belting out the riff from 'Layla', Joe Public will only want to see that behind him is the river flowing serenely toward the hills in the distance.' He smiled. 'And if we can cue up a flock of geese flying majestically into the sunset that will be just fine.'

'I don't think even your budget will run to trained geese.'

He turned his attention back to the bottom of the bowl of the amphitheatre. 'You see that block of stone at the back of the stage? That looks like some kind of altar?'

'I see it.'

'I guess there's not a hope in heaven of moving that?'

'You guess right. It's carved from the bedrock.'

'Oh, we'll have to work round it, then. Or maybe we can make it some kind of feature of the show.'

'I'll get the art department to look at it.'

'You know, in years gone by Jimi Hendrix or Sid Vicious would have happily smashed their guitars against it. Then we'd have sold the stills to *Rolling Stone* magazine.'

'Perish the thought. The Department of the Environment people would throw us in jail for despoiling an ancient monument. Uh, wait a minute.'

'What is it?'

'It looks as if the show's about to get under way.'

'What show?'

'The local tourist board stage some kind of entertainment for visitors. Want to move on down to the river?'

Sam looked at the people filing down the timber steps where they took their seats on the amphitheatre's sloping sides. 'No, we'll grab a few minutes of it. We might be able to bring a crew in to film part of it so we can drop in a taped insert as part of the introduction.'

'You think your viewers will be interested?'

'Not particularly, but it gives them time to visit the john or finish microwaving the popcorn before the concert gets under way. There, grab a seat. Whatever it is, it's just about to start.'

Chapter Five

One

'Mint?' he asked, offering her the pack as they sat on the seats looking down onto the amphitheatre's central stage.

She gave a little shake of her head. The heavy plait swung. 'I'll stick to my fix of nicotine. Are you sure my smoking doesn't bother you?'

'Not at all . . . oh, dang, that's me, I guess,' Sam said as his phone began to chirp. From his pocket he pulled out the black Motorola phone and thumbed the switch. 'Hello . . . Oh, hi, Joe. Fine. Fine. Yeah, I'm on site now. Yeah, England's great. They're looking after me like I'm a long-lost son. How's Bunty? You don't say . . . Listen, have you got the nod for an overrun?'

Sam recognized this as an anxiety call typical of TV companies. He could imagine there'd been a meeting in the office of the lady upstairs (as the station manager was known). It would have begun sensibly and calmly enough, but as sure as eggs are eggs there's always someone (and that someone is usually very ambitious and chasing your job) who will do their utmost to assassinate you. They don't openly stab you full square between the shoulder blades while snarling, 'I hope you die in the gutter with rats gnawing your nose from your skull.' But it's certainly done in the same spirit. They start by raising quite rational questions about poor weather forecasts for the night of the show; go on to say that there are rumours that TV technicians are about to strike for higher pay; continue with reports that Sting or Eric Clapton is complaining of a sore throat – allegedly; and finish by speculating that sunspots might flare and fuck up the satellite link. With a few of these subtle doubts (all expressed with wide, innocent eyes, yet with the aim of eroding management confidence in the victim) the play works like magic. Station management suddenly becomes like a dog covered with fleas, madly chasing its own tail and yapping wildly until someone soothes it.

So, with Zita sitting beside him smoking, her long, red and oh-so-dangerous nails gripping the cigarette, he sat on the bench calmly telling Joe Kane sitting in his Fifth Avenue office three thousand miles away that everything was fine, everything was under control, nothing to worry about, and, yes, the sky was cloudless and sunny (a white lie really, Sam would concede, a few clouds were now moving like a formation of dark battleships over the horizon); that, yes, the British technicians were happy with their money – more than happy. Sam exercised the talents that had made him the youngest TV director at the station. It was more than simply sitting at the console, saying, 'Camera one: close up of the umpire. Camera two: long shot of the team captain followed by pan to crowd.' A trained monkey could do that. Being a director was all about managing the people around you, making them feel good, and ensuring you got them working with you, not against you. And, above all, it was about keeping the producers happy.

As he talked, he stretched out his legs, enjoying the warm sun on his body. He caught Zita's perfume and found himself watching the way she sat with her knees together, balancing the clipboard as she wrote. Her body looked tautly muscled beneath the tiger-skin leggings and cropped top. Although he devoted most of his attention to his conversation (and a goodly portion to Zita) he noticed the amphitheatre was filling up. These would be mainly tourists bused in from the big hotels in York. They carried cameras, camcorders, shoulder bags, and fiddled with maps, or with the bust of Claudius or Zeus that they'd just bought at the site shop. For some reason Laurel and Hardy, Dracula and King Kong had taken the bench to his right. He guessed they were students of some kind, only it was anyone's guess why they were in costume. He only hoped they weren't going to perform some mind-numbingly boring mime. His idea of a good time was most definitely *not* watching some Marcel Marceau clone pretending to walk into a nonexistent wind or feel their way along a make-believe wall while looking for an invisible door handle. It gave him the willies just thinking about it.

Down on the stage, just in front of the rock altar, a man of around fifty dressed in a white shirt, black trousers and a gold waistcoat stood wagging his finger at the audience. Sam realized he was counting them. Perhaps he got paid per head. 'A bob a nob', as the English might say.

A moment later Sam wound up the telephone conversation, satisfied that in his New York office Joe would be replacing the receiver, satisfied that everything was running smoothly. In a little while the man would stub out his cigar and go tell the lady upstairs that everything was fine and why they managed to get themselves so het up and worried the Lord alone knew.

Sam thumbed the button on the mobile phone. He noticed Zita sitting with her phone resting on the clipboard on her knee. In a very low whisper he said, 'I think the old guy in the fancy vest is about to speak. Best switch off your mobile.'

'You're right, sir. The old guy's speaking in about a minute from now. So if you do have mobiles I'd be most grateful if you would switch them off until the show is over.'

Sam looked up, startled. The guy in the waistcoat smiled up at him from the bottom of the amphitheatre and said in a voice not much louder than a whisper, 'The Romans knew a thing or two about acoustics, sir; this amphitheatre can carry the lowest whisper right to the very back.' The moment the man started speaking the audience dropped silent, although one or two continued to take photographs. The click of the shutters and buzz of the motors advancing the film sounded absurdly loud.

The man in the gold waistcoat gave a sunny smile, and cupped his hand to his ear. 'You hear? Every sound is hugely amplified by the shape of the amphitheatre; after all, if you think about it, we're sitting in something the shape of a speaker cone.' He straightened and beamed at the audience. 'Well, seeing as I have everyone's attention, I may as well begin. Good afternoon. Welcome to Casterton's Roman amphitheatre, known locally as the Watchett Hole for reasons no one can adequately explain. My name is Jethro Campbell, but everyone calls me Jud. Now . . .' He moved back towards the stone altar; as he did so, he drew something Sam couldn't see from his shirt collar. 'Now, when I'm giving one of my talks in a public hall or classroom I usually cry out, 'Can everyone hear me at the back?' to which I get a half-hearted chorus of 'Yesss . . .' Here I like to do something different. Now can everyone hear this?'

He dropped an object (again something Sam could not see). A second later Sam clearly heard a *tink* sound.

'There, ladies and gentlemen,' continued the man. 'You've just heard a pin drop. Not something you hear every day. And that demonstrates how well even the tiniest sound – the tiniest sound of a pin dropping – is not only carried, but amplified. Did everyone hear it?'

There was a buzz of voices from the audience. They were impressed. Again there was the over-loud click-whirr of cameras. The man dropped the pin again. And again Sam heard the *tink* as the sliver of steel hit the rock floor of the amphitheatre. Sam shot Zita a smile. The old guy was obviously playing to the audience but he found himself enjoying it. He might actually bring up a camera crew, after all, to record a taped insert for the programme. These acoustics were something else.

Down on the stage, the man launched into his routine. No doubt he said the same thing two or three times a day to tourists who'd come from as far away as Alaska, Japan and New Zealand, but he was amiable enough playing the role of an eccentric Victorian professor.

'This amphitheatre wasn't actually built by the Romans, even though they'd dug out plenty of amphitheatres in the past, such structures being basically the Roman equivalent of television. No, this is a naturally occurring depression in the rock. The Romans merely added timber seating and stairs. What you're sitting on now is, of course, a modern replacement. And this . . .' He slapped the rock altar with the palm of his hand (the sound of palm meeting rock making a pistol-shot crack) '. . . is something of a mystery. It's certainly not Roman. Later, you can come down here and see for yourselves that it's actually part of the bedrock, which is incredibly tough. A form of granite, which only rarely occurs in Britain. In prehistoric times, or so we surmise, people, probably the Neolithic farmers who occupied the area some four thousand years ago, scooped out what appear to be six shallow bowls in the top of the slab.' He ran his hand inside the hollows on the slab. 'See? Probably no larger than breakfast bowls. You'd get a couple of Weetabix in each one and not much else.'

A ripple of laughter from the audience.

'You'll notice the effect if viewed from above is like a domino. The double three, to be precise. See, two diagonal lines of three? And there in the centre a deep slot has been cut. Again, the uses for this object are shrouded in mystery. But most historians agree there's a ritual significance. That this was used for religious practices. And some have speculated that this is a sacrificial altar.' Heads craned forward, suddenly interested. 'See?' Jud said, clearly enjoying himself enormously (while suddenly adopting a Vincent Price voice). 'Can't you imagine the sacrificial victim being dispatched just here as they lay stretched out on top of the stone altar? Then the internal organs – the heart, the kidneys, the liver, lungs – would be carefully arranged in these stone bowls.' He couldn't resist a devilish laugh. 'While the victim's head would rest just here. So it could stare accusingly at the audience. Now, wouldn't that make for a grisly sight?' He laughed again. 'Or then again, it was more likely the equivalent of the Christian harvest festival and the bowls would be filled with berries, apples, wheat, oats, and probably a drop of the best local beer. The truth is, not many societies indulged in human sacrifice. Ancient cultures were far more humane than the makers of horror films imagine.'

While the man talked Sam Baker once more let his attention wander.

To his left the students in fancy dress – Laurel and Hardy, Dracula, and King Kong in her black-hair costume minus the gorilla head – were smoking roll-ups. They smiled a lot and Sam wondered if they'd crumbled a little cannabis resin into the tobacco first. Not that he had a problem with dope. Once he'd had a girlfriend who'd baked chocolate muffins laced with cannabis. They'd had some great nights on a couple of muffins alone; she'd some pretty laid-back sparrows on her bird table, too.

By now Jud Campbell's history lesson had taken its audience into the eighteenth century when the locals had filled the amphitheatre with leaves, then planted licorice in the leaf mulch, licorice being a useful medicine in those days as well as a substitute for sugar in the form of licorice paste. Or so the helpful Jud informed them.

Sam yawned, glanced at his watch. Ten past two. His stomach told him in no uncertain way it was way past lunchtime. He found himself thinking about that deep-fried fish. His stomach rumbled. He looked round wondering if anyone had heard. The acoustics of this place were damn' near supernaturally good. If you could hear a pin drop then a stomach rumbling would sound like a twenty-one-gun salute. Suddenly he felt like the kid who broke wind in class. All eyes would turn on him as his face burned with embarrassment.

Luckily, at that moment Jud Campbell wound up his show and the genuine applause drowned any grumbling sounds Sam's internal plumbing might have made.

As in any theatre, or cinema, the amphitheatre steps were immediately clogged with people making their escape back to their cars, the bus or the ice-cream van.

'We'll leave them to clear the aisles first,' Sam said. 'After all, we're in no tearing hurry.'

Zita watched the crowds packing the aisle. 'OK. It'll give me time to finish this schedule while I've got the chance.' She pulled the pencil from her hair and began writing on her clipboard. As she did so she sang under her breath.

Beside him the students in fancy dress were talking in a very relaxed (some might say stoned) kind of way. The one dressed as Oliver Hardy giggled, gave the gorilla a playful slap with his bowler hat and said, 'Hmmm . . . hur! That's another fine mess you've gotten me into.'

Sam suddenly realized what Zita was singing under her breath as she neatly pencilled equipment codes onto the schedule.

'Buffalo girls gonna come out tonight, gonna come out tonight . . .' she sang in a whisper.

He looked at her, the hairs on the back of his neck starting to stand on end. His scalp prickled, too.

'What made you sing that?' he asked, suddenly feeling a strange shivering sensation running across his chest, then down his arms to his fingertips.

'Mm?' she asked, still running through her figures. 'Sing what, Sam?'

Before he could say another word the lightning tore from the cloud.

Two

The lightning came with a tremendous *whump!* of thunder, too. Sam froze. A wash of blue light cascaded into the amphitheatre; it was so intense it seemed to bypass his eyes

43

and sear right through his skull to the visual centres of his brain.

His heart convulsed. Instantly he looked round the amphitheatre, his eyes wide, expecting to see charred bodies, splintered seating, heads on fire.

Instead people were looking up at the black cloud directly above. Someone opened an umbrella but there hadn't been so much as a drop of rain.

'Wow!' The guy dressed as Dracula looked at the roll-up. 'Was that lightning or was that something I just smoked?'

Oliver Hardy shot his only line. 'That's another fine mess you've gotten me into.'

Sam swallowed. His mouth felt strangely dry. 'You were right about the weather,' he told Zita evenly. 'We'll get someone at the office to ring round the local farmers and have them on standby with their tractors.'

She shot him a concerned look. 'Are you OK, Sam?'

'Sure, don't worry. I haven't a phobia about lightning or anything. I just don't want rain to bog down our OB trailers when we set up.'

'Bloody English weather,' she said with a smile and picked up her mobile phone. 'I'll get Liz right onto it.'

Most of the people had left the amphitheatre as Zita dialled. The four in fancy dress were the last to pick their way slowly over the bench seats: gorilla girl forgot the gorilla head and had to come back for it, still smiling that I-love-the-whole-wide-world smile that comes with pulling on a little dope.

Sam eased another mint from the pack. The cloud appeared to be beating a retreat. The sun returned to shine brilliantly on the amphitheatre. Jud Campbell was in the process of picking up his only stage prop: the pin, which he carefully stuck back into his collar. In the background a millionaire's huge launch bobbed gently at the riverside moorings.

Sam looked back at Zita, the phone to her ear. She nodded at him. 'It's ringing. Liz shares the same office as me, so she should be— Oh.' Her eyes shifted from his face as she concentrated on listening to the voice in the earpiece. 'Oh, hello. Liz, I need you to . . . wait a minute.' She frowned, suddenly puzzled. 'Who am I speaking to, please?'

Sam listened to the conversation, only hearing Zita's half of it. 'Hello, who is this, please?' she repeated, sounding more angry than puzzled. 'No, You misheard me. What's your name? Oh, look, just let me speak with Liz Pearson . . . she's out? Oh, no – no message. Never mind. Good-bye.'

Annoyed, she used one of the red-for-danger fingernails to stab the button that terminated the call.

'I take it you got the schoolkid on the work-experience programme?'

'No.' Zita stared at the telephone in something that was a blend of wonder and disbelief. 'You're not going to believe this, Sam.' She looked at him. 'But, if I didn't know better, I'd swear I've just had a conversation with myself.'

Chapter Six

One

Sam Baker gave Zita a reassuring smile as they walked back in the direction of the car. Zita was looking at the phone as if it was a loaded gun that had inexplicably gone off in her hand and blown a hole in some guy's face. For a moment Sam was startled by the look of shock in her eyes.

'That was weird. Big, BIG-time weird,' she said in disbelief. 'I could have sworn that was me on the phone.'

'Don't worry about it,' he said, being deliberately light-hearted. 'Someone will have been passing your office, heard the phone ring, picked it up—'

'And they just happened to sound like me? With this Pontypridd accent?'

'Sure.'

'Perhaps I've been out in this sun too long. Or maybe I'm really sitting in a room with rubber walls and no inside handle on the door.'

At first she'd looked troubled as they'd walked away from the amphitheatre but now he saw she was making a joke of it.

He smiled. 'Or this is all a dream. Any second you'll wake up.'

'Mmm, could be,' she said, smiling broadly now. 'You best pinch me.'

He couldn't help but look down at the way those tiger pattern leggings hugged her legs and oh-so-sassy hips. He wondered just where he should plant that pinch. Only it wasn't PC to pinch a woman's butt. Besides, he never was the pinching sort. Instead, he grinned at her. 'Well, if you're not crazy and you're not dreaming then it must be low blood-sugar levels through lack of food. Come on, let's find some lunch.'

Sam paused to look back at the amphitheatre one last time before he climbed into the car. He pictured where the OB trailers would be sited. Already he could imagine the cables snaking through the grass like a plague of black cobras. The satellite dish angled at forty-five degrees, beaming the TV signals out to the satellite in its geostationary orbit twenty-five thousand miles in space, from where they'd be bounced back to the receiving dish in New York before being pumped out to fifty million homes or more. The sun burned hard. The shadows it cast were dark, sharply defined. The river shone like liquid silver.

At that moment he had a feeling that something in the landscape had changed. It was as if something was there now that hadn't been there before. Only he couldn't quite put his finger on it. Inexplicably the sensation made him uneasy and, despite the heat, a shiver ran up his spine.

Then Sam's stomach rumbled again, impatient for food. Perhaps Zita and he were both in need of lunch. He climbed into the front passenger seat beside her and within seconds they were driving away from the amphitheatre in the direction of town.

Two

Lee Burton stood in the coach doorway, where he watched Laurel and Hardy and the gorilla (headless again) talking on the pavement outside the hotel. Smoking the dope on an empty stomach had made him queasy. Wearing this stupid Dracula costume didn't help much either in the heat of a summer's day.

The black cape and his white-painted face complete with

bright red blood-trickles running down from each side of his mouth attracted the stares of York shoppers, and prompted one youth to quip, 'Transylvania's the next stop down, mate.'

So this is being a travel rep, he told himself for the tenth time that day. For three years he'd worked as a teller at a building society until they'd merged with a rival, then promptly downsized, as the phrase had it – meaning they'd slashed their workforce by almost half. He'd been one of those slashed, and found himself moping around his bachelor flat with a redundancy payment that was dwindling fast and no other prospects. After a boozy lunch over the Situations Vacant section of the newspaper he and a couple of similarly jobless friends had applied for the tour rep positions as a joke.

Gobsmackingly, he'd been hired.

Palm-fringed lagoons beckoned. Or so he'd imagined. He'd anticipated that the company would send him to Barbados, or at least to Spain or Greece. Instead he found himself guiding tourists around the sunnier aspects of Yorkshire. It wouldn't have been so bad but some bright spark at the company had decided it would be more fun for their clients if the reps wore fancy dress and enlivened the coach rides with party games. So there he was as some lanky version of Dracula, complete with cloak and deathly-white make-up.

'What's keeping them?' the driver grumbled. 'I'm picking up another batch from the airport at six.'

'I'll go and ask.' Lee stepped down from the coach, the long black cloak swishing behind him.

Drivers tooted their horns and waved at him. Maintaining the tour-rep smile (thankfully, he'd lost the Dracula fangs in Whitby on a previous trip), he crossed the road to the front of the hotel. There Sue Royston, dressed as Stan Laurel, was extravagantly waving her arms as she talked at, rather than to, the gorilla. The girl in the gorilla suit was Nicole Wagner, a stunning blonde with blue eyes and what seemed like miles of white shining teeth.

Naturally, the most burning ambition of nearly all tour reps was to be an actor. This was the next best thing. You performed to a coach of forty or so tourists. A captive audience who were ready to let their hair down anyway. Lee had met no end of reps who were either applying for theatre auditions or waiting for calls from agents. Nicole Wagner, Lee had learnt, was a rare exception. She was working her way through university. Her burning ambition was to be a barrister. At rest-stops she could be seen writing furiously on notepads, fashioning five-thousand-word essays with titles like *The Law Of Torts – Evolution, Codification and Future Ramification*, or she'd sit hunched in her gorilla suit poring over law journals with (so it seemed to Lee) shriekingly tiny print, no pictures, and titles that were dry as dead Law Lords' bones; typical examples were *Downyweather v Hoggatt Mineral & Aggregates Limited (1904) – Reflections of Ratio Decidendi* or *The Local Government Act 1971: Clause 4(ii) Re-examined.*

'Strewth . . .

Standing close by on the pavement was Oliver Hardy, real name Ryan Keith, a plump twenty-year-old who fiddled with his spotty tie, plastered a wide grin on his chubby face, and who repeated *ad nauseam*, 'This is another fine mess we've gotten ourselves into.'

Nicole tossed back her breathtaking blonde hair. 'If he says that again, I'll kill him,' she said savagely.

The aura of mellow happiness engendered by the dope had clearly worn off, Lee saw.

'The shit's hit the fan,' Sue told him. 'Bloody gone and hit it and splattered all over the fucking place.'

A passer-by shot her a startled look. *That's the first time anyone's heard Stan Laurel use the F-word*, thought Lee, as he sweated inside his Dracula cape. 'Is anyone going to tell me what's wrong?' he asked.

'The receptionist in there . . .' Nicole pointed at the hotel, the gorilla head still clutched in her fist. 'Has just told me that our party on the coach aren't booked in until tomorrow afternoon.' Her eyes blazed with fury.

Sue added, 'The booking office have got their dates mixed up. They've sent forty people to York and there isn't a hotel for them.'

'What are we going to do?' Nicole asked. 'We can't send them back to the hotel in Whitby because that will have been taken by another party.'

'And they can't sleep on the coach,' Ryan supplied unhelpfully.

'Shit.'

Lee felt as though his heart and lungs were sinking down through his chest into his stomach. 'Someone's fucked up royal, haven't they?'

'Well, no one had better look at me.' Sue pulled her copy of the itinerary from her baggy Stan Laurel jacket. 'Look.' She stabbed a finger at the lines of text. '23rd June. The Magnus Hotel, York. Earliest check-in time, thirteen hundred hours.'

'And it's now half-past two,' Lee said. 'The receptionist definitely said we're actually booked in tomorrow? For the 24th?'

'Well, no . . . not exactly.' Nicole ran her fingers through her blonde hair (perhaps as a prelude to tugging it out in frustration). 'She told me we're booked in for the Tuesday the 23rd.'

Lee shook his head, bewildered. 'The 23rd? Today's the 23rd. So what's the problem?'

'No. That's what's so bizarre. The receptionist insists—'

Behind him the coach driver sounded his horn impatiently. When Lee glanced back the man was using his fingers to mime people walking off the coach. Lee shook his head.

Nicole continued, one hand still holding onto her blonde hair. 'The receptionist insisted that today is the 22nd.'

'Monday?'

'Yes.'

'Impossible.'

Sue gave an emphatic shrug. 'Well, I say it's Tuesday.'

'Me, too.' Lee pulled the cloak higher up his shoulder; the thing was a dead weight on his back. 'Yesterday – *Monday* – we were in Whitby.'

'Only the receptionist *and* the hotel manager tell us that *today* is Monday. Either they've gone mad, or it's us.'

Ryan rubbed his plump cheeks with both hands. 'Oh, shit. I knew we shouldn't have smoked that dope. We shouldn't, we shouldn't . . .'

'Oh, shut up,' Nicole snapped uncharitably.

'Oh, come on.' Lee said. 'It can't be the dope. You'd have to smoke a whole bush of the stuff to lose a day like that.'

'Bad dope,' Ryan suggested.

'Bad dope, my foot. We all say it's Tuesday. Agreed?'

They all nodded, and Lee was once more struck by the absurdity of it all. The sight they must have made – a blonde girl in a gorilla suit, Dracula and Laurel and Hardy standing on a York pavement bustling with shoppers – trying to convince each other that it was a Tuesday and not a Monday.

Again the coach driver sounded his horn. This time he jerked a thumb back at the passengers. They were staring out of the window at their reps, obviously keen to unpack, shower, and hit the city's tourist hot spots.

'Damn him,' Nicole hissed. 'Can't he be patient for one minute?'

'Who's going to tell the clients?' Ryan cried, looking woeful in his Oliver Hardy suit and bowler. 'They're going to tear us another set of arseholes, aren't they?'

'Tell them what?' Nicole's eyes flashed dangerously. 'That they haven't got a hotel? Or that somewhere on the road we took a wrong turn and ended up here on a Monday, not a Tuesday.'

'It's the dope,' Ryan whined. 'I said we shouldn't have smoked it. I'm not used to it. This's a bad trip we're having. We need to lie down and drink plenty of—'

'Look, just take it easy,' Lee told him. 'Everyone, stay cool. We all know it's a Tuesday. OK?'

They nodded.

'So, if we know it, then it must be the hotel that's mistaken—'

'But I've just stood and argued it all out with them.' Nicole wound her fingers in her hair. Lee watched in fascination, expecting her to start tearing out great golden handfuls. 'The receptionist told me it's Monday. Then the manager told me it's Monday. They even showed me the diary.'

'They're the ones who are mistaken,' Lee insisted. 'Look, there's a newsagent. I'll go buy today's newspaper, then we'll march back in there and shove it under their idiot noses. OK?'

They all let out sighs of relief as they realized this would be the solution to their problem.

Lee fished some coins from the pockets of his tight Dracula trousers. 'Just wait here.' The driver honked. 'Ryan. Tell him that we've had a problem and we'll be unloading our people in the next five minutes.'

Ryan gave such a sharp nod that his plump cheeks wobbled.

'Good man,' Lee told him, smiling. 'Right, I'll be back in a minute.'

Lee ran across the road, dodging a motorbike and open-top tourist bus. A young kid pulled at his mother's hand and yelled, 'Look! There's Batman!'

Lee wished again that he didn't have to wear the absurd Dracula cape that billowed behind him as he ran. The thing already had holes ripped in it where he'd caught it on bushes, fences and God knew what else.

Steeling himself against curious stares and jibes, he ducked into the shop, bought the first daily newspaper he put his hands on and came back out onto the pavement.

Sue in her Stan Laurel costume and Nicole in the gorilla suit, with her blonde hair tumbling lusciously down the fake black fur, stood across the road, arms tightly folded.

But at last he had the answer to all their troubles clutched in his hands. Already he was imagining walking into the hotel and holding up the newspaper with all the righteous majesty of Moses revealing the Ten Commandments to the children of Israel and saying, 'There. *Tuesday!* It says so in thick black letters on every page.'

Half-way across the road Lee couldn't resist looking at the newspaper. There, below the paper's name, the *Daily Mail*, was the day and the date.

Monday.

He stared at it in a kind of bug-eyed amazement.

Monday?

So the newspapers have got the day wrong too, was the thought that went instantly whirling round inside Lee's head.

He flicked through the pages, believing in his heart of hearts that some typesetter had mistakenly keyed in the wrong date before the newspaper presses had started rolling late on Monday night. But no. Monday. Monday. Monday, 22nd June. The day and date headed every page.

He looked up from the paper to his two colleagues on the pavement, wondering how he was going to tell them that by some crazy fluke they'd all forgotten what day it was.

But he was never going to get the chance.

At that moment a petrol tanker hammered along the road behind him. The bow-wave of air pressure pushed him forward.

The next second a tremendous pull yanked him back off his feet. At the same time there was the sensation that his head was being torn from his neck.

The sky flew somewhere under his feet; a bellowing roar filled his ears. Then he was lying on his back.

Only he was still moving.

The road surface slid under him, buffeting the air from his lungs. He felt no pain, only astonishment that such a thing was happening to him.

It only took him a moment to realize what had happened. The truck had caught his cape as it had thundered by.

Now he was being dragged, head first, beneath the massive silver cylinder of the petrol tanker.

He managed to turn his head to look to the front of the truck. Past the criss-cross bars of the truck's subframe he saw the twin rear wheels of the tractor unit. The cape had somehow caught itself on the mudguard.

If he didn't release the cape from around his neck he knew he'd either be strangled or have the flesh scraped from his back by the road's abrasive surface.

But Lee's fatal error was that he didn't think through the consequences of simply releasing the cape's catch from around his neck.

And not for a moment did he envisage what would happen if he stopped dead while the truck kept on rolling.

He was acting on instinct. The instinct to get that choking collar from around his neck.

His fingers scrabbled at the button on the collar, trying to push it through the looped piece of cord.

The truck rumbled like thunder.

With a peculiar detachment he marvelled that he could see the legs of shoppers blurring by.

At last the button slipped out through the loop.

Snap!

Suddenly the cloak had gone.

He slid to a stop on his back.

The bottom of the truck kept on moving above him.

That was when he realized his big mistake.

Although he still lay on his back in the road, his head jerked up in time to see the twin rear tyres of the truck slamming against the road towards him.

At that moment the truck driver must have braked.

The wheels slowed.

He's going to stop; he's going to stop; he's not going to run me over: those were the words hammering joyfully through Lee's head.

The truck did stop.

Only not soon enough.

Still on his back, Lee raised himself up on his elbows to watch the two huge tyres as black as the gates of death come rolling forward and pass between his splayed-out legs. They crunched up over his groin, shattering the pelvic bone, before stopping on his stomach.

The bolt of pain wrenched him up into a sitting position. His face slapped against the hot rubber of the tyre. Yet despite it all some small part of his brain coolly compared the deep zig-zag cut of the tyre's tread to the jagged lines of valleys on a map. It even marvelled at specks of a white, chalky grit adhering to the rubber.

And he knew, without a shadow of a doubt, that he was going to die there in the road.

Slowly, remorselessly, the rear wheels bore down on him, bursting his stomach, crushing his liver and kidneys.

He screamed.

But no sound came out.

Only blood.

It burst from his mouth in a great gush of crimson.

Chapter Seven

❦

One

The man who sold ice creams from his candy-striped van in the amphitheatre car park returned home to find a man lying on top of his wife in their bedroom. It was clear enough what was happening. The stranger was digging himself into her as if convinced that if he could only get in deeply enough he'd hit a big red button inside her belly that would set off every klaxon, bell and siren in Casterton. Probably make the Town Hall floodlights flash, too, and then the lady Mayor would sing *All Things Bright And Beautiful* from the top of the clock tower.

Sarah wasn't complaining. She was giving her lover loud enough encouragement.

In the open doorway of the bedroom the ice-cream man stood open-mouthed, and unnoticed by the two lovers. His hand clutched the edge of the door so tightly he felt his fingers must surely sink in through the plywood panels.

At that moment he didn't know what appalled him most.

His wife's enthusiastic and noisy infidelity, or the fact that her boyfriend had the insolence to wear the ice-cream man's pyjama top.

He couldn't take his eyes from that pyjama top. Lost in her own universe of pleasure his wife's hands clutched at the striped fabric, pulling it tight across the man's broad back.

This was too much.

The man who sold ice creams stepped back through the bedroom door and onto the landing, shaking his head, his chest so tight with shock he could hardly breathe.

Right now, more than anything, he wanted somehow to blindly stagger downstairs and get away from the house. But he found himself leaning forward to peer through the crack where the door was hinged to the frame.

Oh, God Almighty. This was like seeing the aftermath of a terrible car smash. He was shocked, revolted, horrified. But he knew he had to look.

They'd finished by this time. With a satisfied groan his wife's lover lifted himself up, then rolled onto his back to gaze contentedly at the ceiling.

That's when the man who sold ice creams knew he'd lost his mind.

Because the man who lay there all sweaty and red-faced in bed was no stranger. The ice-cream man found that he was staring at an identical copy of himself.

Two

Jud Campbell, the historian who'd lectured in the amphitheatre, returned to his narrow boat where he lived with his wife. He unbuttoned his gold waistcoat as he walked.

The boat was moored on the river bank just a moment's walk from the amphitheatre itself. He soon noticed a flash river cruiser moored behind his own boat. It had been secured pretty badly, too. The aft lines were loose, allowing the boat's arse to drift outwards where it might get clipped by other passing boats.

A blond-haired man, dressed in a white dressing gown, sunned himself on the deck of the big cruiser. He was drinking from a can of beer and smoking the biggest cigar that Jud had ever seen.

'Excuse me,' Jud began politely. 'I noticed your aft lines are slack.'

The man pulled on the cigar before shrugging. 'So?'

'The stern of your boat's being pulled out by the current. There's a chance you might get hit by a passing boat.'

The man wasn't interested. 'Seem OK to me.'

'The river's plenty wide enough at this point, but there's a sandbank just out there and it'll force the bigger river traffic close to the shore.'

'Oh, fuck off,' the man said casually and returned to gazing out over the river while sipping his beer.

Jud shrugged. He believed he was being polite and neighbourly. If the arrogant twat wanted to sit there with the boat's arse dragging out into the water where it'd get crunched by one of the big river barges then it was his lookout.

Shaking his head, he walked up the gangplank onto the narrow boat where he paused to wipe a mark off its brass bell. The *Tiber-Lizzie* was Jud's pride and joy. A magnificent seventy-footer, it was powered by a new Mitsubishi four-cylinder diesel; the boat boasted a waxed pine interior, stem-to-stern carpets, fitted kitchen, Eberspacher central heating and an all-steel hull painted in a cool, unflustered oak-leaf green. Along the full length of the cabin's exterior Jud himself had painted a fine dragon in red and gold. And there, studded like jewels along its flanks, were the brass porthole frames that Jud would lovingly polish every week without fail.

Jud had heard that when men reach forty-something they transfer their affections from their now-grown-up children to gardens, dogs, aviaries or aquariums (but rarely to wives); he guessed his time had come and he'd switched his affections, and his desire to nurture, to the *Tiber-Lizzie*. His wife would sometimes click her tongue and tell him he was obsessed to the point of madness with the thing. But secretly she was pleased he sunk his energies into what was, after all, their home, and not into cultivating a fixation on which dog or nag would be first across the finishing line, gambling away their life savings in the process.

In the cabin he found Dot sitting in front of the portable TV while scowling with surprising ferocity at the *Radio Times*.

Pleasingly plump in the way that Arabs are supposed to find so attractive, she was normally so cheerful that Jud found himself experiencing a mild sense of shock at her angry expression.

'They've got it all wrong, Jud,' she snapped.

'Got what all wrong, dear?'

'I want to watch *Columbo* but I've got this *Through The Keyhole* rubbish instead.'

'You've got the right channel?'

'What do you take me for, Jud? Of course I've got the right channel.'

'Maybe the magazine is wrong?'

'This is the *Radio Times*,' she said primly. 'It is never wrong.'

'Oh,' he said mildly again while slipping off his waistcoat before carefully folding it into a tissue-lined box. His wife referred to his waistcoats as 'stage gear' and he looked after them with scrupulous care. 'Perhaps the tennis overran. They might have substituted a shorter programme so they can get back on schedule again.'

'Jud. Don't treat me like a simpleton.' Her voice was actually softening now she was no longer bottling up the frustration here alone on the boat. 'Look, it's all gone to buggery. Today's Tuesday.' She shook the TV guide. '2:45, it says here. *Columbo*.'

'And we've got *Through The Keyhole* instead?'

'Yes, and according to the *Radio Times, Through The Keyhole* was on yesterday afternoon, Jud. *Yesterday*.'

'They'll have made a mistake. Or maybe their videotape broke.' In their thirty years of marriage – a placid, easy-going marriage as comfortable as a good pair of slippers in front of a roaring log fire – Jud Campbell had been forced to recognize, and accept, that his only rival for his wife's affection was Peter Falk. Her *Columbo* hours on Tuesday and Thursday afternoons were sacrosanct. 'Maybe it will be on later?'

'No.' She scowled at the television as if by the intensity of her stare alone she could see into the black hearts of the programme schedulers who were playing this evil trick on her. 'They've messed everything up. They must be having a bad hair day, every single one of them. Look.' She picked up the remote and stabbed a button. 'Look, they've even buggered up Teletext.'

'Looks all right to me. What's wrong with it?'

'Look at the date at the top.'

'Oh.'

'See!' Her grey eyes blazed in triumph at proving her point. 'Look at the day at the top of the screen! Can't they get even that right? I ask you.'

Jud looked at the top of the Teletext screen. The time was right. But the date was wrong.

It should have read Tuesday, 23rd June.

Instead the date mutely announced: Monday, 22nd June.

His wife nodded, now more satisfied than annoyed. 'They've buggered up royal.'

Three

'Who was the guy in the bacofoil waistcoat?' Bony Harris asked the blond-haired man lounging regally on the deck.

'Some cretin prattling on about slack lines or something.'

'They do look loose; I could check—'

'I'm not interested in them. Get me Shitter Brown on the phone.'

'Sure, Mr Carswell.'

'You know, Bony,' the blond-haired man's eyes were hard and tiny as if someone had substituted shiny glass beads in their sockets. 'I'm on holiday but I've been sitting here and grinding my teeth. I'm paying that wet fart Rossman to waste my money running radio ads that don't pull in any punters, for Christ's sake. That last radio campaign cost me nearly ten thousand pounds, but it didn't put a single extra body into the Manchester club. Ten thousand! I might as well have brought it here and fed it to the fucking ducks.' Carswell seethed.

Bony Harris knew his boss was poised for one of his regular eruptions. When Carswell went into a fit of incandescent anger anyone in the wrong place could get blasted off the payroll. Thank God it was going to be Rossman.

Carswell looked at the can of beer as if it disgusted him, or maybe it was thoughts of Rossman that put a godawful taste in his mouth. 'I'm going to tell Shitter Brown to get Rossman to clear his desk and then see that he's thrown out into the street. Let some other poor schmuck look after the charity case, because I'm sick and tired – *sick and tired*! – of being screwed by time-wasters. Ach . . . what is it with this beer? It's disgusting.'

He threw the can of beer onto the banking, where it foamed onto the grass.

'Well, in a couple of hours Rossman can go home to his shit-tip of a house and lick his wounds. But when you get to my position you can have them licked for you. Isn't that right, Bony?'

'That's right, boss.'

'I'm going down below now, Bony. You stay up here and telephone Shitter Brown.'

'OK, Mr Carswell. Do you want me to check those lines?'

'No.'

The man stomped down the steps into the cabin. A girl of around seventeen sat watching *Through The Keyhole*. She had long black hair and wore a white dressing gown identical to Carswell's. Shaking her head, puzzled, she said, '*Columbo's* supposed to be on. They've changed it without—'

Carswell walked across to the television where he punched the power button with his finger. Then he nodded briskly in the direction of the bedroom door.

Four

In York Ryan Keith sat on the steps of the Magnus Hotel and wept. He knew he looked completely stupid sitting there in his Oliver Hardy costume, the bowler hat gripped in his two hands, his plump head hanging down loosely, while tears dripped onto the pavement.

'This is another fine mess . . .' he blubbered. 'This is another fine mess . . .' A purple wedge of hysteria tried to separate him from sanity. Any second now he'd run screaming down the street. A plump Oliver Hardy in baggy trousers that came up his chest as far as his armpits, a white shirt and spotty tie and, over that, a charcoal-coloured jacket. And he'd be running and screaming and crying because his friend Lee Burton lay crushed under the back wheels of the truck. A crowd gathered. Someone had rolled up a cardigan and put it under Lee's head. A priest was reciting the last rites and drawing little crosses in the air over his head. And blood was everywhere: it dripped down the deep zig-zag tread of the tyres. It ran down the road in a big stream of thick, glistening red that was the colour of mashed strawberries.

And worst of all, his friend was still conscious.

Lee knew what was happening to him; he knew he was dying as he lay there under the back wheels of the truck looking from face to face with this look of surprise like someone had pinned a note on his back reading PLEASE KICK ME.

Ryan Keith couldn't take any more. No. Not a single solitary fucking second; not with his friend lying crushed and bleeding.

So he, Ryan Keith, made a miserably pathetic sight. A plump young man in an Oliver Hardy costume sitting weeping on the hotel steps. The tears dropped in coin-size splotches on the pavement.

So what?

So what if today had started out a Tuesday only to turn into a Monday somewhere along the way?

So freaking what?
He didn't care. He couldn't take any more.
'This is another fine mess . . . another fine mess . . .'
He couldn't say any more. The sobs made his whole body pump up and down. His tears fell like rain.

Chapter Eight

One

The girl sang: *'Buffalo girls gonna come out tonight, gonna come out tonight, Buffalo girls gonna come out tonight . . .'*

Sam Baker blinked. Just now it had felt as if a whole river of sunlight had poured in through his eyes. He blinked again, but spinning discs of light still clung to his retina.

Blinking hard, trying to squeeze out the light as if it was shampoo that had got into his eyes, he shook his head.

'Buffalo girls gonna come out tonight, gonna come out tonight.'

Sam Baker was dreaming a weird dream. Of course, most dreams are weird. They make no sense to anyone but two-hundred-dollar-an-hour shrinks. His own common-or-garden recurring dream had him locked into the studio's gallery, directing the live TV programme from hell when all the screens on the editing console became so defocused he couldn't tell the football from the stadium, but manfully he'd struggle to make sense of the distorted shapes as he hollered instructions to the PA sitting at his side. 'Cue camera three. Close up camera two. Cut to camera one . . .'

This dream was different. There wasn't an editing console in sight. And all he could see were lights. Green ones, white ones, red ones, spots of light, stripes of light. He crushed his eyelids down, blinking his hardest.

A moment later he opened his eyes and looked round. The lights were gone.

A ghost girl sang softly to him. *'Buffalo girls gonna come out tonight, gonna come out tonight. Buffalo girls gonna come out tonight, gonna come out tonight . . .'*

The ghost girl smiled sweetly then disappeared. She left behind a bottle of Jack Daniel's whiskey on the wooden bench. Lying as it did on its side, it glugged out its contents onto the hard grey pumice stone that formed the floor.

It's a shame about that whiskey, he thought wistfully. *It's a real shame it's all going to waste, spilling on the floor like that. Someone should pick it up.*

This being a dream, it never occurred to him that he could be the one to rescue it.

Feeling calm, completely relaxed, he looked up from the whiskey bottle as it spilled its beautiful brown liquor onto the stone floor.

He felt no surprise he was back in the amphitheatre once more. Or that he was alone there.

But he knew it was time he should be leaving the place. He didn't belong here on these hard benches. He shouldn't be gazing down onto the circular stage area with that stone altar looking like a big black domino.

Sam stood up. The bottle of Jack Daniel's whiskey still lay on its side on the bench, the liquor still pouring with a loud pattering sound (which sounded pretty much like a man urinating on the floor). He stepped over the whiskey as it streamed down the sides of the amphitheatre, and headed for the timber steps that would take him out to the car park.

As he reached the steps he happened to look back.

His dream had supplied a new image.

Planted firmly in the altar was a large wooden cross that was probably a good ten feet high. Hanging on that cross was a man. He had dark hair and wore red shoes. Tied around his waist was a filthy white towel.

He cried out to Sam Baker.

Although Sam could make out no words, the tone of the

crucified man's voice showed he was clearly begging Sam for help.

Sam knew he must help the man. Help him now. Not stand there beside the glugging whiskey bottle. But the mechanism that drove the dream wouldn't tell him what to do.

Instead, he walked slowly down the steps, watching the man on the cross all the time.

The man carried on crying out for help. But Sam still couldn't make out the individual words: maybe they were foreign; maybe they were somehow distorted out of all recognition. In any event, he could not understand them, he only recognized the tone: begging, pleading, wanting desperately to be released from unbearable agony.

The man's head thrashed from side to side. He arched his body as if the wooden cross had become red-hot and he was trying hard to tear himself away from it.

Sam walked slowly down towards the cross. He looked up at the man in dumbfounded awe.

The man hadn't been nailed to the cross. Instead the cross bristled porcupine-like with long, slender spines. Someone had forced the man against these until they had penetrated the fleshy parts of his body to impale him there, like a butterfly spiked on a thorny rose branch. Lethally sharp spines erupted bloodily from the man's arms, legs, stomach, chest, throat.

So that's what it feels like to be struck by lightning. The words weren't really logical, and didn't make a whole lot of sense, but, nevertheless, they were the ones that slowly circled Sam's brain like goldfish in a bowl.

So that's what it feels like to be struck by lightning.

But then again, did *it feel like that?* Sam wondered as he walked to the foot of the cross that had been slotted into the hole in the centre of the altar like some peculiarly thorny Christmas tree planted in its ornamental holder. If you're struck by lightning do you feel the electrons punching through your skin and muscle and veins as if they were those wickedly sharp spikes?

The man with red shoes writhed on the cross and looked

down on Sam with big brown eyes as soulful and as pain-filled as those of any martyred saint.

Again the words spun around his head: *So that's what it feels like to be struck by lightning*.

One spike jutted out through one of the man's nipples. Like a dripping overflow pipe, blood beaded from the point to fall at Sam's feet. Big splotches of juicy, living red violating the clean grey pumice stone floor.

The man looked down at Sam. He'd stopped calling out and he fixed Sam with those big brown eyes that brimmed with hurt and sorrow.

Sam'd had enough. He didn't want to stand and watch the man dying on the cross any more.

He wanted no more of this amphitheatre. He longed to go home.

Without looking back, Sam turned and walked away from the hanging man.

He ran lightly up the wooden stairs to the top of the amphitheatre.

The car park had gone. It had vanished along with the green Yorkshire pastures and the church.

In front of him were more amphitheatres, all the same as the one he'd just left. It was like standing in a lift with mirror walls. One where you can see your reflection repeated ad infinitum: a million *yous* all stretching away for ever and a day.

So it was with the amphitheatres. They stretched away one after the other.

He turned round and around like he was beginning some kind of dance. All he saw were amphitheatres looking like inverted spots in the face of the Earth, running away world without end to cover every damn square inch of the planet.

Then, as dreams are apt to do for no particular reason, the dream machine that pumped the images through his head suddenly stopped.

Waking, he opened his eyes.

But, at that moment, he strongly suspected the dream hadn't really ended.

Two

He looked to his right. Zita sat on the bench. She wore sunglasses and was jotting figures down on the clipboard. Under her breath she was singing, *'Buffalo girls gonna come out tonight, gonna come out tonight . . .'*

To his left sat four young people in fancy dress – Dracula, Laurel & Hardy, and a blonde girl in a gorilla suit, minus the head.

Sitting around the amphitheatre were around twenty people. Another twenty or so had clogged the narrow staircase that led to the top of the amphitheatre and the car park.

In the centre of the stage, pushing the pin into his shirt collar, was the middle-aged guy in the gold waistcoat who'd given the history lecture.

Through the V-shaped cleft in the amphitheatre Sam could see a large luxury cruiser moored to the bank. Behind that was a narrow boat with a dragon painted in swirling gold and red lines on its sides. And there was the wide stretch of the river itself shining in the sunlight with the gently swelling hills beyond.

Hell, I'm becoming an old man at the age of twenty-six, Sam told himself. *I sit here for twenty minutes and I doze off in the sunshine. Not only that but I have the weirdest dreams.*

But the weird dream wasn't of him walking down into the amphitheatre where the man in red shoes hung from the cross of huge thorns.

No. The really weird dream was of him leaving the amphitheatre with Zita, then sitting with her in a café eating a piece of battered cod along with a pile of chunky golden chips which she'd insisted on dousing with vinegar. 'That's the way we eat them across here,' she'd told him with one of her big she-tiger grins that it would take a brave man to ignore. 'Then we have afters.'

'Afters? What're afters?' he'd asked, leaning back to avoid the reek of vinegar.

'Afters is pudding. Y'know? A sweet?'

'Oh, right.'

'And this café does a really fab spotted dick. Are you going to have some?'

'Spotted dick?' He'd raised a disbelieving eyebrow. 'Don't know. Sounds a tad raunchy to me.'

'You'll love it, trust me.' And she'd ordered it anyway before he could say yea or nay.

Now that dream had the solid ring of reality to it. The café sat in the middle of a row of shops. Trucks and buses lumbered by outside. The café's owner had cutened the place up with pictures of puppies. Later the spotted dick appeared: it turned out to be a great eldritch hunk of cake, spotted with currants and raisins, that wallowed batrachian-like in a bowl of steaming custard.

And just like in any café rooted in reality, customers came and went, including a tramp with ginger hair and a boiler suit who bought (or cadged for nix) a cup of soup and a hunk of chocolate cake. The next high point involved a man in a security guard's uniform knocking a bowl of sugar from the table onto his knees and saying, 'Oops, I thought I was sweet enough already' – which raised a laugh or two from some of the other clientele and a weary shake of the proprietor's head as he came from behind the counter with a dustpan and brush.

But nothing weird happened in that dream. The café-owner didn't turn into a huge bat and go flapping slowly away over the rooftops of Casterton. The spotted dick didn't turn into eyeball pie. Zita was still Zita, a feisty PA with a glossy-auburn plait that was as thick as a ship's cable.

Sam Baker would have readily bet his best shirt on the fact that the meal in the café was no dream.

But here he was in the amphitheatre with the hot sun streaming down, Zita jotting notes against the equipment inventory, tourists streaming back to the waiting coach and cars.

He looked round, shielding his eyes with his hand against the dazzling sun.

Only something wasn't quite right.

And everyone knew it.

Other people were standing, looking round at their surroundings as if convinced something was askew but weren't exactly sure what.

Sam saw half a dozen men scratching their heads as they looked round. A couple of women slipped sunglasses down their noses in order to scrutinize the amphitheatre with their naked eyes, suspecting, perhaps, that the polarized lenses were playing sneaky tricks on them. The body language of everyone there had a kind of 'Do-you-see-what-I-see?' message running through it as clearly as a name through seaside rock.

Sam scanned the skies, half-expecting that the audience had seen a spaceship whirling by.

The sky was empty except for a pair of heron gliding by on stiff, extended wings. Even the thunder cloud had gone.

At that moment he heard a gasp.

He looked to his left. Sitting beside him was the guy in the Dracula outfit, complete with white-painted face and red lipstick daubed around his lips for blood.

He made the sound again, a sudden gasp as if he'd been punched in the stomach. He even clutched his belly and doubled up. Gasping, croaking, sobbing, he tugged his knees up to his chest then rolled forward.

He'd probably have somersaulted all the way down to the bottom of the amphitheatre if Sam hadn't caught him by the cloak.

'Get it off me!' the guy screamed hysterically. 'Get it off me! It's hurting! It's—'

His body jerked with convulsions. Sam saw that the man was in agony. But why? Sam couldn't see anything wrong, unless the guy's appendix had just exploded somewhere in his gut.

'*Get it offffff!*'

In that inverted cone of rock with its perfect acoustics the man's screams were so loud they were as painful as they were shocking.

Everyone turned to stare.

'Do you know what's wrong with him?' Sam asked a chubby man of around twenty dressed as Oliver Hardy. The chubby man stared, sweat running down from beneath his bowler hat.

Sam wrestled the screaming man back onto the bench.

'Hey, listen to me . . .' Sam panted. 'What's wrong with your buddy?'

'Drugs,' mumbled Oliver Hardy, shocked. 'Stupid drugs. I said we shouldn't have . . . not on an empty stomach. Oh, Jesus . . .' Oliver Hardy pushed his fists into his eyes and rubbed like crazy. 'I'm out of my head, oh Christ, I'm out of my head. I'm hallucinating. *Help me . . .*'

Sam watched appalled as the man dressed as Oliver Hardy collapsed sobbing, his arms over his head as if the sky was just about to come tumbling down.

Meanwhile, the guy in the Dracula costume still convulsed in Sam's arms. 'He's fitting,' Sam called back over his shoulder to Zita who by this time was on her feet and trying to stop Dracula beating his head on the timber bench-back.

'He's not the only one,' she said in voice which, although calm, was charged with tension. 'Take a look.'

Sam looked up.

The world had gone crazy. Gut instinct had told him that a few short moments ago. This was the proof.

'What's happening, Sam? Why are they doing that?'

Sam followed Zita's gaze. 'I don't know . . . I really don't know.'

From dream to nightmare. It had only taken a moment.

Three

People were sitting back down in the amphitheatre seats (some standing on the steps sat down on those, too). They dropped down onto their backsides quickly, almost bruisingly, as if they'd just been hit by a particularly bad piece of news. Even though the sun was hot many were shivering and either folding their arms tightly across their chests or wrapping their arms around their shoulders.

This wasn't cold, though, Sam realized: this was shock.

The convulsions of the guy in the Dracula cape had all but subsided. Now he was shivering as though someone had dunked him in a vat of iced water.

'Oh, my God,' Zita breathed. 'Is this what they call a situation or what?'

'Let's just say the shit's gone and hit the fan,' Sam said in something close to a bewildered daze. 'Only for the life of me I haven't a clue what shit, or what fan.'

Some of the people were crying – that went for grown men as well as grown women. A woman behind him had stuffed her knuckles into her mouth and was biting hard to stop from screaming out loud. Her eyes had silvered over with tears.

An old man in a baseball cap beside her rocked backwards and forwards, wearing an expression that suggested someone had stuffed half a lemon in his mouth and he didn't know where to spit.

The only time Sam'd seen something comparable to this was when a bomb had torn through a crowded market place. Not seen at first hand, of course: he'd been editing footage piped in from a satellite link in Asia. There'd been gory shots of torn bodies. Shattered market stalls. A dog's severed head lying in the gutter. Lots of blood slicking paving slabs, making them look as if they'd been enamelled red. And there had been close-ups of survivors moments after the blast. There were expressions of shock, confusion, fear, horror, even more confusion, and a lot of people just looking at each other as if to ask: 'Did this really happen, or did I dream it?'

He was seeing those same expressions here.

Only there had been no blast.

But there was no doubt about it. They'd all just experienced nothing less than a king-sized trauma. And, yes, *hell*, *yes*: these people were in shock.

Chapter Nine

One

Sam eased the guy in the Dracula cape back gently. 'How're you feeling?'

The man straightened and looked down at his stomach as if expecting to see a marching band come right through his flies, playing the theme from *Monty Python*.

'Where is it?' asked the man. Sam couldn't tell if his face was white with shock beneath that stage make-up caked all over it. But there was something pretty colourless about his voice. As if he'd just experienced full-blooded terror.

'Where's what?' Sam asked gently.

'The truck, of course. It was right there.' He touched his stomach. 'I felt the tyres . . . Christ, it was awful.' He looked up at Sam, his eyes strangely glittery and wild-looking. 'Christ, all that blood. That blood on the road. And people just standing there watching me like I was—'

'Take it easy,' Zita said and stroked his shoulder. 'You must have dreamt it.'

The words 'You must have dreamt it' provoked the strongest reaction yet from the girl in the gorilla suit and the girl in the Stan Laurel costume. They'd been staring glassily at their friend in the Dracula cape; now both were stung from their trance. They looked at Zita sharply. Then at each other.

The blonde girl shook her head, as if she was trying to get

her head round some huge mathematical problem. 'He can't have dreamt about the accident.' She gripped a handful of her blonde hair as if she might rip it out, then looked up at Sam. 'No, Lee didn't dream it. Because I did.'

Two

After the blonde girl had claimed to have dreamt about an accident – a truck snagging the guy's cape and whipping him under the wheels where he was crushed – there followed a strange conversation. At least, Sam found it strange. Because all four people in fancy dress claimed to have had the same dream. The chubby guy in the Oliver Hardy costume complete with shabby bowler hat rocked backwards and forwards, sobbing, while saying over and over, 'It was the drugs. I tell you it was the drugs. And I told you we shouldn't have, didn't I? Not dope. Not on an empty stomach.'

Sam turned to Zita who sat shaking her head in a kind of stunned disbelief.

'I admit it,' Sam said in a flat voice. 'This has got me beat. Are we mad or dreaming? Or both?'

'Search me, Sam . . . search me.' Her only concession to showing her own shock was to rub her jaw with a trembling hand.

Sam looked round at the tiers of seating. 'Some of these people look pretty shaken. But for the life of me, I still don't know what happened.' He turned back to her. 'The sensible thing is to bring in the emergency services and let them sort it out.' He pulled out the mobile phone.

'And tell them what?' Zita asked, puzzled.

'To send medics . . . ambulances.' He shrugged, which was an expression of his own bewilderment rather than unconcern. 'Some of these people should go to hospital.'

'But what are they suffering from? A shared bad dream? Déjà vu? An unpleasant premonition? As far as I can see, no one's been physically hurt, have they?'

'I agree. But—' There seemed to be no rational statement

74

to tag on after the 'But.' What could he tell the emergency operator? That fifty people had just experienced unpleasant 'feelings'? That probably rated far lower in priority than trying to call out the fire engine to rescue a cat stuck in a tree, or the local head case complaining to the police that Martians were vacationing under his bed.

Nevertheless, Sam told himself as he thumbed the phone's call button, these people have just had one almighty shock to their senses. Just what was it? Toxic vapours wafting from some factory over the hill? Supersonic shock wave? Spontaneous neural disruption? Who knew, perhaps even a kick in the pants from the invisible man? *Something* had happened. These people needed help.

He dialled and held the mobile to his ear.

What he heard were electronic burbling noises.

He tried again.

'Damn it,' he said scowling at the phone, then he looked up. 'Wait a minute, the emergency number across here isn't 911, is it?'

Zita gave a little shake of her head, the plait swishing. '999. You'd best ask for ambulance, but God knows what you're going to tell them.'

'I'll cross that bridge as and when.' Sam managed to shoot her a small smile. 'I'm a director. I bullshit great. 999, you said?'

She nodded as he keyed the numbers.

'Hell and tarnation,' he grunted as the melodious burbling played in the earpiece again. 'I'm not getting through. The battery's still good, though. It must be bad reception down in this damned hole in the ground.'

'I got through earlier.' She switched on the phone. 'I'll use mine.'

She tried a couple of times, sighing with frustration at each failed attempt. 'No joy,' she said pressing her red lips together and giving the phone an angry glare. 'My batt's OK, too. It must be bad reception after all.'

'Well, perhaps we won't need to call anyway. People are

starting to come round. Whatever hit them seems to be passing.'

'But what *did* hit us? I just feel as if someone's popped an electric blender inside my head and stirred my brains.'

Sam paused, thoughtful. 'The last time I felt anything like this I'd been sitting in a tree when it got struck by lightning.'

'I remember you saying. But you weren't hurt?'

'Nope, not one bit. My eyebrows got singed clean off, that's all. My friends weren't so lucky, though. They were dead before they hit the ground. Lightning's strange stuff.'

'You think we were struck here in the amphitheatre?' Zita looked round and Sam could imagine she was looking for areas of scorched ground and trails of smoke. Not that there were any to be seen. Outwardly everything appeared normal.

'Maybe.'

'Thank God, no one was actually hit.'

'Everyone's moving now. Come on,' he said, feeling more cheerful now that he was rationalizing the living daylights out of what moments ago had seemed a mystery of impenetrable strangeness. 'Weren't we going to eat fish and chips?'

Three

They'd reached the car park of the amphitheatre. The car lay ahead, the heat-haze imbuing it with a wobbly, spongy look as if it couldn't make up its mind whether to be solid or soft as jelly.

Sam tried his phone again.

Again there was only the slightly melodious burbling in his ear.

'If there is an electronic storm brewing somewhere it might be knocking out the signal.'

Zita had stopped, her arms folded, her eyebrows knitting together as she thought hard. 'Sam,' she said in a low voice, as if only now seeing something that had been staring her in the face. 'I'm not hungry now.'

'It'll be the shock, come on.' He shot her a reassuring smile. 'I'll treat you to a big mug of tea with plenty of sugar. You'll be right as a . . . Zita. Zita? What's wrong? Do you feel all right?'

She was running her tongue round in the inside of her mouth as if chasing a piece of unswallowed food. 'Sam. I'm not hungry, because I've just eaten. I can still taste the fish.'

'No, we were just going to—'

'Going to eat. I know. But I feel full, don't you?'

'I'll probably get my appetite back on the way.'

'Sam.' She walked forward, gripped him by the arm and turned him round. Her big, dark eyes were serious. She'd got hold of the tail of some humdinger of a mystery and she was trying to pull it out. 'We *have* eaten. Remember?'

Sam felt the smile on his face tighten as it became unnatural and forced. 'That's not possible. We've just come from the amphitheatre. Before that we were walking round the site.'

She shook her head as if fishing for the words that would explain lucidly the confusion she was feeling. 'But later we ate at the café in Casterton. Fish and chips followed by spotted-dick pudding. You remember that, don't you? Or have we been sharing the same dream, too?'

At that moment, Sam could have believed the ground had opened up just one step away from his feet. He could have believed that a pit, sheer-sided and oh-so-dark, plunged all the way down to hell. Or to insanity: he just didn't know which.

He could pull back, pretend that he'd dreamt it all when he nodded off in the amphitheatre, or he could take the verbal equivalent of a decisive step forward and risk tumbling all the way down into dark, shrieking oblivion.

He looked at Zita.

She'd slipped off her sunglasses and was looking levelly back at him.

Hell.

He'd grown up honest and truthful. Particularly to himself. Self-deception is the worst breed of lie of all.

He'd have to take that step forward and risk the consequences of the pit that lay, not in the tarmac in front of him, but inside his head.

He licked his suddenly dry lips.

He tasted vinegar.

His stomach told him that he'd recently eaten.

Carefully, as if it was something he rarely did, he raised his arm and looked at his watch for a moment. 'It's now two o'clock. But in here' – he touched the side of his head – 'it feels later. So gut instinct is telling me my watch is slow, or it stopped for a while, because it seems to be working fine now.' He spoke slowly and carefully as he studied his watch because he was mindful of that pit in his mind. He didn't want to precipitate a fall into what must be madness by speaking too quickly or without giving due consideration to what he would say next. 'Also. I remember the café had pictures of puppies on the walls. And a man in a security-guard uniform who knocked a bowl of sugar onto his knee and he said?' Sam pointed at Zita for the answer that would decide whether he stayed sane or fell into that shrieking pit of madness.

'He said: "Oops, and I thought I was sweet enough already." Then everyone laughed.'

The dark pit disappeared. Sam knew he was sane. But he knew, also, that he had no explanation for what he'd experienced.

He found himself staring into Zita's deep brown eyes. He realized it was as if they were wordlessly exchanging information, about what they'd seen, about what they felt, about just what in God's name they could do now.

'You know what's happened, don't you?' she said.

He nodded. 'The question is, what happens *now*?'

'Go back into town. We'll go back to the café. Ask if they remember us. Ask subtly, that is, so they don't write us off as raving lunatics. After that . . .' She gave a shrug. 'Any ideas?'

'Yes. We either contact the newsroom and file the most amazing story they've ever heard—'

'Which will make us rich – or get us fired.'

He nodded. 'Or we forget all about it.'

He climbed into the passenger seat beside her. He'd done this before, but this was no eerie sense of déjà vu.

'We can decide what we do later,' he said, with a small smile. 'But first you can tell me all you know about time travel.'

Chapter Ten

One

Lee Burton sat in the amphitheatre. He pulled open the Dracula cape to give himself a clear view of his stomach. There were no back tyres of a petrol tanker crushing his stomach and kidneys to jelly. There was no blood. There was no pain now.

But the memory was still there, burning with a white-hot ferocity inside his head.

He'd been crushed by that truck in York. He was certain of it. He'd puked blood against the treads of the tyres. That gush of red had burst from his mouth like an explosion.

A priest gave him the last rites.

Only now he was back in the amphitheatre again with the sun beating down. For some reason Ryan Keith sat blubbing like a baby at his side, still clutching the Oliver Hardy bowler in his two plump hands.

Sweat trickled down Lee's chest beneath the white frilly shirt. The Dracula cape pressed down on his back, seeming as heavy as a hot sheet of lead.

And he felt like he'd just staggered off the mother of all roller-coaster rides. His head spun. He felt disorientated.

But, oh my God, it felt so sweet to be alive.

Two

Zita swore. She tried turning the key again in the Range Rover ignition. The starter motor turned, cylinders even fired, then the engine ran unevenly again for a moment or so before cutting out once more in a series of spluttering coughs.

Sam looked at her. 'It sounds as if there's a blockage in the fuel line or the ignition timing's out.'

'Shit,' she said forcefully. 'This car's less than a year old. It can't crap out on me. It bloody well can't.'

Sam opened the car door. The heat inside the car from the sun was greenhouse-like. 'Best leave it for a few minutes. The carburettor might be flooded.'

'Sam, I don't flood engines,' she said dangerously. 'I don't flood engines, I don't stall at traffic lights, I don't try and drive away with the handbrake still on.'

'OK,' he said soothingly, climbing out. 'We'll leave it for a moment, then try it again. If it still won't start then we'll call out a mechanic.'

She climbed out and slammed the car door on her side, glaring at it furiously before walking round the front to lean against the cow catcher bolted to the front.

Sam slipped on his sunglasses again and looked round the amphitheatre car park. People were streaming steadily from the amphitheatre itself. Most headed in the direction of a coach parked across the far side of the car park. Some had gone to the ice-cream van. But the whole scene was shot through with strangeness. There was an undeniable peculiarity about it.

The body language of the people was still all wrong. They looked as if they'd just walked away from a bomb explosion. Their expressions were dazed. Some stood and stared at their surroundings. Others repeatedly checked their watches; sometimes they listened for the tick, their faces the image of bewilderment. A couple were prodding the keys of their mobile phones and, Sam saw, they were having no luck whatsoever in getting through to loved ones, work places, the police or whoever they were phoning.

Would-be customers at the ice-cream van were having no luck either. The man who sold ice creams was sitting on the ground outside his van shaking his head. Sam might have been mistaken but he thought he heard the man muttering: 'I've just seen myself. I've just seen myself . . .'

At that moment an elderly man with a walking stick and wearing a hearing aid hobbled up to Sam.

'Excuse me, young man,' asked the man as he fiddled with the earpiece of the hearing aid. 'Can you tell me what day this is?'

'Tuesday.' It should have been a peculiar question; only Sam didn't think it was right now. The normal world had just flipped a somersault and Sam felt he was now a passive observer waiting to see what would happen next.

The old man cupped his hand behind his ear. 'Pardon. I'm sorry, my gizmo . . .' He tapped the earpiece of the hearing aid. 'This thing seems to be on the blink. Monday, you say?'

'No,' Sam said loudly. 'Tuesday.'

'Oh? Tuesday? Oh, I see . . . I could have been sure it was . . . oh, I'm sorry to have troubled you, young man.' Mumbling, the old man hobbled away.

Sam watched him go, struck by the look of terror on the old man's face. The old boy was probably convinced he'd just noticed the first signs of Alzheimer's and all the horrors it would bring. Forgetfulness. Confusion. Incontinence. Asking for lunch at midnight. Calling his daughter by his wife's name. Crying at night because he was afraid of the dark again.

But, deep down, Sam doubted if it was Alzheimer's. Surely this was no senile dementia. Or, if it was, then it was as contagious as a head cold. Because he'd experienced that same confusion ever since he'd opened his eyes in the amphitheatre just fifteen minutes ago. And he'd seen it on the faces of everyone there.

'That old guy thought he'd flipped his lid, didn't he?' Zita said in something near wonder as she watched him limp in circles around the car park, confusion written large in his frightened eyes. 'He thinks he's cracked up.'

'And I figure we all know the feeling.' Sam felt a strange

itchiness in his thumbs – those thumbs that were actually extraneous fingers with twin joints. They sometimes did this when he was stressed or excited: his nerve endings jangled like tiny electric bells. *Damn' mutant hands,* he told himself, feeling suddenly downright cranky. The 'thumbs' itched harder.

But wouldn't this make one hell of a story if he could convince the editors back in the newsroom? 'Zita,' he said, feeling the tension build. 'Remember a couple of minutes ago? I asked you what you know about time travel?'

'Yeah, I remember. But the only one and true shining fact I know about it is that it's impossible.'

'You sure? We travel in time every day, don't we?'

Her forehead creased. 'Of course we do. But time travel is strictly a one-way street. And we're moving at a fixed speed, too. From now into the future.'

'But what does that wheelchair guy say?'

'What? Professor Hawking, the astrophysicist?'

'Yeah. Hasn't he been telling us all for years that every once in a while time doesn't do what it's supposed to do? That it can hare off in different directions, or simply take leaps forwards or backwards?'

'But don't you have to travel through a black hole for that to happen?'

'But I *do* know that it's a hard scientific fact that speed warps time. Einstein said it. The faster you go, the slower time passes. It was proved in 1971 when a couple of scientists put four atomic clocks on a plane and flew them round the world. When they were compared with clocks on the ground the scientists saw that the airborne clocks showed that time on board the aircraft had slowed down.'

Sam noticed that Zita was giving him what his auntie used to call an old-fashioned look. He smiled. 'No, I wasn't particularly nerdy as a kid, but like most boys I soaked up useless facts like a tissue soaks up snot.'

'Charming turn of phrase there, Mr Baker. But if I remember rightly those atomic clocks on the plane only differed from those on the ground by nanoseconds. Am I right?'

'You are right. What's more, if you spent your whole life flying on an aircraft you'd only be younger than your identical twin on the ground, say, by one ten-thousandth of a second.'

'Which still doesn't explain what happened here.'

'No, it doesn't. As far as I can see we will find all the evidence of time travel we need by driving into Casterton and simply asking a cop the time, or finding a church clock.'

'If we can get the car to work.'

'We can catch a damn' bus if need be.' Sam felt himself in gear now. 'What time do you make it now?'

'Two-fifteen.'

'Same here.'

'But do you remember what time we were in the café?'

'Around three-ish.'

'So you think we've somehow slipped back in time by about three-quarters of an hour?'

'Sounds crazy, doesn't it?' Again Sam sensed that deep, dark pit opening up inside his head. Painfully he realized what the old man with the walking stick had felt. That same tottering on the edge of insanity; that frightening tug of vertigo; as if at any moment you'd slip and fall into a pit of crimson madness where you'd gibber and scream because you knew deep down that there was no way you'd ever make that long climb back to sanity again.

He took a deep breath and wiped his face. His cheek was slick with perspiration. 'Yes, it does sound crazy, doesn't it?'

'Totally. The only thing is . . .' Zita paused. 'I'm beginning to wonder if it's true.'

'That's you and me both.'

'Hell, don't you feel as if your head's just about to explode?' She gave a jangly laugh as hysteria tried to get its teeth into her. 'This kind of thing doesn't happen to nice girls from Pontypridd.'

'Why don't we take a walk? I don't think we're going to

learn much here.' He noticed a few other drivers were having no luck in starting their cars. Whatever had crapped out their car's ignition was contagious. 'We could head across to that old church over there.'

She shot him a questioning look.

'Don't worry. I'm not praying for salvation – yet. But we could check the time with its clock tower. Unless you can see the church clock from here, that is?'

She shook her head. 'The walk'll do me good anyway. Besides . . .' She scanned the people still milling as aimlessly as frightened sheep in the car park. 'This lot are beginning to give me the willies. Can't you can just sense the hysteria beneath the surface?'

He'd sensed it, too. The man who sold ice creams was sobbing silently into the palms of his hands. A dozen men were running their hands through their hair with a kind of desperate intensity, as if anticipating that The Bomb was about to fall at any moment. The tall, thin guy dressed as Dracula was standing on a picnic table and was slapping his stomach while pumping out a bizarre affected laugh: 'Who . . . ha-ha . . . who . . . ha-ha.'

Some of those people were coming apart at the seams. And, Sam realized, it wasn't a pretty sight. He didn't want to be here when the floodgates opened. 'Come on, Zita,' he said in a low voice. 'Let's get away from here.'

She nodded gratefully. They set off on foot across the car park, not looking back at the aimless yet edgy crowd circling around.

Three

A moment later they left the blacktop of the car park (which smelled strongly of tar in the heat of the sun) and walked across the grass. It was coarse, extravagantly curly and reminded Sam Baker, quite absurdly, of the pubic hair of a girl he'd once dated. That hair had felt dry and springy against his cheek as he'd lain with his head across her middle.

What on Earth made me think of Jay Lorenz's pubic hair? He pondered this as he walked with the cat-like Zita beside him. It was probably a safe memory, he told himself. Somewhere secure he could retreat to after the weirdness of the last hour. Already his mind was looking for a refuge in the comfortable, unthreatening past.

He scanned his surroundings as he walked. But this looked reassuringly normal. The fuzzy grass that reminded him so much of Jay's pubes ran away into the distance. Beyond the meadows, a good ten minutes' walk away, was a fringe of trees. Beyond that was a road where a few cars swished by, windows glinting in the sunlight.

In the distance he could see a pair of microlight aircraft crawling across the sky from a nearby airfield, the pilots making the most of the fine summer's day. And there, directly ahead, was the church, built from a creamy lime-stone that looked as soft as Cheshire cheese. The church was ancient, with a low square tower at one end, a black slate roof and a walled graveyard that was clustered tight with headstones all leaning this way and that after years of subsidence and erosion. He couldn't yet make out the time on the clock face.

Zita walked in silence. He guessed she was doing the same as him, struggling to digest the events of the last hour or so.

Maybe time had flipped back, he told himself. Maybe once every so often it did just that. Hadn't the universe once been a tiny speck of matter the size of a pinhead just before the Big Bang that started it all? Aren't our bodies made from the same stuff as stars?

He noticed that a dead pigeon lay there on the ground in front of him.

Its head had completely gone, either shot off or chewed away by a cat. It lay oozing blood from the severed neck onto that pubes-like grass. That pigeon was made of the same stuff as stars too. The cosmos recycled everything. Stars into planets. Rock into soil. Soil into plants. Plant seeds into pigeons. Pigeons into . . . whatever.

He stepped over the headless bird and walked on, wondering just what other strangeness this universe was capable of.

Four

A moment later, Sam Baker saw that the church clock didn't contain any stunning evidence for a backward flip through time. He watched as it chimed half-past.

'Exactly the same time as my watch,' he told Zita, feeling his heart sink. He was convinced some extraordinary event had taken place. Now the clock was mutely telling them nothing had happened after all, that due to collective hysteria brought on by a hot summer's day or – who knew? hypnotic suggestion? a contagious insanity? – they'd simply imagined it all.

'Unless what affected us affected the church, too,' Zita said. 'What if the whole world took a backward jump of two hours?'

'There goes my exclusive, for one thing.' He gave a small smile. 'Come on, let's walk up to the road. I noticed a pub up there. I think we could do with a beer.'

'Or two.'

'With whisky chasers.' His smile broadened.

They'd only been walking a moment or so when they saw the grey-haired man in the gold waistcoat who'd given the lecture in the amphitheatre. Sam remembered the man's name: Jud. (*So at least it can't be some freaky kind of Alzheimer's that's grabbed us all and scrambled our brains*, Sam told himself, feeling reassured on at least one point.) Jud strolled towards them, but not in a straight line, more of a long curve. He walked, sometimes glancing up at Sam and Zita, but more often scanning the ground with an intense expression on his face that suggested he could have been looking for a dropped wallet.

Zita glanced from the gold-waistcoated man to Sam, who raised his eyebrows.

So Jud had had his senses addled, too. Because he was

walking along what appeared to be an invisible curving line while sweeping that curly pubes-like turf with his eyes.

The man looked up at them.

'Good afternoon,' he said civilly. 'Weren't you two in the amphitheatre for my little talk?'

'That's right. We enjoyed it,' Sam said cautiously, not wanting to appear an idiot by blurting out: *My-God-I-think-we've-just-zipped-back-through-time-two-hours-whaddya-say-to-that!* 'We were just walking up to the pub on the road. It got a little on the warm side down there.'

'Turned out fine, didn't it?' Jud agreed, still preoccupied with scanning the grass. 'Uhm, this might sound odd, but do you mind confirming what day it is today?'

Zita spoke in a careful voice as if not wanting to incriminate herself. 'Tuesday.'

'Mmm . . .' The man returned to scanning the ground.

Sam looked at Zita. She met his glance. He knew she was thinking the same thing. That the man was confused and that they should move on.

But before they could walk on the man sounded another meditative 'Mmmm . . .' while standing there, hands on hips, staring down at the grass. 'Yes,' he said. 'Tuesday. I would have said the same. But I have a feeling – a strong feeling – that we're both wrong.' He looked up at them, his eyes sharp and anything but confused. 'Not mistaken, I should emphasize, but wrong.'

'Why? Isn't today Tuesday?' Sam asked intrigued. 'What makes you think that?'

'Oh, excuse me. I'm forgetting my manners. My name's Jud Campbell. But you'll know that already, of course. Delighted to meet you.' He held out his hand. Zita shook it without hesitation, saying her name. Sam followed suit. The man's hands were large, powerful, yet surprisingly gentle. Labourer's hands, he thought. 'Sam Baker.'

'Delighted,' Jud said smiling, his blue eyes bright and friendly.

Sam repeated his question. 'You said you thought today wasn't Tuesday. What made you say that?'

'I certainly believed it to be Tuesday.' He tapped his watch face with a large, strong, finger. 'This tells me it's Tuesday. But a few moments ago – or at least it seemed to me a few moments ago – I went back to my boat. That's it, the narrow boat on the river. My wife was trying to find her programme, *Columbo*. She adores Peter Falk. The funny thing is, she discovered that instead of Tuesday's programmes the BBC, and every other channel, were broadcasting yesterday's, that is, Monday's programmes. Peculiar, isn't it?'

'Most peculiar.'

'And perplexing. At first, to be completely honest with you, when I opened my eyes at the bottom of that amphitheatre half an hour ago I thought I'd got sunstroke. I've never felt so dizzy in my life before. I saw everyone looked the same: disorientated, confused . . . but I expect you felt likewise. At least, I suspect you did?' He looked at both Sam and Zita. They both nodded. 'Good, then I've not gone barmy. On the way up the steps I chatted to some of the other visitors, then took a walk out here to clear my head. That's when I came across one or two strange things that weren't here before.'

'Such as?'

'If you're in no tearing hurry,' Jud said, 'would you mind taking a look for yourself and seeing what you make of it?'

Sam looked at Zita then nodded. 'OK.'

'I should warn you,' he added, 'you'll need a pretty strong stomach. Some of it's horrible. You still game?'

'Lead the way,' Sam said, wondering what the man intended showing them. He and Zita followed in silence. The sun burned down, birds sang. But already Sam could see something on the grass ahead – a *something* that didn't look quite right. His thumbs began to itch again, and the words from some half-remembered school lesson came to him:

> *By the pricking of my thumbs,*
> *Something wicked this way comes . . .*

Chapter Eleven

Jud unbuttoned his gold waistcoat as he walked. 'Do you know what a palimpsest is?' he asked.

'Search me,' Sam said, not taking his eyes off a black mound lying on the grass ahead of them.

'Some kind of document?' Zita hazarded.

Jud smiled. 'Close, but no cigar. Palimpsest. In the old days they'd write on parchment. It was expensive, so they'd use the same piece over and over. For instance, you'd write a letter on it to a friend. He or she'd read it, wash off the ink, then write their own letter on the same piece of parchment, send it back to you and so on. The same piece of parchment might have dozens of letters written on it, one on top of the other. You could still see the faint handwriting beneath, looking like ghost images. This piece of ground, right from the river to the road, is something of a palimpsest: it's been used over and over. Before that stone church there was a wooden one. Before that it was a Roman temple. Before that there was a neolithic one on the same site. You can go down into the church crypt and see a well there, right in the middle of the floor. That's where Iron Age folk left their sacrificial offerings. See that cobbled section of road across there? That's Roman. At the top of the field is the line of a prehistoric track, probably one of the old pedlar tracks that have criss-crossed Britain for the last twenty thousand years or so; the road still follows the route. These couple of hundred acres have revealed ten thousand years of human habitation, right down to flint arrowheads and bone fish-hooks that we've dug out of the river bank. And that bump in the grass across there is what's left of a hermitage. Roger Rolle himself lived there in the thirteenth century. Heard of Rolle?'

They shook their heads.

Jud continued in his gravelly voice. 'Rolle was a mystic. That is to say, he believed he'd managed to find some kind of hot line to God. He wrote a few books about his experiences before the Black Death put an end to him in the thirteen hundreds. Now then.' He stopped ten paces from the black mound on the grass. 'What do you two make of that?'

Sam saw Zita wrinkle her nose. But, credit to her, she didn't turn and run. Sam's stomach turned over and he instinctively covered his mouth and nose. There was no mistaking what he saw.

'It's a cow,' Sam said. 'Or, at least, it's half a cow.'

He took a step closer. The cow had been cut clean down the middle. The front half lay on the grass: forelegs, shoulders, neck and head. Where the cut had been made two bluish organs that looked like plastic bags sagged from the front half of the body. Sam guessed these were the lungs. While a brownish football-sized piece of meat tucked in the middle was the heart. From it, two white arteries the size of hoses protruded. Both were neatly cut. A huge pool of blood had turned the grass a sticky brown mess. Flies hovered above it while yet more swarmed eagerly over the entrails, feeding.

'Jesus, what a mess,' Sam breathed.

'The cruel bastards,' Zita said. 'Who'd do a thing like this?'

'Who indeed?' Jud echoed. 'Just one thing, though: where's the back end of the cow?'

'Poachers?' Sam suggested.

'Messy way to steal a cow, isn't it?' Jud said, thoughtfully. 'You'd think it'd be easier to steal the whole animal and butcher it later. And how on Earth do you cut a living cow that size so neatly in the middle of a field. Look, someone could have come along with a huge axe and *bang!*' He mimed chopping with one arm. 'Sliced cleanly in two, like you'd cut an apple down the middle.'

The flies buzzed even more hungrily to form a blue-black mist above the exposed internal organs. Sam could smell the raw meat. 'You said there was something else, Jud?'

'There is. Follow me.'

They followed again.

Jud talked back over his shoulder at them. 'Are you noticing what I'm noticing?'

Sam looked down at the grass where Jud was pointing as he walked. 'I don't see anything,' Sam said. 'Only grass. What is it?'

'Bear with me. I don't want to lead you to any conclusions, if I can help it. I'd prefer that you reach them yourselves.'

Sam stared hard at the crisp, spongy grass. He saw nothing unusual.

Zita, folding her arms, looked too, sharp eyes probing. She didn't say anything but Sam had the feeling she was seeing more than him.

'Here's another curio,' Jud said, like he was pointing out an interesting archaeological site. 'Take a close look at that bottle on the grass.'

Sam dutifully looked. 'It's broken,' he said.

'Not broken.' Jud pointed one of his thick fingers at it but didn't touch it, any more than a cop would touch anything on a fresh crime scene. Sam realized that for Jud the cow and the bottle were evidence. Evidence of what, exactly, he didn't know. 'Take a closer look,' Jud invited. 'Does it look broken to you?'

Crouching, Zita peered at the bottle where it lay, minus its neck. 'It looks as if it's been cut with some kind of saw.'

'A clean cut at that. In fact, would you say as clean a cut as whatever bisected that cow?'

Zita nodded.

'A cut cow? A cut bottle?' Sam asked.

'We're amassing some strange anomalies here, aren't we?' It was the kind of thing someone could have said with a broad grin. Only Jud's face was deadly serious. 'Come on,' he said, 'just a little further. I've one more thing to show you.'

It only took a moment to reach it.

'Oh my, God.' Zita put her hand to her mouth and her eyes went wide.

It was the front part of a bike. For an instant Sam wasn't sure why she found a bike's handlebars, connected by the fork to little more than a half a front wheel, so shocking. It lay on the ground, part of the tyre lying beside it like a black snake. But then he looked more closely.

This time he saw.

This was worse than half a cow spilling its insides back there on the turf.

There was a human hand still grasping one of the handlebars. The attached forearm had been severed midway along. A watch still encircled a wrist that was slick and red with blood. The fingers had uncurled a little from the rubber handgrip on the handle-bars. Sam found himself hypnotized by those still fingers. The fingernails gleamed a bloodless white in the sun. Fine hairs bristled across the back of the hand, which was suntanned and dotted here and there with brown freckles.

'Again, you'll notice a clean cut,' Jud said in a flat voice. 'It looks as if a surgeon's amputated it, doesn't it? No ragged edges, no torn skin . . . are you all right?'

Zita had turned away from it.

'Just give me a moment,' she said taking a deep breath. 'I'll be fine.'

A thought occurred to Sam. 'What time does the watch say?'

Jud crouched down, tilting his head to one side. 'Ten to three.'

'The same as mine.'

'And mine.'

'Jesus H. Christ.' Sam murmured, staring at the front of the bike frame where the hand still gripped the handlebars. Hell, the thing could have been a perverse work of art. 'Not a pretty sight, is it?'

'No, not one bit,' Jud agreed.

'I guess this one's for the police to sort the nuts from the screws.'

Jud shook his grey head. 'I don't know. I've a feeling this might be one case that's beyond them.'

Zita said, 'Jud?'

'Yes?'

'It's the grass, isn't it? It's two different lengths.' She looked at Sam. 'Don't you see it?'

Sam stared down at the ground.

Call me dense, stupid or just plain myopic, he told himself, mystified. But he saw nothing wrong with the grass.

He gave a puzzled shrug.

Jud walked away from the severed hand half a dozen paces or so, then he stood and looked back in the direction of the amphitheatre and the river.

'When I was a boy,' he said, 'The fair would come every year to the park. I enjoyed it like any other boy – or girl, come to that. But what fascinated me was when they packed up the rides and went. On the way to school on the morning after they'd gone I'd rush to the park and stand and look at the grass where the caravans and the rides had been. To me it seemed . . . I don't know, magical. You could see the ghost patterns of the rides and the caravans and the candy floss stalls in the grass. Do you remember? The grass was always longer where the rides had been. You could stand in a perfect circle of longer grass where the roundabouts had stood. There was nothing magical about it, of course. The grass had just been forced where it had been covered by the rides and the caravans. It had grown faster than the rest of the grass. It was a paler green, too.'

Sam looked back down at the turf.

'This is all the same shade of green. But you see it now, don't you, Sam?'

Sam looked. 'I see it,' he said feeling a burst of wonder. 'It's longer at this side of the bike than the other. By no more than half an inch. But it's definitely longer.'

'You'll find it's the same at the bottle with its neck cut off and the half a cow.' Jud rubbed his jaw thoughtfully. 'Also, I'd bet you a week's pay packet that you'd find the line that marks the boundary between to the two different grass lengths runs exactly – *exactly* – along the line of the cuts in the bottle, the cow and that poor devil's arm.'

'You've got an explanation for that?' Sam asked.

'I have.' Jud nodded. 'And, Mr Baker, Miss Prestwyck, I'm pretty sure it's the same explanation sitting right there in the front of your minds right now.'

Zita said slowly, 'It's time, isn't it? It's all gone wrong.'

Chapter Twelve

One

Instead of going to the pub on the main road as they had originally planned, Sam and Zita returned to the amphitheatre with Jud Campbell. The sun blazed down. A heat haze shimmered across the grass, blurring and deforming the once straight lines of telegraph poles that marched across the meadow. Tourists were sitting on benches or on the grass. A good number had bought cold drinks from the visitors' centre.

It seemed that none of the cars or the coach would start. At least three of the cars had their bonnets propped open. A man wiped his oily hands with a rag while staring at the engine, clearly at a loss over which cable or wire to push or pull next.

That atmosphere of agitated confusion seemed to have spent itself. People looked calmer. The man in the Dracula cape had bought a coke from the vending machine and, as far as Sam could see, seemed pretty much in control of himself.

Jud said to Sam and Zita, 'Would you two help me out here?'

'With what?'

'With those.' Sam nodded across the fifty or so people. 'We've got to find a way of keeping them here for a while.'

'Why? What's the problem?'

'I feel as if we should all stay here for a while, until we know what's going on.'

Zita gave a surprised laugh. 'You sound as if you want to keep us all in quarantine.'

'Quarantine?' He nodded, serious. 'Yes, good way of putting it. Quarantine. That's exactly what I do mean.'

'But why?' Sam said. 'Surely these people have had a bellyful, of today. Why not let them go home or back to their hotels to freshen up and sink a few beers? I know that's what I'd like to do right now.'

'I don't think you've thought through the implications. The grass immediately surrounding the amphitheatre is about half an inch longer than the grass out there on the meadows. In this dry weather that's round about a week's growing time. Do you follow?'

Sam nodded. 'Go on.'

'Well, have you ever heard that phrase "I'm so busy it's a wonder I don't meet myself coming back?" A bizarre and meaningless phrase, I know. But right now I think it might be extremely meaningful for all of us.'

'Damn,' Sam breathed as the penny dropped.

'I'll second that,' Jud said firmly. 'All we know for sure is that the universe has suddenly gone all cock-eyed on us. To all intents and purposes we've abruptly gone off in the wrong direction. But it's not a case of where are we—'

'But *when* are we,' Zita finished.

'Exactly.' Jud nodded, his blue eyes locked hard onto Sam's. '*When* are we.'

'You're suggesting we keep everyone here till, when? Hell freezes over? God's fixes his wristwatch? What?'

'Or maybe we should commit mass suicide?' Zita's eyes flashed dangerously. 'So we don't infect the rest of humanity.'

She'd been deliberately flippant to the point of sarcasm but Jud looked at her levelly. 'Mass suicide? That's an option.'

'Shit.'

'But one way down the list.'

'Suicide? You can't be serious?'

97

'Miss Prestwyck. Imagine what would happen if a man walked up to you and said "I've come back in time to you from precisely one year in the future". Yippee, you might think. He might know the winner of every horse race, every winning lottery number; how the stocks and shares are going to perform for the next twelve months. But what about the downside? What if he showed you a photograph of your gravestone six months from now?'

'That's a pretty persuasive argument,' Sam agreed. 'OK. Shall we decide what we are going to do next? And how we're going to convince these people that it's in their best interests to do as we say?'

Two

I died.

I died. Those were the two short words that orbited the deep-rooted conviction in the centre of Lee Burton's head.

I died.

He stood holding the can of iced coke in both hands.

I died.

But this wasn't heaven. The cape still felt heavy on his back; incredibly heavy so that the cord dug into his throat. Sweat still trickled down the inside of his shirt. His shoulders itched. The sun still dazzled.

But there's no doubt about it:

I died.

He looked round at the others. There were the tourists from his coach; other visitors who'd arrived by car; the sobbing ice-cream man. The three reps in costume.

No one knows what happens when you die. Not to your soul, anyway. Every culture has its own idea of heaven. Didn't the Egyptians face Osiris who weighed the dead's sins against their good deeds? And depending on which way the scales tipped you either went through the door to the glory of everlasting life or, if judged a sinner, you were torn apart by something with a man's body but with the head and jaws of a crocodile. Then there were all the other beliefs. Christians were whisked away into the clouds to some woolly kind of paradise, while Hindus were reincarnated for another tour of duty on Earth.

But nobody really knew.

He told himself: *I was crushed to death beneath the wheels of the truck in York. So why am I back here?*

The obvious answer was that his return to the amphitheatre with all these people was some kind of test.

But what on earth was expected of him?

Had he sinned in the past? Was he expected to make some kind of amends, or apologize to someone he'd hurt?

But who?

He was an easygoing kind of guy. A big softie, really, with all the malevolence of a puppy. He was the kind of person who'd always get voted first in a nice-guy contest.

But, nevertheless, he was now convinced he was being tested. If he failed the test he'd go someplace bad. If he did well, and did what was expected, what then? Perhaps he'd be taken up into the hereafter.

He took a swallow of the cold drink.

That was it.

He'd go with the flow. He'd keep his eyes open and when the crunch came he'd do the right thing.

He looked up, squinting towards the sun. Maybe that blazing disc in the sky really was the eye of God. Watching him. Monitoring his every move. Examining his every action. Reading the emotion written across his heart like a lawyer reads the small print in a contract.

Maybe his good deeds were being weighed against the bad. Just like with those dead Egyptians. When he was fourteen he'd visited the tombs in the Valley of the Kings and seen those wall paintings with his own eyes. The three-thousand-year-old images had remained inside his head like they'd been superglued. He'd stood in the cool airless tomb, his eyes locked onto the painting of the dead Egyptian with the green post-mortem face, the body wrapped in white bandages. And there would be Osiris, the Egyptian God of the Dead, weighing the dead man's good and bad deeds. Good on the right scale. Bad on the left-hand scale.

I'm dead, Lee told himself, *and this is a test.*

He saw Jud Campbell walk purposefully towards him.

OK, Lee, old buddy, he told himself, *I think the test is just about to begin.*

Three

'Fancy a drink?' Sam asked Zita.

'I could murder one. I hope this is where you pull out a hip flask full of brandy?'

He gave a faint smile. 'Sorry. I'm going to grab a coke from the machine. Want one?'

'You couldn't make it a Perrier, could you?'

'You've got it.' He walked across the sunlit car park to the vending machine that backed up against the visitors' centre. Above him the sky, a perfect blue, signalled it was going to be a great summer's day.

But which day? he asked himself. He felt his head would detach itself from his body any second and go bobbing away as light as a balloon into that perfect blue sky, taking his sanity with it.

Hell, he needed sugar in his blood.

He fumbled for a moment with the unfamiliar change. A Japanese man of around forty-five said, 'That stuff fooling you too? Here, let me.' He took the coins from Sam's open palm and fed them into the machine.

'It's funny money.' The Japanese tourist smiled. 'Takes some fucking time to get used to. Like the climate. And the food. And what they do to the clocks and calendars I don't fucking know. Now choose your drinks.'

Sam smiled, nodded, and pushed the big chunky buttons, each with a picture of the canned drink – a boon to the illiterate or the foreign tourist. As the cans boomed, rolled and clanked into the dispensing slot below the Japanese tourist grinned again. 'You German? Deutsch?'

'American.'

'Good. Maybe you can explain to me, please, why the British fuck with their days? I got up today — it was Tuesday. I came to this hole in the ground. Then I go back to my hotel and the porter tells me it's Monday. Now I don't know fuck. Only that my watch says Tuesday. Tell me, sir, why do the Brits fuck around with their time?'

Sam smiled back and shrugged. 'Inscrutable island race, I guess.'

'Me too. Thank you. Good day, sir.' The man bowed his head.

Now that was a peculiar exchange, Sam told himself as he strolled back towards the Range Rover. He saw Zita looking under the bonnet. The Japanese tourist had been talking in a light-hearted, probably even deliberately whimsical kind of way about the peculiar habits of the natives. But he'd already latched onto the fact that the continuity of time was all over the place. Like anyone else the Japanese man didn't want to blurt right out and say, '*My God, time's gone all peculiar!*' and then risk looking stupid if everyone else insisted nothing was amiss. That today really was Tuesday, 23rd June.

'Here, grab this.' He handed Zita the drink. She pulled the tab while still looking down into the engine.

'See anything the matter with it?'

'Nothing. Looks perfect.'

'All the other engines were knocked out at the same time as the phones.'

'Do you know anything about cars?'

'The great internal combustion engine? No. Zilch. Do you?'

'I took a car-maintenance course at school. But I think this problem goes beyond dirt in the fuel feed or a flat battery.'

She took a deep grateful drink of the sparkling water. 'Ooohhh . . . that's good.'

'What's Jud Campbell up to?'

'He knows those four in the fancy dress. Apparently they're travel reps who came in on the coach.'

'What does he want them to do?'

'Just help him calm down their clients and suggest they all wait here while someone goes into town and finds out what's happening.'

'It should work for a while. But it won't be that long before those people get restless and start asking why the driver doesn't either fix the bus or call out the local garage.' He pulled out his phone and pressed the keys. 'I think Jud is onto a loser if he reckons he can keep all those people corralled here for ever. Ah, that's better . . .'

'You've got through?' Zita dropped the hood of the bonnet.

'Well, I'm through to the speaking clock. Listen.'

Zita stood beside him and he held out the phone so she could hear the male voice reciting the hours, minutes, seconds.

'Still not brilliant,' she said. 'It sound like someone frying eggs.'

'*Third stroke . . .*' Crackle of interference. '*. . . sponsored by Accurist . . .*' More interference snapping and clicking. '*Fifty-eight and forty sec–*' A whiz, crackles. Then the three bleeps of the speaking clock.

Zita said, 'It sounds better than it was, anyway.'

Sam held up a finger as the automated voice ran on to the next announcement. On this occasion, although the voice was still distorted by interference, they made out the time: '*At the third stroke, the time sponsored by Accurist will be: Two fifty-eight and fifty seconds . . .*' Sam thumbed the button, cutting the voice. 'Two fifty-eight,' he said. 'Call it three o'clock. I make it five to.'

'Maybe this thing . . . this temporal anomaly is sorting itself out?'

'Maybe.'

'But don't you think it's a real possibility? If our watches are telling us it's five to three and the speaking clock says it's three o'clock, as near as damnit.' She looked relieved. 'That's only a difference of three or four minutes.'

'I don't know,' he said. 'I just don't know. But if the phone's working the car's electrics might have sorted themselves out. Want to give it a try?'

Zita popped the can of water onto the car roof, climbed in and turned the key. The engine started and ran. Not evenly, Sam noted. It sounded rough, and kicked out a lot of black smoke from the exhaust but it was still idling of a kind.

When other drivers saw Zita's success they immediately tried their own cars. But they soon found out that their motors were still refusing to fire. The coach stayed dead, too.

Zita had an answer. 'The Range Rover's a diesel. So there are no spark plugs to ignite the fuel. Diesel combusts by compression.'

'So it looks as if their spark plugs still aren't sparking. Well, that's probably for the best if we want to keep the people here for a while.'

Zita climbed out of the car, leaving it ticking over. She grinned at him. 'But it might not matter soon if we're catching back up to British Summer Time. Another half-hour and everything could be back to normal.'

'I hope so,' he told her. 'I really do.'

He looked down at his hand with its long finger where the thumb should be. The skin covering the two joints was tingling like fury again.

And again the lines from the half-remembered lesson came to him:

> *By the pricking of my thumbs,*
> *Something wicked this way comes . . .*

Chapter Thirteen

One

Jud returned with a tall man of around twenty. It was the guy dressed as Dracula, complete with black cape, frilly white shirt, corpse-white make-up and lipstick-drawn blood trickles down the sides of his mouth. It was also the same guy who had freaked out in the amphitheatre, clutching his stomach and yelling wildly about a truck.

Sam Baker stood by the Range Rover's open passenger door and watched Jud amble up, his gold waistcoat flapping open.

'I heard you'd started the car,' Jud said, wiping the sweat from his forehead. 'Are you going into town now?'

'May as well?' Sam said and looked at Zita who nodded before climbing into the driving seat. 'We'll be back in about an hour.'

'I've asked this gentleman if he'll go along with you. His name's Lee Burton. He's a rep with Coast and County Tours.'

Sam tried not to stare at Lee Burton in his Dracula costume but it was hard not to. The cloak looked so big it seemed to weigh the man down.

Sam said, 'Well, I don't know if we need any help, Jud. We're only going to take a look round, maybe buy a paper, and . . . you know.'

'It's all right, Sam. I've talked to Lee, here. He's aware of the situation. But you might need an extra pair of hands, even if it's only to push the car if it breaks down again.'

'How are you feeling now, Lee?' Sam asked, looking him up and down. 'You took a bad turn in the amphitheatre a little while ago.'

'I'm fine now. Believe me, I'll do anything to help. *Anything*.'

Sam saw Lee smiling through his fake blood, but he also heard a throbbing desperation in the way he said 'Anything.'

'Come on, Sam,' Zita called as she grabbed her can of water from where she'd left it on the car roof. 'The engine's missing again.'

'Just a minute.'

'If we wait any longer we might not go at all.'

'OK, Lee,' Sam told him. 'Hop in the back.'

'Good luck,' Jud said and Sam knew he meant it.

'Thanks. See you soon. Less than an hour. Promise.'

Sam climbed into the passenger seat and belted himself in. Lee Burton climbed in the back, cloak rustling.

'I'll do whatever I can to help,' Lee insisted. 'Trust me.'

'OK, Lee,' Sam said reassuringly. 'You're on the team.' He twisted round in the seat hand extended. 'My name's Sam Baker. This is Zita Prestwyck.'

Lee still looked jangled as he shook Sam's hand. He glanced nervously left and right through the windows as if he expected to see tigers or lions or something equally lethal stalking him through the grass.

'Lee. Jud says he told you that something a little strange happened today.'

'I know *everything*.' Lee spoke in a heartfelt emphatic kind of way that increased Sam's unease. They could have been on their way to assassinate a president, the nervy way he was behaving.

'Take it easy.' Sam spoke in a calming voice. 'Enjoy the ride.'

'Yeah. Sure. I'm fine. *I'm fine*.'

The man wasn't raving, Sam saw, but there was an

edginess, even excitement, as if he anticipated astonishing times ahead.

Zita had reversed the car out of the space and now drove forward across the car park with the can of iced water gripped between her inner thighs. Ahead ran the lane that would take them up to the main road. Jud Campbell watched them go. A shrinking figure, hands on hips, gold waistcoat shining in the sun.

Suddenly, Sam heard a loud thump as something hard clunked against the car body.

'Jesus, what the hell is he doing?'

Sam snapped his head back to look through the windscreen.

A blond-haired man of around forty, with all the confidence of a cop, was slapping the bonnet of the car to tell Zita to stop.

'What do you want? I nearly ran— *hey!*'

The man deftly opened the back passenger door and swung himself into the seat beside Lee. 'You don't mind if I hitch a lift, do you?'

'You don't know where we're going.' Zita sounded outraged.

'You'll be going to that little town over the hill, won't you? Well . . . that's where the road leads, doesn't it?' He spoke with a brisk confidence.

'But you can't just—'

'Oh, come on, sweetheart,' he said in a voice that made Sam think of velvet covering steel. 'I'm not taking anyone's place, am I?'

'No, but—'

'And I'll pay for the bloody petrol if you're hard up. Twenty do it?'

He reached into the breast pocket of his white linen jacket.

'Oh, never mind,' Zita said through her teeth. 'We'll drop you off in town.'

'Now, there's a sweetie.' The man smiled. It wasn't a nice smile, Sam thought. The eyes possessed all the qualities of dark glass beads. They were hard, cold. His clothes were expensive-looking, as if he sent the linen suit away to have designer crumples carefully added every couple of weeks.

Probably the kind of man who gets rich by trampling across the backs of others, Sam told himself. A man who hailed from the blitzkrieg school of commerce.

Sam asked conversationally (while noticing Zita was grinding her teeth in silent fury), 'I didn't see you in the amphitheatre this afternoon.'

'Amphitheatre? Oh, that hole in the ground back there? So that's what it was? No, I was lying back and . . . just enjoying life as she comes.'

'On holiday?'

'If you can call it that. I run my own company, so holidays usually end up a pain in the derrière. That's why I need to get into town and make some business calls. The bloody cellphones have gone haywire; the bloody cruiser engine's kaput, too. My Man Friday has vanished into thin air. Why I ever thought a holiday cruising the open sewers of sweet England would be relaxing God alone knows.' He lounged back looking a lot like Charles Dance in his best English-aristocrat pose, arm through the window, his long fingers toying with the edge of the car-door frame, blond hair fluttering in the slipstream. He shot a sidelong glance at Lee in the Dracula costume. A dismissive glance, Sam thought. And no doubt he was filing Lee in the mental folder marked *Prat*.

'Wonderful weather,' the man said, smiling coldly out through the window. 'Oh, to be in England when the sun is shining.'

Sam was going to introduce himself, then thought better of it. The man seemed content to ride in the back of the car, looking like an English lord. Meanwhile, Lee ducked his head up and down, looking this way and that like an anxious bird on the lookout for the hungry red fox. Zita concentrated on the driving. The engine dipped, occasionally misfired, but it seemed to be holding out.

So Sam sat back and watched fields stream by, while listening to the rumble of the Range Rover's big tyres on the road surface.

Ahead lay the suburbs of Casterton, a sturdy town of solid-looking sandstone houses that had sweated its money out of wool and coal mining. The clock tower of the town hall stood high above the skyline, the perfect example of municipal power building.

Zita shot him a look which as good as said, 'Well, here goes.'

Seconds later the town-centre traffic swallowed the car.

Two

Zita asked the blond-haired man, 'Where can I drop you?'

'Over there, by the bank.' He wasn't so much asking a favour as giving directions.

Zita nodded. 'OK.' Sam Baker noticed the way she muttered darkly under her breath. She didn't like their arrogant passenger one little bit.

'You might as well drop me in the same place,' Sam told her.

'It's a double yellow.'

'I won't be a minute. Keep the engine running while I do what I have to do.'

'Let me help,' Lee said eagerly. 'I want to help.'

'Don't worry, Lee,' Sam said easily. 'I can handle this one. Aren't you hot in that cape?'

'Roasting.'

Sam sounded deliberately light-hearted. 'This isn't a formal occasion, Lee. Take it off before you cook.'

'Uh? Oh, sure . . . sure.'

The blond-haired man in his white linen suit raised his eyes to the ceiling. Sam realized here was a man who didn't suffer fools lightly. Not that he'd have described Lee Burton as a fool; only as someone who'd suffered a hell of a shock and was still disorientated.

Lee fumbled with the button. 'It's awkward to undo. The button's too big for the catch. Stupid costume, really . . . but we all have to wear them. I don't know which is worse. Laurel and Hardy or—'

'Thanks for the lift,' the blond-haired man said crisply as Zita pulled over to the kerb. 'Enjoy the rest of your day.' With that he climbed out and walked quickly away along a pavement crowded with market-day shoppers.

Zita murmured, 'Is it just me? Or does that guy make the hairs on the back of your neck stand on end?'

'You'll always wind up with one who flunked charm school.' Sam smiled. 'Don't worry about it, he's gone now.'

'Bloody fastener,' Lee muttered, preoccupied with un-buttoning the cape. Something that he was failing to do with his fumbling fingers.

Sam opened the passenger door and paused while a bus rumbled by. 'I'll be right back.'

'Where are you going?' Zita called.

'I'll buy a newspaper and check the date. If it shows it's Tuesday then as far as I can see this anomaly is sorting itself out. According to the town hall clock we're only about five minutes behind the rest of the world.'

'OK,' Zita nodded. 'I'll sit here with my fingers crossed.'

Sam joined the crowds of shoppers on the pavement. He tried not to run, but he was so eager to get his hands on today's newspaper that he walked quickly, weaving round old ladies pulling shopping bags on wheels, couples with babies in buggies, children who'd suddenly stop in front of him to unpick the paper from another toffee.

He felt frustration growing inside him like a ball of hot rock. He wanted that newspaper in his hands. He wanted to see the day and date written on the top of that paper. Ahead of him was a wooden stall covered with newspapers and glossy magazines.

Sam walked even faster towards it.

A customer was buying a newspaper from the vendor. Instead of taking it away, he stood there in front of him, reading it.

Again frustration burnt the pit of Sam's belly. *Come on, move it!* He wanted to buy a newspaper. Now!

The customer turned to him.

'Hello there again,' the man said in a low voice.

It was the blond man in the linen suit.

Sam stared at him.

'Great minds think alike, don't they?' The man held out the newspaper. 'I don't think there's any need for us to buy two. Why don't you have a look at mine instead?'

Three

In the back of the car Lee Burton still tried (and failed spectacularly) to unfasten the Dracula cape. But his mind wasn't really on the job.

This is all part of the test, he told himself. *God's testing me. He's waiting to see if I do the right thing.*

He still glanced repeatedly through the window, searching for a sign of the real test to come.

But what was expected of him?

Should he telephone his brother in Canada and admit to stealing cash out of his brother's money jar ten – or was it twelve – years ago? Was that what was expected of him? A confession?

Then there was the girl he'd been engaged to a couple of years ago. He still blamed himself for the break-up of the relationship. But it was really Anne who'd walked out on him.

Maybe if he'd tried harder? Bought her flowers? Spent more time with her? She'd always wanted to go to the West Indies. Maybe he should have cashed his premium bonds and—

Oh shit, this stupid button. Perhaps he was doomed to wear this ridiculous black cape until the end of time.

In the front of the car the girl in the tiger-skin leggings hit the radio pre-sets, listening to one radio station for a second or two before impatiently switching to the next. If she was looking for something she hadn't found it yet.

Perhaps everyone was the same, he told himself. Maybe when you die you enter some kind of halfway place between heaven and hell where your past life is assessed. Then maybe you're given a test. Depending on how well you perform you're either raised to heaven. Or dumped, screaming, into the pit of hell.

Yes. That's it, Lee told himself, kneading one hand against the other. *This is the test. This is the test.*

He scanned the street. Buses, cars, trucks clogged it. People crowded the pavements. A red-haired tramp picked slices of bread from a litter bin. Meanwhile, the sun flooded the scene with a brilliant light.

His test must come soon.

It must . . .

He froze.

His eyes widened.

Here it was.

Here was his test.

He could see it with his own eyes.

In a second he'd shoved open the car door.

'Hey!' Zita shouted. 'Lee! Where are you going? Lee!'

Lee didn't hear her. This was it. This was his big chance to prove himself. He ran across the road, not hearing the sound of horns sounded by angry drivers, or the screech of tyres.

God Almighty Himself was putting him, Lee Burton, to the test. He'd let nothing get in his way.

Four

Sam Baker stood on the crowded pavement and stared. The blond man held out the paper.

'Go on, take it,' the man said calmly. 'It won't bite you, will it?'

Sam took the paper. He took it almost reluctantly. This is something he'd wanted to do in private, like opening the envelope that contained the results of an exam or a job application. The idea of someone scrutinizing his expression as he looked at the paper made him feel strangely vulnerable.

He opened the newspaper and looked at the day beneath the title.

The drumming of the traffic seemed suddenly distant.

Tuesday.

Air escaped from his lips in a relieved hiss.

Tuesday. It was Tuesday after all. The sun had been too strong in the amphitheatre, that was all. Somehow they'd imagined it. A collective hallucination. There'd been no backwards flip through time.

Then his idea of reality went all pear-shaped again.

Damn.

Because now he'd seen the date alongside the word Tuesday.

He stared at it, feeling his hands tighten around the newspaper until the pages began to crackle. His twin-jointed thumbs began their outrageous tingling again as if tiny insects burrowed through the skin.

> *By the pricking of my thumbs,*
> *Something wicked this way comes . . .*

'You know,' the man said in a low voice, 'staring at it like that won't change the date. So the question is: Just what the hell is going on here?'

Sam let his arm drop. The date on the newspaper was 16th June. When Sam Baker had climbed out of his hotel bed that morning it had been Tuesday, *23rd June*.

He pushed by the man and scanned the other newspapers on the stall, his eyes darting wildly from one front page to the other.

'I've already done that,' the man said. 'They all show the same date. The sixteenth.' The man's sharp glass-bead eyes fixed on Sam. 'So I repeat my question: What on Earth is going on here?'

Five

Lee Burton ran across the busy road. His eyes had locked onto a man who stood outside the small branch office of a building society.

The building society was the same company he'd once worked for. The coincidence wasn't lost on him.

In fact, he knew it wasn't a coincidence at all.

This was preordained. The conviction that this was his God-given test burnt inside of him.

Because, as he'd sat in the back of the car, with Zita browsing through the radio channels, he'd happened to look across the road at the building society.

There he'd seen a man, apparently reading the name plates on the wall next door.

Lee Burton's eyes had seemed to undergo a marvellous transformation at that moment. It was as if they'd developed the ability to act like a telephoto lens. His attention had zoomed in on the man in the brown leather jacket as the man had lowered his head and slipped on a black balaclava hood. Then the man had drawn another small object from his pocket and had held it in one hand.

Lee's mind had quickly sifted its vocabulary and pulled out the identifying word: *gun*.

This is it, he thought with a blaze of excitement and wonder.

His test had come.

In five seconds flat he was dashing across the road.

He wasn't aware of the traffic or the crowds of shoppers watching this tall, stick-thin man running through the centre of town with a black Dracula cape rippling straight out behind him. Or his white make-up. Or the blood trickles drawn in red lipstick down his chin.

Nothing else mattered.

He was focused on his challenge.

The building society was being robbed.

He had to stop it happening.

It was as simple as that.

The armed man had already entered the building society by the time Lee burst through the door.

Behind the counter the three cashiers were standing back with their hands raised while the gunman shouted instructions. A couple of customers lay on the floor.

'Get down!' the man yelled as Lee came through the door. 'Lie down!' The man's eyes widened in surprise behind the balaclava when he saw Lee standing there, panting in the Dracula costume. 'You! Down on the floor!'

Lee held out his hand, while slowly advancing. 'Give me the gun . . . come on, give me the gun.'

'Get down, you bloody moron,' the man bellowed and pointed the revolver at the centre of Lee's frilled shirt. 'Down! I won't tell you again! *Do it!*'

The cashiers stared, mouths open in horrified O's.

Lee ran forward, determined to grab the gun.

The robber grabbed him by the cape and swung him against a wall. Then he immediately stood back, pointing the gun at Lee again. 'Are you crazy or what? Don't make me use this on you.'

Lee turned round, held up his hands and walked towards the robber.

'I'm warning you. I'll blow a hole right through you, d'ya hear, you fucking lunatic?' The robber looked agitated now. He shot glances at the door, ready to run without the money. 'Keep back or I'll fucking drop you.' He cocked the revolver.

'I'm already dead,' Lee Burton told the man. He felt strangely calm. He held out both arms, hands open, palms upturned. 'I only want the gun.'

'I'm warning you!'

'You can't kill me. I'm already dead.'

The robber's eyes were huge shining discs behind the holes of the black balaclava.

He aimed the gun at Lee's chest.

Then pulled the trigger.

Lee felt something snag against his chest. As if someone had just reached out and plucked at his shirt.

There was no pain.

He'd not even heard the report of the gun. But when he glanced down he saw a wet patch of crimson spreading across the white shirt.

'You can't kill me,' he repeated, still walking forward. 'Give me the gun.' The customers and cashiers were screaming but it was all thin-sounding and seemed to come from far away.

'Bastard . . . you stupid bastard.' The robber was close to screaming himself.

He fired again. This time Lee gasped. A tremendous bolt of agony seemed to light up his bones from the inside. He gritted his teeth and clutched at his stomach. He looked down. Blood poured over his fingers as freely as water squeezed from a sponge.

At that moment he collapsed into the middle of the carpet.

Chapter Fourteen

One

Lee Burton heard screams. He opened his eyes to see the logo of the building society he'd once worked for woven into the carpet – the letters WRBS sitting inside a yellow disc. His blood was soaked into it, like red wine soaking through kitchen tissue. And he saw a pair of green trainers.

A voice said, 'I warned you I'd shoot, didn't I? *Didn't I?*'

He rolled over and looked up at the hooded face; the eyes stared back at him, wide with horror. He smelled the sharp tang of gunsmoke drifting on the still air of the building society. Lee smelled soap, too. In a disjointed way, the realization that the robber had washed himself using perfumed soap was astonishing. Bank robbers should smell of stale sweat, engine oil, possibly a little whisky, too, not Pear's soap. Lee shook his head. It felt fuzzy, as if he'd been sitting in a hot stuffy room too long. He was slipping into unconsciousness.

No.

He couldn't allow himself to go to sleep on the carpet there.

Lee tried to take a deep breath. But his chest felt so tight it was as though someone had wound a huge rubber band around it. 'Give me the gun. You must give me the gun.'

'Fuck you, you stupid bastard.'

The robber backed away.

Lee dragged himself to his feet. The Dracula cape felt as heavy as iron on his back. He wished he could take it off. Only he couldn't. That button . . . that stupid button . . . he'd have to change it for a smaller one . . .

No . . . wait . . . he'd got something to do.

Test.

Assignment.

'Oh, my God . . .' Lee said under his breath. 'The test's not over yet. He's getting away.' Suddenly he yelled, 'He's getting away!'

He looked round groggily at the shocked faces of the staff and customers.

'Don't you see?' he shouted. 'This is my test. I can't let him get away!'

He lumbered at the door, threw it open.

The robber ran along the street, pushing shoppers away, yelling, waving the gun.

Any second now, he might start firing, Lee thought. *There're innocent people. Children . . .*

Come on, he told himself. *You're still being tested. The sun is God's eye. He's watching you. Evaluating you.*

Lee charged after the robber. Now his chest and arms felt strangely numb. Only his stomach stung as though a giant wasp had planted its stinger through his navel.

Shoppers backed away quickly from Lee, opening a path as he ran. Face white with the corpse make-up; black cape flapping extravagantly behind him. And, covering his shirt, a crimson stain that soaked the white cotton frills from his throat to his belt.

He ran as hard as he could; the cloak was like cast iron weighing him down. He could hardly breathe. Blood bubbled from his nostrils every time he exhaled.

And he thought of his mother. How would she react if she saw him like this? Her youngest son, dying on his feet? He knew she'd remember him as a baby. When she'd stayed up all night with him when he'd had the whooping cough that had nearly killed him. She'd stroked his forehead while murmuring gently to him. She'd remember the occasion, after a spasm of coughing that sounded like someone blowing on a whistle, when he'd stopped breathing and she'd wept and prayed and hugged him. Then she'd gently pinched his nostrils and blown into his mouth, forcing air through his swollen throat, inflating his lungs that were congested with sputum. She'd brought him through it alive.

But I'm already dead now, he told himself. Blood sprayed from his mouth like crimson aerosol paint with every breath as he ran. *I'm already dead.*

The robber ran to a waiting car, threw open the door, swung himself in.

Lee heard the man yelling: 'Go! Go! Go!'

The driver slammed the pedal to the matting. Wheels screeching, filling the street with smoke, the car rocketed forward.

No . . . no . . . Lee stopped, panting out gobs of blood. He could never catch the car. He'd failed his test.

And all the time the sun burned in the sky, scrutinizing his every action with an unwaveringly judgemental glare.

Hell waited for him now. A screaming hell of eternal damnation, pain and loneliness.

No, wait . . . He saw the car had taken a left. The only way now was for the car to join the ring road that curved around the town before heading north to join the motorway.

Lee visualized that curved road. It hugged the town centre close for half a mile yet. For another minute or so the getaway car would be the road's prisoner.

A huge burst of energy revitalized Lee. Despite the bullet holes in his stomach he ran across the pedestrian precinct. The cape blew out horizontally behind him. Shoppers stumbled back from him in shock. A scared child started a wailing cry.

He cut down an alleyway, leaping over discarded boxes.

Ahead, he could see the section of ring road the getaway car had to follow.

He pumped everything into that hundred-yard dash down the alleyway to the ring road.

Seconds later he was there. Calmly, he walked out into the road.

Now he went to stand on the white lines that separated the two northbound lanes of the road. Cars, taxis, trucks screamed by him, horns bleating. They didn't trouble him. He waited serenely for the car to come. A tall, thin man with bright, shining eyes that gazed levelly into the flow of oncoming traffic, his black cape wafted this way and that by the slipstream. His white shirt bloomed redly in the sunlight. The blood stain seemed to form a red bull's-eye there.

Lee Burton awaited his destiny.

Two

Sam Baker returned to the Range Rover where Zita sat impatiently drumming her fingers on the steering wheel.

He wasn't alone.

The blond man had returned with him.

'Where's Lee?' Sam asked as he handed Zita the newspaper.

'God knows,' she said. 'He just climbed out of the car and ran across there like the Devil himself was after him.'

'Never mind him.' The blond man's voice was crisp. 'Take a look at the paper. At the date.'

Zita raised her eyebrows at Sam. 'It's OK,' Sam told her. 'He knows.'

'I know what happened,' the man said. 'That we've just been picked up and dropped backwards by precisely one week.' He climbed into the front passenger seat and snapped on the seat-belt. 'But I don't know *how* it happened. Just how fifty people can be transported back in time. And it's the *how* that fascinates me.' He shut the door then popped his blond head through the open window. 'You best hop in the back, Sam old boy. Unless you want leaving behind.'

Sam's eyes met Zita's. Why did it feel to him that the blond-haired man had just taken charge?

Three

Lee Burton stood there beneath a sun that was the eye of God.

Or at least that's what Lee told himself.

A huge eye, burning with fire, and with the power to see him down there on the road.

This my test, he told himself. *I have to get this right.*

Calmly, he faced the cars and trucks as they flowed by him at either side. Engines snarled in fury; horns blasted. The slip-stream tugged, then pushed him until he rocked on his heels.

Behind him the cape rippled and snapped like a sheet on a washing line.

The getaway car must come this way.

Only then could he complete his test.

He didn't see the drivers' faces. The cars were a blur. He awaited only that white BMW, with the green sun-strip across the top of the windscreen.

He didn't have long to wait.

Hurtling along the curve of the fast lane came the BMW, its big tyres eating the road tar between himself and the car.

Here it comes.

Lee waited for a taxi to pass by before stepping into the centre of the fast lane.

Now the white BMW bore down on him. He could see the two men through the windscreen, the green sun-strip across the top of the glass. They stared at him through the eyeholes of their black hoods in sheer disbelief.

As if re-enacting the part of some dotty policeman in an old Ealing comedy, Lee Burton stood there in the fast lane of the bypass, facing the oncoming car, and raised his hand to stop it.

The BMW was boxed in by trucks in the slow lane. It couldn't swerve to avoid him.

It sure as hell wasn't going to stop.

I'm dead, Lee told himself.

I'm already dead.

The car can't hurt me.

Even so, that half-ton of steel, glass and plastic hurtling towards him seemed solid enough.

And he seemed human enough.

He could hardly breathe. His stomach hurt. Blood ran from the bullet holes in his skin. And, at that moment, he was gripped by a near-overwhelming urge to urinate.

He felt human enough. All too human.

The car roared at him. The two men's eyes blazed at him like pairs of headlights.

But this is a test . . .

He couldn't run away from it.

The car was nearly on him.

At that moment he ran.

Not away from the car.

Towards it.

He ran hard, cape flapping, breath coming in liquid-sounding squirts through his throat.

Before the car hit him he dived up over the bonnet straight at the windscreen. Already, he'd gripped the cape in one fist and dragged it up over his face to protect himself as best he could.

There was a tremendous concussion that swept the breath from his body.

When he breathed in it wasn't air that entered his body but pain. Spikes of white-hot agony that tore through every cell of his anatomy.

He heard screams, but they weren't only his own.

Opening his eyes, he saw that he lay in the torn shreds of the cape. He realized he was inside the car, lying with the top half of his body through the glass almost on the lap of the gunman himself.

'Finish him!' the driver screamed.

The bank robber fumbled the gun from his jacket pocket.

Meanwhile, the car lurched from side to side as it sped along the road. The engine howled.

It's a test, it's a test, Lee thought dazedly.

The robber had now pulled the gun clear of his pocket. He aimed it at Lee's head.

Instead of going for the gun, Lee reached up, grabbed the front of the driver's mask and tugged it down. Immediately, the top of the balaclava covered the driver's eyes.

'I can't see! I can't see!' the driver bellowed. 'Get him off me!'

Lee watched the other man point the gun. The muzzle dug into the flesh between Lee's eyes.

Then there was a concussion and the car was turning over and over . . .

Four

Lee Burton opened his eyes.

He lay on the grass. Above him, the sun, which was God's great radiant eye, blazed down.

He turned his head to the left. The white BMW lay upside down on the grass. A steel fence lay crumpled around it. The driver hung suspended by his seat belt. He'd pulled off the balaclava and hung there, groaning. A trickle of blood ran from his nose up his face to his forehead to drip onto the car roof.

A front tyre slowly turned. Steam hissed from the smashed radiator.

Lee turned his head the other way.

There was a railway track. The gunman lay across one of the tracks as if asleep.

He's dead, Lee told himself. But a second later the man groaned and moved one arm.

At that moment came the rumble of a train. It came nearer and nearer with a clattering roar.

I've failed, Lee told himself. *I've killed him. I shouldn't have done that.*

The train tore by.

But it ran along the furthermost track, which was a good ten feet from the gunman.

The gunman tried to move but it was clear to Lee that the man had smashed both legs when he'd been thrown from the car.

Lee's own body felt pretty badly broken up, too. Blood drenched him. He could barely breathe. One arm was bent back at the elbow. His legs were numb and wouldn't move when he tried to stand.

He realized that he was lying on a grass strip that separated the ring road from the railway track. The grass was spattered with dandelions and daisies looking like confetti after a wedding. Also, there were splotches of red. These were scattered like crimson rubies on the grass and glistened richly in the sunlight. When Lee sneezed there were suddenly more of them.

By now, the gunman appeared to have lost consciousness on the track. In any event, he lay there quietly without moving.

In the distance Lee heard another train. He didn't doubt this would tear along the track to slash the man's body in two.

This is part of the test . . . this is part of the test . . .

The words drummed through Lee's head.

Part of the test . . .

Agonizingly, he began to crawl towards the unconscious man.

The train sounded louder.

Lee dragged himself across the stone bed of the track, up onto the rail.

At that moment the man opened his eyes and turned his head towards Lee.

The man screamed. A scream of pure terror.

Just for a second, Lee imagined he was looking through the robber's eyes at himself. What a sight he would have made. A long, skinny young man, wearing a Dracula cape, his shirt soaked in blood, legs broken, yet still crawling forward like some indefatigable nightmare predator, determined to claim his victim come what might.

The robber screamed again. 'Leave me alone! Leave me

alone!' The voice came out croakily from a mouth full of smashed teeth, vomit and blood. 'I'm sorry I shot you. Please believe me, I – I'm sorry . . . I'm sorry. Leave me alone, I won't do it again.' He sounded like some snotty-nosed kid caught stealing apples from an orchard. 'Please! I won't do it again, I won't—'

The robber tried his damnedest to jump up and run. But Lee saw the man had broken enough bones in his body to leave him as incapable of movement as a jellyfish stranded high and dry on the beach.

The sound of the train grew louder.

The ground vibrated, rattling Lee's teeth together.

A blood-red mail train thundered around the bend in the track.

This is it!

Do or die.

Grabbing the man with his good arm Lee rolled him off the track.

The man was safe now.

Lee himself dropped back, bloody, exhausted, broken. He looked up at the sun, hoping to see some wink of approval.

Instead, he heard the approaching roar of the train.

He turned his head to the left and saw his broken arm lying across a rail that shone like silver in the hard sunlight.

The train thundered by.

Lee watched the steel wheels cut through the arm at the elbow.

The severed hand and arm lay on its back between the tracks. The fingers twitched and danced and grasped.

Feeling detached from reality, Lee marvelled. It reminded him of days by the seaside when he'd catch a crab in a pool. If he turned it on its back it would move its legs in exactly the same kind of way as those waving fingers.

As he lay there darkness swelled like a tidal wave and engulfed him.

Chapter Fifteen

One

'Where the hell have you been? I couldn't stop them. They've all gone.' Jud Campbell had greeted them with these sharp words when he ran to meet the Range Rover. It was a little after half-past five. He looked harassed, tired. Speckles of perspiration on his face glittered in the still-hot sun. Now he carried the once-immaculate gold waistcoat roughly balled in one hand. 'What happened to Lee? Surely you never let him go, too?'

Sam Baker climbed out of the car, the newspaper rolled in his grasp. One look told him that the amphitheatre's visitors had deserted. With the exception of the ice-cream van and their Range Rover the car park was empty.

'That fool you saddled us with ran off and got himself shot,' Carswell snapped. There was little sign of gentlemanly English cool now, Sam realized. The man's glass-bead eyes blazed nastily.

'Shot?' Jud's eyes widened. 'Shot? How?'

'With a bloody gun, of course.' Grant Carswell slipped off his white linen jacket. 'My God, I've had a gutful of fools today.'

With that he walked angrily away. Sam didn't doubt that if a puppy had got in the man's way he would have kicked it as hard as he damn' well could.

Jud called after him. 'We need to talk about this. We've got to get together and find a—'

'Leave him,' Sam said. 'He's the kind of guy who does exactly as he pleases.'

'Oh, what a hell of a day.' Zita rubbed her temples.

'What happened?' Jud asked again.

Sam sighed. 'For some reason Lee decided to play the hero. He went haring off, confronted a gunman and got himself shot. We managed to track him down to the local hospital.'

'It doesn't look good,' Zita said. 'I told them a little white lie, that we worked for the same company. As far as we can gather he'll be lucky to survive the next twenty-four hours.'

'Oh, Christ.' Jud shook his head. 'He can't be more than twenty-five. Poor man. He was just so desperate to go with the two of you. He kept saying he wanted to help, that he wanted to do the right thing.'

'If you ask me, he was more than a little flaky,' Sam said. 'I think the whole situation had knocked him off track.' He looked round the deserted car park. 'What happened here?'

'I couldn't keep them. Whatever affected the electrics of the bus and the cars must have sorted itself out. When I tried to explain to them that . . . that—'

'Time had gone skew-whiff?'

'Yes, they wouldn't listen. They drove off.' Jud looked at Sam and Zita with wide horror-filled eyes. 'Can you imagine? Those people will be like a plague virus. They don't belong to this time any more.'

For a while no one spoke. With an unspoken accord they moved to a bench in the shade of a tree.

At last Sam broke the silence. 'I remember as kids we'd sit around campfires and ask ourselves questions that would drive you half-crazy trying to answer them. You know the kind, trying to describe how big infinity really is. The big favourite was: could you go back in time before you were born and murder your own grandfather?'

'Ah, scientists call it the Grandfather Paradox,' Zita said. 'The general consensus was that even if time travel was possible you couldn't go back in time and kill your own grandfather, because if you did, you'd never be born, therefore you couldn't go back in time in order to pull the trigger. Like you say, if you thought about it too much it would drive you insane.'

Jud shook his head in frustration. 'I should have found some way to keep those people here.'

'What could you do, short of holding them at gunpoint?' Sam tapped the rolled-up newspaper gently against the point of his chin. 'Besides, is it our problem? As far as I can see it's going to take a whole busload of scientists to figure out what happened today.'

'I think it *is* our problem,' Jud told them with feeling. 'I believed it was our duty to contain those people, hold them here in quarantine until we could convince the powers that be about what has happened.'

Zita said. 'That we – the people who were gathered in the amphitheatre – have somehow come adrift in time?'

'Yes. A tough one, I know. But I should have tried harder. I really should have.'

Sam handed him the paper. 'We bought this in town. It shows just how adrift we really are.'

Jud nodded. 'I know. We're one week adrift. We've jumped backwards seven whole days.' He glanced at the newspaper. 'When you didn't come back I checked the television's teletext service on my boat. It took a while for the reception to get back to normal, but when it did I saw only too clearly that it was last week's news, last week's programmes and last week's date. Tuesday, the sixteenth of June.'

Zita shook her head. 'That means I can jump in the car, drive back to my flat, walk in through the door and give the other me a hell of a shock.'

'No,' Sam said. 'That won't happen.'

'You don't think we can meet ourselves as we were one week ago?'

'I don't know if there're any physical laws that would prevent it. But think about it, Zita; think back to last week.

Did you see someone who looked exactly like you – and who claimed to be you – come sailing through the door with a cheery hello?'

'No . . . no, I didn't.'

'Earlier you used the mobile in the amphitheatre. You said at the time that you could have sworn you found yourself speaking to someone who sounded like you on the phone. Do you remember that?'

'Now that I do remember.' Zita said, her eyes lighting up. 'I was in the office, busy writing up the costings for a documentary commission. The phone rang. I answered it and I heard this woman asking for Liz. I told her, no, Liz wasn't in, that she was speaking to Zita Prestwyck. I realized it was a mobile and the link wasn't too good; only this stupid woman insisted on claiming she was Zita. I took it she'd misheard me; anyway, the call made no sense whatsoever and after a while she hung up. I was so preoccupied getting my figures to add up I dismissed it entirely.' She gave a watery smile. 'I guess that stupid woman was me.'

Jud rubbed his jaw. 'At least it demonstrates that if we don't remember actually meeting ourselves in the past it shows we've had the common sense not to try and find ourselves as we were a week ago.'

'A little difficult for me,' Sam said. 'This time last week I was in New York.'

'Well, as long as you don't try and telephone yourself.'

'No danger of that. I'm still trying to get my head round what's happening now.'

'But we don't know what the others will do, do we?' Jud asked thoughtfully. 'I counted fifty-two people in the amphitheatre. I guess perhaps there were half a dozen or so just outside it who were also transported. What are they going to do now? Just what on Earth are they going to do?'

At that moment Sam Baker mentally stepped out of himself and saw their small group as if from a distance. Perhaps from the top of the church tower across there on the grassy incline. There was the amphitheatre and acres of

rolling meadow bathed in sunlight. The river with Carswell's millionaire launch moored behind Jud's homely
narrow boat with shirts and brightly coloured towels
hanging from a washing line.

And there, in the car park, three lost, bewildered people.
Zita, looking as if she was suffering from the mother of all
headaches. Jud Campbell, tired, harassed, and as worried as if
he'd been left in charge of a child who'd become lost in a
wolf-infested forest. And himself, Sam Baker, sitting with
his hands in his pockets, his chin almost touching his chest as
he stared at the tarmac wondering what the hell they should
do next.

Two

It was as though they'd fled the scene of a natural disaster.
But unlike a physical hurricane that tears through a town,
flattening houses, hurling cars about, knocking people off
their feet, this particular psychic storm had torn through
their minds.

The tourists sat on the bus feeling emotionally bruised.
They didn't move and none of them felt inclined to discuss
what they'd experienced.

The driver of the County and Coast Tours bus muttered
to himself as he drove. He stared glassily through the
windscreen. Once he missed a red light. Drivers sounded
their horns; a car missed him by a whisker.

In the front seat of the bus Nicole in her gorilla suit and
Sue as Stan Laurel tried to decide where to go.

'I mean we can't just take the coach back to the office and
say, "Sorry we're a week ahead of schedule," can we?'

'I was in the office last week,' Sue said in a small voice.
'They'd asked me to stand in for Toni Burke in admin. If I
go back I'll meet myself. I was wearing that silly dress with
the pink flowers.' She pushed her fist into her mouth and a
hard, machine-like laugh came clacking from her throat.
Yet her eyes had a scared cast to them, like she'd just found a

severed hand in her shoulder bag. 'I'll say hello to myself. What then? Ask myself to go out for a coffee and talk about what I'm going to do about Graham? I mean, I can hardly tell him he's got two identical girlfriends now, can I?'

Nicole sat with the gorilla head clenched in her two hands. She felt dangerously hot in the stupid suit that bristled with black nylon fur. And here was Sue, going over the edge. Oh, Lord, she didn't feel far behind.

In the seat behind her, Ryan Keith sat with his face in his plump hands, the Oliver Hardy bowler still wedged on his head.

Behind him the passengers sat and stared at the passing scenery. Dumb from shock, Nicole guessed.

At one point on the drive to York a man had slapped his wife.

A full-blooded slap straight across her face.

No one knew why.

No one asked.

No one reacted.

It was as if it had never happened.

Then both husband and wife had sat there in silence. Only her cheek was now a brilliant red and tears filled her staring eyes.

They were all coming apart at the seams.

Because each and every one of them knew time had come adrift.

Nicole ran her fingers through her beautiful blonde hair and tried to imagine what had happened.

The best she could come up with was that the present – *the here and now* – was like a group of rafts all tied together. These rafts drifted steadily down a river which was time. For some reason their raft of *now* had somehow broken away. It had gone spinning away from the rest of the here and now, away from the rest of the world of the twenty-third of June, and somehow it had been stolen away on another current that ran backwards. That raft had floated a whole seven days back, from the twenty-third of June to the sixteenth.

My, doesn't time fly when you're having fun? The saying suddenly seemed extravagantly absurd.

Like Sue beside her, Nicole found that her fist had made it into her mouth and that she was biting her knuckles. Whether it was to stop herself laughing out loud or plugging a scream that threatened to erupt from her throat she just didn't know.

But right then a crazy idea struck her. A neighbour of hers had died suddenly on the twentieth of June. Mr Thorpe was a cheerful sixty-year-old who lived with his wife of forty years in a house full of cats. Every spring he'd bring Nicole sticks of fresh pink rhubarb from his garden and glowingly tell her what marvellous crumbles they'd make. On Saturday afternoon he'd just clutched his chest and rolled over dead in his chair.

It occurred to her, seeing that today was, as far as the rest of the whole wide, shining green world was concerned, the sixteenth, she could see him alive and well again (at least, outwardly well if you discounted the artery ballooning in his chest) – *and she could talk to him.*

She bit her knuckle harder.

Wouldn't that be a scream?

To talk to a man who she knew would be dead within days.

She screwed her eyes tight shut as the world gave a slow, sickening spin around her.

But the idea that occurred to her now – the overwhelmingly powerful idea that rushed through her skull like an express train – was that she could save his life.

She could get off the coach. Take a taxi to Invicta Parade in the suburbs of York, somehow persuade Mr Thorpe that he should go to hospital. A quick test would reveal the man's swollen artery on the verge of rupture. They'd operate. Take a section of healthy artery from his leg. Cut out the damaged section in the region of his heart; then splice in the strong section. Why, he might live for another twenty years.

Nicole stared out of the window at the houses and hotels

on the edge of York. Her reflected eyes, wide with astonishment, stared back at her.

God, yes. She could do that. She could save his life.

She climbed to her feet.

'Bill . . . Bill!' She struggled out of her seat. 'Bill! Stop the coach. I have to get off!'

Three

The man who sold ice creams found himself down by the river bank. He wasn't exactly clear how he had got there. Only that he'd been wandering aimlessly in a daze. Birds swooped above the surface of the water catching insects. The 'plop' of a water rat slipping into the river sounded overloud to his jangled nerves.

He looked round, eyes creasing into two thin slits against the brilliance of the sun. Through the V-shaped cleft in the grass slope he could see the timber seating of the amphitheatre.

It was deserted.

He realized he must have left the ice-cream van unlocked.

But at that moment he didn't give a merry chuff. He was just coming to terms with seeing a man humping his wife.

But it wasn't just any man.

Now that he'd thought about it for a bit it wouldn't even seem so bad if it had been a stranger or . . . or the bloody window cleaner, if it came to that.

No, the man he'd seen had been none other than himself.

That's something you don't expect, he thought, for the twentieth time since coming to his senses a moment ago.

Not yourself. You never expect to walk into a room and see you there as large as life, do you?

He knew the Germans had a word for meeting your exact double: *Doppelgänger*. It meant 'double walker'. If you met your doppelgänger it was a bad omen. It probably meant you'd die soon.

Another rat plopped into the water by his feet where it swam just below the surface, leaving a muddy trail.

'Doppelgänger.' He rolled the unusual word across his tongue. 'Doppelgänger.'

Was that it?

He'd seen himself.

His own doppelgänger.

Did that mean he was he going to die soon?

Jesus Christ.

Forty-five years old. That isn't old, he thought. *I don't want to die at forty-five.*

A few yards ahead of him an old man stood on the bank looking out across the river; he leaned forward, taking his weight on his walking stick.

Beyond the man a couple of boats bobbed at their moorings on the water. One was a huge white launch on which a blond-haired man in white linen trousers and short-sleeved shirt sipped from a glass.

The man who sold ice creams gnawed his thumbnail. It was already rough and frayed from being chewed, but he worried at it nonetheless, turning the problem over in his mind. He'd seen a God-given sign of his own death, his doppelgänger. What should he do? Was there a way to escape it?

The old man looked up as the ice-cream seller slowly walked towards him.

'Fine weather,' the old man said with conviction. 'There's nothing like a summer's day.'

The ice-cream seller managed a nod accompanied by a tiny grunt.

'You know,' the old man continued almost as if he was talking to himself. 'I can remember a summer's day like this when I was four years old. My father brought me fishing to this very spot. He was a big man, arms like tree trunks, and when he was fishing he'd wear this straw hat, you know? A straw boater? It wasn't the thing you'd normally see a working man wear in those days. I think he found it somewhere, but he'd always insist on wearing it when he fished . . . a bit thin on top, I suppose . . . didn't want the

sun to burn his scalp. Anyway, he wore that boater and cast
his line into the water while I sat on the bank eating plums –
big soft purple plums, sweetest things I ever tasted. I
remember it all as plain as day. I remember the juice
trickling down my fingers. And I remember my father
stood just there by that tree stump. Course, it was a sapling
then, more than seventy-five years ago . . .'

The old man talked on in a voice that was low, slow and
even soothing. The man who sold ice creams listened. The
normality of an old man remembering sunnier, happier days
was reassuring. He found himself listening eagerly as if the
voice was a lifeline thrown at him across the seething chaos
of his stormy mental seas.

'My father tilted the boater like so.' The old man echoed
the action. 'So the brim came low over his eyes. He smoked
a cigarette – gave him a lot of pleasure it did, too. There was
no harm in cigarettes in those days, or eating meat, or even
drinking a cup full of cream if you wanted to. At least,
nobody thought there was any harm in it. People weren't
scared by what they ate or what they smoked. They knew
nothing about tar levels, cholesterol, saturated fats and
nonsense like that. It was all different then. Better. You
left your back door unlocked when you went out. Children
played in the streets. They were safe. And I remember sitting
right there on that bit of banking with those plums on a
summer's day seventy-five years ago, and I remember it as
clear as crystal. A brass band played marching songs over
yonder in the amphitheatre. There were girls in pretty
dresses that were so long they touched the ground. My
father caught a pike that was as big as me. Monster of a fish it
was, and a devil of a time he had reeling it in. As he was
dragging it up the bank just there, he bent down to grab it
by the gills and his hat fell off in the water. He loved that
straw boater. And, you know? The current took it out into
the middle of the river. A chap in a boat had to fetch it for
him.' The old man smiled, his face creasing into a thousand
lines. 'I wish I could live it all over again. And you know, I

wouldn't change a thing. I'd love it. *Just love it.*' When the old man said the word 'love' his whole body seemed to swell. He didn't so much say the word as will part of his soul into it until it appeared to pulsate with an energy all of its own. 'I loved growing up here. I can remember it all as clear as people remember yesterday.' His face darkened. The smile vanished. 'But you get old. And you can't remember what you did yesterday. You can't remember what you did five minutes ago. My mother went the same way. You know, Alzheimer's? You forget the names of your family. You forget you drank a cup of tea five minutes ago and you sit there asking over and over for another cup. It sends people barmy. No . . . I wouldn't inflict that on my worst enemy. I won't let myself go like that.'

With that the old man walked decisively forward into the water.

The ice-cream seller felt as if he was snapping out of a trance.

The old man floundered forward. In five paces he was out of his depth and swimming forward, blowing out his cheeks with the effort, his breathing noisy, then spluttering as he took in a mouthful of water.

The ice-cream seller pulled off his shoes as he ran into the river's shallows. There he snatched up the old man's walking stick that drifted on the current and held it out to him. It was a useless gesture. The old man was by this time a good twenty yards off shore. There the water had a blackness about it that spoke of cold depths.

'Grab this!' the ice-cream seller cried. 'Come on, swim and grab this.' Even as he shouted the words at the old man, who was still swimming out towards the middle of the river, he knew that what he shouted made no sense. The old man hadn't fallen into the water simply by accident. He'd walked into it deliberately. Just as he now swam out into the deepest part deliberately.

This was suicide.

The ice-cream seller couldn't swim.

Wildly, he looked round.

He saw the man on the launch standing on the deck while sipping a drink from a glass.

The man'd seen everything.

The ice-cream seller ran splashing through the shallows towards the launch.

'Can you see him? *Can you see him*'

The blond man didn't react. He stared back, sipping his drink.

The ice-cream seller shouted: 'Untie your boat; we've got to rescue him. He's going to drown out there! *He's going to drown!*'

The blond man gave a little shrug and sat down on a lounger on the deck.

Stunned, the ice-cream seller looked for anyone else who might be able to help. He ran wildly up the grass slope in the direction of the car park. All the time he was shouting.

He glanced back to see the old man who now swam on his back with a lazy stroke; he was gazing at the sky with a look of wonder on his face.

Four

Sam Baker had just that minute bought a drink from the vending machine by the visitors' centre when he saw a man in a white uniform running across the car park, shouting wildly while pointing back at the river.

Zita had gone to wash her face in the ladies' – and to beat her head against the cubicle doors if the fancy took her, she'd told him. He'd hoped she'd been attempting a little whimsy but he half wondered if she, too, had sensed that pit of insanity opening its deep, dark throat at the back of her mind.

Now a man in white, with red and yellow stains on the front of his jacket, was running barefoot towards him across the tarmac.

Maybe that insanity was well and truly infectious, after all.

Jud looked up from where he sat on the bench. 'That's Brian. What's eating him?'

'Probably the same thing that's eating us all,' Sam said, hearing the bitterness in his voice. 'You don't go through the experience of sliding back one week and come out the other side all happy-smiley.'

The man shouted. 'In the blasted river! There's an old man. He's drowning!' He gestured. 'I can't swim and that stupid jerk on the boat won't bastard well do anything.'

Jud threw his waistcoat to one side and ran across the car park. Sam followed. The man in white didn't wait and ran back down the slope in the direction of the river. The bare soles of his feet were blackened with dirt.

At the bank all three stopped. Sam scanned the water but saw nothing. Apart from the two moored boats there were no others on the water. A pair of swans glided serenely by.

'He was there.' The ice-cream seller pointed. 'Out there in the middle. Just swimming on his back.' He ran down into the water until he was up to his knees, then stopped and turned his head this way and that like a nervous kid getting ready to cross a busy road. 'He was there! You believe me, don't you?' He looked back at Sam. 'There's his walking stick . . . oh, Jesus. He must have gone under. We've lost him!'

Sam noticed Carswell standing, resting his elbows on the safety rail of the launch. He had a large glass tumbler in his hand.

'Did you see anything?' Sam called.

Carswell nodded, then took a swallow from his glass before returning to his lounger.

Sam Baker stiffened as if someone had just slapped him. He couldn't believe what he'd just seen. Carswell looked about as concerned as someone seeing those two swans on the water.

Sam walked in angry strides to the foot of the gangplank. 'There's a man in the water. You mean you saw it and did nothing?'

'Don't trouble yourself about it,' Carswell said dismissively.

'What the hell are you saying, Carswell? That you've just sat there and watched a man drown?'

'I sat here, but I didn't watch.'

'You callous bastard.' Sam took five more angry steps up the gangplank and onto the deck of the boat. 'Why didn't you try and help?'

'The old man knew what he was doing. He deliberately took his own life.'

'But you—'

'But nothing, Baker. Why the hell should I interfere in another man's decisions if those decisions do not have any impact on my own life? And, by the way, Mr Baker, I didn't invite you onto my boat, did I?'

'You know where you can stick your fucking boat, Carswell.'

'He wouldn't help,' the man in white was saying in a dazed voice. 'He wouldn't lift a finger.'

Sam scanned the river from the deck. From there he could see more of the broad expanse of water that stretched out more like a lake than a river at this point. The water was smooth, unbroken.

There was no sign of an old man.

The current must already have drawn him down. Nevertheless: 'We could still make a search of the river if we use both boats,' Sam said. He glared at Carswell who stretched out on the lounger and rotated the glass between his two palms so the ice chinked against the sides.

'No can do, Mr Baker. The man wanted to die. I drink to his sensible decision. And I, for one, wish more people would follow suit. Now, Mr Baker, kindly get yourself off my fucking boat.'

The man's once polished accent had vanished. The tones were raw, with a dangerous edge. And his glass-bead eyes began to flash dangerously. Sam saw clearly enough the crude violence simmering beneath Carswell's skin, like molten rock ready to blow the top from a volcano.

'Don't worry, I'm going,' Sam told him, disgusted.

Jud was already untying the lines to his narrow boat. 'We'll use mine,' he shouted. 'If we head downstream we might still be able to pick him up if he's on the surface.'

Five

He wasn't. The old man must have got what he wanted. A quick and, Sam hoped, a relatively painless end to his life. Jud Campbell returned the narrow boat to the mooring. By this time the sun was dropping towards the hills.

Jud told them that people who drowned in the river would remain submerged for a week or so before floating to the surface. In days gone by men would stand on the river banks and fire guns over the water in the belief that the vibration from the shots would loosen the bodies from the hold of the river bed. Now the police dragged the river with cables or sent in the divers.

Sam watched Jud deftly tie the mooring rope to the metal ring set into the timber landing posts. 'I suppose we should report this?'

'Report what exactly, Sam? That we saw an old man drown in the river? If they can't find the body but somehow trace the man's identity from his walking stick, what happens when they call at his house? Remember, there are two identical copies of the man now. One lying on the river bed – and one at home, probably grilling a kipper for his tea. If we weren't charged with wasting police time they'd laugh in our faces, as likely as not. Ah, here comes your friend.'

Sam turned to see Zita walking down the grassy slope to the timber landing stage.

'I saw you go out on the boat. I take it you weren't running out on me. What happened?'

Sam told her. Occasionally he shot glances at Carswell's launch moored behind Jud's far more modest and homely narrow boat. The man himself sat drinking on his lounger.

Every so often a girl of around eighteen, wearing a little black dress, would come clicking in high stilettos across the deck to pour him another drink. Once Carswell squeezed her leg. It didn't look like a gesture of affection; rather a pinch intended to hurt.

Sam Baker liked the man less and less.

'Right,' Jud said gently. 'Can I offer anyone a drink and perhaps something to eat if you've the stomach for it?'

Brian Pickering, the man who sold ice cream, shook his head. 'Thanks, Jud. But I think it's time I was going home.'

'Is that wise, Brian? After all, you're going to find an identical copy of yourself there.'

'I'll work something out.' He grinned, but to Sam it looked more like a frightened kind of snarl. 'The wife won't know which way to turn with two husbands, will she?'

'Just take it easy with her, won't you? It won't be easy.'

'Don't worry about me, Jud.' Again he tried to speak lightly, but there was a distinct waver in his voice. 'I'll be all right.'

'Sure you will,' Jud said kindly. 'See you later.'

For a moment they watched Brian Pickering go. A stumpy man, half walking, half running up the slope back to his ice-cream van in the car park.

Sam felt for him. He sensed the man's anticipation of meeting himself. Clashing with that was probably a hefty wedge of fear, too.

Zita was astonished. 'How could you let him go like that? Imagine the shock of seeing what is basically a carbon copy of yourself coming through the door!'

'I don't think we need worry about him,' Jud said evenly. 'Something will happen to Brian Pickering between here and Casterton.'

'How do you know that?'

'Because he never met himself. After all, he never mentioned meeting himself to us, did he?'

Sam nodded. 'Point taken. But tell me, Jud. Where were you on June the sixteenth?'

'Twenty miles upstream . . . fortunately. I'd taken the boat to have her engine serviced. So there's no immediate danger of me coming face to face with myself.' He smiled. 'Who's for that drink?'

He stood back on the landing stage and held out his hand towards the gangplank, inviting them on board.

Sam Baker took one step forward.

But he was never to have that drink.

Because at that exact moment, whatever had happened earlier in the day went and happened all over again.

Chapter Sixteen

One

The dream was the same.

Sam Baker sat alone in the amphitheatre. Planted squarely in the centre of the stone altar, which in turn stood in the middle of the amphitheatre stage, was a huge wooden cross. Spikes sprouted from the cross like thorns on a rose bush. And impaled on the spikes was the young man with red shoes and a dirty towel tied around his waist.

As he hung there, the spikes punching through his flesh in twenty different places, he looked beseechingly at Sam.

Blood pooled in the bowls scooped out of the stone altar.

In a dreamlike way, Sam stood up.

> *Buffalo girls gonna come out tonight,*
> *Gonna come out tonight,*
> *Buffalo girls gonna come out tonight . . .*

The softly-sung words appeared to leak from the stone beneath his feet. They were so sweetly intoned, the voice little more than a whisper.

He opened his eyes.

People sat in the amphitheatre seats. Instantly there was a kind of startled *OH!* sound as people experienced that sharp burst of shock when they realized they were back again.

It was as if every man and woman was attached to the

place by a long, long piece of elastic that allowed them so far before pulling tight and jerking them back into their seats.

Following the *OH!* there was a moment or so of stunned silence as they absorbed what had happened to them. Then a rising buzz of talk, shot through with glaring threads of panic.

He felt a hand grip his forearm.

He turned to see Zita staring at him with wide frightened eyes.

'Sam, it's gone and done it again, hasn't it?'

He nodded. 'There's no question about it . . .' He glanced round. 'But the only question is: how far have we gone back this time?'

He heard a moan beside him.

Sitting there, dazed, glassy-eyed, was Lee Burton in his Dracula costume. He looked as if he was just coming round from one hell of a knockout punch.

Sam looked for any sign of the massive injuries that Lee had suffered. The doctor's description had been vivid enough to give Sam a good idea of what he must have looked like. Just hours ago – or so it seemed – Lee had lain in casualty, with tubes running into his arm, nostrils and mouth. Lumpy dressings stained with blood from the bullet wounds were taped to his torso. His left arm had been severed at the elbow. The heart-monitor would have shown the erratic lines of a heart heading into a one-way pattern of defibrillation with the bleeps chattering out faster and faster until there was that one long terminal *Bleeeeeeeeee* . . .

But here he was again.

Intact.

The white shirt without so much of a drop of blood marking it.

And Lee was looking down dazedly at his two hands resting there in his lap.

Without a shadow of a doubt the mechanism that had dragged them back through time had brought them back whole. Just as they had been when they'd first walked into the amphitheatre at midday, June the twenty-third.

Sam quickly examined the knee of his chinos; they were a light tan colour. Earlier, he'd noticed dirty marks there about the size of a penny. It might have been drips from a coffee cup in the café. Now they were gone.

Quickly, he checked his watch. It showed a now-erroneous time and date. *1 p.m., June 23.*

Maybe this was the hereafter? Maybe they'd go round and around on some kind of temporal fairground ride for ever and a day. Never getting any older, never dying; hell, never even seeing their clothes wear out.

Sam looked down at the centre of the amphitheatre. Jud Campbell was standing there, looking round at the audience, his gold waistcoat neatly buttoned and as immaculate as the first time Sam had seen it. He had one arm slightly raised, his index finger pointing. Sam saw he was counting the audience again. He seemed in control of himself and when he saw Sam and Zita he waved at them to join him.

Two

'So it's happened again,' Jud said, calmly enough, as Sam and Zita joined him beside the stone altar.

Zita said, 'But what we don't know is *when* are we now.'

'Hopefully back where we started,' Sam said. 'Back to the afternoon of June the twenty-third.'

'You really think so?' Jud raised his eyebrows doubtfully.

'I don't think so, Jud. I just hope so, that's all. But I reckon we need another run into town so we can buy a newspaper all over again.'

'The weather looks the same,' Zita said. 'Clear and sunny. At least we haven't been dropped into the middle of winter.'

'So we're still in the summer,' Sam said.

'But which summer?'

Sam felt suddenly cold, despite the heat of the sun. Which summer, indeed? What if all this went even more haywire?

What if they were whisked so far back they saw a Tyrannosaurus Rex come stomping over the hill, looking for brunch?

Sam licked his dry lips and closed off those distinctly unnerving thoughts. 'The upside to all this is that we're being brought back in one piece. In fact, whatever brings us back also repairs any damage we might have suffered before the last time jump. Do you see Lee Burton up there? There's not a mark on him. He looks pretty shook up, though.'

'Hell,' Zita said, 'from what we heard in the hospital he'd been reduced to a pile of raw mincemeat; it was only a matter of time before they pulled the plug on the life-support machine.'

Sam gave a watery smile. 'If this freaky game is the guy upstairs's doing then at least he doesn't want to lose any of his players.'

'I don't know,' Jud said, rubbing his jaw thoughtfully. 'Call it monomania but I count everything. When I wash my socks I count them, when I peel potatoes I count them. And I always count the people in my audience. When I first counted this lot there were fifty-two. Now there are fifty-one.'

'We've lost one?'

'Looks like it. And if my memory isn't playing any strange tricks I think it was a gentleman who sat just there at the foot of the steps.'

'Don't tell me,' Sam said. 'He was old and carried a walking stick?'

'That's exactly what I'm telling you. I remember because he was fiddling with a hearing aid before the talk.'

Zita looked at Sam. 'That old boy in the car park. He carried a stick and he was complaining that his hearing aid wasn't working properly. Remember?'

'I remember. And I'd wager any money that the two were one and the same. I'd also wager that it was the same old boy the ice-cream vendor saw walk into the river to commit suicide.'

'So don't do anything too reckless,' Jud said. 'It seems at the moment that the rules of the game are if we're hurt we come through the next time jump in one piece and as good as new.'

'But if we're killed we're out of the game,' Zita added.

'Well, at least it's good to know some of the rules.' Sam watched the audience once more filing out of the amphitheatre. 'But *is* this some kind of game? And if it is, what's the object of it?'

'And how do we win?'

Sam headed across the amphitheatre's stage.

'Where are you going,' Zita asked.

'I'm going down to the river to talk to our Mr Carswell.'

'That bastard. What on earth for?'

'Right,' Sam said. 'He's a bastard. But he's one hell of a smart bastard. Maybe he's got his own ideas about what's happening.'

Three

'1978.'

That was how Carswell greeted Sam Baker as he walked briskly towards the boat.

'Permission to come on board? Sam called, but didn't wait for an invitation before running up the gangplank to the deck where Carswell stood with his drink in hand.

'It looks as if you're coming anyway, Mr Baker.'

Sam glanced back to see Zita following. Jud was hurrying back to his own boat to find his wife.

'The year of Our Lord, 1978,' Carswell repeated in such a light-hearted way that Sam thought *Dear God, the bastard is actually enjoying this.*

'Shit,' Zita breathed. 'That means we've gone back more than twenty years.'

Carswell looked at the drink in the glass. 'More than twenty years and the tonic still hasn't lost its fizz. Remarkable, hmm?'

'Damn remarkable,' Sam agreed with feeling. 'What are your thoughts about all this?'

'Time travel?' He took a drink and appeared to relish the taste with such pleasure that it could have been the elixir of life.

'Well, what occurs to me immediately,' Carswell continued, 'is that in a vehicle-repair shop in the East End of London, not far from where the shining commercial palaces of Canary Wharf will be built in a few years, is one twenty-year-old youth with oily hands and blond hair like this – only much thicker – draining the sump of some rich man's motor while dreaming of bigger and better things.'

'How do you know the date?'

'I've just listened to the radio. The pop music is definitely late Seventies.'

'So? It might be a station playing golden oldies.'

'And, Mr Baker, the DJ just announced he was playing a newly-released single that turned out to be a rendition of *My Way* by none other than the Sex Pistols' Sid Vicious.'

'You sure that was released in 1978?'

'It was. In the July of 1978 to be precise – the original summer of hate. Although you'd never find me engaging in such a pastime I could beat you hollow in a pop-music trivia quiz.' He tapped his blond temple. 'I retain information. Dates, places, names, even what people say down to every nuance of speech. Not bad for a Cockney boy, is it?'

'OK. I believe you.'

'I don't care whether you do or you don't. By the way, your mobile phones won't work. That particular communications system won't be introduced to this country for several more years yet.' The eyes, still cold and beady-looking, swivelled towards the cabin steps. Again that expression of barely-contained rage flared into his face. He went to the cabin door and snarled down the steps. 'Is that meal going to take all day, or what?' He drained the glass. 'I'm going to change, then eat. See yourselves off my boat, won't you?'

With that he went down the stairs.

Zita looked at Sam and rolled her eyes. 'Charming as ever.'

Sam sighed. 'Come on, we might as well find Jud.'

'Do you think Carswell's right about the year?'

Sam nodded. 'Though I hate to admit it, Carswell's probably always right.'

'And insufferably arrogant with it, too.'

'I'd back you to the hilt on that one.'

'After we talk to Jud, what then?'

'Another trip into town, I guess. I think it's time we tried to find someone who can help us.'

'Who?'

'Search me, but we'll never find anyone unless we start looking now.'

Four

Lee Burton was finally free of the Dracula cape. He'd stood in the hot sun in the amphitheatre car park and fought the button until his finger tips stung, but at last he prised the damn thing through the loop of chord.

'And good riddance to you,' he told the cape as he stuffed it into a concrete waste-bin. After that he went to the toilet block where he scrubbed the deathly white make-up and fake blood from his face.

Just minutes earlier he'd come to in the amphitheatre as if he was waking from a dream. Ryan Keith had sat beside him in the Oliver Hardy costume, his plump face running with sweat and he was staring in a kind of horrified fascination at the people in the amphitheatre, as if they'd sprouted bright green lizard heads from their faces or something. Nicole and Sue were talking to each other in low worried voices.

But Lee'd had enough, God damn it.

He'd done his best. He'd tackled the robbers. He'd been shot, he'd broken bones in the car crash, his arm had been severed by the train wheels.

Now he was whole again.

Had he passed the test?

If the sun was the eye of God glaring unwaveringly down at him, then the Almighty had seen everything.

But had he passed the test?

Shit. He didn't care any more.

He was going to go into town and get well and truly rat-arsed.

After drying his face and hands on paper towels he left the toilet block, then headed off along the access track to the main road where he knew he'd find a bus stop.

Behind him, the man who sold ice creams was sitting on the ground, his back to the van, his head in his hands. People were milling around the car park. The bus driver was trying – and failing miserably – to start the bus: the starter motor cranked away uselessly.

Lee walked faster.

It was a beautiful summer's day.

The white church shone bright in the sunlight.

Bees buzzed among the wildflowers in the meadows.

And right now, God knew, Lee Burton was going to enjoy life to the hilt. Even if it killed him.

Five

'It's 1978 . . . it's 1978. I heard those people talking down by the river. We're back in 1978. The month's July.' The middle-aged woman walked up the amphitheatre steps. She was smiling with sheer happiness and telling every-one she met: '1978. My Frank must be still alive. Isn't that wonderful? I lost him in 1991. He'd only gone to the bathroom when I heard this bang. He'd fallen back against the door and . . .' She went on up the steps, beaming so happily her cheeks looked as tight as balloons.

'At least someone's cheerful,' Sue said. 'Want one?' From the packet of her Stan Laurel jacket she'd pulled a packet of cigarettes. 'Oh, damn. I've just realized. If it's 1978, some-where I'll still be in nappies.'

Nicole took a cigarette. Inside the hairy black gorilla suit it felt like a furnace. She threw the gorilla head onto the stone floor. 'Yeah, and Freddie Mercury's still alive.'

'And Cary Grant.'

'And Peter Sellers.'

'I never cared for him much.'

'Didn't you? I thought he was brilliant in *Being There*.'

There was a pause, then Nicole blew a jet of smoke through her lips. 'My God, we nearly had a normal conversation about normal things, didn't we?'

'So what happens now?'

Nicole merely shrugged.

They smoked in silence for a moment. Part of the audience had already streamed out of the amphitheatre. The rest sat and talked or stared mutely into space. They all knew now that they'd been dragged back here from whatever they had been doing. Like dolls on a long piece of elastic. They could go only so far before being snapped back into their seats.

Nicole pushed back her long blonde hair. She felt peculiarly calm. She guessed the real description of her condition was that she was resigned to what had happened.

It only seemed a few minutes ago that she was on a burning quest to save the life of old Mr Thorpe who lived next door. She'd jumped off the bus in York and had run through the streets in her stupid gorilla suit, all the way back to Invicta Parade. She'd pounded on the door until Mrs Thorpe had opened it. She'd been surprised to see Nicole standing on the step in her gorilla suit but that surprise had turned into something close to shock when Nicole had dramatically demanded to see Mr Thorpe. In any event, it turned out he'd just walked down to the local supermarket for a loaf of bread.

Nicole had been running down the street drawing honks from passing drivers and shouts from school kids when suddenly she wasn't running any more.

She was sitting in the amphitheatre again.

Cooking in that damned ape suit.

What do you do in a situation like this? she asked herself. Do you sit and wait and hope that whatever's clogged the arteries of time frees itself?

Do you go out and make the most of it? Drink, laugh and love until the cows come home? Or do you find some professor – the loony kind with the wild and woolly hairstyle – who can straighten all this out for you?

Or do you throw a rope over a tree branch and end it all?

Suicide. It seemed such a simple and elegant solution to everything.

Suicide.

There was a rope, she knew, in the luggage hold of the tour bus.

Why it was there she wasn't sure. To tie more luggage on to a roof-rack? Or maybe it was supplied by the National Euthanasia Society of Great Britain for just such a crisis as this. When your boyfriend leaves you pregnant and penniless. Or you're fired from your job, maybe. Or if the universe turns all contrary on you and flicks you back through time like a child flicking a tiddlywink button.

She found herself grinning. *Yes, that's it. The answer to all my problems.*

She plucked a length of white cotton from the black furry leg of the gorilla suit; almost idly, as if she'd just made an everyday decision like what to eat for lunch or what blouse to wear on a date.

'I'll be back in five minutes,' she told Sue – which was a bare-faced lie, of course. Then she went to find the rope.

Six

The Range Rover started at the eighth attempt.

'Thank the Lord for that,' Zita said.

'What else do we need to thank the Lord for?' Sam Baker asked, pushing the mobile phone into the glove compartment. (When he'd tried dialling out of curiosity all he'd got were the clicks and hisses of static.)

In the back of the car Jud leaned forward. 'At least there's less electrical interference this time round.'

'Is that a good sign or a bad sign?' Sam asked. 'Until we know what the hell's happening we could keep rolling back through time until we reach Year Zero.'

'That's, hopefully, what we're going to try and find out.'

Zita powered the car through the car park exit onto the track that led to the main highway.

A moment later they all felt a bump in the road. 'The roadway was on two levels,' Zita said. 'I didn't notice that before, did you?'

Sam shook his head. 'The road surface is different, too; it's pebbles that have been rolled into the road tar.'

'So it looks like we've left the road of 1999 behind for the road of 1978.' Jud Campbell looked through the back window. 'See the grass? It's far longer here, too.'

Zita glanced in the rear-view mirror. 'At least we're starting to get see the extent of the land area that's made the jump with us.'

'Roughly, my guess is it comprises the amphitheatre at the centre, the car park, visitors' centre, a chunk of river, a few acres of grassland and a hundred yards or so of access road. As far as I can guess, the church lies just inside the affected area.'

They passed Lee Burton who was marching hard along the road, head down, his expression set in determination. Sam didn't suggest stopping to pick him up. No one else did, either.

They joined the main road to town.

In the back, Jud said quietly, 'This time I think we're going to notice one or two changes.'

Seven

The driver never asked why Nicole Wagner needed access to the luggage hold. He simply pushed a button on the dash, then went back to jabbing the pre-sets on the bus radio. The sound of the Bee Gees' *Stayin' Alive* filled the bus.

Inwardly Nicole was grinning as she climbed off the bus in her gorilla suit. The luggage-hold doors hissed open on their hydraulically driven supports. There lay the orange nylon rope, neatly coiled on top of a suitcase.

That internal grin widened. At that moment she realized, in a disconnected this-doesn't-affect-me kind of way, that it felt like she had a grinning clown locked away inside her head. The clown grinned and grinned behind his cherry-red nose. Of course, it wasn't a real grin – it was only painted there as a mask to conceal the real expression of despair and helplessness beneath.

Right now, she acted on autopilot. Someone else pulled the strings that moved her arms as she picked up the coil of rope and walked slowly towards the trees.

This was the right thing.

She was certain of it. So what if the stress of recent events had triggered a self-destruct mechanism?

Putting her head through a noose was the simple and elegant solution to all her problems.

A tiny voice in the back of her head protested. Perhaps it was the shock of what had happened to her – the backward skip through time – that was to blame; maybe the shock had screwed up most of the people in the amphitheatre, too; they couldn't think rationally; perhaps if she only took the time to have a coffee and think things through she wouldn't take her own life.

But no . . .

The voice was too small and far too feeble.

In the distance now she could hear the Bee Gees song pumping from the bus. *Stayin' Alive*? Wasn't that an exquisite irony?

In the back of her head the clown's grin grew wider and wider. He began to rock backwards and forwards, quivering with a manic laughter. The rope felt good and strong and thick in her hands. Now she only needed to find a tree with a branch sturdy enough to hold her weight.

Eight

William Bostock was arguing again with his wife of thirty years. They'd habitually yelled at each other at least once a day since their only daughter had run away from home ten years before. Not that the daughter's story had turned into high melodrama. They had never tracked her down to a whorehouse where she cavorted furiously for the price of a heroin fix.

No, nothing that purple. Daughter Tina had only run as far as Pontefract where she'd found work on a Woolworth's check-out. Now she was married to a quantity surveyor and lived in a comfortable house overlooking the racecourse.

But her leaving had thrown William's and Marion's relationship out of kilter. There was some marital problem that neither could even identify, never mind resolve.

Instead they yelled.

Now William followed Marion away from the amphitheatre. He was a short, sturdy man in a cream polo shirt and polyester trousers; above his belt a beer belly blossomed (already heading for that fat-man fold-over that would in time obscure his privates when he looked down at himself). Lately, he'd begun to notice his own body odour or, to put it a little more plainly, his armpits stank of sweat: a sharp, stale smell that enveloped him in an aura of armpit stink. At first he found himself walking faster to outpace the smell. When he found that didn't work he began to slosh huge amounts of aftershave onto his chest and armpits. Now stale-sweat smells mated with Superdrug Sport For Men to give birth to a truly potent odour that made people pause and look at him as he walked by in the street.

Marion Bostock was a short, plump woman of fifty with large breasts that had grown soft and pudding-like over the years. On her nose rested thick brown-rimmed glasses that gave her the look of an owl, or so William thought. An ever-staring, ever-judgemental owl that criticized everything he did.

The eyes were still huge as she snarled at him, 'I told you I never wanted to come on this holiday, didn't I? I knew – I just knew it would end in disaster.'

'How the hell could I foresee this?' he said feeling his cheeks burn. 'Rain, yes. Losing our suitcase, yes. But not this, you stupid woman.'

'Stupid, am I?'

'Of course you bloody well are. All you want to do is nag, nag, nag . . . it's the only time you're happy.'

'The only time *you're* happy is when you're with your cronies with a drink inside you.'

'Too bloody right.'

Instinctively they headed away from other people to where they could yell at each other in relative privacy.

'And I haven't forgotten you hit me on the bus, William Bostock. I'll never forget that.'

'Well, you were driving me—'

'But to hit me? You do realize that's the first time you've raised your hand to me?'

'Marion, I—'

'And it will be the last, d'you hear? The last!'

By this time they'd entered a clump of trees some way from the amphitheatre.

'Oh, shut up,' William said. 'I'm sick of hearing you . . . day after day after—'

'You're sick of hearing me?'

'Yes. Bloody sick.'

'That's rich.'

'But true.'

'I have to listen to you moan about work every time you come home.'

'It's a treadmill at that factory; it's—'

'You moan about it, you say you hate it.' Her eyes flashed, passionate with anger. 'But you never stop talking about it.' With that she turned and walked briskly along the path through the woods, her soft pudding-like breasts no doubt bouncing heavily up and down as she went, thought William bitterly, picturing the way they moved independently of her when she marched away angrily like that. Which was one of her favourite tricks.

'Where are you going now?' he sneered. 'Home?'

'Somewhere you won't find me.'

He ran after her. His leg muscles were so tight he ran stiffly, his legs hardly bending at the knee at all. Anger – sheer, blazing anger – had caused every muscle in his body to tense until he felt he was running in a suit of armour.

'Marion—'

He only meant to grab her by the arm to turn her round.

Whether she thought he was going to slap her again he didn't know. In any event she got one in first: a surprisingly muscular slap that caught him across the forehead and eye.

He lurched back, the eye stinging, filling with tears.

He found he could hardly see.

She raised her hand again. Alarmed, he stepped back, but some obstruction wouldn't allow his foot to move. With his balance gone he tripped backwards and sat down hard on the earth floor.

Suddenly, even under the canopy of branches, everything seemed over-bright to William. A great rush of energy surged through him.

With it came rage.

An awful tidal wave of rage that swamped all reason, all logic, all conscience.

He jumped onto all fours and crawled like some fast woodland animal, his eyes swivelling left and right as he searched for something in the dirt.

Got it, got it, got it!

The words machine-gunned through his head.

Got it! Goddit-godditttt!

Ahead lay a pebble the size of a tennis ball.

It was brown and shiny and – God, yes, yes – hard. Hard as flint.

He grabbed it in his right hand, jumped to his feet.

His wife had stopped to stare at him, her eyes ridiculously huge behind her glasses.

Old Granny Owl.

Crimson flashes burst in front of his eyes.

Old Granny Owl, come here!

He didn't so much run at her as pounce.

In fury he swung the hand that gripped the pebble down at her.

Clunk . . .

Quite a gentle sound, really. Like someone patting a baby's pillow for its head when it was laid down to sleep at night.

Gurfff . . .

The grunt came from her mouth like a fart.

Old Granny Owl!

He hammered at her head with the pebble.

His arm blurred with speed.

It all seemed so effortless and easy to William.

Thud-thud-thud . . .

Marion staggered backwards until she clunked against a tree trunk and couldn't retreat any further.

She looked up with what seemed to him a kind of gormless surprise at the pebble coming down again and again.

William watched as if he stood outside himself as her forehead split under the hammer-like blows. The wide expanse of creamy forehead just opened like cracks appearing in a frozen puddle.

Her soft pudding breasts wobbled to the rhythm of the blows.

Blood gushed in a thick red stream down her face. Some poured into her mouth. It bubbled as she made that farting sound with her lips.

Still he beat.

The lenses of the owl glasses shattered.

But still – amazingly to William – they stayed on her face.

He hit again. Slap in the middle of that bloody forehead.

Only this time instead of the soft thud there was a sharp crack. Like someone snapping a bamboo cane.

Instantly she dropped at his feet.

And then she lay still. Knees together and bent, arms down by her side.

He was grunting for breath; his chest felt empty of everything – not just air, but bones and guts and lungs and heart.

He looked up.

What he saw didn't register at first.

Because it was an impossible sight.

At least, impossible here in this patch of trees in Yorkshire, England.

Maybe he was dreaming. He blinked.

The image remained.

A gorilla with a coat of shaggy black fur stood on the ground watching him. In its hands it held an orange jungle creeper that snaked up into the branches.

He glanced down at the lifeless body of his wife, the smashed owl glasses still perched primly on her bloody face.

Then he looked back at the gorilla holding the jungle creeper.

This time his powers of recognition came back to him.

What he really stared at was a girl in a gorilla suit holding a rope, as if she was going to climb into a tree. What was more, she was one of the four travel reps on the coach. They'd all been in fancy dress.

He glanced back at his dead wife.

And he knew he couldn't allow the girl to leave the wood.

Chapter Seventeen

Nicole Wagner had stood and watched the man murder his wife with the stone.

The shock of witnessing such an act of violence had stunned her. As though someone had tent-pegged her feet to the ground she stood there, just holding the rope that she'd thrown over the branch as a prelude to hanging herself.

Now the man stared back at her, his own eyes wide with shock.

She saw he was panting with the exertion of beating the woman's head until it resembled raw liver.

Grey sweat-stains formed half-moons beneath his armpits on the cream polo shirt.

The pair were man and wife. Yes, she remembered them from her bus. They were always arguing.

The man coughed, then looked round at the deserted wood. His eyes suddenly became crafty.

Nicole let go of the orange rope and backed away slowly, one step at a time, the big gorilla feet making a swishing sound across the dry earth.

The man held up his hand (the one without the pebble, she saw). He smiled; it was an absurdly warm smile at that.

'Wait a moment,' he said in a friendly voice. 'I want to have a word with you. I need you to tell them I— Wait!'

But she wasn't waiting.

At that moment her mind snapped into focus. The grinning lunatic clown in the back of her mind evaporated.

Now she realized she didn't want to kill herself.

She didn't want to die, full stop.

She turned and ran through the wood. She ran as hard as the ridiculous gorilla suit would allow.

'Come back . . . I just need to talk to you. Only for a moment . . . a few seconds . . . *please*.' The cajoling voice gave way to a desperate shout. He ran after her, blundering through the undergrowth. It sounded like a ferocious bull chasing her.

She ran hard, her arms windmilling, the gorilla costume snagging on twigs and leaving clumps of long nylon hair behind.

'Wait!' The man yelled. 'Wait!'

The crashing became louder.

He's catching up, Nicole thought, panicking; *he won't let me tell the others*. He'll use that pebble on me.

The thought of that heavy pebble cracking agonizingly against her own skull pushed her faster.

Tree trunks seemed to leap out to stand in front of her. She zigged and zagged to avoid them, her legs growing weaker and more watery by the second.

Then, with horrifying abruptness, the ground suddenly ended in front of her.

Dizzy with shock, she stopped and stared. Just two paces from her own feet the ground had been cut away.

Below her was a good thirty-foot drop into an ancient quarry that was dotted here and there with half a dozen trees. There were no people she could see. On the quarry bottom rabbits scampered for cover, startled by the sounds of the chase from above. And that quarry bottom, scattered with boulders and clumps of nettles, seemed a long, long way below.

It certainly wasn't the kind of distance you leap and live to tell your grandkids about.

The man blundered through the bushes behind her, coughing and gagging as he fought to breathe. The sun blazed: his face had become a blotchy red, yet his nose was oddly white, as if it was made from plaster of Paris.

Nicole turned to her right and ran up the steep incline.

Immediately she thought: *What a stupid thing to do. I can't run uphill in this ridiculous suit. It's heavy; it's like running wrapped in a fireside rug. He'll catch me now. Then he'll break open my head like an egg.*

He's crazy enough to do it.

And he was. There was no doubt about it. He made barking sounds now; his eyes were wild. He gripped the pebble hard, because the pebble was slippery with Marion Bostock's blood. And he'd need a good, tight grip on the pebble when he used it on her.

He was ten paces from her and closing fast.

Growing close to the sheer rock face of the quarry from the ground below was a horse chestnut tee. Perhaps thirty feet high, it was soft and green and billowing as a cloud. The uppermost branches, she saw, were level with her feet.

The man clumped towards her, swearing; raising the pebble.

Nicole judged the distance.

It was a crazy leap.

But she had no choice.

Cutting to her left she ran as hard as she could towards the edge of the cliff. Then she leapt.

Her body followed a downward curve. Arms held out as if she was some great hairy bird, she closed her eyes and gritted her teeth.

Behind her the man snarled in fury. 'Stupid-stupid-stupid . . .'

Then she heard the godalmighty crashing and snapping of twigs and branches as she landed on top of the horse chestnut tree. Her momentum carried her down into the green heart of the tree, a dizzying breathless dive, cracking twigs, ripping away leaves in a spray of green, then bumping against the thicker branches before coming to a sudden — and bone-jolting — stop.

Chapter Eighteen

One

Lee Burton stood at the bus stop on the main road to Casterton. He looked round at the fields of potatoes, wheat and sugar beet, all drenched in dazzling sunshine. The only building he could see was the Plough Inn; a typical country pub, whitewashed walls, black slate roof, with a small car park and a children's play area complete with swings and slide.

On the walk up here from the amphitheatre he had realized that whatever mechanism had pitched them back through time had just gone and done it all over again. He clearly remembered being shot, how he'd caused the robbers' car to crash and losing his arm on the railway line, then how it'd all gone dark until he opened his eyes in the sun-filled amphitheatre again.

He hadn't a clue how far they'd travelled back in time. A few hours? A few days?

But as he stood there and saw the cars running by on the road he knew it must be much further than that.

He saw an old Ford Capri.

Rather, it should have been old. It should have been a superannuated rust bucket with a clapped-out motor. But this was a gleaming new model. The registration would have given him an approximate date but he realized he just didn't care that deeply anymore what year this was.

Shock still numbed him.

He wanted to get into town, then get a few drinks down him.

No. Scratch *a few*. He wanted lots and lots.

A double-decker bus rumbled up the hill and stopped with a hiss of hydraulics. The door opened.

At least the bus didn't look that much different to the buses he was familiar with. He climbed on and handed the driver a fifty pence piece.

'Casterton, please.'

'Ent ya got any less, son?' the driver asked.

'How much is it?'

'Eighteen new pee.'

Lee forced his hands into the tight pockets of the black trousers he was hating more and more with every passing minute.

The driver drummed his fingers impatiently on the steering wheel and hummed while Lee fiddled with small change, eventually counting eighteen pence out in copper.

'Don't forget your ticket,' the driver told him as he went to find a seat.

Seconds later, Lee sat absently rolling the ticket into a tube as he watched the passing scenery. Most of the cars he couldn't even identify, but he'd seen them often enough in old TV programmes from the Seventies.

He still felt a glassy indifference to it all. At first he ascribed it to the shock of nearly dying twice in what would have been the space of a few hours. The physical pain of both incidents was still pungently real to him. He still found himself rubbing his stomach where the bullets had punched holes through the skin.

But now he wondered if it was more than pure shock that made him feel this way: he was indifferent to his surroundings; this was a sense of detachment from reality. *Perhaps I feel like this because I've lost control of my life*, he thought. *Something else pulls the strings now.* Here he was, riding on the bus to town. Only at any second he might blink and find himself back in the amphitheatre with the rest of his accidental time travellers.

The only reality he could centre himself on was his thirst, and his longing for that first mouthful of beer.

Two

Nicole Wagner climbed down the trunk of the tree. The hefty gorilla suit repeatedly snagged on branches.

She panted hard, her long blonde hair messed, knotted, the strands speckled green with pieces of leaf.

She guessed that, after hitting the top of the tree, she'd fallen perhaps halfway through the branches before landing face down on a more unbending – and unforgiving – branch. Her boobs and stomach ached furiously from the collision.

Right now the only thought in her head was to get down to the ground, then run.

William Bostock would soon realize she hadn't broken her neck. Soon, he'd find a way down into the quarry.

'C'mon, c'mon, Nicole . . . faster . . . faster,' she panted to herself. She had to get out of the tree. She had to run.

Back to the amphitheatre. That would be best. People there. Bostock wouldn't dare touch her.

She looked down through the web of branches. There was the ground, perhaps eight feet below.

Just swing down, holding onto the bottom branch, dangle there, for a second, then drop to the ground.

Then get the hellfire out of there. Run.

She sat on the lowest branch above the ground; little thicker than her wrist, it creaked and swung beneath her. Her feet moved as though she was sitting on a playground swing.

She took a deep breath. Almost there . . .

'*Gerr-darn-here!*'

The animal-like roar startled her.

She cried out as Bostock lunged out of nowhere to grab at her foot.

He must have found some path down into the quarry more quickly than she'd thought possible.

Now he clung to one of her feet.

She screamed as he pulled.

Instantly he'd pulled her half off the branch by her foot.

Her rump was no longer seated on the branch: it rested in midair. The only thing stopping her falling to the ground below, and a certain bloody and painful death at Bostock's hands, was that she'd instinctively grabbed the higher branch in front of her face.

This was as thin as a child's arm and so springy it bent with her weight.

Screaming, she kicked with her free leg. But Bostock stood with both feet firmly planted on the ground and was tugging her by her left ankle. With every pull she dropped by about a foot or so as the flexible branch bent.

Every time he straightened his legs (ready for the next tug) the springy branch lifted her back up by a foot.

Christ . . . the man was like a bell-ringer; she was the bell rope.

Up and down, up and down . . .

And it felt as if her shoulder joints would pop from their sockets.

She couldn't hold on.

She'd have to let go . . .

The pain was immense now in her arms and back.

She couldn't breathe.

He pulled down hard.

Down she went like that bell rope.

Then suddenly she shot back up, almost catapulted back into the tree by the branch in her hands.

He's let go . . .

Dazed, she shook her head, trying to understand why he'd released his grip.

Nicole glanced down as she swung there like a gymnast. He was sitting on the ground. Gripped in his hands was one of the feet from the gorilla costume. He was glaring at it while swearing loudly.

Thank God, she thought gratefully. The elasticated foot had slipped off, dumping him rudely into the dirt.

With an effort she drew her knees up to her stomach as she hung there so he couldn't reach her feet. (She knew he wouldn't just give up and go away. No, would he hell! He looked to have the temperament of a bull-dog as well as the look of one, with his flattened face and short thick limbs.)

The branch whipped her up and down as she hooked one leg over it before hoisting herself into a sitting position.

Safe for the moment, at least now she could regain her breath.

'Get down here!' he snarled as he hauled himself to his feet.

She looked down. Bostock's foreshortened body looked stubbier than ever; his upturned face glistened with sweat; his eyes burned with fury.

'Get down.'

She shook her head, an emphatic *no*. She didn't want her head broken open with a bloody rock.

This time he changed tactics. He couldn't reach her so he jumped up to grab the trailing ends of a connecting branch. As soon as he had a grip he tugged at it, shaking the whole branch she sat upon, like he was trying to shake apples from a tree.

Quickly, still sitting astride the branch like it was a horse, she worked her way towards the trunk where it was thicker.

Soon it hardly moved at all, no matter how hard he tugged.

For the next five minutes she sat there watching tensely as he tried everything he could to either dislodge her or reach her.

After furiously swinging on every branch he could reach, in the vain hope of dislodging her so she'd fall out of the tree, he began picking rocks out of the long grass and throwing them at her.

But she moved again until the branches formed a shield between herself and him. No rocks even touched her.

Next on his agenda was to try and climb the trunk of the tree to reach her.

Although powerful-looking Bostock was very short, and not at all agile. It didn't help that there were no real hand- or footholds on the tree for the first six feet or so of the trunk.

He did manage to grab hold of a branch just below her which would have made a half-decent handhold.

However, as soon as he'd curled his stumpy fingers around the branch Nicole climbed down the tree until she could reach them.

Then, taking her weight on her bare left foot, where the gorilla foot had been pulled off, she used the other foot to stamp down on his fingers as hard as he could.

After the seventh or eighth stamp on his knuckles he swore loudly and let go, slithering down, face against the trunk of the tree, the bark scraping his chin and nose.

He swore louder.

'I'll get you!' he yelled.

Nicole was trembling from her bones outwards but she managed to say in such a calm voice it surprised her, 'No, you won't.'

'I will, you bitch.' He looked suddenly crafty; his eyes gleamed up at her as he stood there, head tilted back, watching her. 'I'm not leaving here. And you can't stay in that tree forever, can you!'

She stared down at him, not replying.

He said in an oily voice, 'Well, I'm prepared to stay here for as long as it takes.'

'They'll catch you!'

'No, they won't. No one will find Marion for days yet.' Smiling, Bostock lay down flat on his back on the grass, his hand pillowing his head, looking for all the world as if he was enjoying a sunny day in his back garden. Now he could watch her comfortably, without tilting his head back.

Nicole crouched down on the branch with her back to the main trunk of the tree and stared right back at him. His eyes were quite insane. She saw that clearly enough. Mad, bad and dangerous were the words that ran sidled through her brain. Mad, bad and dangerous.

She knew she had no other option. There was nothing else she could do. They were both in for a long wait.

Three

Ryan Keith got a lift into town from an Australian couple who'd been at the amphitheatre. Immediately he went into the nearest supermarket. The name of the store, Hillards, was unfamiliar to him. It smelt different from other supermarkets – a strong floral disinfectant, he supposed. Some of the products on the shelves looked unfamiliar, too, but in that state of mind he didn't stop and look more closely. Gazing at goods on display wasn't why he was here. Moving like he was on autopilot, not noticing other shoppers grinning at his Oliver Hardy costume, he picked up two bottles of vodka, then headed for the check-out.

The sweetest thing imaginable right now was to get completely out-your-skull wrecked.

Once the girl had punched the till buttons he handed her his Visa card. Then he waited as she laboriously pulled a credit-card slip printer from a shelf beneath the till; she slotted the card into it; rested a carbon slip over the top; then struggled for a moment to slide the pressure bar over the top.

It was all taking a very long time. Ryan was conscious of that. The bowler hat made his head itch but he didn't think to remove it.

He merely waited.

That sweet-looking vodka glinted like holy water in the bottom of his basket.

The temptation to simply open a bottle right now was nearly overpowering. His scalp itched even more: centipedes could have been nesting in there the way it felt, their multitudinous pointy feet digging into his scalp as they scurried through his hair.

'This card isn't right,' the girl said.

Ryan looked at her, frowning in a woolly distant kind of way as the words sank in. Eventually, he responded, 'You take Visa, don't you? It said so on the door.'

'Yes.'

'It's valid. It doesn't expire until the end of April next year.'

The girl gave him a puzzled look, then glanced around her as if half-expecting some camera crew to pop out, complete with a presenter to tell her all this was a riotously funny practical joke. *Oliver Hardy presents duff card to checkout girl. Cue studio laughter.*

There was no one there she could see. No hidden camera, no presenter wearing a cheeky *Gotcha!* grin.

Patiently, but a little louder as if to make sure her voice was picked up by a hidden microphone (she still thought this was some kind of elaborate set-up), the girl said, 'The card expires April 1999. But it's the "valid from" date that's wrong. It's valid from January 1996. See?'

'So?'

'Well, the year is 1978, isn't it?'

'This is 1978?'

'Yes.'

What the man in the Oliver Hardy suit did next took her by surprise.

With an explosive yell, he cried: '*Shit!*'

Then he grabbed a bottle of vodka in each hand and ran for the door.

Chapter Nineteen

One

Zita parked the car in the centre of town. The summer day had brought out enough shoppers to thicken the flow along the pavements.

'Good heavens to Murgatroyd,' Zita said in something between wonder and disgust. 'Will you just look at those fashions? Did we ever wear anything as drab as that?'

'So this is what passes for Seventies chic?' Sam said, wrinkling his nose. 'There's every shade of brown and grey you could possibly think of.'

In the back of the Range Rover Jud eagerly wound down the window. Sam saw the man's head was turning left and right so much it was a wonder he didn't sustain friction burns on his neck from his shirt collar. 'Heavens above,' he said again and again in tones of sheer amazement. 'Look. The Crescent's still a cinema. What's it showing? Damn, old-man eyes I'm getting. I can't see what's on.'

'*Jaws*.' Sam said in a low voice. 'What we might describe as *Jaws One*, still well away from the cruddy sequels.'

'Heavens above . . . heavens above. You know, I can't believe Casterton's changed so much in twenty years. Look at the shopfronts! All that drab plastic. Old Harker's the ironmongers. Look, they've still got buckets tied up on strings and you can see . . . oh, there's Woolworth's. See the old sign? Who's betting they still sell loose biscuits by the pound?'

Sam glanced back at Jud Campbell. The man was like a kid who'd been treated to a day at the fair; one who'd excitedly look this way and that, naming every ride, and where even a humdrum candy-floss stall was suddenly a thing of magic and wonder.

Meanwhile Zita stared in that fascinated way at the clothes the people wore. Sam, too, couldn't help but marvel that the pavements were full of people in clothes that were either dark brown, coffee-coloured or a lighter brown that was the same tone as a used tea bag. For all the world he could have been looking at a stream of water that had been churned up into a muddy brown. The nearest thing he saw to colourful clothing was a girl in a pullover that was a kind of washed-out powder blue.

These were the fashions that taste forgot. In the space of twenty seconds he saw half a dozen middle-aged men who fancied themselves as Elvis Presley look-alikes (that is to say, the sad Elvis from his bloated middle years); they had the same blowdried quiff stiffened with hairspray, the same side-burns and steel framed sunglasses, while their shirts were unbuttoned as far as swelling midriffs to reveal gold medallions nestling in dark thickets of chest hair. On the other hand, much of the younger generation looked like refugees from the cast of *Saturday Night Fever* with clunking platform shoes, huge wing-tip collars, and flared trousers. Most striking of all was their tightly permed hair. This did give them an Afro look, but the effect was marred by so many spotty, dough-pale faces which peeked from beneath these magnificent dandelion locks of hair.

Hell, he thought, *we've only rolled back twenty years and already the world looks different.* Not just a *bit* different. But strikingly different. The muddy brown clothes, the ugly plastic shop-fronts; the cars were different too, although he could have named only a handful because most were of British or European make, not American. Even so, he recognized the odd VW Beetle, boxy Volvo or occasional Datsun.

Meanwhile, in the back Jud was in a kind of ecstasy and speaking in tongues as far as Sam was concerned. The man was clearly recognizing cars that had long since vanished from the British roads.

'Singer Gazelle. I bought one of those. Cost me £75 and had an engine like a mule; only thing was, the bottom rotted out of it . . . Hillman Imp. Christ, look at that, a Ford Cortina. A Mark 1 Ford Cortina in metallic paint. My God, that was the car that used to turn heads. Metallic paint was virtually unheard of then . . . and mopeds. I've never seen so many mopeds. Not a satellite dish to be seen. And there's Dirty Harry – there, the tramp, lying on the bench with a bottle of cider in his hand. Hell, I think he's the only one who's never changed. Still wearing the filthy boiler suit and Wellington boots! There's Hillards supermarket. They were taken over by Tesco in— *Oh my God*,' he pushed his head out of the window. 'The man on the bike! The man on the bike! It's Tony Newell, he was sports editor of the *Casterton Gazette*. Oh, my dear God. He died in 1991. I was at the funeral. Dear God, I was actually there when they lowered the coffin into the . . . good grief . . . good grief . . .' Jud suddenly leaned back into the seat, looking as if someone had just planted their knee in his stomach. He looked winded. His breath was coming in hard tugs. His blue eyes watered. 'My God . . . oh, my God . . . this is really quite incredible. I didn't realize it would be such a shock. I'm seeing – *actually seeing* – people who have been dead for years.'

Zita looked back, her brown eyes showing concern. 'Are you OK?'

'A bit overwhelmed, that's all.' He placed both hands on his ribcage and breathed deeply. 'I don't think this heat's helping much.'

'Can I get you a cold drink?' Sam said, opening the door.

'That would be very welcome, thank you.'

Zita looked back at Jud and said gently, 'Best close the window. I'll turn up the air-conditioning. You'll soon feel better.'

'Air-conditioning? The wonders of modern technology.'
He leaned back and gave a smile that seemed suddenly
weary, tremendously weary. 'Air-conditioning. If we travel
any further back you will be able to take a patent out on it
and become millionaires.' He closed his eyes and chuckled.
'But somehow I don't think money will do any of us much
good in the long run.'

Sam was in the process of opening the door when he
paused and asked. 'Money won't do us any good? What
makes you say that?'

Jud had closed his eyes and rested his head back on the seat
so his face was tilted up at the car's ceiling. 'Already you
have notes and coins in your pocket that are no longer legal
tender. You should check coins carefully before you pay for
anything.' He opened his eyes and gave a little smile. 'After
all, how are you going to explain carrying a 1990s coin in
1977?' The smile widened as he closed his eyes. 'And, Sam, if
you should meet someone who looks a little like me, only
with darker hair and more of it, be nice to him. I was going
through a rough patch in 1977. In fact, I spent most of
August that year in plaster of Paris up to my crotch.'

Sam grinned. 'I'll do my best.'

'You will. You'll do your best.' Jud opened his eyes again.
'By the by, if you've developed a taste for English beer
you'll find they do a very nice glass of mild in the Gryphon
Hotel. And be sure to go into the public bar, not the lounge.'

Jud closed his eyes again as if he was ready for a nap.
Sam looked at Zita; she looked back and raised her
eyebrows. To Sam, what Jud had just said all seemed
pretty enigmatic – as if there was far more meaning loaded
into those few words than met the eye – or rather, in this
case, than met the ear.

Sam gave a little shrug at Zita's questioning expression.
Maybe Jud had just got himself a little over-warm and over-
wrought. This was probably a bigger shock for him. After
all, he knew the town; they didn't.

Sam said, 'I'll see you both in five minutes.'

'Don't forget the beer in the Gryphon Hotel, Sam. And take care.'

Sam shut the door, then crossed the road to join the stream of people in their muddy brown clothes.

Two

Ryan Keith was a man on the run.

On the run in a town he didn't know. And in a time that was unfamiliar to him.

As he'd run from the supermarket, carrying the bottles of vodka, he'd heard a shout. Glancing back, he saw two men chasing him. They wore burgundy-coloured nylon smocks with the name of the supermarket written on the breast pocket.

They looked young, physically fit.

Ryan knew they were far fitter than him. When he ran his plump face wobbled like jelly, his stomach heaved against his white shirt. The Oliver Hardy bowler hat stayed on his head by luck rather than design.

No way could he outrun them.

'Oh, Christ, oh, Christ . . . oh, no,' he sobbed under his breath as he ran along the street. He didn't like this world he'd fallen into. He was terrified of what would happen when the two supermarket workers caught him.

He was sure they'd knock him around before they handed him over to the police. They did that, didn't they? Shop-lifters received rough justice.

He sobbed louder as he ran; tears filled his eyes, he imagined only too vividly that first kick to his softly-rounded belly.

'Oh, why does everything have to happen to me?' he panted under his breath as he ran.

'This is another fine mess . . .' he began to tell himself before suddenly snapping, 'Shut up, you idiot, shut up . . . don't let them catch you. Christ, I don't want to get hurt . . . I don't want . . .' That was when he turned a corner and ran into his old friend Lee Burton.

Three

Nicole Wagner looked down from the tree at the man.

He lay flat on his back in the grass and stared back at her. A Red Admiral butterfly sat on a dock leaf by his head, warming its wings in the sunlight. Doves called softly to each other in the woods above the lip of the quarry.

To all intents and purposes the man, Bostock, was her jailer now.

She knew that the moment she climbed down from the tree he would pounce on her and beat her head to the colour of raw mutton.

The quarry was deserted. Even the rabbits had fled the commotion when she had leapt from the top of the rock face and into the tree. Nevertheless, every few minutes she carefully stood up on the branch to look out across the quarry towards the river in the hope someone would be strolling by. She saw no one. She was certain no one would hear if she shouted.

The man below her (who was probably deranged, she told herself) smiled benignly, as his wife's blood and brains slowly dried on his otherwise white polo shirt. She found it hard to look away from those brown stains because, she realized, if she wasn't very careful her own blood would contribute additional patterning to the shirt.

So she sat there in her big black shaggy ape suit and watched the sun sink slowly towards the horizon.

And she wondered what he would do when darkness at last fell.

Chapter Twenty

One

Sam Baker left the car in which Jud lay back, his head against the seat, looking all but overwhelmed. Zita appeared composed and had given Sam a little reassuring wave when he'd glanced back.

Hell, so this is 1978, Sam told himself. To be precise, this is the twenty-third of June, 1978. He'd seen the date on newspapers slotted into racks outside a newsagent's.

And this was a world full of people dressed in muddy brown clothes. Men wore Tom Jones hairstyles with hefty sideburns. They seemed noticeably plumper, too; their faces looked particularly rounded and full. He paused, pretending to look into a shop window, but really he was studying the reflection of those passing by. And he realized he was actually experiencing something close to shock at seeing so many teenage girls smoking. Already he was seeing different patterns of human behaviour even though they'd only scrolled back twenty years through time. In the 1990s there had been a growing gut feeling that smoking in public was becoming something mildly distasteful, like chewing gum in church or wearing a swimsuit in a shopping street: it certainly wasn't illegal or shockingly ill-mannered, but it just wasn't seen as 'the done thing'.

Sam lingered a little longer. Suddenly, in close up,

the faces of 1970s people fascinated him. Women wore pale blue eye-shadow which gave their faces a different look. Hairstyles were over-neat in a fussy kind of way. Young men wore flares and wide ties. Although punk fashions must be just around the corner, as far as time was concerned, they hadn't arrived yet in this northern backwater.

As he stood watching the reflection of people passing by in the big plate-glass window he saw another reflection. And he realized someone was staring at him.

He turned his head slightly and saw it was the tramp Jud had referred to as 'Dirty Harry'. He was a thin man with curly ginger hair and a beard. He was dressed in workman's orange overalls and Wellington boots that were turned down at the top so they looked like rough-and-ready ankle boots. In one bony hand he gripped the neck of a bottle of cider.

Sam guessed the man must have been in his mid-forties. But what was most surprising was that the tramp stared hard at Sam's face as if recognizing a long-lost friend.

Dirty Harry took a couple of unsteady paces towards Sam. He raised the bottle, uncurled one filthy finger from the neck, then pointed a fingernail that was brown with nicotine – or something worse – at Sam. He made a jabbing motion with the finger, trying to put a name to the face.

Sam gave the man a nod that was definitely cautious, non-committal, then he began to walk away. Like most people the last thing Sam wanted was to be buttonholed by the town nutcase.

Then Dirty Harry spoke to Sam. It was as if he'd kept the words bottled up for years; suddenly they burst from his lips in a rush. 'See, wretched little man, how the delights of carnal lust cover up the terror of the coming damnation! Before your heart can burn with the love of Christ – the love of Christ! – it will have to get rid of its appetite for all passing vanity, whatever – whatever . . . A mind on fire with the spirit of Christ finds its sole nourishment in its love of eternity . . .'

With a very weak smile Sam broke eye contact with the mad tramp and began to walk away. Others in the street barely gave Dirty Harry a glance. Perhaps to make eye contact was an invitation to the man to harangue you.

'Love of eternity, and its gladness in joyful song. The heart that has turned to fire – turned to fire! – embraces nothing of the world, but strives always to pierce heaven.'

Dirty Harry hurried to stand in front of Sam, blocking his way. The man's eyes blazed.

'I'm sorry, I haven't got any change,' Sam lied. But then he wondered if it would have been wiser to pass the man a few coins, then hurry on.

'I know your face. I know it, I know it . . .' The tramp spoke in a low voice that was full of awe, as if he'd just met some famous rock star. '*I know it.*'

'I'm sorry, I think you must be mistaken. I don't live—'

'You don't live at all! Wretched little man, hiding from the terror of the coming damnation – no, I'm sorry, I'm sorry. I don't know why I said that. I didn't want to, but – but I am alight with the flame of heavenly vision and – and no, no.' Suddenly he looked ashamed of himself and his voice dropped. 'My apologies, sir. My tongue escapes me sometimes. Too many times. No, wait . . . I wanted to tell you something of great importance. Huge importance.' His eyes suddenly clouded. 'Only I forget; I have a memory that runs round and around the mulberry bush and won't allow me to catch up. But aren't there many with such a problem? Many, many are the same.' He looked up, his eyes suddenly brightening. 'Did I tell you, sir? That I am many. I am indeed numerous. I am beyond counting. A line of *me* would stretch from Casterton to the gates of Constantinople itself. Now . . . I'm sorry . . . I had something to tell you . . . something very important . . . very, very . . . oh dear, oh dear.' With his free hand Dirty Harry pushed his fingers jerkily through his beard as if he'd find the words in there; the filthy fingernails probed and pushed through the knots of ginger hair.

Sam eased himself around the man and began walking quickly away; even so, the smell of the man, an unwashed-hair smell, had already lodged itself in his nostrils.

Behind him the man still stood in his orange overalls, cider bottle in one hand, the other hand fumbling through his beard as he muttered to himself, as if trying to recall a message he'd once learnt verbatim long ago.

Sam saw a shop just ahead where he could buy the soft drinks.

He'd almost brushed aside his encounter with Dirty Harry when he heard a shout behind him. Glancing back, he saw the man's face light up with pleasure. 'I remember,' he called after Sam. 'I remember. You've got to get away from it; you've got get away from the Watchett Hole. If you don't, you're all going to die. Did you hear that? All going to die!'

The man's voice dropped. Muttering to himself he returned to his bench where he'd left carrier bags full of his possessions.

Shaking his head, Sam headed for the shop. But he would never make it as far as the door.

Two

'Sam! *Sam Baker!*'

When Sam heard the voice as he crossed the pavement to the shop he thought for one surreal moment that the tramp had called out his name.

Instead, he saw Lee Burton rushing at him across the road. His face was white and his black hair looked as if it had been brushed with a wild ferocity until it stood up from his head.

'Sam!' Lee sounded scared. 'They're going to take him apart in there. Everyone else is just going to stand there and watch. They're just going to let it happen.'

Sam shook his head, bewildered. 'Let what happen?'

'Some thugs have got hold of Ryan – the guy in the Oliver Hardy suit – they're going to beat the shit out of him. He spilt their drinks; he didn't mean it; but they're going to—'

'Where?'

'Back there in the hotel bar.' Lee panted. 'I was looking for a cop, then I saw you were—'

Sam looked up at the white-painted building standing four storeys high in front of him. 'That's the one? Oh, shit.'

Sam's heart sank when he saw the sign in foot-high letters above the entrance:-

THE GRYPHON HOTEL

Suddenly Jud's words, heavy and potent with hidden meaning, came back to him. Just five minutes ago Jud had said: 'If you've developed a taste for English beer you'll find they do a very nice glass of mild in the Gryphon Hotel. And be sure to go into the public bar, not the lounge.'

'Come on,' Lee said quickly. 'They're going to kill him!'

Sam still stared up at the hotel: a premonition oozed through him. It wasn't a pleasant sensation; it was cold and slick and turned his skin to tingling goose-flesh.

At that moment Sam reached a decision. Even though he didn't really know Lee Burton (now without his Dracula cape) or the plump Ryan Keith he did feel a kinship with them. They were a clan of travellers now – even though they were travelling in time. They'd have to look out for each other.

As he ran across the road he called to Lee, 'He's actually inside the Gryphon Hotel?'

Lee nodded. 'They're going to tear the poor sod apart.'

Again Sam spoke and again he knew full well what the answer would be. 'He's in the public bar?'

'Yeah . . . wait. How did you know that?'

Through clenched teeth Sam said, 'Hang on tight, Lee. I think we're in for a bumpy ride.'

Three

By the time they were through the lobby and had reached the door of the public bar Lee had managed to tell Sam that he'd found Ryan Keith running through town, chased by two supermarket employees. He'd grabbed Ryan and had managed to get him away from the two men by hiding in the hotel. Only Ryan, naturally clumsy and now even clumsier from exhaustion, had then blundered into a group of mean-looking youths at the bar, spilling their drinks. It hadn't helped when a panicky Ryan had given them a banknote that wouldn't be legal tender for ten years.

That's when the shit had really hit the fan.

And that's when Lee had rushed off to find help.

There would be no help to be had from the hotel's usual occupants. It was a seedy, run-down place where rooms could be rented by the hour and fights in the bar were a more frequent event than the toilets being cleaned.

Sam could already hear a high-pitched warbling cry. (*Any betting that's Ryan Keith?* Sam asked himself. It sounded as if they were carving his nuts with a penknife.)

The bar was a gloomy cave of a place after the brilliant sunshine outside. It stank of beer and cigarette smoke. The boards were bare, sticky underfoot. *Hell . . . a den of strife and trouble if ever I saw one*, he thought.

Around half a dozen men in their late teens were gathered around a pool table. They could have been fascinated by a tricky shot into a corner pocket – but then Sam saw a pair of feet sticking out over the table and he realized that they must have Ryan Keith spreadeagled there like a sacrificial offering.

Again Sam heard a high-pitched, 'No-ooo . . . let me go-ooo . . .' It sounded like the bleating of a terrified sheep.

Sam glanced at Lee who stood panting at his side.

Hell, this was a suicide mission. From the amount of denim and shaven heads Sam could see this was nothing less than a skin-head gang. More fruit of Seventies culture. They looked like mean bastards. This wasn't going to be easy.

Sam decided to take as tough a line as he could muster. 'OK, break it up. That one's ours.'

One skinhead jerked his head up. 'Who the frig are you?'

'His pal, *pal*. Now let him go and there'll be no trouble.'

Now the rest of the gang were taking an interest in Sam. One leered. 'A yank? And a homo in a frilly shirt? Which planet are you two from?'

'Look,' Sam said, 'We don't want any trouble. We—'

'Well, that's exactly what you've got. You've got trouble! Big trouble!'

Another skinhead scowled. 'Let's take the fuckers' heads off.'

'Oh, shit,' Sam murmured. 'Showdown at the OK Corral.'

The gang left Ryan on the table as they started to advance towards Sam and Lee. The door swung open behind Sam; he glanced back, half-hoping it would be a bunch of coppers charging in to save the day. Instead, in walked a man of around thirty. The hair was darker, the face unlined, the figure leaner, but his identity was unmistakable.

'Jud . . . Jud Campbell,' Sam spoke the words before he could stop himself. *My tongue sometimes escapes me . . .* Shit, Dirty Harry had put it perfectly. He realized he should have kept his mouth shut.

'Oh, hello,' Jud said. (At least, the younger version of Jud Campbell did – the older one sat in the car not five minutes' walk from here.) Then he paused, obviously not recognizing Sam. But in the next second he weighed up the situation in the bar: that there was one hell of a fight brewing.

Behind the skinheads Ryan rolled off the pool table like he was climbing out of bed with a hangover. His head hung so low his chin almost rested on his chest. He looked exhausted.

But at that moment, when he looked as he could do nothing more than curl up on the floor, he suddenly charged at the backs of the skinheads. Sam saw this was no heroic attack from the rear: the man merely wanted to push his way through to the door, then make good his escape from the hotel.

Again Ryan's natural clumsiness brought him into contact with a skinhead, knocking the thug forward into Jud.

All hell broke loose.

Sam saw the ferocity in the eyes of the skinheads as they lunged forward, swinging their fists.

He backed away easily from the clumsy punches. Lee wasn't so lucky and he was soon embroiled in a slugging match with a stumpy skinhead with arms as long as a gorilla's.

Although this wasn't Jud's fight, and he was already halfway out of the door into the lobby, a skinhead dived at his back, swinging blows at the side of Jud's head.

It was a big mistake.

Jud simply stopped, turned and fixed the skinhead with such a hard stare that the skinhead stopped slugging.

Sam remembered shaking hands with Jud, and clearly remembered those powerful labourer's hands. If anything, the young Jud Campbell looked even stronger, with hugely powerful arms and bulging muscles under the white cotton shirt.

The skinhead took another swing at Jud. It caught him on the cheek with a thin cracking sound. Jud didn't flinch. But that was when his eyes began to burn.

Before Sam could fully take it in, Jud's huge arm swung up, catching the skinhead a tremendous blow on the chin. Instead of a crack Sam heard a loud pop. The skinhead shot backwards to land flat out on the pool table.

Sam took the opportunity to plant a punch on the nose of the skinhead in front of him who'd watched open-mouthed as his friend had become airborne.

The punch knocked the kid back, but not down. He looked back viciously at Sam.

Sam realized the contest would be reduced to a grim slugging match, but he still hadn't appreciated Jud's sheer muscle power. The man was wading into the skinhead gang. Just one of his punches was enough to floor any of the thugs.

Soon they were retreating to the back of the bar in confusion – and in more than a little pain, with a few wiping bloody noses. Jud pushed their retreat harder, picking up stragglers like they were rag dolls and throwing them at their mates.

'Get out!' he roared. 'Get out! And if I see your ugly faces round here again I'll tear them off and stuff them down your bloody throats!'

Realizing they were no match for the raging bull of a man, they ran for the door at the back of the bar. Finding it locked, they rushed forward frantically once again.

Like panicked cattle they were only thinking of running away, but catching Jud off balance they shoved him backwards over an upended table.

He fell awkwardly.

Sam immediately saw the man's face screw up in pain.

One of the skinheads who was last in the mad scramble to escape saw that the man who'd made mincemeat of the gang was at least temporarily disabled. As Jud lay flat on his back in a pool of spilt beer, clutching the upper part of his thigh while grimacing in pain, the skinhead grabbed a glass from another table, then doubled back.

Sam saw that the skinhead's intention was to smash the glass into Jud's face.

In one second Sam had crossed the floor of the bar. As the skinhead raised the glass, Sam shoulder-charged the youth right in the middle of his back.

With a startled 'Uph!' the youth went crashing forward, landing face down in a mess of upturned chairs, the glass smashing in his own hand.

Sam saw blood pouring freely from a cut in the palm of the youth's hand.

'Oh, bastard, bastard, bastard,' groaned the skinhead, climbing to his feet. Then, clutching his bloody hand to his chest, he decided enough was enough and ran for the door.

The young Jud lay on his back. Despite the pain, he said through gritted teeth, 'Thanks for that.'

'The least I could do, Jud,' Sam said gently. 'Thanks for saving our necks back there.'

'Christ . . . they can be little toe-rags at times. Thing is . . . thing is, they'll grow up to be good men one day. Ack . . . I reckon I've busted my leg. Hurts like shit . . .'

'Take it easy,' Sam said kindly. 'Lee, pass me the towel from the bar. No, one of the dry ones. Thanks.' He took the towel and rolled it into a pillow before placing it carefully under Jud's head. 'We'll get you an ambulance, Jud.'

'Hell, I think I need one. First time in my life as well. I'm usually pretty resilient when . . .' Jud broke off and looked up, narrowing his eyes. 'Wait a minute . . . how do you know my name?'

'Don't worry about that now, let's get you fixed.'

'Christ, I hope I'll be able to walk again.'

'Don't worry, buddy, I know you will.'

Again Jud gave him what could only be described as an old-fashioned look. 'Are you sure I don't know you?'

'Not yet, Jud. Not yet.' Then Sam scanned the bar. 'Oh, no. Where the hell did Ryan run off to?'

Lee shrugged. 'He just legged it when the fighting started.'

'Christ, and after we saved his nuts, too. That guy's got a yellow streak up his back that's wider than an eight-lane freeway. You stay here with Jud, I'll phone for an ambulance.'

The bar staff had disappeared sharpish when the fight began so Sam climbed over the bar, found a phone, dialled 911, clicked his tongue as he remembered the right number, then dialled 999.

Ten minutes later, as Jud was stretchered into the back of an ambulance, Sam and Lee walked back to the car where Zita fumed impatiently. There was no sign of Ryan Keith. He'd done a bunk, Sam guessed. At least the gang had done him no serious harm.

The older version of Jud, wiser, greyer, a little heavier around the jaw, stood leaning back against the car.

He smiled broadly at Sam before slapping his leg.

'I always know when it's going to rain because this starts to ache again.'

'You son of a gun, you remembered, didn't you?' Sam said, smiling. 'You remembered we'd met before.'

'I did.'

'Why didn't you say something?'

'What could I say? That you'd get into a fight in the Gryphon Hotel? That I – or at least a younger version of me – would be there to give you a hand?'

'Something like that would have been fine by me. You know, it was scary back there.'

'Sure it was. But what do you suggest? That I try and change history?'

'Why not?'

'The repercussions could have been enormous.'

'Those hoodlums could have killed us.'

'But it turned out all right in the end, didn't it?'

Zita flicked back her plaited hair. 'Are you letting me in on this secret, boyos? Just what on earth happened back there in the hotel?'

'Tell her on the way to the library, Lee.' Sam said. 'It's time we started to try and find out just exactly what's happening to us.'

Chapter Twenty-One

One

The library didn't close until eight. But by ten to the hour library staff were jingling keys and asking the public to make their way to the exits.

Long before then Sam had to concede, at least privately, that there was little in the books that could help them. Scientists were hard-pressed to describe adequately the nature of time. Even the great Professor Carl Sagan conceded in a science book aimed at the ordinary reader that 'Time is one of those concepts that is profoundly resistant to simple definition'.

Certainly there was nothing that could explain why fifty or so people had come adrift in time. And why they were slipping further and further back into history.

As they returned to the car in the library car park Jud said, 'You know, the more I weigh up what's happened to us the more I think about the time-slips of folklore.'

'Folklore?' Zita echoed as she thumbed the remote, unlocking the doors of the Range Rover. 'You're not going to say we've been bewitched by fairies or the wicked witch of the west?'

'Right now, I'll grab any half-decent explanation with both hands and hang on tight.' Sam opened the door. 'Even fairy stories, because I feel as if I'll go completely nuts if we don't get to the bottom of this.'

'Same here.' Lee unbuttoned the collar of the white frilly shirt. 'I went into town today with the intention of getting drunk. And it still seems a good idea right now.'

When they were in the car Sam turned in the front passenger seat and said, 'Ok, Jud, if you've got a theory I'm all ears.'

Jud composed his thoughts for a moment. In a play-ground behind the car park children shouted and laughed on the swings; a girl chased a black dog with a bright yellow frisbee in its mouth.

'Folklore is riddled with time-slip cases. In the past they've been treated the same as ghost stories. You must have heard plenty of them. You know, a couple driving through the countryside become lost. They find an old inn, stay there, and are surprised to see the other occupants are wearing old-fashioned clothes and there's no electricity, only gas lighting. Later the couple will try and find the inn again, only to learn that it burnt down fifty years ago. One of the most famous examples is the case of Charlotte Moberley and Eleanor Jourdain who visited Versailles while on holiday in 1901. There they saw people in old-fashioned clothes and saw buildings they subsequently discovered no longer existed. Later Miss Jourdain wrote that as she entered the grounds at Versailles she experienced an "eerie feeling" as if she'd "crossed a line and was suddenly in a circle of influence". There are some people who've concluded the two ladies somehow found themselves centuries back in time when Versailles was a royal palace.'

Zita said, 'But had the ladies really travelled back in time or were they were seeing ghosts, or at least claiming to?'

'No, not really. The buildings and the people were solid. Your modern ghost-hunter is more likely to attribute the couple's experience to a time-slip. That is, due to some anomaly in the cosmos the palace of two hundred years ago suddenly slipped forward through time.'

'Or the two ladies slipped back in time,' Sam said.

'Oh, come on,' Zita said. 'Fairy stories. Nothing but fairy stories.'

'Look at any half-decent book about the supernatural,' Jud said. 'There are dozens of similar accounts. In 1991 a farmer in Scotland looked out of his window to see a dozen or so men walking by his house dressed as Roman soldiers. He thought they were youths in fancy dress. When he went outside to ask them what the hell they were playing at there was no one there. And there have been cases of people waking up in old houses in the middle of the night and noticing that furniture has been mysteriously rearranged, or that there is a fireplace in the bedroom where there was no fireplace when they went to bed. When they get up in the morning the room is back to normal. These people experienced time-slips; somehow they either saw back through time, or were actually transported there.'

'Time-slips, my foot,' Zita snorted. 'Dreams or alcohol abuse, more like.'

'It's something,' Lee said.

'It's rubbish,' Zita said with feeling as she slammed the gear into first and drove out of the car park. Sam guessed she was pissed off because they'd found no answers. Now she drove aggressively, as if questions about what had happened to them were rising like ghouls from the road, and she, Zita Prestwyck, was intent on flattening each and every one of them beneath the fat tyres of the Range Rover.

Jud said, 'It's my belief that the amphitheatre and an area of land surrounding it have come adrift in time. Remember the front half of the cow, the neck of the bottle and the remains of the cyclist? I think they were straddling the boundary when the time-shift occurred.'

'You mean just half of the cow and part of the bike and the cyclist's hand were transported back?'

'That's what it looks like to me.'

For a while they fell silent as they digested Jud's hypothesis. Meanwhile, Zita drove faster. Insects splattered on the windscreen.

A moment later, Lee leaned forward. 'Is it a bad time to ask a question?'

'Shoot,' Zita snapped.

'Where are we going?'

'I'm going to do what I should have done hours ago. Have a damned good meal and plenty to drink.'

She slipped into top gear and barrelled the car along the country lane. By this time the sun was setting behind the hill. This was the end of a summer's day in 1978, Sam reflected. Somewhere in America a junior version of him was probably playing with his toy cars in his parents' New York apartment. It would be another six or seven years before that lightning strike in Vermont would knock him out of the pear tree and kill his two friends.

Earlier Jud had said he didn't want to interfere with history, that even though they'd come back in time he'd do nothing to change past events.

Sam Baker wasn't so sure. The extra fingers that served as his thumbs began to tingle again.

Now they had the opportunity to play God.

What could they do?

What *would* they do?

Two

Right now Nicole Wagner wanted time to go head over heels again. She wanted it so much she ached from head to toe. She wanted to find herself sitting there in the amphitheatre with the rest of them.

She'd be safe there.

She knew it.

She shifted her position in the tree so she could see what Bostock was doing. For the last ten minutes he'd been searching the ground around the tree. He'd even gone as far as the abandoned car that lay at the bottom of the rock face. When he'd reached the car, which seemed a good, healthy distance to her, she'd begun to climb down out of the tree in the hope she could outrun him to the river. Once on the river bank she might see someone.

But Bostock had seen what she was doing and he'd run back, laughing and holding up his arms like a parent ready to catch a child jumping down.

Instantly she'd clambered back into the safety of the branches.

Well, temporary safety, she told herself. It would be dark in an hour or so. She knew he'd try something then to get at her.

After a while she'd become so hot in the gorilla suit she'd wriggled out of it.

Even though she wore a T-shirt and cycling shorts underneath the outfit, Bostock had wolf-whistled and clapped. His mad eyes had watched her every move as she'd pulled herself out of, the great woolly bitch of a thing. And, God, could she murder a drink! Her throat had dried out completely. Even her tongue felt rough and leathery.

Just then Bostock returned from foraging around the tree; in his hand he carried a hefty stick. He rapped the trunk with it.

Instead of making a thudding sound it rang like a gigantic tuning fork.

'Solid iron,' he called proudly. 'You could break coconuts open with this.' He sounded loonily cheerful. 'Come down, blonde girlie.'

'No.'

'Promise not to hurt you.' He beamed up at her with a sunny benevolence. 'We can talk.'

'No.'

'Come down here. I won't do anything to you.'

She shook her head.

'*Bitch*.' He slashed at the tree trunk with the iron bar. Nicole felt the vibrations run through the tree into her hands and feet. 'Bitch. I said, come down here. Now!'

'Go away . . . please.' Nicole's voice was a dry croak. 'Just leave me alone.'

'But you saw what I did to Marion. Now people are going to believe you when you tell them I killed her. They won't believe me when I say how she used to go on and on at me, ridicule everything I ever said and did. Never satisfied, always comp— Hey! What are you doing? Shut up! *Shut up!*'

But Nicole had seen a man strolling by the river with his hands in his pockets.

'Hello!' She yelled as hard as she could. 'Help! Help! Up here! This way! I'm over here!'

Already the man had heard and was looking round. She jumped up and down on the branch and waved.

'Shut up, shut up, shut up . . .' Bostock looked round wildly, not sure who she'd seen.

She hissed down at him. 'That's scared you, you bastard, hasn't it?'

'Shut your mouth now . . . be quiet.'

'Will I hell. You're going to get caught, and they're going to take you to jail and bury you there forever.'

'Shut up!' He was almost pleading now. His eyes looked wild, frightened.

'Over here!' Nicole yelled at the man on the river bank. 'Help! I'm in the tree!'

The man paused, tilted his head to one side.

She jumped up and down on the branch, waving, shouting.

The man still stood there, cocking his head to one side, no doubt hearing the distant cries and wondering just what on earth was going on.

Maybe it's kids fooling around, he'd be thinking.

Suddenly Nicole realized that he might just shrug his shoulders and walk on along the river bank.

She'd be stranded here until after dark.

Then no doubt that homicidal maniac Bostock would find some way to reach her; he'd bring that iron bar down on her head. After that, he'd bury her body in a shallow grave alongside his cooling wife.

'Hey! OVER HERE!' She shook a branch vigorously. 'Help I'm here! Please help me!'

'Shut it,' Bostock hissed, striking the tree trunk with the iron bar. 'Shut it, or I'll shut it for you.'

He's going, he's not going to stop, he thinks it's kids, were the panicky thoughts whirling round her head.

The man, still with his head tilted to one side, walked a pace or two in her direction. Nicole snatched up the gorilla mask and waved it over her own blonde head. All the time she was shouting.

Now the man walked more quickly towards the tree. He still had his head tilted to one side, obviously wondering just what the deal was.

Then she recognized the man. Brian Pickering, the ice-cream man in his caterer's white suit.

'Brian! I'm here! In the tree. Brian! Help!'

Now Brian realized there was something wrong. He was a stumpy man, but he broke into a surprisingly rapid jog through the scrubby bushes towards her.

'Bitch! Bitch! Bitch!' Bostock spat in frustration. With that (and a look of white-hot fury) he was gone.

'Oh thank God, thank God,' Nicole croaked, her throat sore now, painfully sore.

Bostock had run for it.

She couldn't wait to get out of that tree.

Brian Pickering had almost reached the tree now and was looking up at her in amazement.

'Nicole? Nicole, is that you?'

'Yes.'

'What on earth are you doing up there?'

'Oh, just help me down, please. He was going to kill me.'

Brian held up his arms. In the dying sun his ice-cream seller's white suit seemed to gleam like shining armour.

'Who was going to kill you?' He looked baffled as if unsure whether this was some leg-pull.

'Bostock . . . one of our tour group.' Nicole lowered herself down from the branch, ready to jump the last eight feet or so. Her whole body was shaking now. A watery sensation filled her stomach.

But, Jesus-sweet-Jesus, the relief was enormous. Brian looked so solid and reassuring as he stood looking up at her with concerned eyes, his hands outstretched to help her down.

'Bostock killed his wife in the wood . . . he was— *Brian!*'

'*Neee – yah!*'

Bostock materialized from the deepening gloom.

As if he was swinging a baseball bat at a ball, he swung the iron bar at the back of Brian's head.

Brian didn't even make a noise as he staggered groggily from the blow. Nicole watched his body go all rubbery as he slumped face forward against the tree. With a yell, Nicole hoisted herself back into the branches, every fibre or her muscles quivering.

She saw Bostock raise the iron bar high over his head. It glistened wetly in the gloom. She knew what would happen next.

Screwing her eyes shut, she hugged herself against the tree trunk. Although she saw nothing she heard Bostock's excited grunts, heard the iron bar smacking against Brian Pickering's skull, and felt the vibration of the blows transmitted up the tree and into her body.

'No, no,' she whispered over and over. 'No, no, no . . .'

Then she began to sob. She felt helpless, alone, vulnerable. And night was falling fast.

Three

Ryan Keith jogged along the road from Casterton to the amphitheatre. He was exhausted. His legs ached, a stitch pierced his side. He'd hardly stopped running since leaving the Gryphon Hotel. For quite a time he'd repeatedly shot looks back over his shoulder with huge terrified eyes.

He expected at any moment to see the mob of skinheads chasing after him to beat him to a pulp on the road.

It took a while but he eventually realized they weren't in hot pursuit after all.

Nevertheless, he still ran. He didn't want to take the risk of being spotted in town.

Now it was nearly dark. The road was flanked by fields. Only the occasional car passed him. Once someone honked at the sight of the plump round-faced youth in an Oliver Hardy costume. He'd jumped and yelped at the sound of the horn.

A mile out of town he'd passed a tramp striding purposefully along the road. He wore orange overalls, Wellington boots, and sang the hymn *Jerusalem* with loud gusto. Every so often he would pause to drink from a bottle of cider. Then he'd draw the back of his hand across his mouth in a hugely dramatic gesture to wipe the drops from his ginger moustache and beard.

For a moment Ryan slowed down. Would the tramp attack him, too? Anything was possible in this crazy, topsy-turvy world.

As a child he'd watched the old Benny Hill TV shows. They always ended with Benny being chased by old men, blowzy women, policemen and pretty girls in high heels and stockings. Those chases always fascinated Ryan, and he'd imagine what it would be like to be pursued like that, with people shaking their fists after him. Now he knew. Today the whole of humankind seemed out to get him. It was horrible. Now even that tramp might chase him, laughing gutturally and making horrible suggestions about cuddling together under the bushes.

If Ryan's shadow had been visible he'd have been frightened of that, too.

Taking a deep, controlling breath he began jogging again.

Jogging as fast as he could, so he could get by the scary tramp.

The moment he passed the tramp he heard a bellow.

'I know no pleasure sweeter, than in my heart to sing you a song of praise, Jesus, my love . . .'

Dear God, thought Ryan in deep, deep terror. *It's happening again.* He ran harder, feeling his stomach pull heavily from side to side beneath his shirt.

Behind him the tramp held up the cider bottle trium-
phantly while shouting, 'We shall sing to Christ with sweet
voices and delightful melody. His love conquers all things.
Therefore let us live in love, and in it die!'

Shit, shit . . .

Ryan gasped for breath as he ran. Any second the tramp
would run after him, grab him, and haul him into the
bushes.

'Wait . . . wait,' the tramp shouted. 'We need to speak
. . . listen to my words. I know you. *I know you!*'

Ryan ran on, shaking his head in terror, his breath
coming in sobbing grunts.

'Listen to me!' shouted the man. 'You've got to get out of
that hole in the ground . . . the Watchett Hole! If you don't,
it'll be the death of you. Did you hear that, my mate – ee –
oh? You'll all die!'

Closing his ears to the shouts, Ryan ran on.

Four

From her perch in the tree, Nicole Wagner peered
down cautiously through the leaves. On the ground,
gazing up at her once more, was Bostock. In the gloom
his face appeared to glow whitely until she could almost
believe she was looking at a replica of the moon lying on
the dark ground. His eyes were merely shadows in his
face.

At times she wondered if he'd fallen asleep there, with the
iron bar laying diagonally across his chest.

Then, as she was thinking of sneaking down from the tree
and making a run for it, she'd hear him click his tongue.
He'd wag a finger at her as if to say, 'Don't worry, girl, I've
still got my eye on you.'

And from her high vantage point she could see the darker
stains on the earth, the broken grass stalks and trampled
nettles where Bostock had dragged the body of the man
who sold ice creams into the bushes.

Now she felt cold as the night air closed around her like a hand. Taking the gorilla suit, she held it to her chest, buried her face in the synthetic fur and prayed for a guardian angel.

Five

Ryan Keith no longer walked straight. He moved in long zigs and zags, and he was muttering to himself. Every so often sobs would judder through his body so strongly he had to stop. Then he'd unscrew the cap from the half-bottle of brandy he'd bought from an off-licence on the edge of town.

He was so drunk he thought at times he'd simply barf the whole lot into the gutter. But somehow he kept it down. Now the alcohol was singing through his veins.

Above him stars appeared in the night sky. Bats swooped around the street lights.

'Top of the world, ma,' he said thickly to himself. 'I'm top of the world . . . no, wait . . . that's Cagney,' he muttered, suddenly preoccupied with the role he'd been playing as a tour rep for God knew how many days, months, years or whatever. He hiccupped.

Still walking in those long zags that took him into the road, and the zigs that took him tottering into the hedge bottom, he said to himself, 'My name is Oliver Norville Hardy. Pleased to be at . . . at your surface . . . no, service. *Service*.' He gave a giggle that was actually closer to a cackle. Manic-sounding. He blundered against a telephone pole and banged his forehead. 'Doh!' He rubbed the bruised skin. 'Oh, Gabriel, blow your horn.'

Six

In the public house at the end of the lane that led from the road to the amphitheatre, Zita, Lee and Sam sat round the table. Jud had already left them to walk back to his narrow boat where his wife would be waiting.

'I've never been so hungry in my life,' Zita said, watching the waitress bring plates of ham salad to the table. 'That first mouthful's going to taste like heaven.'

Sam smiled. 'Believe it or not, but we haven't eaten in over twenty years.'

'And it damn' well feels like it,' Zita said.

Sam watched her pick up the knife and fork and eagerly cut a triangle of thick York ham. 'Boy, am I looking forward to tasting this.'

She raised the fork to her mouth.

At that moment Sam felt his skin crackle, as if static was running across it; his fillings tingled uncomfortably. He just had time to breathe, 'Oh, God.'

And the pub was no more.

Chapter Twenty-Two

◆◇◆◇◆

One

This dream was all lights. Green ones, white ones, red ones, turquoise, vermilion, pinks – electric pinks of every different shade and hue. Colours pulsed, merged. Strands of colour were drawn out from pulsating blobs until they resembled veins or arteries created from coloured light.

A ghost girl sang softly. 'Buffalo girls gonna come out tonight, gonna come out tonight . . .'

Sam Baker blinked hard and opened his eyes.

Instantly the lights vanished.

The amphitheatre lay before him. He sat in one of the upper tiers of seats.

The amphitheatre was empty – with the exception, of course, of the man hanging from the cross in the centre. Again, Sam noticed the huge thorns punched through the fleshy parts of the man's body. They held him there, like a butterfly pinned to card.

Sam struggled to wake up. But it was the same as diving into deep water, then finding you can't swim to the surface. Like some evil water sprite is pulling you down by the feet. Sam's lungs felt airless and a huge weight began to bear down on his heart.

Above him the sky was a dark grey, blotched here and

there with red patches as if someone had sprayed the cloud with droplets of blood.

Then, in the dream, the tramp he'd seen in town earlier was standing just half a dozen paces from him.

The tramp, Dirty Harry, was exactly the same. Dressed in orange overalls, black Wellington boots, ginger hair, beard; those intense eyes stared at Sam.

'I know you now,' the tramp said. His voice was low, urgent-sounding. 'Do you remember me?'

Sam didn't respond.

You needn't talk back to dream characters, he told himself, *they don't mind. They don't mind at all.*

'Come on, sir,' Dirty Harry urged. 'Wake up, wake up. Do you remember me?'

Perhaps the dream tramp would go away if Sam humoured him.

'Do you remember me, sir?'

This time Sam acknowledged that he did with a nod.

'And you will recall what I told you? You must get away from this hole. If you don't you will die. Already the integrity of the transport is breaking down. For the time being . . . if I can be permitted such a meaningless phrase . . . the entire area comprising the amphitheatre and the surrounding meadows has been transported cleanly. But this will soon start to disintegrate. Do you follow me?'

Sam stared at the ginger-haired tramp who now spoke so clearly.

Funny what dreams can do.

'Please hear my words, Sam Baker. Because here I can speak plainly, God has allowed that. It is only in the outside world that my thinking becomes confused, and then my tongue escapes me. I babble. I find myself en-mazed in bewilderment. Now let me try to explain what has happened to you.' He took a steadying breath. 'If it helps, imagine that at this moment we are travelling on a train between stations. You have just left one station that was the year 1978, now we are headed back to another station. At the moment we are still travelling backwards, but at any moment we will stop again, and you and your fellow travellers will alight into another time.' Dirty Harry looked up at the sky; bluish flashes like lightning bursts lit the clouds.

Sam's skin began to tingle. He could smell ozone in the air.

He felt it coming.

Shadowy figures were appearing all around him, growing more solid; now he saw their features – eyes, noses, mouths – becoming more pronounced on their faces as if he was seeing a photograph developing in a bath of chemicals.

'Jesus Christ, forgive your poor servant Roger Rolle!' Dirty Harry suddenly shouted. 'I am too late. I'm too late! I have the blood of innocents on my hands.'

The world suddenly snapped into sharp focus. The grey sky was gone; the sun shone.

And that was when the screaming started.

The blood, too.

Two

This time there was pandemonium in the amphitheatre.

Sam had reached the top of the stairs in a kind of daze, almost as if he were sleepwalking, when suddenly the world had snapped into hard focus. People milled around him.

Then came the piercing screams of men and women in agony.

He looked round, wondering what the hell was happening. It sounded as if people were having their throats cut, but Sam could see no signs of violence.

Then a man of around fifty blundered into him.

Sam looked up to see what at first he took to be a man with a bird on his shoulder, furiously flapping its wings and screaming. The man was screaming, too.

Dazed, Sam thought: *We're being attacked by blackbirds.*

Sam reeled back from the man who was clawing at his own face and shrieking so loud that Sam's eardrums vibrated painfully.

But then he saw what was really happening.

It didn't make sense.

And what he did see was sickening.

Because now he saw that the bird wasn't on the man's shoulder. It had actually become part of the man's head. The black feathered head of the bird protruded from the man's cheek, just below his eye. The bird's head turned frantically, the yellow beak open wide in panic, and it was screaming.

The man turned. A wild spin round and round as if he was trying to dislodge the shrieking bird. One of the bird's wings had erupted from the side of the man's head where his ear should have been. The wing flapped frantically, feathers filling the air like black snowflakes.

The man now lunged forward at Sam, his eyes locked on him as if begging for help.

Sam recoiled at the sight of the man's panic-stricken eyes and the equally terrified eyes of the bird. The bird's neck writhed and stretched, almost snake-like, from the man's cheek.

The man clutched at Sam's shoulders. He opened his mouth. And Sam saw that filling the man's mouth was a dark feathered lump; as he tried to speak a yellow bird-leg suddenly sprang from between his lips, the claws opening and shutting in a spasming motion. And all the time the wing growing out of the man's head where the ear should have been flapped like some mutant version of the helmet of the god Hermes.

Then the man was gone, running and screaming, while trying to claw the bird out of his face.

Sam looked around at the terrified people. There was no sign of Zita. He ran towards her car in the car park, thinking she might have headed there for some reason.

Now Sam noticed that a couple of trees had erupted through the otherwise smooth tarmac. A tree had fused with a car. The whole thing resembled some weird kind of sculpture.

There was more screaming. He looked in the direction of another tree. The sight was as shocking as the bird-man.

A woman's head protruded from the trunk of the tree. One arm was thrust from the side of the trunk; she was waving desperately, and all the time she was shrieking in agony, her mouth a huge 'O' shape.

Sam paused and stared in shock. At first glance it could have been almost a comic image. He'd seen plenty of old TV shows with people disguised as trees; the sort where, so he can creep unobserved right up to the enemy, a soldier wears a cardboard tree trunk. His arms form the branches and he peers out through a hole in the trunk. This could have been a perverse version of the same. But Sam knew that here the woman's body was fused inside the timber body of the tree, and that her face now stuck out from it, looking something like a head part-way through the neck-hole of a tight jersey. The pressure had distorted her face. Blood had begun to run from her nostrils and mouth. The bark below the face was stained red.

The woman's face twitched, the eyes bulged, her tongue protruded from her mouth as the pressure of the wood surrounding her tightened like a giant hand crushing a moth. Then she stopped crying out. Her eyes stared sightlessly. The only movement now was the blood falling from the tip of her nose like water from a dripping tap.

'Zita!'

Sam advanced on the tree-bound body.

Had Zita made it halfway across the car park before their backward slither through time had come to its abrupt stop? Only the solid matter of the past – the trees, the bird and goodness knew what else – was occupying the same space as some of the time travellers. So if anyone had had the misfortune to occupy the same space as a tree or a bird they would have become fused with it.

He approached the tree with the face sticking out from the bark like some toadstool growth. Distorted by the crushing effect of the surrounding timber, it had become

purple with congested blood; the dead eyes bulged agonis-
ingly from the face; the tongue pointed from the lips as
stiffly as a stick.

It could be Zita; the face appeared young. Swallowing
down a filthy taste in his mouth, Sam looked more closely at
the collar of bark that framed the head. Then he saw a wisp
of black hair.

Zita's hair was a rich chestnut colour. So the poor wretch
wasn't Zita. But what a ghastly, miserable way to die.

He backed away from the dead face in the tree; suddenly
it seemed disrespectful to turn his back on the tree-bound
corpse.

Only when he was twenty or more paces from the tree
did he turn away.

As he did so an elderly woman clutched at his arm; in a
shrill voice she demanded, 'Have you seen my husband? He
had a bee in his eye.'

Sam shook his head. The bad taste in his mouth wasn't
going to go away yet.

The woman hurried on, searching for her lost husband.
Again he heard her call out to someone. 'Have you seen my
husband? He's got a bee in his eye. He's allergic to bee
stings.'

The car park was a seething mass of people. His head rang
with their panicky cries. For all the world it looked like
someone had thrust a stick into an ants' nest and given it a
flipping good stir.

Taking a deep breath, he skirted the amphitheatre, then
headed down to the boats moored at the river bank.

Three

Ryan Keith opened his eyes in the amphitheatre. He knew
instantly he was back where he'd started. He should have
still been drunk – completely stoned on the brandy, in fact: it
only seemed a second or so ago that he'd been stumbling
along the country road, drinking from the bottle.

But now he was here. He was completely sober. The bottle had gone from his pocket.

The Oliver Hardy bowler hat sat levelly on top of his head.

Around him people were yelling like their pants were on fire.

Ryan was determined not to get involved in any more trouble.

He folded his arms and sat firm on his seat.

He wasn't going to get into any more messes – *fine or otherwise*.

Four

Nicole Wagner awoke after the time-slip to find herself sitting there in the gorilla suit again with the hairy nylon head in her hands.

Whatever mechanism it was, whether supernatural or some weird kind of science, that dragged them back through time restored them to exactly how they were when they'd first sat down in the damned amphitheatre at midday on the twenty-third of June 1999.

Yes, she thought, *everything is back in its original place and condition*. She felt the bump of her watch through the gorilla suit's hairy sleeve. She'd lost the watch when she'd jumped into the tree; a twig had ripped it from her wrist. She rubbed her arms and chest. The soreness from the bruises had vanished as if by magic. She didn't doubt, too, that her hair would have that just-brushed look.

Oh, shit . . .

Bostock. Where was he?

Suddenly tense, she scanned the seats on the tiers opposite her. Bostock had been sitting there. Along with his wife. Of course, the wife's seat was empty because he'd killed her.

But she expected to see Bostock.

The seat was empty.

It was too much to hope for that he was dead, too.

She guessed he'd probably come to his senses faster than she had and had probably fled the amphitheatre.

But the fact remained that he might come looking for her. In his crazed state, he saw her, Nicole Wagner, as the sole witness to his crime. At the first opportunity he'd make sure that she'd never be able to accuse him of the murder.

Nicole anxiously scanned the seats, half expecting to see him clambering down towards her.

But there were only more confused tourists. Somewhere at the top of the amphitheatre she heard screams. Maybe Bostock was launching some crazed attack on other people. *God, I hope so*, she thought, *at least then he might forget me*. Instantly she felt guilty she'd thought that way. She was a law student, for God's sake. Her professional integrity demanded that she uphold the law.

She stood up and headed for the stairs. Come what may, she had to see what was happening. Even if the world had gone topsy-turvy she believed she had a duty to see Bostock brought to justice. He couldn't be allowed to get away with murder.

Five

Lee slowly came to his senses. As he blinked and licked his lips he looked round the amphitheatre.

Yes. It's gone and done it again, he told himself.

He was sitting there in the damned Dracula cape again. And no doubt he had the white spook make-up plastered all over his face, complete with blood trickles down his chin drawn in lipstick.

So, he asked himself, blinking up at the sun. *What year is this?*

Six

'My guess is that this is the early Fifties or possibly the late Forties,' Jud called out as Sam walked down the banking towards the narrow boat.

Sam watched Jud retying the lines that moored the

narrow boat to the landing stage. 'What makes you think that?'

'I've only had time for a quick look round, but you'll see the road to the amphitheatre is no longer metalled. It's just a rutted track. I've checked the television.'

'What's showing?'

'Nothing. Until the late Fifties the BBC had a monopoly on television broadcasts in Britain and unlike the United States there was only one channel. And that was restricted to a service that ran from about four in the afternoon until around midnight when the whole service was shut down. Ah, can you just tie the line around the metal ring on the landing stage? Thanks.' Sam caught the line Jud threw him and tied it. He didn't use any elegant sailor's knot, just a simple under-and-over as if tying a shoelace.

'That do it?' Sam asked.

'Fine for a landlubber.' Jud forced a smile but he looked none too cheerful. 'I've been working my way round the radio stations. All I'm getting in English on medium and long wave are the BBC Home Service and Light Programme. I can't find the BBC's old Third Programme. But seeing as that didn't go on air until the late Forties that might be no surprise; I've heard a mention of George the Sixth who was king until his death in 1952.'

'Any music?'

'Some classical, which doesn't help much when it comes to trying to fix the year. On the Light Programme I've heard a Sinatra record and a couple of show songs. So until we find a newspaper or hear a specific date on the radio we're going to be guessing. Hello, it looks as if we've got company.' Jud finished tying the last mooring line as Sam heard the sound of an approaching motor. It was a low throbbing sound like someone beating slow time on a big bass drum. Around the bend in the river lumbered a barge loaded with limestone.

'OK, Sam. Come aboard,' Jud invited. 'I'll make us a coffee and then we can chew the fat.' He waved to the boatman at the tiller of the barge as it ploughed slowly past upstream. The boatman, dressed in a striped shirt and black waistcoat, waved back. But it was plain that he was astonished to see the big white 1990s motor launch moored behind the narrow boat. The boatman also looked up in the direction of the amphitheatre where people still milled round. Whether he'd noticed how agitated the people were – or whether he'd seen what to him must have been some pretty freaky fashions – Sam couldn't tell, but he still twisted his head back to watch as the barge ploughed its way upstream.

'I had to retie the mooring lines because, as you probably noticed, the river level is a lot higher than it was in 1999. The grass is noticeably greener, too.'

'The rainfall must've been heavier in the Forties.'

'You're probably right, Sam. Come on down below.'

Sam hesitated. He didn't want to simply walk away and leave all those agitated people to their own devices. He couldn't get the images out of his head: the man with the bird growing through his face. Or the girl, how she'd become embedded in the tree trunk. Jud must have noticed the expression on his face.

'I've seen it, too. Dot and Zita are out helping some of the victims.'

'You've seen Zita?'

'She came down to the boat straightaway. My wife trained as a nurse so I guess she's our only medic. The last I saw they were helping a man with grass growing through his feet. You've heard the phrase "rooted to the spot": this poor sod was – literally. Now, do you take milk?'

'Black,' Sam responded, dazed. Jud was taking this pretty coolly.

'Watch how you go down here,' Jud said, leading the way down into the cabin. 'I've already had to mop out a bucket or so of water. And there were a couple of fish slapping about the floor. Makes you think, doesn't it? There they were swimming happily about in the river when the boat materialized around them. Hell . . . will you take a look at that? Turns your stomach, doesn't it?'

Sam looked down as Jud bent to peer at something where the cabin wall met the floor.

'It looks like a roach.' Jud said as he pulled a metal fish slice from a rack beside the cooker before crouching down again.

A fish head protruded from the cabin wall just above the floor. The eyes bulged, the mouth hung open. Dead, obviously, it was frozen there in the steel hull of the boat. The fish had been swimming beneath the surface of the river when the boat had simply materialized there, trapping it in the wall. Now it looked like some quirky fisherman's mascot.

Oh, hell, there's some weird shit going down today, Sam told himself.

'Fortunately the molecular structure of the metal hull is far more dense than the flesh of the fish,' Jud told Sam as he used the fish slice to scrape the fish head from the wall. 'Otherwise it would have left a hole in the hull and we'd now be at the bottom of the river. See, the hull's still intact, but you can see a little of the bone locked there in the metal. Looks like a fossil, doesn't it?'

Sam sat down on the sofa.

God, yes, really weird shit.

'This hasn't happened on the other jumps back through time,' Jud said, scraping the mess into a plastic bag. 'For some reason the whole area that's trapped in the time-slip isn't jumping as cleanly as it did. We're being . . . con- taminated is the best word I can find, by objects and animals from the past.'

'I've seen examples of it, and believe me, it isn't a pretty sight. As far as I can tell some of the people have materialized and found themselves occupying the same space as a tree or a bird.'

'Which shows that whatever mechanism is shoving us back through time is starting to go out of kilter.'

'Dirty Harry told me pretty much the same thing.'

As Jud poured the coffee he looked up, frowning. 'Dirty Harry? The tramp from town?'

'Yes.'

'He's here?'

'Well, at least he came to me in what I took at first to be a dream. But now I think it was a kind of transitional state during the time-jump.'

'I get that, too,' Jud said, handing Sam the mug. 'All I see are bright coloured lights and a kind of ghost image of the amphitheatre, only it's deserted. What did he have to say to you?'

Sam told him about what Dirty Harry had said – what little there was of it.

'And you say Dirty Harry was coherent?'

'Quite coherent. Unusually articulate, I'd say. And he seemed to have a pretty good idea what was happening to us. And the consequences of not getting away from the amphitheatre.'

'Did he say anything else?'

Sam shook his head. 'Nothing that I— Oh . . . he did mention his name; his real name, that is. But I guess you know that?'

'No. Townsfolk have always known him as Dirty Harry. What name did he give?'

'He said: "Jesus Christ, forgive your poor servant Roger Rolle."'

Jud's eyes widened. '*Roger Rolle*?'

'Yes.'

'Well, if you'd told me that name a little while ago I'd have written it off as one of Dirty Harry's delusions. Now I'm not so sure.'

'Why's that?'

'Because Roger Rolle was a mystic – that's a kind of Christian shaman.' Jud handed Sam the coffee cup. 'And he died close on seven hundred years ago.'

Seven

Nicole Wagner shed the gorilla suit as she ran. By the time she reached the car park she was down to her black cycle shorts and T-shirt; she stood there pushing her long blonde hair back from her face so she could see properly.

The ice-cream van still stood by the visitors' centre. Of course, there was no sign of Brian Pickering. She'd seen Bostock club him to death with the iron bar. So that meant Pickering was out of the time-travel game now.

She was observant enough to notice that there were changes now. Before, the car park and several acres of grassland had been transported cleanly back through time. Now it looked as if chunks of car park were missing. Here and there, trees grew through the tarmac. A strip of grass ran lush and green from one side of the car park to the other, as if someone had neatly cut the car park into two halves then pulled them apart a yard or so to allow the grass to spring through.

She passed a car from which a timber telegraph post sprouted through the centre of the roof. She could almost imagine a photograph of it appearing in *The Times* captioned 'Vampire Car Staked In Yorkshire.'

Raising her hand to shield her eyes, she scanned the car park and the meadows beyond. Over by the church she saw a running man. He clawed at his face, and there seemed to be a bird on his shoulder; at least, she thought she saw a single black wing flapping. Of Bostock there was no sign.

At first she thought she could simply call enough people to her and tell them that Bostock had murdered his wife and was intent on killing her. Then, with a kind of posse, she could have tracked him down and made a citizen's arrest before handing him over to the police. But it wasn't going to be that simple.

These accidental time travellers were preoccupied. An old man clutched his eye while a woman of around the same age guided him by the arm. He was muttering something about a bee sting.

A couple of men were, for some inexplicable reason, draping a checked travel blanket across one side of a tree trunk. One of the men was weeping.

The girl in tiger-pattern leggings and with the heavy plaited hair was running across from her car with the first-aid kit in her hands, her face serious, determined.

It was as if a whole mountain of shit had just hit the world's biggest fan.

There was nothing for it.

She'd have to find Bostock alone.

Eight

Sam followed Jud up onto the deck of the narrow boat. 'So just who was this mystic Roger Rolle?'

'You're pronouncing Rolle as if it rhymes with dollar; I always pronounced it as if it were French – Roll-Hay. But now I think about it, Rolle as if it rhymes with dollar sounds how a medieval Yorkshireman would speak it.'

'So you figure that, somehow, this tramp they call Dirty Harry and the mystic Roger Rolle are one and the same?'

Jud shrugged. 'As well as a mystic, Rolle was a hermit, which meant he probably lived in some crude wooden shack in the middle of a forest seven hundred years ago. If I mentally conjure up the image of a medieval mystic, Dirty Harry would actually fit pretty closely; you can imagine someone with a shaggy beard and wild, staring eyes who'd gabble away eighteen to the dozen about subjects most people couldn't comprehend in the slightest.'

'So you think he was crazy?'

'Not crazy as such. Probably "very intense" would be a better description. Certainly eccentric. Very eccentric, at least to twentieth-century sensibilities. He wouldn't shave, he might not wash, he'd probably fast for weeks on end. He'd be so pre-occupied with whatever wonders were happening inside his own head that at times he might seem to be in a trance – or he might talk excitedly to himself.'

'Come to think of it, I remember when we first met that you pointed out the church and told us that Roger Rolle's hermitage was close by there.'

'Indeed. It's not possible to be that precise about Roger Rolle's life. After all, records of that time tended not to be especially accurate or complete – lots have simply been lost over the centuries. But to give you a potted biography of Rolle we can say with reasonable certainty that he was born around the year 1300 in the village of Thornton in Yorkshire. He came from a poor family, but he was so unusually intelligent that one Thomas Neville, the Archdeacon of Durham, sponsored his education at Oxford university – you see, even seven hundred years ago Oxford and Cambridge were England's most important seats of learning. After that, he came home but quickly decided to become a hermit. It's said that he fashioned a hermit's habit out of his father's rain hood and two of his sister's dresses – one grey and one white. As to his character, he was described as a fiery young man who was certainly no shy, retiring monk, and was apt to passionately insult and abuse anyone who offended his vision of Christianity. He also had the peculiar ability to write away furiously, page after page on one subject, while simultaneously lecturing at length and equally passionately on an entirely different subject.'

'Well, if that was an identikit picture I imagine it could fit Dirty Harry pretty closely. When did Rolle die?'

'Some say he died on Michaelmas Day 1349 at a little place called Hampole south of here. But that was probably writers trying to tidy up his life with a few invented facts.'

'You mean he simply disappeared?'

'Apparently so; although for centuries afterwards there was a cult surrounding the Rolle personality and a good many miracles were observed to take place where he'd lived. Miraculous healings of the sick; visions; appearances by angels, that kind of thing.'

'Then as far as I can see we should be tracking down Dirty Harry, or Roger Rolle if that's the real name, and asking him what the hell has been happening to us; and where this jaunt back through time's going to end.'

'I couldn't have put it better myself.' Sam turned quickly to see Carswell standing on the river bank. 'Mr Rolle sounds as if he could be a useful man to know.'

Clearly, Carswell had been eavesdropping on the conversation from his own boat. 'I don't know how easy it will be to find him,' Sam said coolly; he wanted as little to do with Carswell as possible. Even though the man smiled, and spoke in a soft voice, his eyes always looked angry, as if he was on the point of unleashing his rage on someone.

'Well, there's no point in wasting time here. From what I saw earlier, every time we make one of these leaps back through time people are going to die some pretty disgusting deaths.'

Carswell's eyes drilled into Sam's face. 'You've seen the pretty girl in the tree?'

Sam nodded.

Carswell cocked his head to one side as if springing a little surprise. 'That pretty girl was my . . . niece.' The pause before 'niece' was telling.

'I'm sorry,' Jud said and he meant it, too.

Grant acknowledged the condolences with a nod. 'Me, too. But this is the real world. Shit happens. Now, hadn't we better start looking for the mysterious Mr Rolle?'

Chapter Twenty-Three

One

'Wait . . . Nicole, wait! Where are you going?'

Nicole turned to see Lee Burton running across the car park towards her. The big vampire cape flapped out behind him like a black sheet; his face was white with make-up.

'Nicole. I wondered what had happened to you. I opened my eyes . . .' He panted breathlessly while trying to feed the cloak's big button through the undersized loop around his throat. 'When I opened my eyes and I saw you weren't there I thought something had happened to you.'

'It very nearly did.'

His eyes widened and he stopped struggling with the button.

'Why? What happened?'

'Here, Lee, let me,' she said and unfastened the button. 'Have you seen anything of Bostock?'

'Bostock?'

'He was on our coach. A short, stocky man. He was sitting with his wife towards the back, and—'

'Oh, yes,' Lee said remembering. 'He was always arguing with his wife, wasn't he?'

'That's the one.'

'Why are you looking for him?'

As they crossed the car park she told him what had

happened, how Bostock had murdered his wife, then Brian Pickering, that he had tried to kill her, and how she intended to track him down.

'Is that wise?' Lee said. 'After all, he sounds insane.'

'We can't let him roam round here. Who knows who he'll attack next? And, remember, he'll want to shut me up once and for all. I'm the only witness.'

'Poor Brian Pickering.' Lee shook his head. 'He was a bang-up guy. Did you know he used to be a professional footballer until his knees gave out?'

'Well . . . Bostock must have smashed his skull to pieces.'

'The bastard.'

'I'd appreciate some help finding him.'

'Sure, but if he's that dangerous we should be going after him mob-handed. Not just the two of us.'

'OK, we'll try and round up some others. What shape are Ryan and Sue in?'

'Sue's fine. But all Ryan's doing is staring into space and saying "This is another fine mess you've gotten me into."'

'His one and only line, huh? Sounds as if he's getting flakey.'

'Him and a dozen or more others you can mention. Have you seen the state of them? They're all pretty badly shook up.'

'Yeah,' Nicole gave a weak smile. 'All time travel should come with a government health warning, shouldn't it?'

'Are you sure you're OK?' He touched her arm lightly.

'I'm fine. You go back to the amphitheatre and see if you can muster people to look for Bostock. He's probably in there,' she said, nodding in the direction of the wood.

'You could come back with me' He scanned the trees, then shot her a concerned look. 'I don't like to think of you alone here with that maniac on the loose.'

'Don't worry. I'll be fine. Look, I'm still standing in the car park. All those people are just fifty yards away.' She smiled. 'What harm can come to me here.'

'OK' He sounded reluctant. 'I'll be five minutes. Now stay there. OK? Don't go anywhere.'

Well, she thought, watching Lee's lanky shape moving back across the car park, *I've got the makings of my posse; so, Mr Bostock, watch out, watch out, wherever you are . . .*

Two

Before Jud left the boat he told them he needed something from the cabin.

Carswell sniffed. 'I wouldn't bother bringing any money. I haven't a clue what year this is, but my guess is we're in the days of pre-decimal currency. Now it'll be pounds, shillings, pence and all that.'

'No, not money, something else that's far more important,' Jud sounded enigmatic enough to prick Sam's curiosity but he didn't comment.

'So what do you make of the United Kingdom, my American friend?' Carswell asked.

'I liked it better when it was 1999.'

'Don't worry, you'd have to go back another two thousand years before you found the Brits indulging in cannibalism or anything as unsavoury as that.'

'Everyone ready?' Jud asked, stepping lightly from the narrow-boat. In his hands was a cardboard wallet of the kind in which you'd store documents. 'Then shall we begin our trip into post-war Casterton?'

Three

Sam Baker drove the Range Rover into town. Carswell sat beside him in the front passenger seat. Jud Campbell was in the back.

And, hell, the world was looking different now. Lots, lots different.

A dirt track now connected the amphitheatre with the main road. As Jud pointed out, the amphitheatre only became a tourist attraction in the late 1960s. With this being sometime in the 1940s the amphitheatre was, as far as the locals would be concerned, a hole in the ground occasionally visited by a student writing his or her thesis on Roman Britain.

He wished Zita had come with them. He found her presence reassuring. But she'd stayed to help Jud's wife take care of the tourists who'd been injured by the latest jerk through time. Some were suffering from shock – which was purely a psychological reaction to what was happening to them. Then there were the grotesque injuries. Like the man with the bird fused inside his head, and the man with grass growing through his feet. The latter probably wasn't seriously hurt but Jud's wife had urged them to find antiseptic creams in town.

Sam joined the main road to town. It looked pretty much the same as it had in 1978, or in 1999 for that matter. Of course, the road signs were different. It seemed narrower. And there were great clumps of horse droppings scattered here and there.

Jud noticed, too. 'Horses were still commonly used for transport right up into the 1950s. So watch out, you'll probably find a few horse-drawn delivery vehicles on this road.'

Sam eased the Range Rover down to forty. He didn't want to compound their problems by running the car into the ass of some carthorse ambling along the road.

The fields at either side of the road, Sam noticed, were smaller; there were far more hedges, too. On the road itself there were few cars. And what vehicles there were looked pretty much like museum pieces: boxy cars that seemed peculiarly high, with running boards and spoked wheels, and painted in colours that were predominantly black or grey. The sole exception being a cream-coloured sportscar driven by a jaunty-looking man with a handlebar moustache and a leather flying helmet.

Carswell said, 'I think our own vehicle is going to turn heads. An electric-blue Range Rover in 1940s Britain is going to stick out like the proverbial sore thumb.'

Sam nodded. 'I think we'll just have to live with that interest. If anyone asks, just say it's an experimental car from the States. I think they'll buy that, don't you?'

'Wait – wait! Stop the car,' Jud shouted suddenly from the back.

Sam braked hard and the car skidded slightly on the carpet of horse crap that covered most parts of the road. 'What's wrong? Jud? Where are you going?'

'Back in a minute.'

Carswell said coolly, 'If he's going to be jumping in and out of the car every five minutes then perhaps we should drive on without him.'

Sam frowned. 'He knows what he's doing.'

'Does he? Maybe he's losing his marbles, too. You know, time travel doesn't appear to be agreeing with most people.'

Jud came running back to the car, his gold waistcoat flapping open as he ran. 'See this? Yuk, bit of a mess I'm afraid.'

'Hell, Jud, what's that smell?'

'What's left of someone's fish-and-chip supper, it looks and smells like to me,' Carswell said dryly. 'That's one souvenir we could safely leave behind, don't you think?'

'No,' Jud said. 'Look, in days gone by fish and chips were wrapped in old newspapers. This should give us a pretty accurate date. Uh, I think vinegar was even more pungent in . . . let's see.' Jud peeled back a corner of the newspaper from a clot of cold chips and scraps of batter-covered fish skin. The paper was nearly transparent with grease. 'Good heavens, it's wet through with fat.'

'And just think, no one had heard the word "cholesterol" in those days,' Carswell observed in that dry voice of his.

'Let's try further down where . . . ah, got it.'

'You can see a date?'

'Yep. 14th May, 19 . . .' Jud screwed up his eyes to read the blurred print. '1946. That's it: 14th May, 1946 – a Wednesday.'

'The paper might be old if it was used to wrap fish and chips.'

'But not that old – no more than a month at the most,' Jud said, dropping the greasy newspapers back onto the road then wiping his hands on his handkerchief. 'So,' he said, thoughtfully. 'The summer of 1946. That means the war's been over for a year. There's still rationing. And most of the world is undergoing some pretty miserable austerity measures to pay for the war effort.' He shut the car door and Sam accelerated away.

'If Britain in 1946 was hardly a land of milk and honey,' Carswell said, 'do you think we'll just be able to walk into a pharmacy and demand antiseptic cream? We've no cash, remember.'

'That should be our first priority.' Jud still rubbed at his fingers with the handkerchief. 'Perhaps we can find a local doctor who'll—'

'I don't agree.' Carswell's voice sounded crisp, as if addressing a business meeting. 'Our first priority should be to find this Rolle gentleman. From what you say he should be able to tell us what's happening: why we've come adrift in time, and how we can return to 1999.'

'If he can tell us that,' Sam said. 'All he was trying to do was warn me to keep away from the amphitheatre during the time-slip.'

Jud nodded. 'And how do we know he'll be here in the Casterton of 1946? For all we know Rolle, or Dirty Harry, whatever his name really is, might be stuck in 1978.'

Sam cocked his head to one side, thinking. 'But didn't you say that when you saw him in 1978 he looked exactly as he did in 1999?'

'True.'

'Then he might be here in 1946?'

'I really don't know,' Jud said. 'I really don't know.'

'There's only one way to find out,' Carswell said. 'Step on the gasoline pedal, Sam, old boy, and we'll see if we can track down this mysterious fellow.'

Sam glanced in the rear-view mirror and caught Jud's eye. Jud shot the back of Carswell's head a look as if to say, 'You'll be lucky.' Then, shaking his head, he flipped open the cardboard wallet.

Sam, glancing back in the rear-view mirror, saw Jud pull out a sheaf of old photographs. He began to study them each in turn, taking particular notice of what was written on their backs. Sam couldn't see what the photographs were of, but he did see that Jud examined them carefully, very carefully; they were clearly of tremendous importance to him.

'Watch out for the poor gee-gees,' Carswell said with more than a hint of sarcasm.

Sam grunted and turned his attention to the road in front of him. It was busier now as they headed into town. Carefully, he eased the car round a horse-drawn van on which were written the words *Ferringer & Son, Greengrocer*.

The town itself was noticeably smaller than it had been in 1978. There were no high-rise buildings. The only man-made structures of any height were the town hall clock tower and factory chimneys, standing like long fingers of brick. From them black smoke rose. In fact, Sam saw that a haze of smoke hung over the whole town; every household, it seemed, must have had a fire blazing in the hearth grate, despite the fact it was a fine summer day.

Jud noticed, too. 'Looks pretty filthy, doesn't it? I'd forgotten how smoky towns were before smokeless fuel and gas central heating.'

'You must be a cold-blooded race,' Sam said. 'Fires on a warm day?'

'You have to remember that most of these people wouldn't have electric or gas water heaters. The only way they'd have hot water would be to light a fire. Also, I'd bet good money that a lot of these people are cooking meals on coal-fired ranges.'

'Roll on 1999,' Carswell grunted, his voice thickened with distaste.

Suddenly there seemed to be men on bikes everywhere. They wore blue military uniforms.

'Ah, the boys of the RAF,' Carswell said lightly. 'I take it there must be an RAF station hereabouts, Jud?'

'RAF Casterton. Home of 717 Squadron. They flew Wellington bombers out of here until 1950. Then the aerodrome was closed down and ploughed out. The last I saw of it, it was under several acres of wheat.'

'My dear old Dad was in the RAF,' Carswell said distantly, his elbow resting on the door frame, fingers toying with the rubber seal around the window. 'Although I don't think he made it so far north.'

'Where was he stationed?'

'Christ knows. Whenever he started talking about it people left the room. The old boy bored us silly. All I know was he was a grease monkey on Spitfires. Probably Kent or some such place. Just think . . .' He shot Sam a smile. (On Carswell's face it wasn't a pleasant expression; the man's eyes were as nastily beady as ever.) 'Just think, if I knew his base's telephone number I could phone the silly old bugger up and say, "Guess who?"' Carswell laughed.

And as far as laughs went, Sam thought, it wasn't a particularly pleasant one. Carswell was soon lost again in his own thoughts as he absently fiddled with the rubber seal of the window.

Sam turned his attention back to the road that was becoming clogged with slow-moving traffic. There were a fair number of horse-drawn carts and even a horse-drawn postal van. Horse crap littered the streets, lying here, there and everywhere in piles of greeny-brown balls. He could even smell it through the airvents of the car.

The town hall clock showed the time to be just a little after four.

On the High Street there were far more shops than he'd remembered before, each specializing in a specific kind of merchandise – ironmongers, hardware, greengrocers, butchers, fishmongers, a bookshop, a baker's, a confectioner's, a men's clothes shop (specializing in made-to-measure military uniforms, said a sign), then a womens' hat shop, a laundry, a bank, a post office. They all looked pokily small with drab wooden signs and even more drably painted woodwork in dull greens and chocolate browns. Most had their windows covered in whitewash writing that announced 'Coupons welcome here' or 'Nylons on sale – first come, first served' or 'Boys in Blue? Front of the queue!'

'Looks poxy, doesn't it?' Carswell murmured. 'So bloody poxy.'

Jud leaned forward to say in a low voice, 'They've noticed the car.'

Sam glanced to his left, then right. Shoppers were stopping to stare at the car, some open-mouthed. To his right a pair of boys in short trousers (although not so short: they reached their knees) ran after the car, waving and shouting.

Sam heard a thumping sound. When he looked in the door mirror he saw that a man in a blue uniform riding a bike had grabbed hold of the back window frame and was hitching a lift. He had a cigarette gripped between his teeth and grinned hugely as he coasted along.

'Funny old world, isn't it?' Carswell murmured. 'I can't wait to find out what we shall see next. Can you?'

Sam gave a low groan. 'Damn. I think we might just be about to run into our first problem.' Standing in the middle of the road was a policeman. He held up his hand and fixed Sam with an authoritarian stare.

'Well, old boy,' Carswell said. 'You've got a choice of running the constable down or stopping.'

Sam stopped the car.

'You might have made the wrong choice,' Carswell said. 'I hope you're silver-tongued enough to explain why three strangely dressed people, especially Jud in his gold waistcoat, are driving a peculiar-looking car that isn't taxed for this year and bears an incomprehensible registration plate. Good luck, old boy.'

Sam wound the window down as the policeman walked slowly up, poked his head into the car and gave the three of them a look that was both long and searching.

Four

Nicole Wagner stood in the hot sun. She found she couldn't take her eyes off the deep shadows of the woods. She was convinced Bostock was in there.

Probably watching me standing here, she thought uneasily. She shot a look back at the amphitheatre. Where was Lee? He was supposed to be drumming up some kind of posse to go out and look for Bostock. She couldn't bear the idea of Bostock escaping. The little bastard should be brought to justice.

Wait . . .

She tilted her head to one side and shielded her eyes with her hand against the sun.

She saw something move in the wood. It moved quickly. Fleetingly, she glimpsed a figure.

Now, now, she told herself; *is that Bostock running from tree trunk to tree trunk to hide himself?*

She shot a glance back at the amphitheatre. There were half a dozen people or so in the car park. Most had gone to the toilet block or begged cold drinks from the coach driver. The galley boasted a well-stocked refrigerator. (Good grief, he probably even *sold* them the drinks; she hadn't met a tour-coach driver yet who hadn't some wrinkle for earning extra cash on the side. Usually it was spurious detours to destinations not in the regular itinerary: passengers would be invited to make a 'contribution' to the driver for the additional fuel used. Naturally, the money, equalling at least a week's wage, went directly to the driver's pocket. It did not pass GO, nor did it attract the tax man's beady eye).

There he goes again! she thought, looking back to the wood. A figure, nothing more than a dark shape, flitted amongst the trees.

Was that Bostock playing peek-a-boo with her?

Or maybe he would rush out of the wood with the intention of strangling her there and then at the edge of the car park.

Let the sod try, she thought, angrily. *Just let the sod try.*

He was fifty, fat and short-legged. She could easily outrun him. She'd run, yelling blue bloody murder all the way back to the others.

She caught a glimpse of a pale face peeping from behind a tree trunk.

Perhaps if she took a step or two towards him that might tempt him out from the wood. Then she'd let him chase her back to the amphitheatre where Lee and the rest would overpower him. Just what would happen then she wasn't so sure. She had vague ideas of turning him in to the police. *Well, never mind*, she told herself, *I'll cross that bridge when I get to it.*

The face still peered out at her. It was too far away for her to be sure if it was Bostock. Nevertheless, whoever it was seemed peculiarly interested in her.

She took another couple of paces. Now she was on the turf.

The wood lay about fifty yards away from her.

The face ducked back as if shy.

She took another pace forward.

No more peek-a-boo. The owner of the face was staying hidden.

Damn, she thought. *I've scared Bostock away.* More angry than afraid now, she strode towards the wood.

It was far bigger than in 1978, she realized. The whole countryside seemed far more lush, greener. Everywhere there were hedgerows. Birdsong was more noticeable, too.

She slowed as she neared the edge of the wood.

'Come out, come out, wherever you are,' she sang under her breath. Then louder, 'Come on, Mr Bostock, you're not shy, are you now?'

With the faintest of rustlings a figure moved lightly away from the trunk of a huge oak in front of her.

At that moment she was ready to turn and run like hell. But the figure was moving away from her into the shadows of the wood where they hung as thickly impenetrable as a fog.

'Damn you,' she hissed. It was a good thirty or so seconds later that she realized she was following the man. She'd acted on impulse. Only she just didn't want to see the wretch get away scot-free.

Now she found herself under the canopy of branches.

She glanced back. The car park seemed a long, long way away. And here in the wood it was like a different world. Very still. Very quiet. Very gloomy. All that came to her ears was a distant whispering sound from the leaves being stirred in the treetops. A bird called.

Startled, she took a step back.

She bumped back against a tree trunk.

At least, that was the first thought that entered her head.

Only now she realized the tree trunk was soft. And then it breathed into the back of her neck before grunting, 'You've done it now, haven't you, you bitch?'

Her insides turned cold.

There was no mistaking Bostock's voice.

Chapter Twenty-Four

One

The second Bostock spoke the words Nicole Wagner saw his two ape-like arms appear at either side of her to grab her in a crushing hug.

She couldn't believe someone could be so strong. She felt like a little child in his arms. He picked her up bodily so her feet were clear of the ground. Then he was carrying her, half walking, half running. Her head bobbed up and down; she tried to yell but he was holding her around the stomach so tightly she couldn't even breathe properly.

Instantly she felt spearing pains in her chest.

My God, he's going to break my ribs if he doesn't let go, she thought in panic. *I'm going to break like a stick!*

But immediately after that came the realization he was going to take her somewhere quiet. Far away from the others back at the amphitheatre.

Eyes bulging, she saw trees swing out at her, then past her as she was carried deeper into the wood.

Uh, and the pain. She felt sick with it. Her ribs and stomach ached so much she wanted to yell out and beg him to stop. Just stop. She'd promise anything.

But he didn't stop. He carried her deeper into the wood. To somewhere he knew they'd be alone.

Tears rolled down her cheeks; she was so light-headed; he was asphyxiating her with this murderous bear-hug.

She screwed up her eyes to protect them from whipping branches as he blundered through bushes. The shadows deepened; here and there a stray shaft of sunlight penetrated the canopy like a spotlight to illuminate a patch of earth; dizzy, she saw rabbit holes.

Bostock nearly stumbled when he inadvertently put his foot in one.

Please fall, please fall . . . she thought desperately. But he regained his balance and moved on. A dead rabbit lay in Bostock's path; he kicked it savagely aside.

'You're too fucking clever for your own fucking good,' Bostock panted. 'Who do you think you are? Eh? Fucking Wonder Woman? Didn't you know I'd be waiting for you, you stupid cow?'

Nicole tossed her head and her long blonde hair tumbled forward across her face.

'Cat get your tongue, eh? Eh?'

He reinforced each 'Eh?' with a muscular hug. Now she felt the vertebrae of her spine grate together under the pressure. Her heart felt as though it was being squeezed like a sponge. Now she couldn't breathe at all, never mind speak.

'Here should do just fine,' Bostock whispered madly. 'Eh? Just fine, just fine, just fine. Mmmm?'

He'd stopped in a small clearing. She rolled her head back; her skull seemed too heavy for her neck muscles to support it. Above her she saw an irregular patch of blue sky framed by branches. A white dove sat in the tree and cooed down at them as if they were fairy-tale lovers.

'Just fine, eh? You fucking little bitch,' Bostock snarled. She felt his mouth rub against the side of her neck. It was like being nuzzled by a cow. His mouth was sloppy, wet. When he finally relaxed his grip a little, allowing her to breathe, she smelt his body odour, strong and sharply sweaty.

'I think it's time for a little play, don't you?' His hands rubbed her stomach. 'A little play, mmm?'

Suddenly he pinched her stomach hard. She writhed in agony.

'I said, it's time for a little play. Now did you hear me, you stuck-up little cow?'

'Yes . . . yes,' she managed to murmur. Fear as much as asphyxiation had disorientated her; she felt dizzy, nauseous; the trees revolved around her as if she'd just been out on one hell of a bender.

'Good,' he cooed. 'Now, these.' He patted her hip where the lycra cycle shorts hugged her like a second skin. 'Take these off for me, mmm?'

She breathed deeply, her mind clearing. She knew full well what he intended. If she could only get—

'Ah, ah,' he said, scolded. 'No, you don't. I'm hanging onto you, sweetheart dear. We're going to have a little play. Then . . .' His voice turned guttural with rage. 'Then I'm going to break your fucking neck. D'ya hear me? Eh? I'm going to fucking break it, then I'm going to fucking bury you!'

'Please,' she whispered. 'Please, don't hurt me. There's—'

'Hurt you? Hurt you? You're going to wish you were never fucking born. I'm going to—'

Bostock stopped suddenly and gave a little cough. Or at least it sounded like that. Almost the kind of cough you'd make to attract someone's attention.

A moment later she realized he was no longer holding her. She simply stepped out of his arms.

Bostock was standing there in the centre of the clearing. His face was a picture of bewilderment. She saw him running his fingers over the side of his neck as if he'd felt an insect crawling there. When he took his fingers away and looked at them his expression turned to one of shock.

She saw the fingers were red with blood. And as he stood there she watched his polo shirt turn from white to red from the collar downwards. Within seconds the whole left-hand side of the polo shirt had turned to that deep bloody crimson as the blood soaked it.

Bostock's eyes bulged in shock; his lips trembled as if he was trying to speak, but no words came out.

Stunned, Nicole looked round the clearing. She was alone with Bostock. So what had happened to him?

There was a blur of movement as a figure moved with such grace and speed she could barely take it all in. Instantly there came a *swish* as something like a stick buzzed through the air.

This time Bostock cried out.

The figure moved quickly to one side and she saw Bostock clutching that plump beer belly of his. He looked down at it as if he was about to witness something marvellous.

Slowly, with one shaking, blood-red hand, Bostock lifted the bottom of his polo shirt to see his stomach.

He gave a sudden shocked yell.

Nicole closed her eyes.

But it was too late. The image had already burnt its way into her brain. Bostock standing there clutching his beer gut while his intestines slipped smoothly out through his fingers, sloppy with stomach fluid and blood.

It was quite involuntary. She didn't want to do it. But her eyes snapped open.

This time she saw a tall figure standing over Bostock who now lay flat on his back, grunting pig-like.

Again the figure moved with such grace and poise he could have been a dancer.

He was, she saw, holding a long, slender sword. Then, in a strangely delicate way, he assumed an odd pose, holding the sword by the pommel in his right hand, while steadying the blade with just the fingertips of the left hand. Almost comically, the little pinkie of his left hand was cocked outwards as if he was drinking tea at a royal garden party. His eyes were fixed on Bostock who lay at his feet. Then she saw him jab the sword down at Bostock's neck.

Bostock himself gave a huge shudder. His feet scuffed the grass as if he was suddenly trying to run as he lay there. Then he was still.

For one lunatic moment she thought the man who'd saved her was Lee Burton. The figure was tall; he wore a cloak. But as she looked again she saw it was no fancy-dress-shop Dracula cloak, but one in brown wool.

With that same grace he bent from the waist, tore up a handful of grass and wiped the blade of his sword clean before slipping it into a scabbard that hung from a strap across his shoulders.

Later Nicole would curse what she did next. It was naff, so embarrassingly clichéd, but it happened anyway.

She fainted clean away on the ground.

Two

'Is this your vehicle, sir?' the policeman asked as he leaned into the car. The man's face seemed huge. And Sam was so close to it he could see the shaving nicks and the lines of bristles that had escaped the blade. Rolls of fat nearly hid the knot of his tie. Sam also smelled the odour of onions beating out from the man's mouth so richly that he found himself holding his breath, or at least trying to.

'It *is* yours, sir?' the policeman repeated.

'Yes, officer.'

'Oh, American, are we, sir?'

Sam gave a tight smile. He would have nodded but to do so would mean he'd end up head-butting the huge face in front of him.

The policeman looked searchingly at Carswell's white linen suit, then at Jud's golden waistcoat. Then he turned to look at the Range Rover's hi-tech instrument panel and CD player.

'Which button do you press to make it all fall apart, then?'

Sam felt his smile growing increasingly phony the wider he forced it. 'Fall apart?' he echoed, wondering if everyone in 1946 was ever so slightly barmy. Already a crowd had gathered around the car. A boy of around ten had climbed onto the bonnet and was pulling faces through the windscreen.

'It does fall apart, doesn't it?' the constable asked, liberally venting onion breath into Sam's face. 'My wife can't stand 'em but I'll be bringing the kids. It's the smell that puts her off, you know. Smells like dirty britches, she says.'

What the hell was the man talking about?

The man turned his red, razor-nicked face back to Sam so they were only about five inches from eyeball to eyeball. Sam found himself pressing his head further and further back into the head-restraint.

'Although I've got to tell you one thing,' the policeman said, his eyes bulging hypnotically into Sam's. 'You've come too far.'

Too far? Did the policeman know what had happened to them at the amphitheatre? That a hundred or so acres of dirt and grass had come adrift in time and were carrying with them fifty people, like shipwreck survivors on a raft? But how could he?

'Quite a bit too far.' The policeman looked back at the dashboard. 'I bet this does all kinds of funny business, doesn't it? Squirting water. Bangs, flashes, smoke. I love 'em. Kids love 'em an all. Pity the wife won't come. It's the stink she can't stomach.' He shook his head gravely. 'Never mind, eh? One less won't bankrupt you, will it now?'

Still smiling a fixed smile that was starting to hurt his cheek muscles, Sam shook his head in a way that he hoped humoured the mad policeman. On the bonnet the boy had stuck both fingers up his nose while shoving his tongue out against the glass, leaving spitty wet smears.

The policeman noticed. 'Oi . . . clear off.' He withdrew his head from the car and made as if to cuff the boy, but the boy had slithered off the bonnet and run into the crowd singing, 'Nah-nah!'

'Bloody tyke,' grunted the policeman heavily and hitched up the belt of his trousers. Then he looked back at Sam,

'Wouldn't do to have this thing exploding all over the street, would it now?'

'It wouldn't, officer,' Sam agreed pleasantly while thinking: *Please God, won't anyone tell me what on earth he's talking about?*

'Anyway, like I explained. Your lot turned left at the Buttercross. You can't miss them, they're all parked in the parish field. That's the big one down by the bridge.'

Sam nodded and grinned; his cheeks ached outrageously. He couldn't stand much more of this lunacy.

The policeman continued, 'Last I saw, they already had the Big Top up. Besides, you can always follow the elephant shit. Big as bloody cannonballs, it is.'

'Ah, *the circus?*' Sam almost shouted with relief.

'Yes. You *are* with the circus, aren't you?'

'Of course, yes. We got held up back in . . . uh . . .'

'In Selby,' Jud chipped in helpfully from the back. 'This car's just been shipped in from America.'

'America?' The policeman gave an appreciative whistle. 'It looks a fair piece of machinery.' He ran his finger along the door frame. 'Cost a bit, too, I expect?'

'A hundred thousand dollars,' Sam said, lying easily now: he felt the circus story would cover anything.

The policeman, however, stopped smiling. 'How much?'

'Just our little joke, constable,' Carswell said.

'Oh . . . right, right.' The constable chuckled. 'Right, best get you moving or you'll be late for the show. You will be on tonight, won't you? I've got seats on the front row.' He touched his nose. 'I had a word with your boss.'

'Oh, we'll be there, constable.' Sam grinned. 'You'll be amazed what this car can do.'

'I say, don't over-egg the pudding, old boy,' Carswell whispered into his ear. 'Otherwise he'll be asking for a demonstration right now.'

'All right,' the constable grunted. 'Everyone back. Let the car back up the street. Oi, you!' The boy had worked his way to the front of the crowd again. The constable used his meaty hand to cuff the boy round the ear. The crowd laughed and backed away as Sam, still smiling fixedly, slowly reversed.

'Careful what you tell the natives, Sam, old boy,' Carswell said, smiling and acknowledging the crowd with a regal wave. 'In 1946 one hundred thousand dollars is an unfeasibly large amount for any kind of car. Even a circus car that squirts water and falls apart every night.'

'Phew,' Sam said with feeling. 'I call that a stroke of luck, don't you?'

'Well, if he thinks we are with the circus you should turn round and at least head in that direction.'

'Jud,' Sam said glancing back. 'Have you seen any sign of Rolle?'

'None.'

'Well. I suggest we look long and hard, gentlemen.' Carswell examined his fingernails. 'As far as I can see, Mr Rolle is our only hope of extricating ourselves from our predicament.'

'But the antiseptic cream—' Jud began.

'Sod the cream. If we go through many more of these time-slips there's going to be no one left alive to use the bloody stuff.'

Again Sam heard the sound of ice and steel in Carswell's voice. He was a man used to getting his own way. 'Turn left here,' Carswell ordered. 'We can park the car down near the Big Top where, hopefully, it won't attract too much notice, especially now these hill-billies think we're part of the fucking circus. Jud, take off that gold waistcoat. We don't want to draw more attention to us than we need.'

As Sam pulled into the field where the circus had parked its trailers and trucks he noticed Carswell slip something from his jacket pocket.

'Hell, Carswell. A gun? What the hell have you brought that for?'

'Why do you think?' Carswell slipped the cartridge clip from the butt of the automatic. 'Hardly to show it the sights of 1946. This, dear boy . . .' He clicked the clip back into the automatic. 'This is our insurance cover. Unlike you, I don't intend to stand arguing the bloody toss with these peasants.'

Sam exchanged looks with Jud as he climbed out of the car. Carswell was going to be big trouble. The only question was, would it be sooner or later?

Chapter Twenty-Five

One

The three of them walked back into the town centre. Even though Sam didn't know the town particularly well, he was already noticing that the Casterton of 1999 and 1978 was very different from the Casterton of 1946.

It looked a good deal smaller, for one thing. Huddled in back streets were cramped-looking rows of terraced houses, which Jud told him would be demolished in the 1960s to make way for a supermarket and carpark. Children played in the streets with wooden spinning tops, iron hoops, skipping ropes. Three girls had chalked out a hopscotch pattern on the pavement and were skipping along it – at least hopscotch hadn't changed that much down through the years.

The buildings were a grimy black whereas in 1999 the stonework had been sandblasted clean to its original golden honey tones.

The reason for the grime became apparent when Sam noticed a cloud of black smoke and steam appear above the rooftops with a whooshing sound.

'Ah, the age of steam,' Carswell said. 'You'd think it impossible for people to get so sentimental over such filthy machines.'

Sam usually found himself bristling at most of Carswell's remarks, but when he saw the steam-powered loco puffing noisily out from behind the station buildings he had to agree. The engine was black from the encrusted soot; only the silvery piston rods driving the wheels looked remotely clean.

As it passed by along its track unburnt coal dust drizzled down from the sky onto them. Carswell clicked his tongue as he brushed black specks from the shoulders of his linen jacket. 'As I said, filthy machines. Now, shall we try and find our mysterious Mr Rolle?'

He strolled on ahead, looking like a tourist, part curious, part disgusted by what he saw in a foreign town.

Sam saw Jud shake his head after the man.

The commercial areas of town were an ants' nest of activity. This was an age when muscle power was the main way to move materials around the factory yards. And with labour still comparatively cheap the places swarmed with men. The sounds of the town were pretty much the same as in any modern town: voices, car motors, a dog barking, even music from a car radio. The main difference, Sam noticed, was the whistling. The entire male population, from boys to old men, whistled furiously wherever they went, whatever they did. All seemed to be in competition with each other to whistle the most cheerful-sounding tune the loudest.

By the time they reached the shops in the High Street, Sam's ears were ringing. Judd paused by an evening-news-paper vendor shouting the name of his paper on a street corner. It came out as '*Ee-poe!*' but Sam saw the name on the board was *Evening Post*. Jud smiled and Sam noticed a spark of excitement flare in his eye. '22nd May, 1946. So the paper that wrapped those fish and chips wasn't too far out.'

The excitement in Jud's eye grew more intense. He stopped on the pavement, rubbing his jaw and looking up at the town hall clock.

'Five past five.' He continued to rub his jaw as if working out some mental equation that fascinated and yet somehow scared him too. 'You know, I could make it. I really could.'

'Make what?' Sam asked bemused.

'Yes, what are you talking about?' Carswell snapped. 'Are we supposed to be finding this Rolle chap, or what?'

'Yes . . . yes, of course.' Jud sounded distracted. 'But there's somewhere I need to go first.'

'Uh.' Carswell closed his eyes and took a deep breath as if trying to master an anger that raged inside him. 'You do what you have to do. I'll look for Rolle.'

Sam said, 'If you find him, ask him to come back to the car. We'll meet you there if we don't see you before.'

'I'll bring him back.' Carswell smiled and patted the gun in his pocket. 'I can be very persuasive.'

'Dear God,' Jud said, shocked. 'Don't pull that thing on him. He might be the only chance we have.'

Carswell sniffed dismissively. 'If we don't meet before we'll rendezvous back at the car at seven.' With that he sauntered away among the people on the pavement.

'Damn him,' Jud said under his breath. 'Damn and blast him.'

'Well, let's hope we run into Rolle before he does. That is, if he is here.'

'I think all we can do is hope to God he is.'

Sam noticed that Jud glanced repeatedly up at the town hall clock.

'There was something you wanted to do,' Sam prompted.

'If there's time.'

'There's plenty of time. The problem is that it seems to be all pretty much cock-eyed at the moment.'

'True . . .' Jud paused as if reaching a difficult decision. 'Sam, my mother lived in this town in 1946. In fact, she'd lived here all her life until 1947 when she married my father.'

'Uh-oh, Jud.' Sam guessed what the man would say next. 'Is it wise to go find your mother? I take it you weren't even born by 1946 if your parents didn't marry until the next year?'

'I bowed in during 1948.'

'But what on earth will you say to her? You can hardly march up to the house and say: "Good afternoon. I'm your unborn son. I've just popped back from the future to say Hi."'

'No, Sam, I can't. But, you see, my father died of a stroke in 1990. That was quick. He went out like a light when he was mowing the lawn. But my mother died by inches after that. She just sat in her living room and waited to join him. Within twelve months of his death she'd developed cancer in the—you know, down below . . . I just watched her shrivel away to nothing over the next couple of years.' He looked searchingly up at the clock again. 'She died on Christmas day in 1993.'

'I'm sorry, Jud. That must have been hard to take.'

'It was. But the hardest thing was that I never told them that I loved them. Or thanked them for what they had done for me. It's ridiculous, really. But it struck me so hard the day of my mother's funeral that all my adult life I'd never ever said, "Mum, I love you," nor said it to my father, either. Not once. Or ever even acknowledged I was grateful for the sacrifices that—'

He stopped suddenly. His Adam's apple bobbed in his throat. 'Will you look at that? Horse-drawn drays. Look at the size of the shire horses.'

Sam realized Jud wasn't normally one to allow himself to display emotion, and now he was quickly changing the subject as the shire horses lumbered past, pulling the cart carrying barrels of beer.

As Jud watched it pass by with a close interest that was obviously designed to cloak his embarrassment at becoming emotional Sam said quietly. 'Sure, Jud. It couldn't do any harm to say hello.' He shot Jud a smile. 'Say you're a long-lost cousin from Australia or something and that you just happened to drop by.'

Jud looked relieved. 'It's along this way. We'll need to be quick.'

Mystified, Sam followed. Jud still glanced up at the clock in the town hall tower. Why did they have to be there at a particular time? What was so special about five-fifteen on the twenty-second of May, 1946?

'Your mother lived up this way?' Sam asked as he followed Jud, who now seemed preoccupied with some plan of his own.

'No. She lived in one of the little terrace houses not far from where we parked the car.'

'So why are we heading in this direction?'

Jud opened the cardboard wallet he carried and handed Sam a black-and-white photograph.

Sam recognized it as the same one that hung on the cabin wall of Jud's narrow boat. He must have slipped it out of the frame just before they left for town.

Sam Baker studied the print as he followed. It showed a young couple sitting astride a motorbike. They both smiled brightly into the camera. Of course, then neither wore helmets. The woman on the pillion wore trousers, a tweed jacket and a silk scarf. The man, grinning hugely, with goggles pushed up onto his forehead, wore a leather jacket. There was no mistaking the family resemblance.

'My parents on the day they became engaged,' Jud said, hurrying more quickly now along the street that was crowded with workers going home from local factories and offices. 'Look at the back of the photograph, Sam.'

Sam flipped it over. Pencilled on the back were the words: *Jeremy Campbell & Liz Fretwell (and Barney) – our very special day, 22nd May, 1946.*

The date was obvious.

'So they were engaged today?' Sam was starting to get breathless.

'They were.'

Sam looked back at the photo. 'But who's Barney?'

'The motorbike. My father saved for it all the five years he was in the army fighting the Nazis. It became a kind of holy grail for him. He used to tell himself with every week that he survived all the bullets and shells that it brought him one week closer to buying the motorbike; it's a 500cc AJS, which was the Rolls-Royce or Cadillac of motorbikes at the time.'

'He must have really loved it.'

'He did, but he loved something else more. He sold the bike to pay for the wedding.'

'But I still don't understand where we're going.'

'Look at the photograph. Do you see what looks like a castle turret in the background?'

'I see it.'

'Now look up this street. What do you see?'

'Hell, yes. The castle in the photograph.'

'It's not a real castle. It's a nineteenth-century folly called The Rook, built by a certain Lord St Thomas, a chess fanatic.'

'But why—'

'Why now? Why dash up the street at five twenty-five?'

'Yes.'

'Look at The Rook again. No, the one in the photograph. There's a clock set in the wall. What time does it say?'

'Half-past five.'

Jud's eyes blazed as he shot Sam a big happy schoolboy grin. 'That gives us just less than five minutes for me to say hello to my parents.'

Sam paused. This could go badly wrong. He was going to say something to Jud but the man was already hurrying up the street towards where his parents might already be posing for the photograph. Jud half ran with his head down as though, if he had to, he'd charge like a bull through the crowds of workers streaming home. Sam saw that nothing was going to deflect the man now.

Sighing, he followed. He realized full well that the next ten minutes or so could become rather complex.

Two

Nicole Wagner opened her eyes. Above her, branches. Leaves glowed a brilliant green as the sun shone through them. A bird sang in a tree nearby.

It all seemed so peaceful that she could lie there all—

Oh, Christ.

Suddenly she remembered and sat up straight, her heart cracking so hard against her ribs it felt as if it wanted to make a mad dash for freedom all on its own.

'*Bostock.*'

'Lady,' a voice said calmly. 'If that man is Bostock, then he is dead mutton now.'

First she looked across to the figure of Bostock lying flat on his back on the grass. His face and chest were red with blood. The spilled intestines rested in a tangled heap on his legs, like a nest of pink and white snakes.

Then she peered up at the man kneeling beside her. She stared awestruck for a moment. His handsome face, framed by blond curls, was astonishingly angelic. He wore what she guessed was a medieval costume. Brown cloak, dark greenish leggings or hose, with a claret-coloured tunic beneath the cloak itself.

He gazed down at her with his angelic face. 'What strange clothes you wear . . . are you a tumbler?'

She looked at him dumbly.

'A tumbler? An acrobat?' he suggested in a pleasant voice that was as gentle as a parent talking to a baby. He looked into her eyes. 'Pardon me, are you quite yourself yet?'

'Of course she isn't. That gorilla tried to kill her.'

'Hush, demon head.'

She looked round startled. Where had the second voice come from?

But with the exception of Bostock's corpse she was alone with the angelic man.

'Smelling salts. Hold smelling salts under her nose.'

Startled, she looked round again. The second voice seemed to come from thin air. What was more, it was a strange croaky voice. The kind of voice that belonged to someone who might have gargled with sulphuric acid to ruin their vocal cords. And there was a cockney quality to it.

'Smelling salts, I said,' came the voice again. 'She needs smelling salts. D'ya hear me through them pretty-boy curls?'

'I have no smelling salts. Besides, the lady appears well. Her cheeks are rosy. She is awake.' Although the man's blue eyes still studied her face with a concern she found astonishingly gentle, he wasn't speaking to her but to his invisible companion.

'Let me see her,' came the rasping cockney voice.

'No.'

'Let me see her.'

'Not yet.'

'I'll turn my head round if you don't – and bite!'

'Oh, very well.'

The blond-haired man's eyes fixed on hers. 'I'm sorry about this. But I must do as this demon head asks.'

'Demon head – *ha!*' the cockney voice exclaimed dismissively. 'I'm as flesh-and-blood as he is.'

The man stood up and untied a cord beneath his cloak.

Alarmed, Nicole climbed to her own feet and backed away.

'I'm sorry, lady. Please do not be too disconcerted by what you see.'

He gripped a side of the cloak in one hand and lifted it to expose one side of his stomach.

Nicole wasn't sure what to expect; she looked down at his stomach, startled. The claret-coloured tunic came down over his waist to reach his upper thighs.

Then she noticed two things almost simultaneously. One, the tunic bulged just above his right hip, more or less where the appendix would be. A large rounded bulge almost as if he'd concealed a bowl beneath the tunic.

Then, secondly, she saw a strip had been cut from the material to form a diagonal slot maybe six inches long and little more than two inches wide. Through the slot she could see the colour of skin.

She was as much embarrassed as shocked, wondering what the man was trying to show her. She angled her head to one side so her eyes would be level with the diagonal slot cut in the tunic.

Her breath caught in her throat when she realized she was looking at a pair of eyes.

And those eyes, staring wide and brown from the flesh of the man's stomach, looked steadily back into hers.

Three

'There they are.' Jud's voice was hushed with amazement. 'There they are.' He looked back at Sam, his face shining with wonder. 'Those are my parents . . .'

Sam had found himself expecting Jud to rush forward, calling wildly to them – and probably scaring them half to death in the process.

Instead, he stopped thirty or so paces away.

Here they were already on the edge of town. The road rose up a slight incline. At one side were large detached houses, homes to the upwardly mobile residents of Casterton. On the other side of the road was a hill on which stood the mock-castle tower of The Rook. Its clock announced it was now barely two minutes to half-past five. The sun shone brightly.

Sam looked down at the photograph in his hand showing Jud's parents, then in their twenties, sitting astride the motorbike and smiling their youthful happiness at the world.

Sam glanced back to the grass verge at the side of the road. A motorbike – the same motorbike, he saw – was propped up on its stand. A girl in a brown tweed jacket and silk scarf posed by the wall, smiling brightly. A man in a leather jacket photographed her with a chunky box of a camera. Although they were too far away to make out individual words Sam heard the couple laughing as they talked. They were in love. There was no doubting that.

'Jud, wait . . .' Sam said, but Jud was already walking forward. He still stayed on the opposite side of the street but Sam watched him gazing in awe at the young couple.

Sam followed the man, feeling as awkward as he'd ever

felt. He didn't want to intrude on what must be a deeply personal meeting.

Again Sam found himself cringing at what Jud might blurt out. But Jud walked forward slowly, holding his emotions in check. To a dispassionate observer he could have been just a passer-by showing an interest in the camera.

At that moment Jud's father (or father-to-be, more accurately) glanced back after taking the photograph.

He held up his free hand to attract Jud's attention. Then he pointed at the camera, then at the woman now standing by the bike, then at himself.

Sam saw Jud give a slow nod.

There's no reason to rush forward and try to talk Jud out of this. He knows what he's doing, Sam thought with a sense of satisfaction that felt so strange, and yet so heart-warming. This had to be the same feeling that a parent experienced when they saw their child ride a bike without stabilizers for the first time. First would come the anxiety that there would be some hideous calamity as they let go of the child who would peddle furiously away. Then would come a spreading warmth as they realized, both surprised and pleased, that their son or daughter wasn't going to fall off in a bloody tangle of broken limbs after all.

This situation called for a sense of balance, too; of almost defying gravity. A wrong word would lead to embarrassment, if not out-and-out chaos. But Jud was smiling, making small talk about the camera, then the motorbike.

Now Sam stayed where he was on the pavement, leaving Jud to that curious moment of intimacy with his parents, or parents-to-be, who were still in their twenties.

Sam realized he was watching something close to a miracle. Well, yes, as near as damnit it *was* a miracle.

Most people's memories of their late parents are often darkly coloured; of mothers and fathers shrivelled with age, withering away in a hospital bed.

Jud was unique. This would be the last time he saw his parents. But he was seeing them in the blooming-rose tints of youth, with nearly all their adult lives in front of them.

Sam watched as the two climbed astride the motorbike, then smiled with sheer happiness at the camera as Jud clicked the shutter. At that moment the clock struck the half-hour. As the vibrations of the bell faded away a tingling sensation rose through Sam's chest, up his neck and across his scalp.

He glanced down at the photograph in his hand, which was a perfect copy of the real-life scene taking place in front of him.

After taking back the camera from Jud, the father shook the son's hand, a friendly smile lighting his face. Seconds later, the couple rode the motorbike away along the road.

Jud watched it go. He was still standing there when the sound of the bike had dwindled into the distance and Sam could hear it no more.

Four

'Nicole. Where have you been? Have you seen Bostock?' Lee called the words as he ran to her across the car park. Behind him was Susan in her Stan Laurel costume.

'I've been in there.' Nicole jerked her head back in the direction of the wood.

'Bostock?'

'Yes, I've seen Bostock. He's dead.'

'Dead?'

'Disembowelled, throat cut.'

'How? Did you—'

'With a sword, and, no, I didn't do it . . . and don't ask who: a stranger. A very strange stranger.'

She didn't stop walking until she reached the machine that vended soft drinks by the visitors' centre. Then she aimed a kick at it. Satisfyingly, she heard the rolling boom and clunk of a can rolling into the dispenser.

She opened it.

Still cold. Thank God, even though there was no electricity now. Power cables only ran out as far as the boundary of this chunk of 1999 ground.

She looked at Lee and Sue who were watching her with a curious kind of expectancy, as if at any moment she was going to scream shrilly, then run down to the river to drown herself, unhinged by her experiences. But inside she felt a peculiar calmness.

Maybe this is shock, she told herself. *Well, if it is at least it's shielding me from the increasingly surreal experiences.* The memory of what had happened ten minutes ago was still registering at full strength inside her head.

Every time she blinked she saw Bostock lying there with his guts heaped on his legs. Equally strong was the memory of the blond-haired man in medieval dress, complete with a second pair of eyes that peered from his stomach.

All right! Pick the bones out of that one, Salvador Dali . . .

And she remembered how the angelic-faced stranger had kissed her hand before running lightly away into the wood.

Taking the drink she headed for the shade of an oak tree at the edge of the car park. She was aware, in a distant well-it's-got-nothing-to-do-with-me kind of way, that Lee and Sue were firing questions at her, mainly centring on how she felt, and was she OK?

But all she wanted to do was sit in the shade of the tree for a while and drink the Dr Pepper.

(But, oh, how she normally hated Dr Pepper. To her tastes it was a viscous drink, so overloaded with sugar it left an unpleasant film on her teeth. *But hey!* she thought. *These aren't normal times. God or the Devil's gone and rewritten the reality code.* Most important to her right now was that the can was ice cold in her hand, so that was OK; that was very OK.)

As she walked, she scanned the edge of the wood, wondering what other marvels it would spew out. What next after the man with eyes in his stomach? Cavorting men with goaty legs and hooves? Centaurs with the bodies of horses, yet with the smooth muscled torsos of men? And why not mermaids frolicking in the river, splashing everyone on the bank with their fishy tails?

She knew it all could happen. No matter how surreal or bizarre; they were falling into a world full of wonders, miracles and monsters. The conviction was rooted as solidly in her as the two eyes were rooted in the man's stomach.

Oh, crap . . .

She needed that sit-down in the shade. That long sit-down with the earth rock-solid beneath her. The world was turning grey around her; her tongue felt as if fur had grown over it.

She sat with her back to the tree trunk. But not before she noticed that the front wheel and handlebars of a bicycle protruded from the solid timber.

A bike that wanted to be a tree?

Or was it a tree that wanted to be a bike?

Never mind, bikes fused with trees were small fry. She could handle that easy as ABC.

She drank deeply. Then she closed her eyes and waited for her self, the inner 'her', to find its centre once more.

Then perhaps the world wouldn't look so crazy when she opened her eyes again.

Five

When Sam walked back into Casterton he couldn't believe his eyes.

'Well, will you just take a look at our Mr Carswell,' Jud said heavily. 'Doesn't he look the proper English gentleman?'

Part-way along the High Street stood an old cottage set back from the road. In the front garden were half a dozen tables covered with tablecloths that were gleaming white in the early-evening sun. A sign nailed to a tree in the garden ran:

TIME FOR TEA?
TEAS, ICES, SANDWICHES SERVED HERE

And chalked underneath was the stern command *Ration books required for full meals. Sugar subject to availability. Gentlemen who spit will not be served.*

Red writing on a piece of card hanging from the gate stated: *YES! WE HAVE BANANAS! (ONE PER CUSTOMER ONLY)*: the whole tone of that particular sign screamed with a giddy excitement. And when Sam looked at the customers sitting at the tables he saw they were indeed all eating bananas, a fruit that would have been scarcer than Dodo eggs during the war. Now, in post-war Casterton, still grimly shackled to tight rationing, eating a banana was a serious business. They were served finely sliced in dishes. The clientele, wielding forks, ate them carefully one morsel at a time, the expressions on their faces peculiarly intense as they savoured the unusual flavour.

Carswell, however, ate sandwiches made from equally thinly sliced bread that was much closer to grey than white.

He waved a hand, inviting them to sit with him.

'These are unfeasibly disgusting; the cucumber has the texture of recycled latex,' he said, dropping the sandwich back onto the plate. 'But you're welcome to take tea with me.' He clicked his fingers at a girl of around fourteen in a white apron. 'Two more cups and another pot of your tea. Thank you very much, Jenny.'

As she quickly hurried away, he gave one of his tight little smiles that was as cold as a January morning and murmured. 'What I can say, unequivocally, is that the service is as keen as the tea. I recommend you take it with plenty of milk. There's no sugar, I'm afraid. The girl was telling me that the ship carrying the sugar into Scarborough harbour hit a stray mine. Consequently the ocean is a sight more sweet than this Victoria sponge cake.'

Jud frowned. 'We don't have any 1940s currency. How did you—'

Carswell held up the little finger of his left hand. 'I pawned my pinky ring. Don't worry, it's hallmarked 1906 so it won't alert the man to the fact that we hail, in fact, from the latter part of this century.' He spoke in that nonchalant way of his, not caring if he was overheard or not. 'Have you two completed your own mysterious assignment?'

'Yes,' Sam said.

'Nothing too outrageously purple, I trust? No WAAFs ravished senseless?'

Coolly, Sam said, 'Jud wanted to see his parents.'

'Oh? *Sweet*.' Carswell said the word 'sweet' softly but somehow managed to infuse into it enough sarcasm, disdain and contempt to make Sam grit his teeth. Carswell made it clear enough that he dismissed the pair of them as over-sentimental imbeciles.

Sam was tempted to tell Carswell in short bludgeoning sentences that not everyone was a flinty-hearted emotional retard, but he stopped himself. It would be wasted on the cynical Carswell. As the waitress set the cups and saucers in front of Sam and Jud, Carswell said, 'While you were involved with your own doubtlessly important mission I've been making enquiries among the locals.' He dabbed his mouth on a cotton napkin. 'Specifically, I've been asking about any tramps who might frequent the area.'

'And?'

'And there are three. They rejoice under the names of Muddy Joe, Toad Gilbert, and Mr Sixpence. God knows what their real names are. The townsfolk gave them those colourful nicknames years ago.'

'Did you get any descriptions?'

'I've done better than that. Tea, anyone?' Carswell poured the tea, his eyes boring furiously into the brown liquid that streamed from spout to cup.

'Remember, gentlemen,' Carswell said, 'plenty of milk otherwise your eyes are sure to water, I'm afraid.' He sipped his own tea. 'Now . . . Casterton's three vagrants. Toad Gilbert is actually just across there in the market square. You can see him foraging in the market for spoilt fruit and vegetables.'

Jud craned his head to see.

'Don't bother,' Carswell said. 'He's not our man. He looks around seventy and is clearly as senile as the day is long. And we can dismiss Muddy Joe as well. He's of African descent and bald as a badger.' Carswell mused as he sipped his tea. 'Muddy Joe? Clearly no one in 1946 was ticklish about being accused of racial prejudice.'

'Well, that leaves the one called Mr Sixpence. Have you found him?'

Carswell clicked his fingers and the waitress ran obediently across to him. 'Jenny. Mr Sixpence. What does he look like?'

'Oh, him again, sir?' The girl smiled shyly. 'Why on earth do you want to hear about him again, sir?'

'This is for my friends here. I've already explained we're a team of doctors researching the terrible, terrible conditions these gentlemen of the road have to endure. Now . . . Mr Sixpence, Jenny?'

'Well, he wears these bright orange overalls, or flying suit, I'm not sure which. Galoshes. He's got ginger hair – all this way and that.' She gestured near her head to describe someone with wild, stuck-out hair. They call him Mr Sixpence because whenever you see him he says, 'Sixpence. Got a sixpence?' And you hear him babbling away to himself and he says . . .'

The waitress continued talking as Carswell looked at Jud, then at Sam, and raised his eyebrows as if to say, 'We've found our man.'

Six

It didn't take long to find Rolle. They saw him walking along one of Casterton's side streets with a large brown paper bag in his hand. His red hair was a tangle of corkscrews and the knees and elbows of his orange boiler suit were green with grass stains. Sam wondered if the man had been enthusiastically prostrating himself before the Almighty in a meadow somewhere.

Carswell didn't bother with niceties. He simply grabbed Rolle by the elbow as he walked by. He could have been a plain-clothes detective arresting a suspect.

'Let him go, Carswell,' Sam said. 'He's not under arrest.'

'Well, if he's our only hope of getting off this weird carnival ride back through time I'm not letting him slip through our fingers.'

'Carswell . . . we need Mr Rolle's voluntary cooperation.'

Displeased, Carswell nevertheless gave a shrug that said clearly enough, 'OK, you think you know best, but don't come running to me if he disappears.'

'Mr Rolle,' Sam said quickly. 'Do you remember me?'

'From the hole, from the Watchett Hole. I remember, I remember, I remember . . .' He chanted the words in a pulsing rhythm that was as soft as it was fast. 'I've told you, you have to get away from the hole. You'll be integrated, you'll be fused, you'll be mashed if you don't.'

'Integrated?' Sam remembered the man with the bird fused into his face; how both the man and the bird had screamed in agony. 'You mean every time we make the time jump someone's going to end up fused with whatever's occupying the same space when they materialize?'

'I do . . . and the time stream has become a leaky conduit – an oh-so-leaky conduit. Liminals are escaping. Are escaping out into the here and now.' He gave a little chuckle, but his eyes were fixed and serious. 'So how long – how long until Robin of Greenwood rides into the shopping malls of tomorrow-year? And – and how long until you find Caesar in McDonald's? Big Mac, Blood Mac, Dead Mac. I'm sorry, my tongue is slippery as an eel: it escapes me so easily.' He took a deep breath to steady himself. 'Now my blood boils with salvatory . . . salvation; God-given salvatory tasks.' He started to move away from them as if late for an important appointment. 'I've work in the other places.'

'Wait,' Carswell said. 'We haven't finished with you yet. We need to know how to get off this damn' conveyor belt back into history. What's more, we want to return to our own time. 1999. Did you hear me? Nineteen-fucking-ninety-nine; I told you to wait.'

Muttering to himself, Roger Rolle backed along the street, eager to be on his way. Carswell didn't hesitate; he grabbed the man by his arm to stop him going any further. The bag slipped from his hand.

Sam looked down to see a dozen or more brown pill bottles spill from it. There were glass ampoules, too, filled with an amber liquid.

'What have we here?' Carswell said unpleasantly.

'Please, dear heaven, dear sweet heaven, those are for my neighbours. I need them.'

'What the hell is this nutcase talking about?'

'Apologies, sir . . . when I am in the world of now my tongue runs swiftly . . . so swiftly; swiftly ahead of my thoughts.'

Jud crouched down and started putting the ampoules back in the bag. He looked at the labels on the pill bottles. 'Penicillin.' He handed the bag back to Rolle.

'Thank you, sir. These are needed most urgently. Most urgently, sir.' He started to back away again, anxiously clutching the bag.

'And just what are you doing with those?' Carswell said. 'You've enough to run your own dispensary with that lot.'

'It's no business of ours, Carswell,' Jud said. 'I imagine Mr Rolle has his own reasons.'

'Indeed so, sir, indeed so, indeed . . .'

Carswell gave one his irritated grunts. 'We've spent all day looking for him! Just look at him. He's a tramp. Nothing but a scruffy tramp, and as mad as a bloody hatter.' Eyes burning furiously, his hand went to the gun in his pocket. For one crazy moment Sam thought the man would draw the gun and shoot Rolle dead in the street.

'Wait,' Jud said soothingly to Rolle. 'I know you're in a hurry. But we do need to talk to you. Believe me, it is important.'

'No time. I'm terribly sorry,' Rolle said quickly running the words into a single stream of sound. 'I need to hurry — rush, rush, rush. Babies are dying. All dying so quickly now. Buboes swelling up on them, here, here.' With his free hand he pointed to his armpit, then to his groin.

'Buboes?' Jud said, astonished. 'The penicillin is for them?'

'Yes.'

'Please. Won't you let us help you?'

With a twitchy shake of his head Rolle said, 'No . . . no.'

'Can't we take you where you want to go? We have a car.'

'Hah.' The sound was more a breathy expression of regret than a laugh. 'Your car doesn't go that far.'

'Mr Rolle,' Jud said. 'Please, we do need your help. Can we meet you later? All we want to do is talk.'

The red-haired man looked at each in turn; he seemed nervous, even anxious. Sam was sure he'd see that jerky shake of the head again. *No.*

'Well?'

This time they were rewarded with a single sharp nod. 'St Jude's. Eight o'clock.'

'St Jude's. Eight o'clock,' Jud echoed, and nodded. 'We'll be there. Thank you.'

'Are you sure we can't take you somewhere in the car?' Sam asked.

Again the twitchy shake of his head as Roger Rolle began to back away as if already he'd wasted far too much precious time. 'I'm beginning the Jesus Prayer now. For me the way is made open by the Jesus Prayer.'

With that he turned and hurried away, the precious bag clutched to his chest. Sam could hear the ginger-haired man muttering quickly under his breath, 'Lord Jesus Christ, Son of God, have mercy on me, a sinner. Lord Jesus Christ, Son of God, have mercy on me, a sinner. Lord Jesus Christ, Son of . . .'

The voice faded away, drowned by the whoosh and roar of a steam engine pulling into the station.

Carswell fixed Sam then Jud with his piercingly angry eyes. His expression was the sourest Sam had seen so far.

'Well, what a piece of carnival that was. What a waste of fucking time. We'd have had a more meaningful conversation with one of the monkeys down there at the bloody circus.'

Jud began calmly, 'Roger Rolle is—'

'Is bloody mad. It's as obvious as the nose on your blasted face.' Carswell slapped the pocket that carried the gun in a way that Sam could only describe as neurotic; dangerously neurotic at that. 'Lunatic. He should be locked away. And there you two are, nice as pie, politely asking him to help you.'

'Carswell,' Jud began again, firmly but calmly. 'Roger Rolle is a hermit and a mystic. That means he is a maverick, an outsider, he won't behave as ordinary men and women behave. That doesn't make him insane.'

'It does in my book; at least, what I've witnessed.' He forked his fingers towards his eyes as if about to gouge himself. 'These two eyes tell me he's completely insane. Did you hear how he talked? Did you hear that nonsense about the Jesus Prayer, and see the way he ran off muttering gibberish?'

Jud said, 'The Jesus Prayer is a prayer from the Orthodox branch of Christianity. "Lord Jesus Christ, Son of God, have mercy on me, a sinner."'

'You're barmy, too.'

'No. That is the prayer repeated by mystics over and over until they achieve an altered state of consciousness, or a trance if you like. All cultures have their own variant of this – in the East mantras are chanted. Modern hypnotists repeat the same phrase over and over to induce a state of hypnosis.'

'Oh, mesmerism is it, now? Fat lot of good that will do us, Campbell.'

'You still don't get it, do you?' Jud's eyes gleamed in a fixed way. 'Already Rolle's given us a clue, no, not just one, but several clues about how he can apparently travel through time at will. He does it through altering his own state of consciousness. What's more, we've just seen him with bottles of penicillin. He's talked about helping sick people suffering from buboes beneath the arms and in the groin.'

'So?'

'So those are symptoms of people suffering from what has to be bubonic plague.' He looked Carswell in the eye. 'Or what was more commonly known as the Black Death. Mr Carswell, I think we've just been privileged enough to meet our first genuine time traveller.'

Chapter Twenty-Six

One

'Where is St Jude's?' Sam asked as they walked back to where they'd parked the car in the field near the circus.

'It's the little church near the amphitheatre,' Jud replied.

'Well,' Carswell said sharply. 'If you take any notice of the madman you're probably bigger fools than he is.'

'Get in the car, Carswell,' Sam said, irritated by the man's mood.

Jud climbed into the back seat. 'So far, Carswell, Rolle is our only hope.'

Sam started the car. 'And he appears to know how to travel in time – as distinct from us who are just being carried along by the flow.'

Carswell nodded and, staring out of the window, echoed Sam. 'He knows about time travel. Well, we'll have to wait until we can speak with him further at eight.'

Sam scanned the channels of the radio until he hit a station playing big-band swing music.

'Glenn Miller,' Jud said. 'It used to be my father's favourite.'

'Sweet,' Carswell said in a voice sticky with sarcasm.

Sam shook his head. For two pins he'd leave Carswell there to walk back.

'Back to the amphitheatre, then?'

'Fine,' Jud said. 'We'll have a wait of just under a couple of hours until we meet Rolle at the church.'

Then Carswell said something surprising.

'Well, if the evening's still young why don't we stop off at that old inn at the end of the track to the amphitheatre?' Carswell smiled across at Sam. 'I'll treat us to a beer apiece. I think we've all earned it, don't you?'

Two

Lee Burton had thought he would throw up, but oddly the job he had to do wasn't as repellent as he'd anticipated. He'd talked it through with Nicole and Sue (Ryan was still out of it and had taken himself off to sit on the coach where he muttered to himself, his frightened eyes rolling). They'd decided that as tour reps they still had a duty to their clients, whatever the circumstances, no matter how bizarre the situation.

After the last time-slip Sue had noticed an elderly woman apparently asleep on one of the benches. She'd soon discovered the woman was dead. Perhaps the shock had killed her; perhaps she'd materialized with a rat inside her, a rat that had been occupying the same space as her when she'd suddenly popped through into 1946. Who knew?

Not that Lee was going to investigate any further. In any event, she looked as if she'd died peacefully enough, perhaps of natural causes after all.

Nevertheless, she *was* dead. And the three of them had decided to move the body. They'd quickly agreed on using the visitors' centre as a mortuary.

According to the coach radio the time was six o'clock. The early-evening news was just starting on the BBC's Home Service; the opening news report concerned the repatriation of Italian prisoners of war and reminded listeners that it was now twelve months since the war had ended in Europe. The defeated soldiers were going home.

With the help of Dot Campbell and Zita they had carried

the body on a door taken from one of the toilet cubicles up
to the visitors' centre.

It was probably then that Lee found he was distancing
himself from the fact he was carrying one end of a door on
which a dead human being lay. Instead, he concentrated on
the practical problems of carrying the body, manoeuvring it
through the doors into the visitors' centre, then over the
counter and into the museum area at the back. By then the
body might have been no more than an awkward piece of
furniture that had to be moved from A to B.

Not an elderly woman with slightly parted lips that were
turning a bloodless blue and one eye that remained fixed
wide open while the other's lid lay shut.

The little museum area housed a few artefacts that had been
excavated from the site over the years – mainly Roman coins,
bits of pot and a sword blade that was only remarkable
because it had been found lodged in the ribs of a skeleton.

Lee remained quite dispassionate about the business as he
eased the body between two glass cabinets, with Zita issuing
breathless instructions: 'Your end down a bit . . . watch
your back, Lee. Sue, can you push the waste bin aside with
your foot?'

He even found himself reading the label on the skeleton
exhibit.

> ROMAN LEGIONNAIRE'S SWORD – C. AD 200
> LOCATED IN SITU WITH BLADE IN THE
> VICTIM'S RIBS,
> CONSIDERED TO BE THE SKELETON OF A
> WOMAN IN HER TWENTIES.
> SKULL MISSING.
> RITUAL SACRIFICE OR MURDER?

Nicole, with both hands gripping the end of the toilet door
that was serving as a stretcher, flicked back her long blonde
hair with a toss of her head, then tried to blow away the
loose strands that clung to her face.

260

'There's not much room,' she panted. 'But we could put her behind the display at the end.'

Lee nodded. 'Go back straight. There's a space where we can slot her at the side of the monk.'

There at the end of the room was a scene depicting, so a notice said, *The Devotion of Roger Rolle, Hermit, Writer and Mystic (b. 1300, d.Michaelmas Day, 1349)*. There, kneeling before a fake stone altar of fibreglass, was the mannequin of a small pious-looking man, his limpid brown eyes turned up towards heaven in prayer. The figure was dressed in a monk's habit, and the silver nylon hair was shaven into a monk's tonsure.

(*A solar panel for a sex machine* was Lee's sudden inappropriate thought as he manoeuvred the lavatory door on which the dead woman wobbled plumply at every movement.)

'There, got it,' Nicole said as she dropped the door the last inch (so as not to trap her fingers) onto the raised stage area that carried the tableau of the hermit. 'Just shove it from your end, Lee.'

With a last heave he slid the door onto the stage, knocking the fibreglass altar back against the wall.

Oddly, the tableau of the kneeling monk didn't look at all out of place. If anything, he now looked to be praying over the dead body of the woman. A moment later Jud's wife covered the body with a dust sheet she'd found at the back of the museum area.

'You say there's another body still out in the woods?' Sue asked Nicole.

Still breathless, Nicole nodded. 'Bostock. But he deserves to lie out there and rot.'

'It's a shame we can't just phone for an ambulance and let them take care of it.'

'And then start having to answer some awkward police questions?' Nicole shook her head. 'We've got to manage this ourselves.'

When Lee spoke he was surprised at how businesslike he sounded. 'Did anyone see what happened to the man with the bird in his face?'

'As far as I know he's still alive,' Dot Campbell said. 'But how long he can survive like that, I don't know. Certainly the blood groups will be incompatible. I imagine the bird will die first and decompose. Then septicaemia will set in, which would kill the man in a few hours.'

'Dear God, what a way to go,' Sue said, and swallowed as if a filthy taste had leeched across her tongue. 'Imagine. A bird growing out of your face; its flesh and bones fused with your flesh and bones.'

At that moment Nicole thought about the man in the wood with the pair of eyes peering from his stomach. And as she walked away from the visitors' centre she began to wonder about that.

Three

'What do you think?' Jud asked.

They sat in the tap room of the inn that stood at the junction of the dirt track leading to the amphitheatre.

Sam sipped the beer. It was flat, warm, and tasted particularly bitter. In fact, it was very much like every other British beer he'd tried before. He was getting a taste for it now, but he didn't feel competent enough to say whether it was great beer or if it tasted like something a tom-cat had passed.

'Not too unpleasant,' Carswell said. Which, coming from him, Sam realized, was probably high praise indeed.

Jud licked his lips before taking another swallow. 'I don't know,' he said, 'I imagined something full-bodied, richer, stronger.'

'Remember,' Carswell said, sipping the beer, 'this is the austere post-war period with rationing and belt-tightening still much in evidence. Now, would anyone like anything to eat?'

Sam glanced at Jud as Carswell studied a chalked menu that offered pork pie, sandwiches and something called Rabbit Bake. Why was Carswell suddenly on a charm offensive? He seemed to have completely changed, mood-wise, on the fifteen-minute run back from town. Why was he buying them drinks, inviting them to eat? For heaven's sake, he'd even concealed that sour expression and was actually being charming.

Sam realized from the expression on his face that the same questions were going through Jud's mind.

Needless to say, he knew the maxim 'There's no such thing as a free lunch.' And he was positive that Carswell would do nothing for anybody unless he'd identified a profitable return for himself. So what was Carswell's game? What did he want from them?

'I think I'll take the pork pie,' Carswell said. 'Anyone like to join me?'

Sam and Jud shook their heads and thanked him.

'No? All right,' he said mildly. 'Anyone for another beer? No? Just say when you're ready for more. I still have a fair amount of 1940s currency left. There's no point in allowing it go to waste, is there? Now, you know, this beer is starting to grow on me. More hoppy than the ones I'm familiar with. What do you think?'

While Jud and Carswell chatted about the beer, Sam allowed his gaze to run round the pub. It didn't look much different from other English pubs he'd visited. There was no jukebox, of course, nor any gambling machines. The chairs weren't cushioned and the whole place looked in need of a lick or two of paint. There were half a dozen or so other people in the bar. A couple were in RAF uniform. Across the room a middle-aged couple sat at a table. They were drinking half-pints of beer while shooting glances in Sam's direction. The woman was clearly talking about him, even holding her hand against her mouth in such a secretive way it was nothing less than theatrical. The man wore a thick moustache and black-framed glasses.

Sam looked down at his own light-coloured chinos, loafers, and open-necked cotton shirt that was the colour of a well-ripened lemon. Well, the clothes stood out as much as the Range Rover, which they'd taken the precaution of parking down the track behind a clump of bushes.

After a few moments the secretive couple drank up and left, the woman still looking him up and down as if she couldn't quite take in the clothes he was wearing.

In the meantime Carswell had been to the bar again, his own white linen suit attracting curious glances from the RAF men.

When Carswell had returned with the drinks he said, for no real reason, 'I hated my father, you know. The man was either drunk or chasing women. I don't know why my mother put up with him, but whatever he did she had an excuse. At weekends he'd stagger in at breakfast time covered with cuts and bruises, his clothes torn . . .' He wiped foam from the rim of his glass, then licked his finger. 'That wasn't just an occasional event. It happened nearly every week. He used to get into fights, I suppose. I suspect he was actually allergic in some way to alcohol and it made him act like a madman. Anyway, this went on year after year. But one day, when I was eight years old, I asked my mother why he came home in such a state.' Carswell leaned forward with his elbows on the table. 'And do you know what she said?'

Sam shook his head, puzzled why Carswell was baring his soul like this.

'She said my father was employed by the Lord Mayor of London, and that he had a very important job.' He looked from Sam to Jud. 'She said he was employed to fight the Devil's Serpent.' He gave a colourless smile. 'Can you believe that? To protect us kids from the truth – that dear old Dad was a drunk, a brawler and an adulterer – she invented that outlandish story. She told us all that this monstrous serpent of the devil was as long as six London double-decker buses; that it would come slithering out of the Thames every weekend intent on tearing Westminster Abbey down stone by stone. But every week my father would be standing on the Abbey steps, waiting for him. The monster serpent would attack, and dear old Dad would fight him all night until dawn; that's when, she said, the serpent's power would fade as the sun rose. Then it would go slithering back to the river where it would lurk until next time.' Carswell chuckled, but his eyes were glazed and fixed as he remembered. 'And, of course, my father would always be there the next weekend: waiting to do battle with Old Nick's serpent. Some part-time job, eh?'

'Your mother wanted to protect you.' Jud took a sip of beer. 'It's important for young children to respect their parents. Even to see them as superhuman or heroes.'

'Well, I can appreciate that. But do you know what my mother did to drive the story home – perhaps to give it that little extra veneer of truth? She told me that one day I'd work for the Lord Mayor, too. That when my father retired, it would be my turn to stand guard on the Abbey steps, and to fight that big old serpent with all my might.' His voice rose louder. 'So that was to be my destiny. To stagger home every weekend – dishevelled, dirty, my eyes blackened, blood dripping from my nose onto the kitchen lino, because, God, I remember that as clear as day. Seeing those drips of blood leading through the kitchen, through into the hall, up the stairs to where the old bastard would collapse into bed. You know, my mother would wash him and tuck him up in bed knowing full well he'd got himself into a fight over some tart he'd picked up. He even came home with love-bites on his neck – you'd call them hickeys, Sam – he'd come home with those, and she'd call us in when he was asleep.' His voice dropped to a rasp. ' "Do you see those," she'd whisper to us, "those bruises on his throat? That's where the serpent coiled round his neck and tried to strangle him." '

Carswell took a large swallow of beer. 'And she drummed it into us how Dad was a hero. That we'd follow in his footsteps. That we'd fight the monster too, and, oh, how proud she would be of us all.' He put the glass down and fixed Sam and Jud with his piercing eyes. 'I had nightmares for years . . . bloody years. As soon as we could my brother and I escaped not just from home but from the East End altogether. My brother found his slice of paradise at the sharp end of a syringe in a hippy squat in Cornwall. I chose a different path. While my friends, well, peer group, I should say, were out on the piss in the local pubs, I educated myself by reading every book I could lay my hands on. I could read two a night. And I'd been into the City enough to realize that people with top jobs spoke with upper-crust accents, not a cockney cor-blimey-where's-me-trousers patois. So I taught myself to speak like an English lord, enunciating 'How now, brown cow' and 'The rain in Spain falls mainly in the plain' until the early hours. Consequently I ended up with an apartment in Belgravia. My brother is dead from being unlucky enough to have bought extremely pure heroin. While my father—' He gazed at the beer glass as if it was a TV screen in which he saw his life being replayed. 'While my father is still working for the bloody Lord Mayor of London. Still coming home with his shirt buttons torn off, still with a bloody nose. In his seventy-fifth year, too, miserable bastard.'

Sam looked at Carswell. The man's face was expressionless.

It was hard to find a response to such a story. He found himself hoping that Jud would speak first. As it was, the voice came from another part of the room.

'Excuse me, sir.' A man had come to stand by the table. Despite the heat of the evening he wore a brown woollen suit that looked a size or two small for him. Even his chin rolled over his shirt collar to hide the knot of his tie. 'Sorry to trouble you. But could I have your name, please?'

Sam looked up, surprised. Two thoughts vied for prominence: one, that he'd been mistaken for someone else. Two, the man thought he was from the circus in town and was trying to poach a couple of free tickets.

Sam nodded. 'Sam Baker. And you are?'

'Oh, my name isn't important, Mr Baker.' Abruptly he stood back. In the doorway were two uniformed policemen;

their high helmets made them look huge in the low-ceilinged bar.

Then the man in the brown suit turned to the man in glasses who'd been sitting in the bar earlier and had returned unobtrusively.

'Mr Blakemore. Is this him?' the man in the brown suit asked sharply.

'Yes.'

'Are you sure?'

'Quite sure. I took the photograph myself two years ago. It was the night of the big Whit Sunday raid.' The man in the glasses fixed Sam with a direct stare. 'Well, you're a cheeky bastard, aren't you? I never thought you'd be brass-faced enough to come back here after what you did. They were my neighbours.' With that the man lunged forward. At first Sam thought the man would attack him. Instead he threw a folded newspaper onto the table.

Sam stared at it, stunned. He heard the brown-suited man say, 'Read the charge, Sergeant.'

'Yes, sir. Samuel Baker, I am arresting you on the suspicion of . . .'

Now Sam hardly heard a word of it. Because he was staring at a photograph of himself – an impossible photograph – plastered there halfway across the front page of the newspaper. It showed him looking back over one shoulder as if caught by surprise.

WANTED FOR MURDER ran the headline in monstrously dark print. *DO YOU RECOGNIZE THIS MAN?*

In sheer astonishment he found himself reading the story as the policeman recited the charge in a monotonous voice; 'That on the night of May the twenty-sixth, 1944, you did, with malice aforethought, unlawfully kill . . .'

Gazette photographer Sandy Blakemore discovered the bodies of the Marshall family in their home in The Rookery, a quiet suburb of Casterton. Sam read on, stunned: *Even hardened police officers were appalled by the brutality of the crime . . .*

Then the newspaper was yanked away from him by the man he now took to be Blakemore. 'You bastard . . . they'd done nothing to you . . .' The detective held out an arm to gently push the man back.

At that moment another policeman stepped forward. Dumbfounded, Sam watched the cop snap handcuffs onto his wrists. The only rational thought going through his head was how heavy they were. And how cold.

Blakemore shouted, 'They'll hang you, do you realize that? You'll hang . . . and I hope you feel it – I hope you feel the *agony* when that rope breaks your neck!'

Chapter Twenty-Seven

One

Sam Baker sat looking down at the heavy steel cuffs clamped around his wrists. They were tight, cruelly tight, and already the fifth fingers that served as his thumbs were starting to tingle. The oval scars where the thumbs had been removed soon after his birth, normally a pink colour, had turned a bloodless white.

The detective said, 'Sergeant, we'll take his two companions in for questioning, too. Birds of a feather and all that.'

It had to happen. Looking back, Sam saw that it had, after all, been only a matter of time.

Carswell pulled the gun.

'Carswell, no!' Jud shouted.

Carswell stood up, pushing the table to one side; glasses crashed to the floor, splashing beer against the policemen's legs.

'Lie down on the floor,' Carswell ordered, holding the muzzle of the gun so it was pointed at the centre of the detective's face. 'Lie down on the floor!'

The detective shook his head. 'No, I won't do that, sir. Give me the gun.'

'Lie down!'

'No, sir.' The detective's voice was very low, soothing almost; he looked Carswell calmly in the eye. 'I think it best if you give me the gun.'

'*Damn it!*'

'You know you'll hang if you shoot a policeman. Now, give me the gun.'

Sam saw the muscle tension begin in Carswell's shoulder. It was as if he was watching it all in extreme slow motion and extreme detail. The muscles coiled, bunched and tensed beneath the white sleeve of the suit. Carswell was squeezing the trigger.

Sam watched as the tensing muscles actually created a ripple in the fabric of the sleeve, running from shoulder to wrist to trigger finger.

The dark blue metal muzzle of the automatic shook slightly.

'Sir, hand me the—'

Sam swung his manacled hands upward, hitting Carswell's arm just below the elbow.

The gun jerked up at the same instant as it boomed.

Sparks seemed to fill the bar; acrid smoke flooded Sam's nostrils.

Above the detective's head the bullet hacked a chunk of timber from the ceiling beam.

'Bloody idiot,' Carswell screamed. For an instant Sam thought he'd turn the gun on him; instead, Carswell tugged his shoulder. 'Run!'

As Sam blundered through the fog of gunsmoke he glanced back to see Carswell and Jud following.

Carswell paused again to fire the gun.

But this time he fired into the wall of the bar, adding to the confusion of the customers, who shouted as they scrambled under tables for cover, knocking over glasses and chairs.

Suddenly, Sam found himself outside. A policeman had left the patrol car and was running towards him.

Sam froze, expecting the cop to pull a gun.

But British cops are unarmed, he reminded himself.

They don't carry firearms.

Even so, the constable was drawing his truncheon.

Sam turned and ran past the side of the building into the back garden.

A family was there, the father pushing a girl on a swing that hung from a tree branch. 'Get down on the floor,' he yelled as Carswell came running across the grass, firing the gun in the air.

Sam heard Jud shout, 'Carswell, throw that damn' thing away. Someone's going to get hurt!'

Carswell didn't listen. He vaulted over the fence and ran.

Jud climbed over the fence and followed.

Sam saw policemen pouring through the back door of the pub. The photographer was there, too. Straightening the glasses on his face, he was hollering, 'Don't let them get away!'

Sam ran at the fence, ready to vault over it. It was only as he put out his hands to grasp the top rail that he realized his hands were manacled together.

The chain links of the cuffs caught on a protruding nail, but already the momentum of his body was carrying him forward.

He made it over the fence, but the chain snagged against the nail, throwing him of balance.

He fell face forward.

The turf came up at him in a green blur.

It looked soft, but the blow it struck was hard.

As he groaned and rolled over, the chain on the cuffs clinking, he looked up at the sky. Coloured lights streamed from it as static electricity crackled across his arms and through his hair.

That was when he realized he'd not been knocked senseless by the blow.

But whatever mechanism had hauled that little group of people back through time was starting all over again.

· Two

Just moments before Nicole Wagner was flung into temporal backflow for the slide down through the months and years to who knows when she had walked into the wood.

She had no intention of finding the body of Bostock. Let him rot!

No. Instead, they were looking for the man Lee'd dubbed 'the birdman.' On the face of it, it was distasteful to give the poor devil such a nickname. But already they'd begun dealing with the horrors of the day by developing a dark sense of gallows humour. If they didn't make a joke of some of the things they'd seen – the old man with the bee squirming in his eye-ball, for instance – they would go mad.

Dot Campbell was certain that the birdman would soon die. That the blood of the bird and the blood of the man would intermingle and poison both of them, either through septicaemia or gangrene.

Nicole stepped slowly across the dappling shadows cast by the sunlight filtering through the leaves.

There, deep in the wood, she found the birdman.

As she looked down at him, she felt the first crackle of static in her hair. If it wasn't for the fact that her attention was held by the poor man's face she probably would have realized what was happening.

The man lay on his back. His breathing was shallow and rapid.

She found her gaze held by his face.

The bird's black wing twitched feebly from the side of the man's head. His eyes were glazed, unseeing; his hair was ruffled and sweaty.

From his cheek just below the eye the blackbird's head and neck hung limply, the yellow beak resting against his nose.

The bird, in panic, must have pecked the man's face. Worse were the cuts around his top lip: they still glistened a shiny red.

For a moment she thought the bird was dead. But then she saw the eyelid slip down over the eyes, turning them a milky white as it blinked slowly.

'Can you hear me?' she asked the man gently. He didn't

stir; if it wasn't for the little tugs of air as he inhaled she would have thought him dead.

He was dying.

So was the bird; the yellow beak parted slightly and she could see the tiny tongue trembling.

A black feather protruded from between the man's lips.

'Are you in pain?'

'He doesn't feel pain any more.'

She turned sharply at the sound of the voice.

The tall man with the blond hair stood there with his cloak gathered around him. He gazed down at the dying man on the ground with the bird crudely, repulsively fused to the face, like some sculptor's sick joke. 'He looks at peace now, doesn't he?'

Nicole stared for a moment at the blond man's beautiful face, then she nodded.

The man came to stand alongside her. For a moment they both gazed down at the dying man.

Nicole said at last, 'I need someone to help me carry him back to the amphitheatre.'

The blond man shook his head.

'But we can help him.'

'No, you can't.' The man spoke gently.

'Why don't you tell her?' It was the sharp cockney voice she'd heard before. The voice that belonged to the eyes in the man's stomach, she guessed.

'I'll stand over him,' the blond-haired man told her.

'Why?'

He looked at her with those gentle blue eyes. 'Because he's one of us now.'

The words had barely left his lips when Nicole felt static crackle through her T-shirt up into her hair.

Lights exploded in her eyes.

And there was the dizzying sensation that she'd suddenly been turned head over heels.

Chapter Twenty-Eight

One

They'd died quickly.

Sam Baker stood beside Zita while they both looked down at the three bodies – two men and a woman, all three middle-aged.

'Hell, what a way to go,' Zita said in a hushed voice.

Towards the bottom of the amphitheatre a mass of brambles sprouted; they hadn't been there before, and had simply appeared at the last time-jump.

As well as the thick purple strands of old bramble growth there were new shoots covered in a profusion of leaves that were a fresh green. And lying there, as if they'd been dropped from above, were the three bodies.

At first glance it looked as if they'd fallen into the brambles and become trapped there. A closer inspection showed that the brambles were trapped *in them*.

It had happened again.

Those fifty or so people in the amphitheatre had been transported back through time. For an unlucky few there was already solid material occupying the same space as they'd materialized.

Sam remembered only too well the fate of the birdman, the girl in the tree; even that fish in Jud's boat, its rounded head bulging from the cabin wall.

Now three more people had suffered a similar fate. Brambles sprouted from their stomachs, legs, chests, arms and faces, as if some mad gardener had planted in their skin blackberry seeds that had sprouted explosively from their bodies.

Sam felt a sick feeling rising in his throat as he saw a bramble stalk as thick as his finger growing wild and green from a man's widely-open eye. Inside, their bodies must be a riot of shoots, thorns, leaves that had interrupted the function of the organs the moment the people had flashed into existence here . . . *whenever* here was.

Lee Burton and Nicole Wagner returned from the visitors' centre with scissors and began cutting through the brambles. It was tough work, but both were adamant they weren't going to leave their clients there, grotesquely dead amid the blackberry plants.

Sam found himself admiring the three travel reps. They were unswervingly loyal to the people their employer had assigned to their care. This must surely be above and beyond the call of duty. Nicole hacked through the tough greenery to free the arm of a corpse; the scissors made sharp clicking sounds. Lee had already caught his knuckles on a briar; blood stood out from the skin in tiny crimson beads.

Ryan Keith in his Oliver Hardy costume still sat on an amphitheatre bench. He was withdrawn from the world. Clearly he had no intention of helping his colleagues. Even though it was impossible to resign his position – in reality the company he worked for wouldn't exist for another God knew how many years – he had, however, resigned emotionally.

Jud walked across to stand beside Sam. Looking down at the three corpses, he shook his head. 'Tragic . . . tragic.' He took a deep breath. 'You know, our numbers are dropping. I calculate a good half a dozen or so didn't make it through the last time-jump. There's these three. Nicole here told us what happened to Bostock. And there're others missing.'

'Any idea what happened?'

'From what the coach driver said, three people got into a

green car and took off at high speed. I can only imagine they were in an accident; all must have died.'

'Otherwise they'd have been back here and in one piece after the last time-slip?'

'Correct.'

Lee looked up as he snipped through a particularly tough briar that protruded from the throat of the woman. 'Sam, would you do me a favour?'

'Sure.'

'There's a toilet door up at the visitor's centre. We used it last time as a stretcher. Would you bring it down here, please?'

'No problem,' Sam said and headed up the steps that led out of the amphitheatre.

Jud followed him.

'What are they doing, Sam?' he asked.

'They're using the museum area of the visitors' centre as a temporary morgue.'

'But why?'

'To store the bodies. You'll have noticed they're starting to mount up.'

'But as far as I can see, when people have died they've simply not come through the time-slip with us. They're out of the game.'

At the top of the steps Sam stopped and looked back down at the two reps cutting briars that held the bodies down in their seats as effectively as the little threads that bound Gulliver to the ground in Lilliput. 'Out of the game,' he repeated, thoughtfully. 'You said that before. Out of the game. Do you think that's what all this really is? Are we just being toyed with by . . . by, I don't know, beings from another dimension? Scientists from the future? Are we just a kind of laboratory rat involved in an experiment we know nothing about? Or maybe it's the Devil. And this is just one of his diabolical little tricks.'

'I don't know, Sam. But it has that feel, doesn't it? We're whisked back through time. When we reappear we are exactly how we were when we first made that jump in 1999.

We're sitting in the same seats or standing in exactly the same positions. We wear the same clothes. If we were hurt in one time period we are suddenly healed when we make the next jump.'

'Nicole and Lee find themselves back in their costumes. Carswell pawned his ring in 1946. Just now he showed me it was back on his little finger. So how does it work, Jud? What's the mechanism that's pulling us back?'

Jud shrugged. 'If anything, we're duplicates of the originals. You can imagine some kind of celestial photo-copier churning out copies of ourselves. We might damage ourselves, we might lose our possessions, we could even burn down the visitors' centre. But don't you bet that after the next time-jump everything is back as it was? The cars are full of fuel, there are drinks in the vending machine. If our clothes are damaged, they're magically repaired.'

'And I opened my eyes to find that the handcuffs had vanished. But the only glitch is that the part of the land that forms our time raft isn't being transported back as smoothly as before. The integrity of transmission is suffering inter-ference. Look, you can see it from up here. You can see how a line of greenery begins near the altar in the centre of the amphitheatre there. As it runs out to the edge of the amphitheatre it gets wider and wider so it resembles some-thing like a triangle, or . . . or even a wedge of pie.'

'And in that wedge of pie . . .' Jud nodded, 'if you're unlucky enough to find yourself sitting in that area . . .'

'You are fused with whatever's occupying the same space. And the results, as we have seen, are pretty shitty.'

As they talked they saw Carswell step off his millionaire launch. He sauntered up the grass slope to the side of the amphitheatre, then followed the edge of the car park. The man jerked his head back at the car park. 'Another car gone, I see.' He'd indicated a car that looked as if a bush was sprouting from the bonnet; even the cabin was filled with greenery.

Trust Carswell to notice the damage to property, not to people, Sam told himself. There were three people lying there dead in the briars, their hearts and lungs full of twisting greenery. But, oh no, the commercially-tuned Carswell would only notice that a ten-thousand-bucks car had been ruined.

Overhead a plane lumbered heavily across a cloudy sky.

'Any idea what year this is?' Carswell asked, sounding almost cheerful.

Jud nodded at the bodies down below. 'We were distracted. We didn't think to run into town this time and buy a damn' newspaper.' He sounded angered by Carswell's nonchalance towards the tragedy. But then, he hadn't given a damn about the girl dying.

Sam shrugged, 'I'm going to get the door.'

'The door?' Carswell sounded puzzled.

'We're using a door to stretcher the bodies of those people down there up to the visitors' centre.' Sam found himself speaking through clenched teeth as if talking to a fool who'd just shit his pants and not thought anything more about it. 'We're using the place as a mortuary. Hadn't you noticed?'

Carswell didn't respond, or even give any indication he'd heard the reply. 'Take a look over the treetops. Those things floating in the sky will give you a clue what year we've alighted in this time.'

Sam was already walking away. He didn't want to talk to Carswell. Moving the bodies was a grisly business, but in a way there was normality about it. After all, the only certainty in the world was that people were born; then, at some point, those people would die. To be involved with moving those bodies was hardly reassuring but, oddly, encountering death like this actually anchored Sam's sanity.

When he reached the visitors' centre he was surprised to find Carswell shadowing him. 'Are you blind, man? Look above the treetops.'

This time Sam glanced up. He paused, surprised despite himself, by what bobbed on the warm summer breeze.

'Barrage balloons,' Carswell said. 'There's probably twenty or more of them. You know what this means?'

Sam didn't want to know. Right now it seemed important to move those bodies from the glare of the sun – and the public view. He went inside to find the toilet-door-cum-stretcher.

Carswell called after him. 'It's wartime. We've arrived back slap bang in the middle of World War Two.'

Even as he spoke the words a siren began to wail in the distance.

Two

By the time they'd moved the bodies the siren sounded again. Instead of the notes rising and falling there was only a continuous tone. 'That's the all-clear,' Jud said as Nicole locked the visitors' centre door.

'I didn't hear any bombs falling.' Lee looked up into the sky, his eyes narrowing against the brilliance of the sun.

'It may have been a false alarm. I expect there must have been plenty of those.'

'Was Casterton ever bombed in the war?'

'Several times. Mainly the target was the airfield. Goering wanted to nobble the RAF so Hitler could invade Britain.'

Nicole left Jud and Lee talking. She walked to the edge of the car park. Now it was clear where the boundaries of this chunk of 1990s land ended and the world of the 1940s began. At this side of the boundary, the Nineties side, the grass was short, no longer than an average lawn. Then suddenly the long grass of yesteryear began. It was probably waist-high, and thick with thistles and nettles. She followed the line of the boundary with her eyes. It followed a curve, and it didn't take any stretch of the imagination to see that it actually formed a circle with the amphitheatre in the centre.

She found herself gazing at the wood where the blond-haired man had saved her life. Was he there still?

Watching her?

As her eyes searched the trees and the deeply shadowed ground beneath the branches she sensed she *was* being watched.

Not by one person.

But by many.

Three

On the deck of the launch Carswell opened the bottle of champagne. With a pop the cork flew out to drop into the river.

Although none of them could be sure of the time they knew it was evening. The red disc of the sun rested on the hills across the river.

'Are you sure you won't join me?' Carswell asked as he poured the champagne into a fluted glass.

Sam shook his head.

'It seems such a waste not to drink it. Because every time I do and there's another one of these little hops back through time, I find the bottle has magically reappeared in the refrigerator. Mmmm . . .' He smacked his lips. 'And it tastes as good as ever.'

With the exception of Carswell, there was an apathy settling among the hardly happy band of accidental time travellers. It was inevitable that there would be another time–leap soon; inevitable, also, that people would be maimed or even die. And there was nothing they could do about it. Their only hope was the man Rolle, but where was he now?

Jud had half-heartedly suggested driving into town to try and find Rolle, as well as discovering the date, but it all seemed pretty much academic to them now. What did it matter what they did?

They were as helpless as kittens swept away on some flood torrent.

Carswell had brought up onto the deck a radio that he'd left playing on the table at his side. The air was full of light swing music with a trumpet taking the lead. Sam had thought the sound quality would be tinny and so full of crackles it would be like listening to someone cooking a stir-fry; instead it was remarkably clear. As lush-sounding as any 1999 radio broadcast.

Sam sipped water from a glass. Above him a two-engined prop-driven plane lumbered overhead with a low *vrooming* sound.

Carswell glanced up. 'A Wellington, if I'm not mistaken. A medium bomber, probably heading east to bomb Germany. And here I am, sitting drinking champagne. Funny old universe, isn't it?'

Sam grunted. Right now it would feel good just to climb into bed, pull the covers over his head and wait until all this was over.

'You know,' Carswell said, 'perhaps what we should be doing is breaking open that stone altar in the middle of the amphitheatre.'

'Why?'

'Because as far as I can see, Sam, old boy, that altar lies exactly dead centre in this circle of land that is being transported back through time.'

'What good would that do?'

'You never know, we might crack open that stone to find the circuitry of some futuristic device.'

'You mean some kind of time machine?'

'Exactly.'

'I don't think it's going to be as simple as that, do you?'

'Well, it's time we tried to seize the initiative rather than just being blown back through time as though we're nothing more than a handful of leaves drifting on the breeze. Listen, I've got the tools to break that stone open.'

'But you won't do it.'

'What's there to stop me?'

'Listen. I sat in the amphitheatre looking down at that stone slab on the twenty-third of June, 1999. It had six bowl-shaped hollows carved on the top, with a slot in the centre.'

'I don't follow.'

'Well, in 1999 it was intact. It hadn't been destroyed then. So you couldn't have destroyed it sixty years before.'

'So what you're getting at is that we're not physically capable of doing anything that changes history.'

'Yes.'

'Therefore we couldn't, say, grab an aeroplane from the RAF station up the road there, somehow fly to Germany, assassinate Hitler and end the war in 1943, or whatever year this is?'

'That's exactly what I'm saying, Carswell.'

'Interesting.'

'Interesting?'

'Very interesting.' Carswell sipped his champagne. 'After all, think about it, the man who controls time controls the world. Imagine if you could travel back in time at will and kill your enemies as children. Or even kill their parents before your enemy is even born.'

'Or what if you travelled back in time and killed your own father before you were born? Do you just vanish into thin air the second you pull the trigger? No, I don't think that's possible.'

Carswell wanted to push the conversation. Sam, however, felt as if his whole spirit had been shot to pieces. After a couple of moments of Carswell suggesting they smash open the stone altar with hammers to prove that you could go back into time and change events – such as destroying an object that Sam had clearly seen in 1999 – Sam was ready to leave the boat to find somewhere quiet to sit and recharge his mental and emotional batteries. He thanked Carswell for the water and had already reached the gangplank when he heard Carswell call him. 'Wait, the news is about to start.'

Sam very nearly didn't stay and listen to it. But as the chimes of Big Ben died on the radio he found himself pausing just to hear the headlines.

'This is the BBC calling the world from London. My name is Henry Squires and this is the news at nine o'clock on

Sunday, the twenty-eighth of May, 1944.' Typical of the BBC newsreaders of the time, the archetypal Home Counties voice was devoid of any regional accent. It reeked of dinner jackets and smart London clubs. Sam, however, found himself listening hard. For a moment he didn't realize what had caught his attention. Something important . . . very important. The twin-jointed digits that served as his thumbs began to tingle outrageously. But why? What was so important about that date? The voice came loud and clear from the speaker: 'Polish troops have captured the fortress of Monte Cassino. The German Gustav line in Italy has been fatally breached and Allied commanders expect rapid advances into enemy-held territory . . .'

The tingling rose to a crescendo until the scars felt as if they were being pricked by dozens of needles.

Sunday, the twenty-eighth of May, 1944.

Suddenly the significance of that date slammed home. Sam caught his breath; he found himself clenching his fists so hard his whole body trembled.

'Anything the matter, Sam?'

Sam looked at Carswell. 'That date . . . did he say the twenty eighth of May?'

'Yes. May, 1944. So, now we know the date . . . what's so special about it?'

'Before the last time-slip I was just about to be arrested for murder.'

'Well, that was 1946, old boy. This is 1944, so I'd say you're well out of it, wouldn't you?'

'No,' Sam said quickly. 'Don't you see? That guy shoved a newspaper at me. It said the murder took place on the night of Sunday, May the twenty-eighth.'

'Well, that's tonight.' Carswell nonchalantly sipped his champagne. 'But you don't seriously intend to do anything about it, do you?'

'A family was murdered. For some reason the police put me in the frame. I saw my photograph in that newspaper.'

'Then stay put. You can even lock yourself in a cabin downstairs until it's all over. Then you can't be blamed, can you?'

'Look, Carswell,' Sam said as if explaining that one plus one equals two to an idiot. 'At this moment that family in Casterton are still alive. But in a few hours someone's going to kill them, now—'

'Ah, ah . . . Sam.' Casterton wagged his finger. 'Despite what you've just told me about the impossibility of changing past events, you're now suggesting that you hare off, heroically save this family who you don't even know, and do exactly that: change history.'

Sam had altered his watch in line with the time given by the newsreader. He glanced at it. 'I can't sit back and let it happen. If I do that I might as well have slit their throats myself.'

He ran to the gangplank.

'Wait a moment, Sam Baker.' Carswell stood up and fixed him with a hard stare. 'Are you sure you won't murder the family?'

'Do I look like a murderer?'

Carswell shrugged. 'What murderer does go around in a T-shirt bearing the slogan *I'm A Killer*?'

Sam didn't hesitate.

He ran from the boat up the slope in the direction of the amphitheatre.

Behind him Carswell called, 'Think about it, Sam Baker. The police suspected you of the killing. They must have had a good reason for reaching that conclusion. Isn't that worth thinking about?'

Four

Even a hare-brained scheme is better than nothing. Those were Sam's thoughts as he ran into the amphitheatre. And while he didn't know exactly what he could do, he decided to drive into the Casterton of 1944.

As he approached the stone altar slab in the centre of the amphitheatre he slowed down. Dusk was gradually becoming night.

Think of it, he told himself. At first these leaps through time had seemed completely random. In 1946 he was being arrested for a murder committed in 1944. Now he was here a few hours before that murder happened. Surely that couldn't be just a bizarre coincidence?

Someone, or at least some intelligence, must have deposited him here to give him the opportunity of acting.

But was that to save the family?

Or, as Carswell had suggested, to kill them?

Was there any chance he might become a homicidal maniac between here and Casterton?

No. He didn't think so.

But *someone* killed the family.

Is there a chance I can warn them? he asked himself as he gazed at the stone slab. *And have I been deliberately put here on the evening of 28 May 1944 to do exactly that?*

But who by?

Whoever's at the controls of the time machine, of course.

Just for a moment, the mental image of a scientist in the distant future shone as bright and clear as a summer's day. A human being with a massively evolved brain yet an atrophied body: he pictured it there, looking like some kind of man-sized foetus, two dot-like eyes beneath a huge, bulging forehead, staring at a TV screen that carried images of what he, Sam Baker, was doing now: standing there in his chinos, lemon cotton shirt and loafers, running his hand thoughtfully over the stone slab.

Then futurity's scientists with those tiny atrophied hands, nothing more than fleshy buds for fingers, would stretch out to key another day and year into their time machine.

Then, *zip!* Before you could say 'Jack Robinson' this band of travellers would be catapulted back through time again. When then? 1923? Or 1903? So he could read in the newspapers that the Wright Brothers had flown at Kitty

Hawk? Or why not back to the English Civil War so they could be butchered by the Roundheads or Cavaliers? Or even further back, into the depths of the Ice Age when glaciers were grinding mountain ranges to paste and this little bunch of refugees from 1999 could freeze to death in some shrieking blizzard.

Sam made a coughing sound. But it was no cough as such. It was something like a laugh – the madcap laugh of someone pushed dangerously close to the edge.

He glared at the stone slab.

Perhaps that foetus-like creature of his imagination in distant futurity was conducting an experiment. Perhaps he, Sam Baker, and his fellow travellers were nothing more than laboratory rats engaged in finding their way through some temporal maze.

Again he thought of them being examined by those two chilling eyes that were no larger than dots on a page. Maybe their performance, their reactions to death, to arrest, to their out-and-out confusion was being monitored by that cold intelligence.

Hey, Sam, but what would really be hilarious would be if we were all taking part in some future game show. Where contestants drop their characters into all kinds of zany, zany situations in the funky past. Then they guess the outcome, place their bets. Woweee . . . what a ratings puller that would be.

Bastard. Sam kicked the slab of stone. The blow sounded like a gunshot.

The impact must have bruised his toes. But he felt nothing.

Nothing physically, anyway.

But at that moment he experienced such a burning rage. He'd never felt like this before, not even when he'd realized his boyhood friends had been cooked alive by the force of that lightning strike.

Bastard . . .

The force of the emotion winded him.

He'd just allowed his imagination to run a little with that idea. The idea that they were being manipulated by some intelligence, either for fun or research. OK, he didn't know for sure, but he sure as hell felt he was on the right lines.

It couldn't be coincidence that he'd been dropped back in time just a couple of hours or so before the murder.

Like Lee Burton before him, Sam had decided that all this was deliberate; that he'd become part of someone else's plan; that he was being tested.

But for what purpose?

And by whom?

Christ Almighty, if he ever got his hands around their necks he'd twist . . . and twist . . .

'You look a little off-colour, Sam, old boy,' Carswell murmured as he sat on the altar stone. 'And if I may go so far, a little wild around the eyes.'

'Shut up.' Sam realized he was leaning forward, his clenched fists resting on the slab; rage flowed like electricity through him.

'What if I don't? You'll kill me?'

Sam expelled the air from his lungs in a rush. 'We're being used. Some bastard's doing this.' He looked up at the sky, half expecting to see some tiny spy camera floating there. 'They're watching us.'

'That smacks of paranoia, but I have to say I suspect the same. So what will— Sam?'

Sam had turned to march furiously away up the steps of the amphitheatre.

'Where are you going, Sam?'

Sam fired back over his shoulder, 'I'm going to give them what they want. *Action!*'

Chapter Twenty-Nine

One

The controllers of this time machine were sitting at arm's length.

Sam told himself this as he drove into town through the gathering dusk. Perhaps if he behaved in a way they found intriguing enough it might lure them out and make them show themselves.

For one near-insane moment he entertained the notion that they might actually be inside the stone slab in the amphitheatre. That somehow they were sitting hunched there like astronauts inside their tiny time capsule, pulling levers, turning dials, keying in new coordinates. Again he thought of them as foetus-like creatures: tiny, wasted legs, their bodies no bigger than a baby's yet topped with huge bulging heads; the tiny pinprick eyes and nearly non-existent jaw and mouth.

And yes, God damn it, couldn't you just see that big pulse beating away there in their big bald heads?

Right at that moment he was ready to seize a hammer and bludgeon his way into the stone slab.

But no, they must be more sophisticated than that. Surely this must be a remote operation. They would be sitting in a control centre, directing the project from there, every so often deciding to turn that dial and send him, Sam Baker,

Jud, Zita, Nicole and the rest rolling back through time to another year.

Of course it was purely imagination. He had no real way of knowing the truth, but, nevertheless, he pictured those time shifters sitting in something like a TV director's control room, just as he himself had done hundreds of times before, mixing live TV transmissions and directing his camera operators to zoom in on one particular player or to cut to a long-shot of the spectators.

But how to coax them out of that control room; how to trick them into revealing themselves? That was the real problem.

The road was deserted in front of him. He pushed the car faster until the needle touched seventy.

Above him barrage balloons hung in the air, looking like huge silver whales dozing in the depths of the sea.

He drove, knowing that he must do something to save that innocent family. But how? That was the question.

Two

Nicole found herself staring into the wood once more.

By now it was almost dark. A moon like a silver fingernail clipping shone high in the sky.

Someone in there was watching her. She was sure of it.

With her left hand holding her right elbow, she paced slowly backwards and forwards along the edge of the car park, hoping that the watcher would show himself.

Himself?

Yes, she was certain. It must be the blond-haired man dressed in medieval clothes. The man with the pair of eyes in his stomach. She remembered how he'd stood guard over the dying birdman, saying, 'He's one of us now.'

One of *us*?

That suggested that there were more of them. What unusual physical attributes did they have?

'Nicole . . . *Nicole*.' Startled she turned.

Jud was hurrying towards her. In his hand he carried a book.

Breathlessly he said, 'I'm not trying to alarm people but I thought everyone should be forewarned.'

'Forewarned about what?'

'I've been checking this.' He showed her a paperback book entitled *Casterton: A Pictorial History*. 'I remembered Casterton was bombed half a dozen times in the Second World War and . . . well, tonight's the night of one of the worst attacks.'

Nicole felt her eyes go wide. 'Do you know where the bombs fell?'

'The Nazi bombers were aiming for the airbase just outside town; however, a number of bombs fell wide. Some of the town buildings were hit.'

'What about here? Are we safe?'

'I think so, but I'm asking everyone to stay inside the amphitheatre. I'm pretty sure that wasn't touched.'

'Do you need any help in telling people?'

'No, that's everyone now. Oh, with the exception of Sam Baker. Have you seen him?'

'Yes, but he drove out of here about ten minutes ago. I assumed he was heading into town.'

'Oh, damn.' Jud took a deep breath. 'Oh, damn and blast.'

In the pause after Jud had spoken a sound like a ghostly wail came rolling across the fields.

'Well, that's the air-raid warning,' Jud said, heavily. 'Let's just pray he keeps his head down.'

Three

A couple of miles outside town Sam braked hard.

There, in the headlights, was a figure. It was hurrying towards him along the centre of the road. Every so often, it would turn and clamp its hands to the top of its head as if anticipating that disaster would strike the town at any moment.

There was no mistaking the figure – tall, orange overalls, fuzz of ginger hair.

Sam rolled the window down while edging the car forward.

The moment he opened the window the sound came in at him. It was the unmistakable rising and falling wail of the air-raid siren.

On the edge of town a beam of light sprang from the ground to play slowly in the sky, as if it was a single brilliant eye looking for danger. Soon it was joined by more and more until a dozen or so searchlights probed the dark sky.

Sam flashed the headlights. 'Rolle . . . Rolle?'

The man wheeled round, staggered for a moment as if dizzy, or drunk, then fixed his eyes on Sam's face.

'Baker? Baker, Baker, Baker man! Bake me a cake as quick as— no, no!' He chewed his finger and shook his head as if determined not to permit his mind to career away. He pointed a dirty finger with all the emphasis of the profoundly drunk. 'Sam Baker. Yes. I remember you, from tomorrow.' He ran his hand distractedly through his hair. *'Tomorrow.'*

'Rolle? Are you going out to the amphitheatre?'

'Yes . . . you'll drive me there?'

'No, I can't, there's something I've got to do in town'

'Pity, pity . . .'

'But Jud's out there at the amphitheatre. You remember Jud Campbell?'

'Yes, I remember, I remember.' He rubbed his jaw, his face the picture of troubled anxiety. 'Grave news, Baker man. Grave news. There's a bad storm coming. There's—'

'You mean an air raid? That's what the sirens are warning, isn't it?'

'Oh, yes, indeed, sir. But it's far worse than this. The integrity of the time stream is in jeopardy. Already the Liminals are escaping into the here and now; like water leaking from a ruptured pipe.' He threw out his arms and made a *whee-eesh* sound.

'I'm sorry, I don't know what you mean. Look, Rolle, we

can talk later, but I've got to get into town. Do you know anything about a family who were— Rolle . . . Rolle?'

But Rolle had already run on, rubbing both hands through that ginger mop of hair.

Sam struck the steering wheel.

Damn. Where was The Rookery, for God's sake?

He glanced at his watch. Almost ten. Already he might be too late. The family could be lying there butchered. What then? He'd stumble on the aftermath. Be spotted by the reporter. Then the blame'd be pinned neatly on him?

He looked sideways through the window. A man in a white helmet was running towards him. Sam was going to ask him directions but at that moment the man blew a whistle. 'Hey! Put those ruddy lights out. What are you playing at?' He came forward, puffing heavily. 'Fer heaven's sake, man, Hitler himself'll be able to see them flaming headlights from his bedroom window.'

Sam killed his lights. 'I'm sorry, I—'

'You'll have the Jerry bombers dumping everything they've got on our flaming heads; don't you . . . hey, what kind of car is this, anyway?' The man's eyes bulged wide in astonishment as he approached the Range Rover. 'Where's the car headlight covers? Surely you know wartime regulations stipulate lights have to be masked?'

'I'm trying to find a place called The Rookery.' Sam sensed the seconds ticking away. 'Can you give me directions, please?'

'The Rookery . . .' the man repeated distantly, taking more interest in the car than the question. His wide eyes took in the lines of the car, reading it like it was a piece of text. 'What model is this? Those number plates don't look right to me. Is it foreign?'

Of course it is, I'm the advance guard of the German invasion, you idiot! The words flashed through Sam's head; it was all he could do to stop them slipping from his mouth.

The ARP warden backed away a little now. He looked suspiciously at Sam.

'Now, now,' the man said in a low voice. 'There's something funny going on here. How'd you come by a car like this? Where are—'

Sam didn't hang around any longer. He floored the accelerator and the car surged powerfully away.

He glanced at his watch again. It was almost ten.

He didn't have much time left. He could feel it in his bones.

Chapter Thirty

One

Sam had driven away from the man and found himself on a deserted country road. There was no traffic at all. Ahead the searchlights probed the sky.

He'd been driving for barely twenty seconds when he saw a woman walking along the darkened pavement in the direction of town.

The temptation was simply to keep driving into town in the hope he'd find someone else who could direct him to The Rookery. But it occurred to him that the air-raid warning would have driven everyone to the shelters. The streets would be deserted.

He pulled up alongside the woman who was walking as quickly as she could.

'Excuse me,' he called through the open window. 'I need some directions.'

'And I need a lift,' she said quickly. Before he could say anything she'd opened the nearside door and climbed into the passenger seat beside him.

'What a stinking awful night,' she said. 'My bus never turned up. I've walked all the way from the base. I've done it before during the day but it's murder at night.'

'The base?'

'RAF Casterton.'

He saw the uniform. 'Oh? You're a . . .' he searched for the word. 'A WAAF?'

'That's right.' She smiled. 'And you're an American? Unless you're a German spy, of course?'

'No, right first time. American.'

'New York?'

'It shows.'

'You *are* a New Yorker?' She shot him a broader smile. Her lips were painted a vivacious red. 'I thought I recognized the accent. I work with an American liaison officer from Brooklyn so I reckoned you must be from the same neck of the woods.'

Sam accelerated the car away. He could almost feel his watch against the back of his wrist, beating there like a tiny heart-beat, pumping away those seconds. Again, it struck him he might be too late.

'I was delayed getting away from the base. You see, I wangled a forty-eight-hour pass so I could be at my sister's wedding tomorrow in Harrogate. She'd marrying a Canadian flight engineer. There's a train leaves Casterton at eleven; at least now I should make it with time to spare. Thanks.'

'I need to get to someplace in town called The Rookery. Do you know it?'

'Rookery, Rookery,' she murmured hunting through her memory. 'Ah, yes. Swish houses on the north side of town.'

'Houses?' He'd assumed it was the name of one house.

'Yes, there's a few of them built around a square. Wowee,' she exclaimed. 'Some car you've got here . . . Mr, uhm?'

'Sam.'

She reached out to shake his hand. He noticed she wore blue cotton gloves to match the uniform. 'Delighted to meet you, Sam. I'm Ruth.' She grinned. 'It's short for Ruthless. That's what my brothers always called me when I beat them at tennis.' She looked back at the dashboard, the instruments all backlit now with a soft green light. 'But, wow, what a car. I've never seen anything like this before.'

'Latest model,' he said, driving harder.

'Military?'

'Of course.'

'Mum's the word. Careless talk and all that. Mind if I smoke?'

'Be my guest.'

'You drive fast.'

'Sorry, I'm in a hurry.'

'Matter of life and death, huh?'

He nodded.

She sighed. 'It always is these days. Look at those search-lights. Once they've got a Jerry plane in their sights . . .' She pointed a finger at the sky as if it was a pistol. 'Pow, pow. Of course, it's either them or us.'

He drove along the deserted High Street, noticing that the windows of the shops and houses were covered with a criss-cross pattern of sticky tape intended to at least minimize injuries caused by flying glass if a bomb landed close enough to shatter the window.

All the street lights were out – deliberately extinguished because of the blackout. In fact, not a glimmer of light shone through the heavily curtained windows of the houses. For all the world it could have been a ghost town, with no moving vehicles, no lights, no people.

Sam, driving on sidelights alone, hoped a horse or truck wouldn't lumber out in front of him. At this speed there'd be a God Almighty mess.

'Deserted again. Bloody air-raid; I hate it when it looks like this,' she said. 'Spooky, isn't it? Oh, take a left here.'

He braked hard, swung the car, and the tyres slid on the ever-present horse droppings that formed a slippery mat on every street.

'What do all these switches do?' she asked, looking down at the dashboard as he accelerated along the side street.

'Lights, heating, CD'

'Seedy?'

'No. CD.' All he wanted to do was be at the house where the murder was going to take place; so without really thinking he hit the play button. Music boomed from the car's four speakers, the massive bass sound vibrating the steering wheel in his hands.

Startled Ruth looked round for where the sound was coming from. 'Wow, that's loud. Who's the singer?'

'Michael Stipe. He's from an American band called REM.'

'REM. That's a new one on me. Is this kind of music popular in America?'

'It will be.' Sam gripped the steering wheel. His muscles were tense. He scanned the blackened street. 'How far to The Rookery now?'

'It's just past that church on your right. There! There's the entrance . . . just where that truck's parked.'

Sam turned the Range Rover into another narrow street that opened onto a square lined with big detached houses. These, too, were all in darkness. The only movement was from the trees in the grassed area of the square. They swayed in the breeze.

Sam switched off the engine and killed the lights.

There were no sirens now. Searchlights silently probed the night sky. Hanging directly above them, a barrage balloon revealed a silvery underbelly when touched by the million-watt beam of a searchlight.

'My train leaves in three-quarters of an hour,' Ruth said, almost warily, as if unsure about Sam now, and why he'd torn through the town's streets to get here. 'I'll start walking.' She climbed out of the car. Yet, despite what she'd just said, she stood there, holding a small suitcase in one hand as if reluctant to leave.

Sam walked slowly away from the car, all the time looking up at the darkened faces of the houses. It was one of these. This was where a man, a woman and their child would have their throats cut tonight.

Unless, that is, he could stop it happening.

But that would mean he would have changed history.

The repercussions would be enormous.

Perhaps he should just walk away now. Let whatever would happen, happen.

Otherwise his actions would alter the future. Even if he could return to 1999 he might find the world completely different because of what he did tonight.

But is a little child going to trigger a nuclear war in 1955?

Would that child from a 1940s Britain have the power to change the world if her life was saved tonight?

Possibly. Often a single individual changed the whole course of history.

He shook his head as he scanned the silent houses. No. Forget the philosophical arguments. He had the opportunity to prevent three murders. That was the bottom line; that was all that mattered.

He couldn't walk away from here now.

Already he could imagine those foetus-like creatures nodding wisely as their stunted little fingers pressed the keys on their time machine or whatever goddamned mechanism was controlling all this. *Ah, yes*, they'd say. *The human being was a coward after all, and far too ignorant and weak to control events around him.*

'Bastard,' he said glaring up at the sky. Again that rage he'd experienced earlier roared through him. It was a rage on the edge of insanity. *Why are we being subjected to this?* Whoever was responsible should have their miserable necks wrung, wrung hard until their eyes popped and they died black-lipped and pissing themselves . . . That dark engulfing wave of fury . . . boundless, insane fury swept down on him. 'The bastards!'

Ruth took a hesitant step towards him. 'Sam? Are you all right? *Sam, don't . . .*'

But that was when he lunged at her, grabbed her by her jacket and dragged her into the bushes.

Two

She tried to cry out; her eyes were bright with terror in the darkness.

'Sam, please, I—'

He pushed his palm across her lipstick-red mouth, stifling the coming scream. Her eyes bulged in shock as he pushed her further back into the branches where no one would see them from the road.

He looked into those bulging eyes to see a premonition of her own agonizing death written there.

'Shhh . . .' he whispered. 'They'll hear you.'

From the way she blinked Sam saw she wished whoever *they* were would hear her, then come running to free her.

He didn't release his grip, holding her in a bear hug with one arm while his other hand still sealed her mouth; he could feel the frightened exhalations from her nostrils blowing against his hand. Her eyes were locked on his, clearly expecting at any moment to feel his hands around her throat.

'Shh,' he whispered again, still not taking his hand away. 'There's going to be a murder committed tonight.'

Her frightened eyes went impossibly round, like milk-white discs.

'No,' he whispered quickly. 'It's not you. Don't be afraid of me. Listen. A family are in danger in one of those houses across there. Do you understand?'

She nodded as best she could with his hand across her mouth.

'I've just seen a man come out of the front door and leave a sack or a bag in the garden. I think he's robbing the place, so that must be the house. But . . . but I'm afraid . . . I'm afraid I might be too late. Now, do you follow me?'

She nodded again. Her eyes looked less terrified now and were fixed intelligently on his.

'Now, I'm sorry I frightened you,' he said gently. 'But I don't want that hoodlum to know I'm here. OK?'

A nod again. The breath against his hand was calmer now.

He let her go, noticing the lipstick had smeared against one cheek. 'It's that house across there. With the green door that's slightly open.'

She nodded, then asked, 'Are you a detective?'

He nearly lied and told her he was, then thought better of it. To explain why an American was serving in the British police would become just too convoluted. 'I was told about this in a bar.' He shot her a look. 'I'm just trying to be a good citizen. That's all . . . Now . . . shh . . . here they come again.'

A tiny amount of light was thrown back from the searchlights by the clouds. It revealed a bulky figure stepping furtively through the door. It carried a holdall of some sorts. Sam heard the clink of glass. The robber was obviously clearing as much as he could carry from the house.

But where were the occupants?

A cold sensation slipped through his stomach. They weren't making a fuss about being robbed.

That was far from a good sign.

The cold sensation intensified as Sam ran lightly across the street and peered through the hedge between the front garden and the pavement.

Hell, this didn't look good at all. A man lay slumped through the front doorway. Even in this light he could see that the man wore a grey cardigan. A curved pipe that he must have been smoking when he answered the knock on the door lay on the lawn beside a flower border. A pool of something dark and sticky stretched out around the man's head on the concrete path.

Sam, peering through the hedge, saw the bulky figure appear again. It didn't step over the fallen man. Instead the figure stood on the centre of his back as if he was a stepping stone and came out into the garden carrying a large brass bowl.

Sam ducked back as the figure approached the hedge from the other side. He heard the clink of the bowl being carefully eased into the sack to rest among glassware.

But there was another sound too. Sam cocked his head to one side, puzzled.

There was the sound of sizzling. Almost like bacon gently frying in a pan. No, not quite. More like sand being drizzled onto paper. The faint sizzling was continuous. And it was certainly coming from the bulky figure on the far side of the hedge.

Sam glanced back at the crouching WAAF, her eyes bright in the darkness.

She shook her head, as if she'd heard the sound, too, and didn't know what to make of it.

When the figure had returned to ransacking the house Sam whispered back. 'Ruth. Go and wait for me in the car.'

'Why? You'll need help here.'

'No, go back and wait there. If I don't come out by, let's see . . . four minutes from now, sound the horn; it's the big round button in the centre of the steering wheel. That should bring people out of their houses.'

'I wouldn't be so sure. Didn't you hear the air-raid sirens? Everyone's going to be tucked up in their Anderson shelters.'

'Well, shout, yell. Do anything to bring the people out.'

'Call the police, Sam, you can't—'

'There's no time. As I said I might be too late already. Now, go.'

He waited until she ran crouching back to the car.

Then, crouching himself, he slipped in through the garden gate, up the path, past the unconscious man (Sam's shoes made sticky kissing sounds as he stepped in the pool of blood) before he was through into the hallway of the house.

These were big houses.

The staircase curved upwards into the darkness above.

Silence.

Nothing to tell him where the robber would be.

And dark, oh, so dark. It was gloomy enough outside but here he could see nothing at all.

He turned until his back was against the wall. There he stood for a moment, his heart hammering like a runaway motor.

Where was the robber now? He could be standing there in the darkness, watching Sam while easing a knife from his pocket.

Sam raised one hand to his throat to protect it from any slashing attack from the darkness.

He eased sideways, deeper into the house, his back still to the wall.

Oddly, a smell of wet wool hung on the air. Underpinning that was a sharper tang of body odour. It was far from pleasant and certainly seemed out of place in this upmarket residence.

He worked his way carefully round a table, feeling the boxy shape of a Bakelite telephone and the plaited strands of the fabric-covered handset cable. Then he touched cold metal.

Again it was a boxy shape, with what appeared to be a funnel attached to one side. Like a blind man he allowed his fingers to slide over the object, sensing its metallic smoothness. Then his finger bumped against a lump at one end. A switch . . . electrical equipment . . .

Bicycle lamp.

The words flashed through his mind.

Thank God for that, he thought with relief. He gripped the lamp in one hand, then moved forward, muscles tense, ears straining for the smallest sound.

Three

The intruder must be in here, Sam told himself as he inched forward along the hallway. *He must be in one of the rooms, plundering more loot.*

He licked his dry lips.

The fallen man in the doorway must have been the father. He might already be dead. That left the mother and eight-year-old daughter. Now where were they?

By touch alone he moved deeper into the house.

Ahead lay the greyish tombstone shape of an open doorway.

Cautiously he moved through it, expecting at any moment to hear a yell as the robber saw him.

He found himself holding his breath; his chest ached, and it seemed his heartbeat went thumping through his ribs to echo with horrifying loudness throughout the house.

His eyes adjusted to a little light coming through an uncurtained window-pane.

It took only a moment for him to realize that the glass was set in a door. Strict wartime blackout regulations would have stipulated that every window should be heavily curtained to prevent any interior lights being seen by enemy aircrews, so why was this uncurtained?

Then he saw that the curtain had been torn down and lay in a dark mound on the kitchen floor.

He breathed in at last – and recoiled at the sharp smell of vinegar in the air.

As his eyes adapted to the dim light being admitted by the glass (again covered with a diamond pattern of sticky tape) he saw what looked like flour spilt on the tiled floor. A glass jar lay broken in the centre of a pool of watery liquid: that was probably where the smell of vinegar was coming from. There were newspapers, too. He could just make out a page of *The Times* with the headline: ALLIED FORCES LAND AT ANZIO.

From the newspaper ran a trail of liquid. It looked black in this meagre light, but he knew instinctively it was blood. As if someone had used a broad decorator's brush, the dark streak ran across the floor tiles.

Sam's gaze followed it. He saw a pair of women's feet; they were bare. He saw trousered legs; then a dark sweater . . .

He swallowed.

The body of the woman lay face down. Her throat had been cut.

Blood spread out at each side of her head on the floor like inky butterfly wings.

The poor devil had been trying to escape when someone had pounced and slashed her throat. Sam's eyes had begun to ache from staring into near-darkness and he was tempted to use the bicycle lamp. But a burst of its light would be a sure giveaway to the robber lurking in some other part of the house.

Hearing a sound, he looked up.

There was a rumbling, like distant thunder. He could even hear the faint cracking sound of the air being torn apart.

He knew that this was no thunder. The air raid had begun.

Through the glass he could see distant points of light moving up into the night sky like stars on the run.

That must be anti-aircraft fire. The troops manning the ack-ack guns around the town were firing at the advancing Nazi bombers.

A flicker of light lit the kitchen like lightning. Then came a rumble that rattled the cups on the draining board.

He looked down at the woman's corpse again.

Where was the little girl?

But already he'd convinced himself he was too late.

So it is impossible to go back in time and change history, he told himself. At some point the newspaperman would take his photograph as he fled the scene.

But where was the killer?

Sam was certain the man was still somewhere in the house.

And the way Sam burnt with anger right now he was ready to deal out some rough justice of his own.

He glanced at his watch. One minute to ten-thirty. Then Ruth would play merry hell with the horn.

Not that it mattered now.

He'd failed.

Three people dead.

If only he'd been quicker.

Damn. He clenched his fists.

At that moment, above the rumble of bombs falling far away, he heard another sound. Much closer.

A sizzling sound. The sound of dry sand falling in a steady drizzle on newspaper.

Sam turned to the kitchen doorway.

The sound itself made no sense. He couldn't identify it.

But he knew who was making it.

It was the robber.

He was approaching the kitchen.

Sam looked round for somewhere to hide.

Four

The sizzling sound grew louder.

From behind a washtub and mangle he saw a pair of feet appear. In the darkness they were just ill-defined shapes.

The feet moved towards the door, then paused.

The sizzling sound remained constant.

Again Sam had the mental image of sand pouring lightly onto paper. He gripped the bicycle lamp so tightly his fingers ached.

For a moment the feet didn't move.

Maybe the robber knew Sam was here?

Certainly the man seemed to be considering some problem.

Sam could even imagine him looking this way and that, half expecting to see a crouching figure.

But then Sam realized the man must be gazing down at that streak of blood on the floor.

It was puzzling him.

But why? Sam wondered.

Why should he break away from looting the house to come and stand looking at that streak of blood?

Obviously it had been made by the woman as she'd

slithered across the floor, her throat cut, as she'd tried to crawl to . . .

To where?

It was rational to assume she'd make for the door out into the back garden.

If she'd been trying to escape, that was.

But no. She'd been crawling *away* from the door.

Sam risked looking round the end of the mangle rollers. Damn. If only he'd brought a weapon of some sort. Then he wouldn't have had to skulk here like a frightened puppy. Even though Sam was barely breathing he could smell the reek of wet wool again. Clearly it was exuded by the man.

The figure stood with its back turned to him. Just a humped, even headless-looking silhouette in the darkened room.

It appeared to be contemplating the streak of blood. Then it turned to look at a door set in the wall. Perhaps a door to a cupboard or a pantry.

The rumbling became louder. Somewhere a dog started a frenzied barking. A series of tremors from the exploding bombs raced through the house, rattling crockery and shaking the pictures on the walls.

Then a sudden silence fell once more.

Sam could hear his own breathing.

At that moment he and the figure reached the same conclusion.

The woman with her throat cut had been trying to reach that low door set in the wall. Because—

The humped figure moved forward towards the low door.

Because that was where the little girl had hidden herself.

Sam stood up as a flash of light filled the kitchen. It was a cold, bluish light; it flickered, transforming what he saw into something resembling a scene from an old silent movie.

The walls switched from being brilliantly illuminated to being plunged into darkness then just as quickly lit again, as if a brilliant strobe light had been switched on outside the back door.

In an instant, the figure had dragged open the cupboard door.

Sitting on the pantry floor, knees hugged to her chest, was a small girl.

This was it.

Sam moved like he'd been shot from a cannon.

'Don't you touch her!' he shouted as he ran across the kitchen floor.

The moment the figure turned to face him the blue flickering light went out.

Instant darkness.

Sam stopped.

The only thing he had in his hand was the bicycle lamp.

He pointed it towards where the figure had been while twisting the switch on top.

The yellow light flashed in the robber's face.

The sizzling sound suddenly increased in volume.

Sam stared at the face.

A shout sounded in his ears.

And he realized that it had been he who'd made the sound.

Because there, in the trembling light of the lamp, was the intruder's face. The sight of it stopped him dead.

It was a large, distorted face; almost a demon-like caricature rather than recognizably human. The nose was beak-like and stubble bristled sharply across the jaw. A heavy blue tattooed line ran across the upper lip, following the same contour as a moustache would. More vertical tattooed lines ran from the bottom lip down to the line of the chin to create a blue beard effect.

But that wasn't the worst of it. That wasn't what shocked Sam Baker to the marrow of his spine.

Standing out from the man's face were three snakes.

They swung slowly from side to side, tongues vibrating from their mouths; that sizzling sound turning into an angry hiss.

Sam took an involuntary step back and thumped against the kitchen table.

He couldn't take his eyes from that face.

The snakes protruded from it as if looking out of holes in a statue's head.

One snake came out of the man's temple like a rubbery horn.

A second came from his forehead, just below the hairline.

A third – most shockingly of all – actually poked out from the man's left eye socket, just where the eyeball should have been.

The little black bead snake eyes set in greenish snake heads were hypnotic. The tongues quivered as the hissing grew louder.

At the same time the man's own tongue came out, aping the snake tongues, quivering too. His single eye stared at Sam: unwavering, mean, hostile.

The figure moved.

In one lightning movement the man grabbed Sam by the throat. Effortlessly he pushed Sam back until he lay flat across the table.

The next second the man raised his free arm. Sam saw in the faint light the gleam of an axe head.

Sam knew he'd only a moment before his head was hacked from his body.

Falling bombs rumbled. Cutlery rattled like nervous creatures in the kitchen drawers.

Sam twisted his head while trying to reach up and grab the arm that held the axe. The arm was thick, muscular.

The man leaned over him, then brushed Sam's hands aside like he was a child.

The snakes stretched out from the man's head, trying to bite Sam's face. The eyes glinted. The furious hissing seemed to drown out the sound of exploding bombs.

Suddenly music crashed through the house.

Sam shook his head, trying to make sense of it all.

The air raid. The snake-faced man.

Now the sound of Meatloaf's *Bat Out Of Hell* was coming through the house in tumbling waves of crashing guitar chords. Pumping bass notes vibrated the windows, drums sounded like worlds colliding: it all came in one hellish extravaganza of sound. Then the operatic vocals came battering over the top of the music.

The music surprised the man, too.

His head jerked up as he listened.

Sam seized his moment.

With one hand free he reached up, grabbed the snake that grew from the man's eye socket and pulled.

The man bellowed in pain.

Sam pulled harder; the snake's body stretched as if it were rubber. He could feel it wriggling inside his clenched fist, squirming, contracting, expanding as that thick, warm body of muscle, bone and sinew tried to wriggle free.

He pulled harder.

The man screamed in agony. Even so, he brought the axe down wildly.

Sam jerked his head sideways as the blade glanced against the side of his face and buried itself deep in the wooden table top.

Now the man clawed at Sam's hand. But Sam wasn't quitting. He pulled at the snake, raising a pyramid of skin from the man's face.

Now blood began to seep from where the snake body joined the flesh of the man's face.

Sam tugged harder.

The blood trickled like red tears down one cheek.

The man shrieked.

And as he shrieked he tried to drag the axe blade from the table.

The music grew louder. At least the drumbeat did, or maybe that was the sound of the exploding bombs fusing with the music.

'Run!' Sam shouted. 'Run!'

Behind the snake-faced man came a light flurry of movement.

Sam lifted his head to see the little girl in her white nightdress run through the kitchen door.

The snake-faced man released his grip on the axe handle: the blade wouldn't shift.

As if swatting away a fly he flicked his hand across Sam's cheek.

The blow knocked Sam's head sideways. He heard his own teeth crunch.

Immediately, he let go of the snake.

Panting noisily, the man gripped the axe handle with both hands to rock the blade free.

Dazed, Sam rolled off the table and ran for the door.

He was part-way through it when the blade buzzed through the air and smashed into the door frame.

Sam ran harder: out of the house, over the prone body of the girl's father, down the garden path to the gate.

Running across the square was the little figure of the girl in white.

As he ran after her he saw another figure. It raised its hands.

He expected to see the axe again. But this time there was a flash.

Sam paused for just a split second to see the newspaper-man he'd seen in the pub – the man with the Buddy Holly glasses. The man lowered his camera and stared at Sam, obviously fixing his face in his memory.

The newspaper man stepped back into the shadows as the burly shape of the intruder crashed through the gate, the axe in his hands.

Sam ran after the girl. The axeman followed.

Chapter Thirty-One

Sam glanced back as he ran across the square of grass. The axeman was following. For the first time Sam saw the clothes the man was wearing. He'd never seen anything like it before. The man looked like some barbarian warrior from the mountains. What was more, the axe was no domestic implement for cutting firewood. This was a battleaxe with a curving blade; the handle itself was tipped by a sharp iron spike for stabbing or eye-gouging.

As Sam glanced back he saw Ruth standing beside the car.

For some reason she hadn't found the car horn. Instead she'd managed to switch on the CD player, then turned the powerful sound system on full. Still, it had been enough to distract the axeman at that crucial moment. Otherwise Sam's head would have been rolling across that kitchen floor like a football right now.

Meatloaf's *Bat Out Of Hell* still blasted out across the square, echoing from the house fronts.

Only no one came out to see what was responsible for the sound. No doubt they were going to stay in their air-raid shelters until the enemy bombers had passed.

Sam ran hard across the grass.

By this time the girl'd reached the church and had climbed through the iron bars of the fence into the graveyard.

A bluish light lit the scene again. It flickered like a silent film, rendering every movement into a series of jerky twitches.

Then Sam saw where the light was coming from.

Something like a drink can lay in the grass ahead. It burned with an intense bluey light, white smoke drifting up from the surrounding turf.

Incendiary, Sam told himself. As well as high-explosive bombs the bombers were also dropping incendiaries. Not much bigger than beer cans, and filled with inflammable chemicals, they were dropped in their hundreds on towns in the hope they would ignite buildings and simply reduce the whole area to ash and cinders.

Another of the little cylinders gave a popping sound on the road in front of him. It, too, began to blaze with a bluish flame, spitting out sparks that set fire to the grass.

Sam ran on, glimpsing every so often the blue-white of the girl's nightdress as she dodged around the gravestones.

Whatever happened Sam couldn't let that monster with the axe catch her.

This had become something of a divine mission for him now. Nothing else mattered.

If he saved the girl, he would change history. Then there would be a chance after all that they might escape this nightmare carnival ride back through time.

Besides that, something more profound, more fundamental, had kicked in now. He had to protect the little girl. He couldn't allow her to be slaughtered as her parents had been.

He reached the graveyard fence at the same time as he heard a tremendous thump from the field across the road.

Although he saw nothing, he certainly felt the shock wave from the exploding bomb.

He glanced back.

The man with snakes in his face was still running after him.

What in hell's name can stop that juggernaut? Sam thought grimly. The axeman was built like a tank.

Even though winded by the bomb blast, Sam made it to the iron fence. It was spiked with imitation spear blades; hoping he wouldn't slip and impale himself on them, he vaulted over.

Ahead, the girl had tried in her terror to hide behind a gravestone, but she was still clearly visible.

He had to grab her, then run like hell; somehow he had to find a safe hiding place.

Behind him the monster climbed the fence; the blade of the axe glinted blue in the light of the incendiaries.

Sam heard the sound of planes passing overhead.

More Nazi bombers, their rough-sounding engines clattered like badly tuned motorbikes.

Searchlights probed through the clouds for them; every so often a salvo of anti-aircraft shells would stream skywards.

He'd almost reached the girl when he heard a yell.

This was female; angry-sounding.

He looked back to see Ruth standing with her arms held out as if she was trying to stop nothing more than a runaway chicken.

Sam's eyes widened when he saw she'd blocked the path of the monster with the axe.

'Keep down,' he told the girl behind the gravestone. 'I'll be right back. Shhh . . .'

He couldn't allow the slender WAAF to face the creature alone.

Already, it had stopped and was looking at her in surprise, head tilted to one side, wondering what possible weapon this tiny woman might have that could stop him.

The whole scene was lit garishly in that blue-white light as yet more incendiaries ignited on the ground around them.

Smoke bit into Sam's nostrils. Behind him the little girl was sneezing.

The man raised his axe, ready to swipe off Ruth's head.

Sam put down his head and ran, intending to cover that

fifty yards or so then simply shoulder-charge the creature. If he could knock it off balance, he might—

He'd taken three paces, no more.

The ground erupted into a column of black in front of him.

He didn't stop dead so much as get flung back by some invisible force that hit him with the force of a speeding truck.

Even as he fell back, the air forced from his chest, he knew what had happened. A bomb had fallen there, right in front of him, to tear up the turf and gravestones.

Hardly able to breathe, he lumbered to his feet.

Ahead, a hole steamed gently.

'Ruth . . . Ruth.'

It hurt to shout.

But it didn't stop him.

'Ruth!'

There, big enough to comfortably swallow a family car, was a crater. Rimmed with a ridge of loose soil, it steamed.

Moving like he was drunk, Sam staggered around the perimeter of the hole while staring down into its centre.

'Ruth?'

He looked around the graveyard. The headstones now lay flat against the ground.

Falling from the dark sky above him were stalks of grass that had been ripped high into the air by the blast. Now they floated gently back down to earth.

A green fibrous snow. He plucked a piece off his sleeve and looked at it wonderingly.

It was then he noticed something resembling a piece of silver foil sticking to his chest.

He pulled at it.

The pain slashed through his nerves to his brain in one searing rush.

He pulled at the shiny silver again.

And again the pain.

Understanding nosed its way through his stunned brain.

The silvery metal was shrapnel that had been slammed into his chest by the bomb blast. He looked at his fingers. Blood reddened them.

On the ground lay an object about the size of a Snicker bar. He picked it up. It was a snake head that had been severed from the monster's head. The forked tongue hung loosely through the jaws.

Sam threw it aside.

'Ruth?'

His voice sounded woolly in his ears. The explosion must have damaged his hearing.

'Ruth!'

He looked towards the iron fence.

Slumped across it was a figure.

'Ruth!'

Running forward he saw the arched torso and the limbs hanging limply to the ground.

There, lying on his back, as if carefully balancing across the fence, was the man who'd attacked him. The axe lay in the road where the explosion had flung it. The railing spikes had punched completely through the middle of his stomach. Spikes protruded bloodily from the clothing.

Even though Sam could see the chest rising and falling in jerky breaths the man seemed unconscious.

Certainly he was dying.

'Ruth!'

Sam turned and walked back towards the crater.

Ahead of him he saw figures in the darkness. He saw the helmets of police, ARP wardens, ambulance men. One of them tenderly held the little girl in his arms.

Even from this distance Sam could see she was unhurt.

All their attention was on the little girl. Sam couldn't hear the reassuring voices but he could imagine them. They were going to give her the best care and love they could. She was one of their own who had been snatched from the jaws of hell.

Already Sam no longer felt part of this world.

Their lives, battles, tragedies would continue. But he would no longer contribute to it. Nor influence it. He was like a football player forced to retire from a game before it was through.

The rest of the team would continue to play without him.

He reached the edge of the crater. There he dropped to his knees. The wound in his chest gushed blood but he didn't feel it.

The ringing in his ears was growing faint.

The world seemed indistinct. Reality was losing its hard edge.

He looked down at the rim of broken stone and earth.

From the debris he picked out a cap.

He didn't recognize the badge but he knew what it was.

'Oh, Ruth,' he whispered. 'Oh, Ruth . . . I'm sorry. I made you miss your train.'

His whole body began to shake.

'I'm sorry, Ruth . . .'

Then, as his blood dripped onto the torn cap clenched in his two hands, the world seemed to twist violently beneath him.

Then it was no longer there.

And he was falling.

Into some other place. Some other time.

Chapter Thirty-Two

One

It was just half an hour after the latest time-slip when Sam and Nicole walked into the museum room at the visitors' centre. As they'd anticipated, the bodies were gone.

'Out of the game,' Nicole said in a flat voice, nodding towards where they'd placed the bodies.

'And yet everything else is the same,' Sam murmured. He ran his hand over his chest. Just moments ago, it seemed to him, he had been kneeling before the bomb crater with a chunk of shrapnel jutting from his ribs, blood pouring down the front of his lemon-coloured shirt. Now here he was, squeaky clean and as good as new. The shirt even looked freshly ironed. Outside the cars and the bus would be sitting there, exactly as they had been on that first time-jump. The fuel in the tanks would be restored to the same quantities down to the last litre.

Perhaps they weren't being transported back through time as such, but manufactured anew with each time-jump – perfect replicas of the original.

'At least it makes room for the next batch,' Nicole said as she wedged open the door, ready for Lee and the others to stretcher in those who'd died during the time-shift this time. Sam tried not to recall the corpses' faces with their surprised expressions, their eyes wide as branches had erupted from their chests and heads like crazy reindeer antlers. Even now Jud would be sawing through the branches to free the bodies of the dead tourists.

Perhaps it was pointless to go to the trouble of moving bodies into this makeshift morgue, but it *felt* right to lay them here. Sure, they'd be gone when the group was next hauled back through time. But humans had disposed of their dead in a ritualistic manner for a hundred thousand years. Rather than burial or cremation, this had all the resonance of those ancient Eskimo rites where a body would be left on the ice to be eaten by polar bears.

Where the bodies disappeared to at each time-slip, Sam didn't know. Perhaps they were all projected into the dim and distant future where the foetal-like descendants of humankind performed autopsies. He could see the bodies laid out on slabs: the hearts, lungs, brains and other vital organs being weighed, before being plopped into jars of formaldehyde ready for the shelf.

The mental pictures of the autopsies and futurity's scientists scrutinizing the eviscerated bodies were all as clear as crystal, even though Sam did realize it was pure imagination on his part. But it was this not knowing *why* they were falling back through time that was getting under his skin. He burned to find an answer; any answer.

Anything was better than wallowing in this dark pit of complete ignorance.

'Here they come,' Nicole said. She was in gear, taking control of the situation, the travel-rep training providing for her, at least, a framework in which to operate from hour to hour.

Lee Burton, together with a couple of other men, came in bearing the weight of a corpse on one of the toilet doors that served as a makeshift stretcher.

Sam helped them manoeuvre the door and its grisly cargo the last few feet over the exhibits and around the display cases. He deliberately avoided looking at the face of the corpse. Even so, he glimpsed one of the dry branches protruding from the forehead like some mutant stag antler.

The latch on the toilet door read 'Engaged'. It was an absurdly small detail, completely irrelevant to what was happening. However, Sam fixed his eyes on that single word that represented civilized normality. And it was infinitely better to concentrate on that rather than look at the grotesquely deformed face of the corpse with a tree branch fused right through its brain.

At that moment Jud appeared at the doorway.

'Sam,' he said, breathless, urgent. 'Rolle's appeared. And I think you should hear what he's got to say.'

Two

Rolle's eyes blazed from beneath his fringe of ginger hair. They looked as wild, as manic, as passionate as ever.

If not downright crazy, Sam told himself as they crossed the car park to where Rolle stood at the edge of the amphitheatre, still dressed in the orange overalls and Wellington boots.

Already he seemed to be holding a conversation with himself, gesturing extravagantly, or clutching his forehead as if he'd just heard bad news.

Carswell appeared at the top of the steps, still immaculate in his white linen suit.

'There's no show without Punch,' Carswell observed obliquely as Sam and Jud walked up.

'So, Mr Rolle,' Carswell went on with a dry smile. 'What do you have to tell us this time?'

Anxiously, Rolle chewed a dirty thumbnail as he spoke. 'Wrong. It's all going wrong . . . completely wrong. I've never seen it like this before. Bluebeards are coming out of their darkwoods . . . darkwoods of their souls. Dangerous now. Very dangerous for all—'

'Oh, what the hell is he talking about?' Carswell snapped. He fixed his glaring eyes on Jud. 'Do *you* have any idea what this means?'

Sam stiffened. The penny had dropped. 'I think I do. Mr Rolle. These Bluebeards that you say are coming out. They

319

are people like us? Who are being moved back through time?'

Rolle's eyes fluttered as he nodded sharply. 'Yes. Yes. Only they stand outside nature.'

'What the hell does—'

'Shh, Carswell,' Sam hissed; then, gently, he asked Rolle, 'Are these men bad?'

'Bad.'

'They are outlaws? Bandits?'

'Yes. They sneak oh-so-stealthily from their hidey, hidey-bidey, hidey—'

'Oh, for God's sake!' Carswell snapped.

'Let him speak.'

'They are starting to come from out of their hiding places.' With a physical effort, Rolle forced himself to speak lucidly. 'They hide outside the normal flow of time. But every so often . . . every so often they enter a time zone to launch a raid. Once they could do this only rarely. Now they strike out at will. They are pirates, time pirates, time is their ocean, they move through that ocean at will, then they strike. They steal, kill.'

'Go on,' Carswell nodded at Sam. 'Interpret that.'

Sam sighed impatiently. 'Don't you see what he's saying?'

'Only gibberish.'

'Carswell, get your head around it. He's saying this has happened before. That people throughout history have been dragged out of their own time. And that, like us, they've been pulled backwards into history. But some of these people have learnt to use whatever mechanism is causing this. Not only that, they're using it for their own purposes.'

'Criminal purposes at that,' Jud added.

'Exactly. They're operating like pirates. Only instead of moving around the sea on ships they're moving through time.'

Carswell considered. 'So you might have fifteenth-century outlaws raiding a twentieth-century post office?'

'Yes, exactly.'

'Now that *is* intriguing.'

Sam continued, 'What's more, I think I've seen it happen.' Quickly he told them what had happened the night of the air raid in 1944. Finding the robbery in progress, rescuing the little girl.

Rolle's eyes narrowed when he heard the description of the huge axeman who'd tried to take off Sam's head. Sam went into all the grisly details, right down to the blue tattoos and the snakes growing Medusa-like from the intruder's face.

'He is one of the Bluebeards,' Rolle said.

'Where does that monster come from?'

'He's no monster. At least not bodily, but as for his soul . . .' Rolle shrugged.

'He was human like us?'

'Of course. Perhaps he was sleeping with his head to the earth when he was twitched back through the years. And then he came into being in the same place as a nest of vipers.' Rolle looked at them. 'You've seen what happens when a body comes into being in the same place as a tree or a bird?'

Jud nodded. 'We have. How many of these Bluebeard characters are there?'

'Beyond my counting. Once, they were locked outside the flow of years but now they are escaping into other time zones. They are like a plague of locusts emerging from the desert to feed upon the farmer's wheatfield; they are like a million rats falling upon a household . . . they are – they are . . .' Rolle lost his grip on lucidity and began muttering to himself, his eyes fixed downwards into the amphitheatre; he rubbed his hands slowly together as if trying to remove a dirty stain; his eyes were troubled-looking.

'Rolle,' Jud said gently. 'What year is this?'

The man didn't hear him and muttered to himself.

To Sam it sounded as if the man was praying – a prayer begging for salvation, at that.

'Rolle, can you tell me what year this is?' Jud repeated.

'Uh . . .' Rolle's eyes rolled; he rubbed his hands harder

together. 'Uh . . . 1865. The year of Our Lord. 18 . . . 1865. This is the year Bluebeards will be unleashed on the world like demons. To destroy; to kill; to burn; to degrade; to violate; to make the sacred profane; to – to . . .' Rolle seemed overcome by a tidal wave of passion. Blasting out a lungful of air, he turned away to stand running his hands through his hair.

Carswell raised his eyebrows, which seemed pretty much to indicate his contempt for Rolle.

Jud said to Carswell in a voice low enough for Rolle not to overhear. 'Carswell, you have to remember that over there stands a man who's mastered time travel. He probably sees himself as the custodian of these gates in time and he now knows only too well that soon there's going to be a mass breakout by this tribe of Bluebeards.'

'And we should be concerned about that?'

'I think we should. Throughout history there are count-less cases of one tribe invading the territory of another, or one nation invading another. What we have here is far more dangerous. The invaders are going to come from the past to invade the present.'

'You mean, they might break into 1990 or whenever and smash up a shopping mall? Come on, Campbell, be serious.'

'I *am* being serious. Think of a river eroding a river bank until it breaks through to flood a town. Now imagine something like this is happening with time. The barriers are crumbling. How soon before the past floods into the present?'

'Well, considering the present is now 1865 and we haven't even been born yet, I don't think we've much to worry about, do you?'

'I'm concerned, yes,' Jud told him. 'We don't know what the repercussions of such a temporal breakdown will be.'

'Look, we've been through this already,' Carswell snapped impatiently. 'We can't change time. Those Blue-beard johnnies or whoever they are won't break out into the here and now.'

'How do you know that?'

'Because we've not read about it in our bloody history books, have we? We know for a fact that Roman legions were never sighted in nineteenth-century London. Viking warriors never raided Heathrow airport.'

'Carswell,' Sam said in a low voice. 'I think we were wrong. Remember I told you what happened during the air raid in 1944? I prevented the little girl from being murdered. Yet in 1946 I saw a newspaper cutting clearly stating that *all* the family had been murdered in Casterton, their throats cut.'

'You're saying you changed history?'

'Yes, that's exactly what I'm saying.'

Carswell paused, his lips pressed hard together. 'Well, if that's the case, Sam Baker, old boy, we'd all better stick our heads between our legs and kiss that little puckered hole goodbye.'

Sam held up a finger. 'Wait a minute . . . wait a minute. We're travelling back through time, right?'

Jud nodded. 'Right.'

'Well, we've already worked that one out, Baker, so what about it?' Carswell snapped.

'Think about it. At first we believed the leaps back through time were completely random. That it was some freakish act of nature, like a lightning strike or an earthquake.'

Carswell sighed. 'What are you talking about?'

'What I'm talking about is that maybe all this is deliberate.'

'Come, come—'

'No, listen to me for a minute, Carswell. Call me crazy but I did wonder if all this was some cruel experiment by some scientists in the future. Maybe a million years in the future. But – and just humour me for a moment – but just suppose that, say, here in 1865 the shit really *did* hit the fan. That time barriers *did* break down and people from different centuries found they could move into a different time zone.

Probably one of the greatest problems of the latter half of the twentieth century was refugees moving in their tens of thousands from war zones into places where they thought they could find food and somewhere peaceful to live. The problems this caused were immense. The local populations couldn't cope with the influx of refugees – there simply wasn't enough food for all those extra people. They began to starve. So what happened? Those refugees who were fit and able turned to robbing their unwilling hosts. Soon there were murders, raids, kidnapping, all kinds of banditry. Now imagine if this were to happen where people didn't just move from one *place* to another, but from one *time* to another.'

'Now that would be the mother of all refugee problems,' Jud said in a hushed voice.

'So what're you saying?' Carswell said. 'That people who are starving in the tenth century are going to up sticks and move into the twentieth century and expect the welfare state to look after them?'

'Partly, yes. But I think it's going to be worse than that. I think you're going to find whole armies coming through from the past to invade the present.'

'Well, my money is on a modern tank regiment, backed up with helicopter gunships, beating the pants off any hairy-arsed barbarians armed with swords and spears.'

'Eventually, perhaps. But that would be in a pitched battle on open ground. But what if a thousand men armed with swords and longbows came out of that amphitheatre right now? For one thing, we wouldn't stand a chance against them. Secondly, neither would Casterton. They could walk into the place, burn every building to the foundations and murder the whole population before sufficient troops could be mobilized to stop them.'

'Bloody,' Carswell allowed thoughtfully. 'But I still don't see how flattening a little town in the middle of nowhere would affect the rest of the planet.'

'Who knows?' Sam replied. 'In the States we're being

engulfed by illegal immigrants from all over the world. They're pouring in across the Mexican border in their hundreds every week. Simply because they're fed this diet of Hollywood films and TV programmes that screams loud and clear, 'Hey, the US of A's the place to be. It's glitzy, it's glamorous, and if you can only get your ass onto American soil you're going to be rich and happy.' So, are the millions of human beings who inhabit the past going to see that this world of the nineteenth century, or the twentieth century, is a land of milk and honey? A place to emigrate to, come what may?'

'Or even a place to invade and conquer?'

Carswell said to Sam, 'Earlier you were saying that you thought that our trip through time was no accident. That we might have been pitched backwards into history as part of some scientific experiment.'

'That's what I thought might be possible. But the more I think about it, the more I'm beginning to suspect that it's more than that.'

'What, then?'

'That we've been sent back in time for a purpose.'

'And that purpose is?'

'To plug this puncture in time. To stop this invasion of people from history marching into 1865 or 1944 or 1946 or 1999, or whenever.'

'You mean this little bunch of tourists is intended to stop them?'

'Yes.'

'We don't make a particularly formidable band of time warriors, do we? A handful of tour representatives shepherding some middle-aged to elderly holidaymakers?'

'Perhaps it's a desperate last-ditch attempt to save the human race.'

'Pretty desperate at that, if you ask me,' Carswell said with a thin smile.

'OK, imagine this . . .'

'More fairy stories, Mr Baker?'

'If you like. Humour me, though . . . please.'

Carswell shrugged. 'OK. Shoot.'

'Picture this. It's a million years in the future. The world is a wreck. I mean, completely screwed. Society's in chaos. The cities are in ruins. All those glossy scenarios we've seen in sci-fi films about us colonizing the planets are in the bin, too. Human civilization is up the spout because there's been a constant flow of refugees and invading armies from different periods of history. Get the picture?'

'Go on.'

'Perhaps this flood from history has affected the whole world. Thirteenth-century Mongol hordes might sweep down from the mountains into modern China. Sixteenth-century Apache and Cherokee warriors rampage in New York in the 1990s.'

'They wouldn't stand a chance. Not against modern armies.'

'Not at first they wouldn't. But the civilization of the twentieth century would be like a human body being constantly battered by a viral infection. It can withstand it for a long time, but eventually the immune system is overwhelmed and breaks down. Maybe the individual illegal immigrants coming into America can't do anything to harm the nation but collectively they're beginning to erode the economy. Every year tens of millions of dollars are spent dealing with the problem. Europe, too, is terrified of an influx of refugees, whether it's Kurds or the dispossessed from the former Soviet bloc. Now, this hypothesis I'm pitching at you says that, in a nutshell, this constant exodus of people from the past will eventually bring future civilizations to their knees. Imagine for a moment that scientists find they can send a bunch of people back in time. Perhaps right to the time that this rupture, or puncture if you like, in the barrier of time occurs.'

'But why not send back a trained team? Why only a bunch of oldies and a few others who just happened to be in the area?'

'I'm not going to be arrogant enough to say I've worked out all the answers. But my guess is that, for some reason, they can't send their own people back as far as this. Perhaps they were forced to take pot luck, snatch up a few people from the amphitheatre and send them back into history in the hope they could plug this hole in time.'

'Well, that's a very interesting reason *why* we've been sent back through time,' Carswell said slowly. 'But just supposing that your entertaining guesswork is all true? How do we prevent this tidal wave of humanity gushing through from the past? Afterall, this time gate's not something we can simply roll a big stone across the entrance of, is it?'

'True.' Sam gave a thin smile. 'Very true. But don't you think we should be considering some solutions? Before it's too late.'

Three

Nicole Wagner stepped into the shade of the woods. Above her, fluffs of cumulus cloud floated against a clear blue sky. After laying out the bodies in the museum room she'd spent ten minutes on the bus trying to tune in the radio.

There'd been nothing but the hisses, snaps and clicks of static. There were no stations broadcasting now; she was certain of that, even though she didn't know what year it was.

Now the woodland stretched out before her: deep, dark and mysterious.

There was a stillness about it now; that, although peaceful, was a little frightening. Almost like entering a ruined building that had a sinister reputation.

She looked round at the towering tree trunks soaring up into a hissing world of leaves and sunlight. While away through the columns of tree trunks the shadows gathered deeper and darker.

Yes, she told herself, *I've got a word that describes these woods.*

Haunted.

They had a haunted feel to them. As if legions of ghosts moved with a supernatural fluidity through those deep shadows.

Why, she told herself, *they are probably watching me even now*.

She took a step back, feeling that haunted atmosphere rolling at her in a cold stream from the depths of the wood.

It wasn't safe in there.

Yet she found herself drawn to it.

There was something – or someone – waiting for her there in the wood.

Someone important.

'So we meet again.'

She nearly screamed at the sound of the voice.

Turning sharply, she found herself looking into the angelic face.

'I'm sorry to have alarmed you, dear lady.'

'You?' she whispered in confusion.

'William Horbury at your service,' he said with a smile and a slight bow. It was the blond man who'd saved her from Bostock.

A muffled voice came somewhere near his stomach. 'Tell her, then get the buggery away from here. It's not safe with—'

'Hush,' the blond man said.

'Hush, my foot. I tell you it's not safe!'

The man gave a smile and a shrug. 'He is right, of course, dear lady. It's not safe at all here in the wood. Nor, dare I say, in your carriages across there by the hollow.'

She glanced back in the direction he'd indicated with a nod of his head. He was looking at the bus and the cars.

'Not safe?' she echoed at last, finding some mental equilibrium.

'Not at all safe. There are all manner of strange men in the woods. Fighting men. Some are clearly Liminals like myself. A fellow melted most peculiarly with a goat, I saw. Some with birds.'

'Which are like me,' came a voice that sounded as dry as paper.

From behind a tree came a man she'd believed to be dead. It was the middle-aged man with a bird's wing protruding from the side of his head, while the head of the blackbird jutted from his cheek. Now both bird and man looked very much alive; the man's eyes were strong, clear. The bird looked at Nicole as though fascinated; its eyes were bright as black sapphire.

Nicole stared, amazed. 'You're all right?'

'If by "all right" you mean I'm still alive, then, yes, I'm very much all right.' He reached up a finger to stroke the head of the bird. He stroked it like a man caressing a favourite pet. 'But I'm different now. This gentleman here has explained everything.' As he spoke a small feather flew out through his lips. Nicole fancied she could see part of the bird's body in his mouth, as if a feathery growth was descending from the plate of his upper jaw.

The coarse voice rumbled from the angelic man's stomach. 'Far be it from me to interrupt happy reunions . . . only we have to get away from this bloody wood.' Horbury pulled aside his cloak, revealing the pair of eyes that bulged through the letter box-like slit in his jacket. 'Unless, that is, we're all happy with the prospect of being cut into a thousand little pieces.'

Chapter Thirty-Three

One

'Exactly what is this danger?' Nicole asked. 'I'll need to warn my friends.' She glanced back in the direction of the car park where she saw Jud, Sam and Carswell talking together. There too was the tramp she'd seen before, standing not far from them. However, he was taking no part in the conversation, just staring across the river.

'Vagabonds, cut-throats, rogues,' William Horbury said as he flicked back his cloak to reveal the pommel of the sword in its scabbard. He rested his hand on it. 'Known collectively as Bluebeards. We need to be vigilant.'

The man with the bird in his face said, 'You should try and get everyone away from this place. You can take William's word for it, there're some pretty evil-looking characters hanging around these woods.'

'We could simply get into the bus and the cars and drive away, but you know as well as I do that when the next time-shift comes we'll find ourselves back in the amphitheatre.'

The eyes in William's stomach widened. 'Well, why don't you show her the way we used to get out of that blasted hole in the ground? Because that's how we all started, you know? We were in that amphitheatre, as they call it. Then – woomph! – we were in another time. And some of us ended up in other bodies – now there's a tale I can tell you, young lady.'

Nicole stared. 'You mean you became fused with William? Like this gentleman became fused with the bird?'

'Exactly. Talk about ruddy nightmare. Nineteen-oh-eight, it were. And me and my fiancée cycled down to that there amphitheatre for a kiss and a cuddle, like. Ivy Marshall, they called her, with all this long black hair – jet black! – stretched all the way down to the back of her knees when she let it all down. Anyway. We were—'

'Sshh . . .' William held his finger to his lips. At the same time he gripped the sword and quietly drew it from the scabbard. 'Visitors.'

Two

The meeting at the amphitheatre had broken up. Jud was talking to Rolle. Carswell had returned to his millionaire's launch that still bobbed there on the river, a gleaming white in the sunlight. From the acid expression on the man's face Sam Baker figured that Carswell thought that the theory was pretty much shite.

With the sun beating down between banks of cloud, Sam walked across to the visitors' centre and helped himself to a drink from the vending machine. Someone had chiselled the door open. It didn't matter. At the next leap back through time the vending machine would be magically restored to its original pristine condition; the shelves would be restocked once more with cans. The only thing lacking now was an electricity supply to chill the drinks.

But apart from that, everything would be exactly like it had been at that moment in 1999 when the world went pear-shaped and they began this weird and wonderful ride back through time.

Sam tugged at the ring-pull on a can of cherry coke; it was sickly sweet, but God knew he was ready for that sugar rush to his brain. If the machine had stocked Jack Daniel's whiskey he'd have taken a bottle and crept quietly away to get blasted.

Were they some unlikely squad of time commandos? For

want of a better phrase, press-ganged by a beleaguered people somewhere in the future to go back and plug a gap in time? To stop a wholesale invasion by armies from remote history?

OK, Christ, it was unlikely. Admit it. But he couldn't figure out any other explanation. And it certainly seemed to make at least a rough fit with Rolle's warning that criminals and robbers were starting to exploit the ability to travel to different time periods to steal from an unsuspecting public.

For the first time in what seemed like days, he felt a pang of hunger. Which at any rate proved to him, at least, that despite these weird, even downright surreal events, he was still a human being, with basic human needs. There'd be souvenir tins of locally produced cake and honey in the visitors' centre. He decided to fill up on some of that while he tried to figure out what he should do next.

Three

William Horbury drew his sword as the stranger stepped out from the forest. The stranger was dressed in a leather biker jacket patterned with silver studs. On his feet were a pair of motorcycle boots; the buckles rattled with every step he took.

'Mr Bumble, as we live and breathe,' came the raw cockney voice from William's stomach. Mockingly it said, 'Did your soft comfy bed catch fire or what?'

'Shh, Bullwitt,' William scolded. Then he turned to the stranger. 'Grimwood, what is it?'

'Those jerk-off bastards are everywhere. They trashed the camp so I came here to find you lot. Who's blondie?'

'The lady is Nicole. She is one of us now; dispossessed; a wanderer; a—'

'Spare me the jerking poetry.'

Nicole found herself staring at the stranger so hard her eyes felt as though they were going to rip from their sockets and fly at his face.

Her first thought was: *he's black.*

But as he walked towards her, scything through the nettles with a stick, she changed her mind.

Not black.

But he's been sprayed with some black liquid, possibly engine oil.

His face was covered with black lumps. Around the size of her little fingernail, they were a shiny black. And they were moving. The man's face was seething with them. It was like looking into an ants' nest or a . . . a . . .

Beehive.

She caught her breath.

The three (four, rather, if you included the face that bulged from William's stomach) spoke quickly together; this was evidently a meeting of men in crisis. As Nicole listened, bemused, making neither head nor tail of any of it, she also found she couldn't tear her eyes from the man they called Grimwood.

At least, that was, she couldn't tear her eyes from that face.

Oh, what a face, what a face . . .

That face was the centre of her universe now. Nothing else existed. Every shred of her attention was locked hard upon it.

Oh, dear God . . . his face was alive with bees. She saw that now. Dozens and dozens of bees – living, squirming bees, with orange and black striped bodies, shiny black legs, glossy heads, quivering antennae and those rounded insect eyes.

Why don't the bees fly away?

Why doesn't he wash them off?

Why don't they sting him to death?

The questions buzzed with an insectile ferocity of their own.

The bees covered the man's face as completely as a mask. They even filled one of his orbits, leaving a sticky white slit that was a mere ruin of an eye.

'You've got a yellow streak up your back, you piece of brown rubbish,' the one she now knew as Bullwitt sneered from William's stomach. 'Why did you let them smash up our camp? I bet they took all the food, didn't they, Mr Bumble? And Mr Bumble stood there and let it shitting well happen. Isn't that right, Mr Bumble?'

'No, that isn't right,' Grimwood snarled. 'And stop calling me Mr Bumble.'

'Mr Bumble, Mr Bumble, Mr—'

'Shut it!' Instantly a hum sounded. Wide-eyed with amazement, Nicole realized it was the bees. The bees were buzzing angrily. Somehow their insectile emotions were synchronizing mysteriously with those of their human host's.

Nicole saw the man's face even become blurred, as if a thin grey smoke had drifted in front of it. She realized the effect was caused by the sudden beating of the bees' wings. They beat in fury as Grimwood himself snarled in fury. 'It wasn't like before, Bullwitt. It wasn't just a couple of Bluebeards trying to whip a can of beans or a packet of bleedin' fags. This time there were dozens of them. They were armed to the teeth. We had to run for our lives – for our freaking lives! – and I'm telling you, never ever call me Mr Bumble again.'

'Why?' Bullwitt asked from William's stomach. 'Are you afraid I'm going to come out of here and fight you?'

'For two pins I'd cut you out of there and kick your bloody head through every piece of shit I could find.'

'Temper, temper,' Bullwitt chuckled. 'After all, you don't want to come out in hives, do you now?'

'I'll kill you one day. I promise!'

'Oh, buzz off.'

'Be quiet, Bullwitt, *please*.'

'But he—'

'I said *quiet*.' William pulled the cloak back over the face, muffling the voice.

'Don't listen to Bullwitt,' William said soothingly. 'He's bitter and frustrated.'

Nicole turned from the bird-faced man to the bee-faced man. Just for a second it felt as if her skull had caved in under the pressure of the bizarre images she was seeing. It wouldn't have taken much to send her screaming back to the others in the car park.

But for the moment, she told herself, *my duty lies here. These men know something. They might be able to help us.*

She tuned in to what William was saying. 'Is anyone from our camp hurt?'

'Kylie was clubbed. Caught her here in the mouth.'

'But she escaped?'

'Oh aye, got clean away, but she's well pissed off at losing her front two teeth.'

'Where have they gone now?'

'They're all leaving this time. They're pissed off, as you can imagine. All our food's gone; blankets, tents; that big box of cigars that Dixie got. All gone.'

'Bastards,' came a muffled voice from beneath the cloak.

The bird wing fluttered from the side of the man's head. 'Can't we all just split up and go home?' His eyes were large and sad-looking. 'I mean, just go back to our own times?'

'Looking like this?' Grimwood pointed to his own beehive face. 'I can hardly see myself walking into the Casterton Social and Welfare club for an afternoon's snooker with a mush like this, can you?'

The birdman shook his head, and dropped his eyes to the ground. Even the blackbird head looked down in sympathy.

'Take heart, Mr Saunders.' William laid a hand on the man's shoulder. Nicole was touched to see it was a genuine gesture of affection. 'We've sworn to be brothers now. You have joined a new family, each one of us similarly blighted.' He squeezed the shoulder and smiled. 'Divinely blighted, we say. Together we shall survive and prosper and make new homes for ourselves. And look.' He nodded to Nicole. 'We have a new sister. Her beauty and her intelligence will enrich our family.'

'A new sister?' Nicole shook her head. 'I'm sorry, I don't follow.'

William tilted his head to one side and looked at her, smiling. It was almost a secret smile as if he was just about to spring a surprise birthday present on her. 'Didn't I make myself clear to you, dear lady? I'm sorry, I do not speak plainly enough, tatter-tongue that I am.'

'Make yourself clear about what?'

'My dear lady,' he told her gently, 'you are one of us now.'

She looked from the man with the face in his stomach, to the man with the bird in his face, then to the man with bees embedded in the skin of his face and throat.

She shook her head. 'Oh no,' she said in a disbelieving whisper. 'I'm not one of *you*.'

'But you are,' William said, smiling pleasantly as if not wanting to frighten her. 'You are divinely blighted. But that's no handicap, you can—'

'No!' her voice sharpened. 'I'm nothing like you. You were fused into other animals during a time-leap. Look at me . . .' She stood before them holding out her long tanned arms; she lifted a leg, each in turn. They stretched down from the lycra cycling shorts, long, lean, golden-coloured. 'Just look. There's nothing wrong with me.'

There's nothing wrong with me.

As she spoke that sentence her voice rose in pitch, ending with a tremor as the first sensation of fear twitched her stomach muscles.

'Please . . .' William's kind smile didn't falter; his eyes were as compassionate as a saint's. 'Please don't be alarmed. But if I may be so bold?'

Gently he reached out towards her, his movements slow so as not to alarm her. Lightly pinching the neck of her T-shirt between his finger and thumb, he began to ease it down from her throat so as to expose her shoulder.

Alarmed, she was ready to pull away.

He shook his head; again, a gentle movement. 'Be still, please. Just for a moment. I won't harm you.' He looked into her eyes. 'There, my lady. Tell me what it is that you see there upon your shoulder.'

Four

That hot summer's day in 1865 wore on. The accidental time travellers – there were about forty in all now – stayed pretty close to the amphitheatre. Well, it could be said more accurately that they stayed near to what creature comforts those few acres of earth could offer.

They helped themselves to drinks and food from the visitors' centre. The driver had now given up charging for snacks from the bus's galley. Every so often he'd pull from his pocket a thick wad of the notes he'd already taken from his passengers (the duty-free beer he'd smuggled in on one Continental trip had been a real money-spinner), then he'd shake his head sadly.

The cash was useless. 1990s currency in 1865? He might as well light a fire with it.

Sam walked round the site, examining the perimeter of the time-shift. It was as if someone had taken an extremely sharp knife and sliced through the metalled road. The fifty-or-so-yard section that ran from the perimeter of the boundary to connect with the car park was the same as it always had been: smooth blue-grey tarmac, complete with iron stormwater grates, neatly painted white lines along the centre and a steel sign warning of playing children at the entrance to the car park: *5 MPH MAXIMUM!*

Where the road left that 1999 chunk of ground the metalled surface suddenly ended. Sam had to step off the higher road and down onto a cart track of black cinder that had compacted down as hard as concrete.

When he turned to look back to where the road abruptly ended he could even see a cross-section of it, built up in layers of shale and limestone that was then topped with tarmac. The whole thing looked like a sandwich cake made up of layers of red, white and black sponge.

In the distance a foggy pall of smoke marked the position of Casterton. No doubt domestic and commercial chimneys still smoked richly. Even on a hot summer's day like this.

After a while Sam returned to the amphitheatre.

Perhaps it was all illusory but at least there seemed to be some sense of safety and security there. Already people, incredible though it might seem, were settling into a kind of domestic routine. Jud and his wife were brewing vast quantities of tea and coffee for their time-travelling companions. Even Ryan Keith seemed to have snapped out of his trance. Still dressed in the Oliver Hardy costume complete with bowler hat, he filled plastic buckets from the visitors' centre water-storage tank and brought it down to the Campbells' narrow boat. There they boiled kettle after kettle on their Calor-gas hob.

Only Carswell remained aloof, watching the proceedings from the deck of his launch with a glass of cold beer in his hand. He looked like a Roman emperor dispassionately watching slaves at work. He wasn't going to filthy his hands by helping out. And he certainly wasn't going to hand over any of his food and drink, although (and both Sam and Jud had noticed it) a good number of people were growing more and more hostile towards Carswell. Already there was talk of simply going aboard the launch and taking what they wanted.

Sam sympathized. But he thought of the handgun that Carswell had pulled in the bar when the police had tried to arrest him.

There was every chance he'd start waving that gun the moment anyone stepped onto his gangplank.

'Where's Rolle?' Sam asked Jud who was carrying a steel pole along the deck of the narrow boat.

'He left a couple of hours ago. He said he had to go somewhere, and that he'd be back later.'

'Has he been able to tell you how we can get out of the amphitheatre during time-jumps?'

'No. At least, not clearly. I think that's going to take a lot more work yet on our part.'

'That's not particularly encouraging. What happens when we make the next time-jump?'

'I think more people will die, Sam. Here, take this.'

Jud leant out from the boat and handed Sam the steel pole.

'What's this?'

'We're building a barbecue.'

'A barbecue!' Sam laughed in disbelief. 'You're kidding?'

'No. We're going to eat out tonight.'

'Where did you get the food for forty people?' Sam took the pole. 'Wait. Don't tell me, you do this trick with five loaves and some fishes.'

'Carswell poured scorn on the people here in the amphitheatre. He wrote them off as just a bunch of ignorant halfwits. But we have a retired butcher among our number. He and another man cornered a sheep up on the hills. I lent him my sharpest kitchen knives and, hey presto, we're just about to roast a whole sheep. Coming?'

'You bet.'

In a way Sam wondered if they were wasting their time (and on every occasion he used the word 'time' in a figure of speech that word would clang back at him). It was possible that at any moment they'd be whisked further back in time again.

Then they'd find themselves sitting back in the amphitheatre seats. The travel reps in fancy dress. Jud Campbell pushing that pin into his collar.

But the people were actually enjoying themselves. For the first time on this roller-coaster ride into history he heard laughter. They gathered wood for the fire. On the river bank Jud, helped by Sam, rigged up a spit on which the sheep could be roasted.

The time-shift didn't come that evening. As the sun sank behind the hills they lit the fire, then roasted the sheep. Sam couldn't remember ever tasting anything as delicious as those hunks of mutton he held in his hands. Perhaps every nerve-ending was making a desperate grab at normality. The barbecue, eating, talking to the others, all smacked of normality.

At one point Jud had carved him another hunk of sizzling

mutton and said, 'You know what you were talking about earlier? About there being a reason for all this? Being sent back through time to save humanity. Well . . .' Jud handed him the plate, his eyes twinkling in the firelight. 'I believe you, Sam. I think you're on the right track.'

'Hell, it's relief to hear someone say it. Carswell dismissed me as some kind of crackpot. He's taken to his boat and looks as if he's going to stay there until hell freezes over.'

'That's his problem. And no, I don't think you're a crackpot. What we must do is sit Rolle down the next time we see him and find out how he manages to navigate through time.' Jud looked up at him. 'You know, I think it's our only hope.'

That was as far as the strand of conversation went. After that they joined the others sitting on the slope overlooking their fire with the still-sizzling mutton. It dropped spits of fat which ignited in pops of blue flame in the glowing embers. Everywhere there was a delicious aroma of cooking meat.

At last people returned to the bus or to the cars to sleep. Jud made up a bunk for Sam in the spare cabin on the boat. Zita slept on a bed-settee in the boat's lounge area. And in the corner of the cabin sat a television. It was completely useless now. A piece of lifeless plastic and circuitry. For Sam, however, it was still a potent symbol of the life he'd left behind. After saying goodnight to the others he found himself lightly touching the top of it, feeling that cool plastic beneath his fingertips. Bizarrely, it was reassuring. Perhaps reassuring in the same way a devoutly religious person would feel when entering a church or synagogue or mosque. Although there was no electricity to feed the set, it still seemed to hum with its own magic power.

Again he realized how bizarre it was, but he wished he could switch on the television. Even if it was just to see a string of old TV ads that he'd always written off as banal. It would be like seeing the smiling face of an old friend again.

Moments later Sam lay on the narrow cabin bunk, feeling

the tilt of the boat under him as the current gently pulled at the hull. A nightbird called from somewhere across the water. In the distance a dog barked; the sound had a near-musical quality that shimmered on the air. Despite everything, he felt a strange kind of contentment that he'd never experienced before.

It might just be eating the first square meal in God knew how long.

Or it might be a feeling of kinship that he was developing with his fellow time travellers now he sensed they were on some kind of quest together. Where it would lead he just didn't know.

He heard a female voice singing. Perhaps it was one of the tourists strolling along the banking in the moonlight. She sang the old hymn *Onward Christian Soldiers*. He couldn't explain why, precisely, but at that moment it seemed hugely appropriate.

> *Onward Christian soldiers,*
> *Marching as to war,*
> *With the Cross of Jesus going on before . . .*

Hearing the words, sung as softly as a lullaby, he drifted off to sleep.

Chapter Thirty-Four

One

The next morning that feeling of normality was reinforced by a good breakfast of fried eggs, bacon and mushrooms. Jud, Dot, Zita and Sam ate sitting at a folding table on the narrow-boat deck. To Sam, even the most ordinary domestic activity became hugely reassuring; like using the pepper-grinder to sprinkle fragrant specks of peppercorn onto the egg yolks.

Jud splashed bacon fat onto his trousers and Dot tutted. 'How many times have I asked you to wear the apron when cooking?' Then she smiled and made a joke of him beating the grease out of the trousers on a rock down at the water's edge. Jud, in that typically English way, talked about the weather, speculating that it was going to be a fine day. 'Good cruising weather' was how he described it. Which would have had a radically different meaning if used casually in a New York bar. Zita asked if she could borrow some shampoo so she could wash her luxuriant chestnut hair. Dot told her that she had a shampoo with henna that she would be welcome to use and that would bring out the chestnut gloss beautifully.

Ducks and swans glided across the still waters of the river. Presently a pair of men, both in white shirts, grey waistcoats and bowler hats rowed by in a boat that looked the size of a lifeboat.

The boat itself was piled with fruit and vegetables. Sam

saw a basket full of strawberries that shone a brilliant red in the early-morning sun. There was also a pole that at first he thought was some kind of stunted mast. Then he noticed there were pheasants and rabbits hanging from it.

'Off to market, I shouldn't wonder,' Jud said in a low voice. 'Ahoy there,' he called to the two oarsmen. 'What have you for sale?'

He stood up and, resting his hands on the guard rail, began talking to the two men. He talked easily, his York-shire accent matching theirs.

The narrow boat and Jud's plain clothes didn't look out of place on a river in 1865, but Carswell's white launch with its sleek lines, radio aerial, satellite dish and radar obviously did. The two nineteenth-century men each removed their bowlers so they'd be free to scratch their heads as they stared at it.

Jud turned quickly back to Sam, Zita and his wife. 'Give me whatever jewellery you're wearing. No, dear,' he said to Dot, 'not the wedding ring or the engagement ring.' He looked at Zita and Sam. 'And if you have anything of too great sentimental value you needn't hand that over.'

'It doesn't matter. We'll get them all back at the next time-slip.' Zita unhooked a gold chain from her neck, then another from around her ankle.

'Which could come at any moment,' Dot added, slipping off an eternity ring.

Sam worked off his signet ring after rubbing butter on his finger. His mother had bought him it for his eighteenth birthday. But Sam realized quickly enough what Jud had in mind. If they were going to be stranded here for any length of time they would need food. Besides, Dot was right; at the next time-jump all their possessions would be restored to them as if by magic.

Jud did all the talking, handing over the jewellery and his own antique pocket watch on a fob and chain. Then he haggled.

Sam had expected the men to talk slowly, in a kind of

farm-yokel 'Arrr, that be a good field of oats' kind of way. But their speech was so rapid that he had difficulty in following it, their words running into each other, and there were more than a few phrases he didn't understand at all. Already speech patterns and language were altering, even though they'd only travelled back a little more than a hundred years.

Ten minutes later the two men were rowing an empty boat away downstream while Sam and Jud began stowing away the foodstuffs down below. The barter had also included a big round cake of a hard reddish cheese. Jud sniffed it and smiled. 'Real cheese; just smell that. Heaven, mmm?'

'You'll never fit all that in your refrigerator. I could ask Carswell if—'

Jud tut-tutted. 'You should never put real cheese in a refrigerator. Real cheese is made up of living organisms. Chilling kills it. You see, we're brought up to eat dead cheese that has the texture of old soap so we don't know any better. Real, living cheese should be served at room temperature – like red wine.'

Sam marvelled at Jud's pleasure over such a simple thing as that block of cheese. Maybe for some time travel had its compensations after all.

Two

Lee Burton found Sue Royston walking away from the visitors' centre with two ornamental tin drums on which scrolling writing spelt out: *YORKSHIRE TEA – THE TRADITIONAL BREW OF OLD.*

She'd ditched the Stan Laurel jacket and bowler but still wore the baggy trousers and tweedy waistcoat.

He said, 'Has Nicole still got the passenger list?'

'As far as I know. Why?'

'I was just going to do an update.'

'You mean cross those that haven't made it off the list?'

She glanced back at the museum room that served as the make-do morgue.

'Well, that's a more accurate way of putting it. Put it down to my tour-rep training but I'd be more comfortable keeping tabs on the clients.'

'Clients?' Clutching the drums of tea to her chest Sue looked round at the people coming off the bus after the night's sleep, or walking out of the toilets shaking their hands dry after washing. 'If you ask me, time travel's a great leveller; the demarcation between service provider and client seems to have blurred one hell of a lot.' She shot him a tired-looking smile. 'Sorry. Yes, I think you are doing the right thing, but where Nicole is I'm not sure.'

'I thought she was with you last night.'

'I haven't seen her today.' Sue's eyes clouded a little as she thought back. 'Come to think of it, I haven't seen her since yesterday lunchtime. Have you?'

'No. And I didn't see her at the barbecue last night.'

'Maybe she found some guy.'

'I don't think she'd just go off like that without telling us, do you?'

'No, that's not like Nicole . . . oh, damn.' A worried expression spread across Sue's face. 'Where the heck can she have got to?'

Three

When William had invited Nicole Wagner to look at her bared shoulder she had frozen. Her heart felt as if it had just exploded into her throat, choking her. Her forehead pricked as perspiration suddenly stood in beads from the skin, cooling immediately so that she felt cold, shivery.

You're one of us now . . .

The words sped round and around in her head like fish trapped in a closing net.

You're one of us now . . .

Before she could bring herself to look at her shoulder she

looked from William's calm green eyes to Tony with the bird's head jutting from his cheek just below his eye, then to Grimwood with what looked like a whole hiveful of bees superglued to his face.

You're one of us now . . .

Fear tastes like aluminium. She'd heard that description before; now she knew the truth of it. Metal flavours ran in tingling waves across her tongue. Her heart pounded harder; the world seemed to retreat into a dark fog around her.

At that instant she knew she couldn't delay the moment any more. She looked down at her shoulder.

Despite clenching her teeth, a moan escaped her mouth. She stared down, all her attention rushing onto an area no larger than a thumb nail.

There, on the back of her shoulder, just about where the shoulder blade begins its outward curve, was a lump.

Her eyes widened until the skin around them stung.

The lump was covered in grey fur.

Hypnotized by the furry lump, she slowly reached out a finger to gently, gently touch it; as if the slightest pressure would cause it to fly into a million pieces.

The fur itself was soft, more like down if anything. But beneath the fur the lump was really quite hard. She pressed a little harder. There was only a numb feeling.

Twisting her head further, until her chin dug down into the crook of her neck, she studied the thing; it could have been a fur-covered boil that had grown out of her skin overnight.

She blinked in disbelief.

Two tiny ears protruded from the top of the bulge.

Two tiny ears that were covered with tiny hairs and ridged ever so slightly with arteries.

You're one of us now.

So, they were right. Her heart thudded in her ears.

And aren't those the two cutest mouse ears you ever did see?

The words spun from some crazy part of her brain; that small part reserved for generating dark humour. The same part that prompts a man who's about to be hanged to quip that the gallows trapdoor doesn't look safe, or combat troops to dress the charred corpses of enemy soldiers in funny paper hats and to squeeze beer cans into the burnt black claws that were once hands. That same well of dark graveyard humour that compels apprentice undertakers to press down on the stomachs of their dead clients until they fart like thunder. Or for trainee doctors to play catch with the kidneys of cadavers in anatomy class; or, or—

The ears twitched.

My God, the ears twitched . . .

She crushed her fingers into her mouth to stop herself screaming and at last turned her head away.

William gently eased the T-shirt back over the hairy mouse head embedded in her shoulder as if he was easing clothing over a graze that was still tender.

'There, my lady. Don't worry yourself. It will not harm you.'

Tony, the birdman, looked at her, his eyes serious but calm. 'It will become part of you.' He stroked the bird-head that jutted from his face. 'You'll learn to live with it. Soon you'll have sensation there.'

She stared at him in shocked amazement. He could feel it himself when he stroked the bird's head?

Grimwood tilted his head to one side. The moving bees made it look as if his face twinkled with black gemstones. 'You'll soon realize why William said you were *divinely* blighted. Stuff's going to start happening to you soon.'

'Stuff?' she asked dazed. 'What stuff?'

Grimwood shrugged while repeating, 'Just stuff.'

Tony took up the explanation. As he spoke she listened with her hand over her mouth, stunned. 'A physiological transformation. You will begin to experience changes in yourself. I'm no expert, just a lab technician at a high school, but as far as I can tell . . .' He stroked the bird's beak thoughtfully. 'The cells of the bird's body fused with mine at not just a cellular level but a molecular level. The DNA of each of us became spliced together. The bird's nerve endings have connected with mine. We share the same nervous system now.'

William added in a soft voice, 'Think of it as a gift rather than a blight upon your body. Soon, a remarkable transformation will take place.'

Four

After breakfast on that second day in 1865 Sam and Jud worked in the amphitheatre. There was a line of greenery there that was shaped like a wedge cut from a pie. It narrowed down to a point at the centre where the altar block stood, and then widened out to the edge of the amphitheatre. But even there the greenery didn't end at the uppermost tier of seating but ran in an ever widening green strip across the car park and out to the edge of that circular area of 1999 land.

Jud and Sam measured the strip of brambles and nettles at the widest point within the circumference of the amphitheatre.

'Twelve feet six,' Sam said, reading off the tape.

'The amphitheatre was only cleared of undergrowth in the late Fifties. Before that I imagine you would have looked down into a hollow that was full of brambles, nettles, bushes. See how straight the line of the undergrowth is? It looks as if a gardener's gone along and carefully trimmed the brambles to form a straight line.'

'So some break's opening up in our chunk of 1990s ground allowing the 1860s to come through.'

'That's about it. With every time-jump it gets a little wider.'

'That's hardly reassuring, Jud.'

Jud reeled the tape into its leather case. 'And my guess is that, because the strip gets a little wider each time, whoever is sitting immediately on each side of it is at risk.'

Sam looked at where he and Zita had been sitting. 'Damn,' he breathed. 'Zita was sitting on my right-hand side just up there.'

'Well, that's too close for comfort. It only looks a yard or so from the green strip there. You know, we're going to have to get a handle on what's happening here, otherwise we're all going to be killed off one by one.'

'So we need to find Rolle and find out how the hell we can get away from the amphitheatre during the next time-jump?'

'Absolutely. But I guess he's going to turn up in his own sweet time, so to speak.'

Sam looked up to see Ryan Keith toiling down the steps in the Oliver Hardy costume. 'Sam, Jud,' he called. 'Have either of you seen Nicole?'

They shook their heads.

Ryan mopped his face with a handkerchief. 'We think she's gone!'

'Gone?'

'Gone walkabout, I don't know; she didn't give anyone a clue where she was going.'

'I suppose she could have gone into town, but she'd have had to go on foot.'

Jud scratched his head. 'And dressed in lycra cycling shorts and a T-shirt she'd stand out like a sore thumb in Victorian Britain.'

'Is anyone looking for her?'

'Lee and Sue and a couple of others have gone into the woods; they're hoping she's just got herself lost in there.'

Sam glanced at Jud, 'If you want to round up a search party I'll go with Ryan and start looking. She can't have got too far.'

Jud went back down into the bowl of the amphitheatre to talk to a handful of people sitting on the bottom tier.

Sam hurried up the steps with Ryan puffing along behind him. He remembered only too well the monstrosity Rolle had referred to as a Bluebeard. They were leaking into other time zones like some dangerous pollutant oozing from a sewer into fresh water.

At the top of the steps stood a stranger. Sam found himself doing a double take at the young man in spectacles and a kind of brown flat cap of soft corduroy who stood holding an unwieldy-looking bicycle while smiling down at them. What was most striking about him was the brilliant white collar of a clergyman around his neck.

'Good morning, there,' the young man said with a bright smile. 'This all looks jolly fascinating. Are you archaeologists?'

Five

Sam looked back at Jud who'd not noticed the new arrival and was busily arranging the people below into a search party.

'Oh, excuse my dreadful ignorance.' The young man thrust out a long tapering hand. 'My name's Hather, Thomas Hather, ah— ahm, more properly the Reverend Thomas Hather, but please call me Thomas.'

Sam shook the man's hand and introduced himself, but stopped short of naming his own profession. 'TV director' would only draw some very blank looks in 1865. Then he introduced Ryan, who raised his bowler hat, automatically falling back into the Oliver Hardy role.

Thomas Hather touched his hat while looking at the top of Sam's head. 'You must be devilishly busy. You are quite hatless.'

At first it seemed a strange comment but then Sam realized that a hundred years ago, whichever side of the Atlantic you hailed from, a man would no sooner go out into the street hatless as he would trouserless.

Sam shot the man his best professional smile, usually reserved for the public and producers. 'I think I must have put my hat down somewhere.'

'Oh dear,' Thomas said quite genuinely. 'Maybe it's, uhm.' He shielded his eyes against the bright sunlight and began scanning the amphitheatre for a mislaid hat. 'My word, you have been extraordinarily busy. It couldn't have been more than a little while since I saw this place last and it was quite, quite choked with weeds and the thickest brambles you've ever seen. Which university are you from?'

'Ah, we're freelance.'

'Freelance archaeologists?'

'Yes,' Sam added. 'Sponsored by a newspaper . . . the *New York Times*.'

'Astonishing. You know, there's so much to be done in the way of archaeology.' Thomas spoke with a breathy kind of enthusiasm. 'There's a Roman encampment across there that I know for a fact has never been properly excavated. Just last year the field was ploughed, yielding pottery, glass and all manner of artefacts. I raked over the soil with a couple of friends and we found twenty-seven different types of coins, including a gold Hadrian.'

The first time the man paused for breath Sam jumped in. 'Ah, we seem to have lost one of our party.'

'Goodness.'

'A girl with long blonde hair. You don't happen to have seen anyone like that on your travels?'

'A child? How distressing. Are you the father?'

Sam took a deep breath. Already English usage between 1999 and 1865 was diverging enough to make it difficult for them to understand each other clearly. 'No, the girl . . . the young lady was around twenty-five. Hair: long, blonde, very curly.'

'No. I've seen no one of that description. But perhaps I could help to look'

'Oh, no. There's no need. But thanks for the offer. I'm sure she'll turn up soon enough.'

The nervous young man nodded back at the church. 'I'm rector of St Jude's as well as St Botolph's in Casterton itself. You see, St Jude's no longer has a congregation: the village it served has long since disappeared. But I still have to call out here once or twice a month. There are some rough sorts who engage in all kinds of foul activities if they get access to the building. There are some who don't respect the property of others as they used to.'

Sam thought: *You should see any town or city of 1999; there's graffiti that would blow your mind.*

'Three times this year, the church has been broken into. Ghastly business . . . ghastly.' He shook his head sadly.

Sam began to walk across the car park, thinking of some way he could politely kiss off the young man and begin the search for Nicole. If there were more brutes like the snake-eyed barbarian he'd encountered in 1944 wandering through the wood, then Nicole might be in real danger.

The vicar pushed his bicycle alongside as he walked. It was a clunky-looking machine with a hard leather saddle, and, surprisingly, there was no visible system of braking.

When the vicar saw the car park his eyes widened behind his glasses.

'Good heavens, when was all this work done? It must have been a good two to three weeks since I was down this far, but all this is extraordinarily quick. You've even built a house and put down a hard-topped quadrangle.'

'We've a lot of resources at our disposal.'

'Your sponsors must be generous!'

'Extraordinarily generous.' Sam noticed the vicar's pale blue eyes darting left and right now as if it had finally begun to dawn on him that something extremely peculiar was happening down on this little stretch of meadow in one far-flung corner of his parish.

Sam noticed how the man's eyes flicked to the bright red Coca-Cola vending machine standing outside the visitors' centre, strayed from it, then locked back onto it with what was really quite an intellectual intensity.

Uh-oh, the man smells something fishy, Sam told himself. Maybe there wouldn't be any real problem. But if the cleric decided that all this paraphernalia he now saw – such as the vehicles, the visitors' centre, the Coca-Cola dispenser, Carswell's swish launch – was a mite *too* strange, he might simply jump on that bike of his and pedal for dear life to the nearest police station.

Explaining everything to a bunch of suspicious nineteenth-century policemen might become a bit too complicated, Sam thought nervously.

As Sam watched the Reverend Hather, he found himself being reminded of someone. Of course, it was absurd. He couldn't possibly have met the man before. He'd have died long before Sam was even born. But there was something about the Reverend's manner. The boyish enthusiasm. The way he'd talk excitedly. How he'd stammer, suddenly break off in mid-sentence and rub his jaw in astonishment. Then it hit him. The man was the spitting image of the late, great James Stewart. Right down to the long, gangling body and the, at times, high warbling quality of his voice.

And the man was no idiot. Sam realized he'd have to play this carefully, and try and find convincing answers to Thomas's questions.

'We're establishing an archaeological dig that might take some months,' Sam lied as casually as he could. 'We're also using the latest equipment available. Shipped in from the States.'

'The States? Oh, I see. You mean, from America?'

Sam nodded as Thomas's lively gaze danced over everything he could see.

Thomas went on excitedly, 'But surely I'd have heard about such a dig?'

'We had to keep it hush-hush.'

'Why?'

'In the past we've had thieves getting to our sites first. They dig haphazardly, thinking they're going to find buried treasure.'

'Oh.' Thomas nodded understandingly.

'Of course, they don't find any gold but what they do is cut through all those carefully preserved layers of archaeological material. Then our work is ruined. Isn't that right, Ryan?'

Ryan nodded so eagerly that his face wobbled. 'Ruined,' he agreed.

'So you approach archaeology as a science, analysing each stratum as it's uncovered?' Thomas said. 'Recording and dating what you find, before proceeding to the next layer?'

Sam gave a tight artificial smile. 'Yes.'

'So you're familiar with the work of Richard Lepsius in Egypt?'

'Oh, yes.' The artificial smile tightened on Sam's face. 'I've read everything of his I can get my hands on.'

'I'd love to hear your theories about the amphitheatre.' Thomas's enthusiasm was like a locomotive running with a full head of steam. Unstoppable. And, Sam guessed, if he put a foot wrong his tissue of half-baked lies would lie smeared all over the track.

Thomas enthused, 'You know that Sir Horace Garston surveyed the area at the beginning of the century? He says that Roman engineers cut the amphitheatre out of the rock around the second century AD, but my belief is that it is actually far more ancient than that, and that the Romans merely utilized an existing geological feature in the land. They probably cleared it of plant growth and wind-blown soils, as you yourselves have done, then added their own timber seating. So my conjecture is that the Romans first occupied the area during the reign of the Emperor Nero. What do you say, Samuel?'

'Sam, eh, call me Sam, please. Uhm . . .' He found himself floundering. 'Oh, excuse me; I haven't offered you a drink.'

'Oh, really, there's no need; I—'

'No problem. Tea, OK?'

'OK? I'm not familiar with the word "OK". Is that a blend of tea?'

Again Sam realized that there were sufficient differences in the language to stir up a hell of a lot of confusion. 'OK. No, no. OK is an American phrase; it's a kind of verbal shorthand for "Is that all right with you?" You can also use the phrase "OK" as a substitute for "Yes" or if you say "I'm OK" that means "I am well."'

'Oh,' Thomas smiled. 'Yes, thank you.' The smile became a grin. 'Then – OK, thank you, I will have a cup of tea.'

Ryan said, 'Best use the galley on the bus. I'll make it. Are you having one, too?'

Sam nodded. 'Sure, thanks.' He glanced back towards the amphitheatre. He didn't want to delay joining the search for Nicole. Already his imagination was supplying unpleasant little scenarios that might account for her disappearance. 'If you'll just excuse me for a moment, I need to speak with a colleague.'

'By all means.'

'Ryan, if you can just look after Thomas for a little while? I won't be long.'

'No problem. I'll make a start on the tea.'

Sam headed back to the amphitheatre. At the top of the steps he glanced back. Ryan had invited the Reverend Thomas Hather onto the coach.

Sam had hoped Ryan would have suggested to Thomas that he sit on a bench while Ryan brought the cup of tea out to him – although God alone knew what an 1860s man would make of styrofoam cups and tea from a foil sachet anyway. Now he could see that Thomas was taking a lively interest in the interior of the bus.

Sam went quickly down into the amphitheatre, feet thumping hard against the timber. *Why is it*, he asked himself, *that I'm sure I'm going to have some very tricky questions to answer the next time I speak to the good Reverend?*

Chapter Thirty-Five

One

When Sam Baker returned to the bus he stopped and stared in disbelief.

Ryan Keith had played the role of host well. Too damn' well, by far.

The bus was deserted apart from Ryan and the Reverend Thomas Hather. The latter sat in the front seat, sipping tea from a bright blue styrofoam cup while Ryan used his Oliver Hardy bowler to point at the TV mounted at the front of the bus.

Sam walked quickly across the car park and stepped through the bus doorway.

One glance took it all in.

Wide-eyed, the cup held frozen in mid-drink, the 1865 clergyman was staring at the TV. A TV that wouldn't even be built in its crudest form by Baird until 1924, and wouldn't exist in the form that the good Reverend was now watching for another hundred years or more.

'What do you think?' Ryan asked brightly, clearly oblivious to the difficulties he was creating.

In near-religious awe Thomas gazed up at the screen. 'All those snakes,' he breathed in disbelief. 'The man hates snakes and yet he finds himself in the tomb with thousands upon thousands of the creatures. What exquisite irony.' The man shot Sam a look of pure excitement. 'Poor Indie has all the woes of Job on his shoulders. To think . . . oh, my gosh, look how he's trying to climb out of reach of the snakes. Just look at the expression on his face: he's quite simply terrified. . .'

The Reverend Thomas Hather's first experience of twentieth-century technology was a TV playing a video copy of an old Indiana Jones movie.

Later, Sam would admit to himself he was surprised by Thomas's fast, almost instantaneous, acceptance of video and television. Sam would have expected a nineteenth-century man to be so startled by a box full of people and sounds that he'd have yelled something about it all being the Devil's work, then fled for dear life. But Thomas took it in his stride. He didn't really believe that there were actual people in the box; he had some grasp of the principles of electricity, even of the rudiments of animation and told them about magic-lantern shows he himself had presented at the town hall.

After watching a few more minutes of television while swallowing the tea in sudden gulps so he wouldn't miss any of the action, Thomas turned his attention to the bus itself.

'You know, I've always thought this would be possible.' Thomas spoke with the gushing enthusiasm of a child visiting a toy factory. 'Just last month I visited my brother in Durham. I travelled on the new express locomotive; speeds reached by that machine have been recorded in excess of seventy-five miles per hour. That in itself is extraordinary, but why must locomotives be restricted to rails, I asked myself? Imagine the network of roads we have compared to the rail network! It occurred to me that lighter locomotives could be built to run on roads rather than rails. They would have to be far smaller and slower, of course, and something would have to be done to suppress the noise and smoke, otherwise all these Snorting Billies would frighten the horses. But can you imagine such machines running through our streets in towns, along roads into the countryside? Such road locomotives would obviate the need for laying costly steel rails from John O' Groats to Land's End.

Now, before I climbed on this omnibus I noticed a small door panel labelled "water". Then I saw the gear levers and the wheel control. Straightaway I told myself that this vehicle is not horse-drawn but powered by steam. Am I right?'

The water inlet on the side of the bus, Sam knew, was where the toilet and kitchen galley tanks were refilled. Again he realised that to patronize this nineteenth-century Englishman would be a fool's errand. 'It's a new process,' Sam said.

'Internal combustion,' Ryan supplied, pleased to be contributing to the conversation.

'Internal combustion? Is it . . . OK?' The Reverend Thomas beamed with delight at being able to use his newly-learnt phrase.

Sam smiled and nodded. 'It works very much OK.' He then went on to give a thumbnail sketch of the workings of a diesel engine, even though Karl Friedrich Benz wouldn't fire up the world's first internal-combustion engine for another twenty years. As he talked he glanced out through the bus window to where Jud was leading two dozen men and women into the wood to search for Nicole. He knew he should be with them. But Thomas's arrival was developing into a knotty problem of Gordan proportions. There was no question of giving him the bum's rush and simply saying, 'I've work to do, so I'll be seeing you,' and waving him goodbye as he cycled away. The man's quick eye was noticing more and more – whether it was technology (he'd spotted a camcorder left on a seat) or fashions (there was a Gola tracksuit in glossy nylon draped over the back of the driver's seat). He'd even seen a jigger of UHT milk on the floor, picked it up and was examining it with an acute air of concentration.

Sam quickly realized that, short of keeping the man locked up in the visitors' centre (a morgue and now a jail?), he'd have to do some pretty nifty explaining. And the bottom line was that the explanation might have to be the truth, the whole truth and nothing but the truth.

Sam glanced out of the window once more as the search party fanned out into the shadows of the trees. Lee Burton was the last into the wood; he turned, noticed Sam watching and gave him a wave.

Twenty-three people went into the wood. Not all of them were going to come back.

Two

William's people had regrouped in a dense part of the wood where water tumbled down a cliff face. They'd obviously salvaged what they could from their destroyed camp.

Nicole felt detached from herself now. As if moving through a dream world she walked down towards the twenty or so people who were laying out blankets, bits of food and knives, or examining broken cooking pots. And there she was, a slim blonde-haired twenty-five-year-old, dressed in lycra cycling shorts and white T-shirt, with the hairy growth of the mouse's head swelling from her shoulder.

Already it had begun to itch, as if mouse nerve endings were bonding with the human parts of her.

This is how my future's going to be, she told herself with no real surprise. The door to her old world had clanged shut behind her. Her future as a barrister would never happen now. No wig and gown. No office with walnut-veneered furniture; no *Halsburies Statutes of England* lining rows of bookshelves; no office politics; no scandals whispered over the photocopier where you learn which of your brother or sister barristers is sleeping with his or her secretary.

She stared at the people laying out travel blankets or sorting through cracked mugs. They were all monsters: like William, like Tony, like Grimwood. They were monsters like her.

And the future she had worked for and dreamed about was all gone.

SIMON CLARK

It had gone, of course, out like the proverbial light, when that first time-slip had so rudely whipped them back from the twenty-second of June, 1999. Only perhaps she hadn't really allowed herself to believe it to be so. Now, as a man with earthworms hanging like pink facial hair from his face looked up at her, she knew that those accidental time travellers were like shipwreck victims clinging to the wreckage. They were all doomed. But they hadn't realized it yet.

A woman with a face full of cats' eyes that were all bright with feline curiosity took her by the arm and led her to sit beside a fire.

Nicole's old life had ended.

Her new life had begun.

Here.

Three

'Who's there?' The bus driver for Town & Country Tours bent at the waist to look under a clump of bushes. The hard wad of banknotes that he'd taken when selling drinks and snacks from the bus's galley dug into his groin. He grunted, pulled at his pocket to reposition the wad, then bent down again. 'Nicole? Nicole, is that you?' There was no reply but he had seen a pair of legs move in the shadows, the feet whispering through the papery leaves.

'Look, Nicole. I don't know what someone's done to upset you, but stop farting around, will you?'

He spotted the legs again, just indistinct shapes beneath the branches of a bush. He glanced round. The rest of the search party was nowhere in sight; they were away to his left somewhere, calling her name.

'Jud's told us all to keep away from the wood. He says it's not safe any more for you lasses.' He recognized a trickle of fear running down his own spine. 'Probably not safe for anyone,' he added.

The bushes parted.

The bus driver allowed his eyes to travel from the feet, up the tree-trunk legs sheathed in some loose woollen fabric, up the enormous chest to a face.

'Aw . . . Christ . . .' the man breathed.

The face was framed by a scraggy ruff of hair. But it wasn't the hair.

Nor the blue tattoos on the upper lip and chin.

It was the snakes rising from the face and the side of the head with an angry sizzling sound, like sand being drizzled onto paper.

'Dear Christ.'

The bus driver stared in horror at the snake that curled out of the man's eye. Its serpent body formed a corkscrew as it coiled, ready to strike.

Hypnotized, the bus driver never took his eyes off the black beady eyes of the snake; even when the huge bear of a man stepped forward, raised the axe, then swung it in a horizontal arc like a batsman slugging a ball.

The axe blade glided smoothly through the entire complex structure of the bus driver's neck – three hundred million years of evolution there, severed in less than a second. Skin, muscle, nerves, oesophagus, trachea, spinal cord, jugular veins, carotid arteries. Ten pounds of head rolled one way, two hundred pounds of trunk and limbs another. Blood rushed over the fallen leaves like spilt wine.

Four

How do you tell a man from 1865 that the man he's talking to is from 1999?

Sam pondered.

You might find all this a bit of a giggle, but we've just hauled ourselves back one hundred and thirty-four years to be here today.

Or:

Hey, guess what, Tom, old buddy? You were long dead before I was even born! Shame you missed out on the Second World War,

Disney pictures, air travel, moon landings, Burger King and zip fasteners.

Cue: freak-out time.

No, that won't do, Sam, he told himself. This clergyman was one hell of a bright cookie. Right now he was crouching down looking through the open door of the refrigerator in the kitchen galley.

'Look at that,' he was saying as he rubbed his fingers along a layer of flaky white frost on the ice compartment. 'It's a hot day in May, and yet here you have ice just whenever you require it.'

'But you have ice?'

'Oh yes, of course. There's an ice factory in Casterton; they'll deliver to one's home – penny a block. But this is so very, very convenient; a box that manufactures ice on an omnibus?'

Ryan said, 'Try one of the beers; they're really cold.'

'Cold beer.' Thomas looked up with raised eyebrows. 'That's rather perverse, isn't it? Ales should be served at room temperature, but then fashions change so quickly these days. I remember my father taking the family to a restaurant in London. Back in the Fifties . . .'

My God, that's the eighteen-*fifties,* Sam thought; *not our Fifties of rock 'n' roll, the Korean war and the advent of teen power.*

'Then my father would treat us to a meal at the Cavour,' Thomas reminisced. 'You know, a bottle of violet wine would be included in the price of the meal and I've never tasted anything so wonderful. Ah, those omnibus windows. How did you come by such flawless plate glass of that size? Incredible, simply incredible.' His pale blue eyes fixed intelligently on Sam's. 'But then, *all* this equipment is extraordinary. Far too extraordinary to support a few people on an archaeological dig, am I right?'

Here goes, Sam told himself. *It's time to give him the low-down on the whole caboodle.* Surely all this technology was positively shrieking out to the man that it didn't belong in the England of 1865? In fact, it didn't belong anywhere on Earth at that time. It was an anachronism with a great shrieking capital A!

As Sam opened his mouth to speak, he heard an urgent thumping sound from the other end of the bus.

He turned to see another stranger. This was a man in a grey suit, complete with a high-winged collar. He was taking off a white straw hat.

'Parson? Oh, there you are, parson. Excuse me. I'm sorry to trouble you but Dr Goldman asks if you can come straightaway. He thinks it's little Harry's time.'

The bright light in the young clergyman's eyes immediately dulled. The smile died. A muscle flickered at the corner of his mouth, twitching one end of the lip. 'Oh . . .' he said in a voice that seemed to ache with disappointment. 'So soon?'

'It looks as if all hope's gone,' the man in the straw boater said. 'Dr Goldman says the little man's lungs have filled up.'

Under his breath Thomas breathed. 'Oh, when the doctors have done all they can then it's time for the poor bloody clergymen to hold their hands and tell them they're going to a far, far better place.' Sam sensed Thomas's muscles knotting in a silent inner rage. 'All right, Ben' Thomas called in a clear voice. 'Thanks for telling me. You have your bicycle?'

'Yes, parson.'

'Best get back to the Middletons as quickly as you can. Tell them I'm on my way.'

'I'm sorry,' Thomas said to Sam and Ryan as he hurried away along the aisle between the bus seats. 'I really have to dash now.'

Sam followed Thomas off the bus. 'What's wrong?'

'There's a boy in the town. A wee lad of five years. He's dying by inches, poor fellow. It's breaking his parents' hearts.' He picked up his bike from where it rested against a tree and turned it, ready for mounting. 'Damn and blast!' The barely concealed fury rose into the clergyman's face, turning it red then white. 'Blast! I hate this. Why can't we do anything more for them? The parents are looking for a miracle to save the boy's life and all I can do is try and comfort them and tell them he'll be happy in heaven. What a miserable specimen that makes me feel, I can tell you.'

'Wait . . . what's wrong with the boy?'

Thomas scowled furiously at Sam, clearly thinking he was merely wasting his time with idle questions. Then Sam saw the young parson's eyes move swiftly to the bus, then back again; this time there was the tiniest glimmer in those pale blue eyes. 'He's suffering from diphtheria. Why do you ask?'

'Look, Thomas, wait here.' The twin-jointed extra fingers that served as Sam's thumbs began to tingle as he was gripped by an outrageous idea. 'I won't be a moment.'

'But I'm expected at the Middletons.'

'Please, just a moment. I have to check on something.'

Sam ran hard. He bounded down the amphitheatre's wooden steps three at a time. The sound of his thumping feet amplified to explosive crashes echoed around the acoustically shaped hollow of rock.

'Damn,' he hissed as he reached the deserted stage area. 'Damn, damn . . .' Jud's wife Dot was nowhere in sight.

For all he knew she might have disappeared into the woods with the rest of the search party.

He raced down to the river banking where he looked left, then right. There was no one in sight. *Crap.*

'You appear in a hurry, old boy.' Carswell's lofty voice drifted down to him.

He looked up to see Carswell standing there on the deck of his launch with all the regal air of a king gazing down from his throne at a commoner.

'Carswell. Have you seen Dot Campbell?'

'You look as if the devil himself's got a whiff of you.'

'Carswell, I'm in a hurry. Have you seen her? Yes or no?'

'My God, on one of your tedious life-or-death quests for the little people, Mr Baker? When will you learn that they—'

'For Chrissakes just shut your stupid mouth. Mrs Camp-bell. Have you seen her?'

'Try the bloody boat, old boy, and all the best to you.' Carswell returned to his seat and picked up a drink.

Sam ran up onto the deck of the narrow boat. 'Dot? Dot!'

'Whatever's the matter?' Zita asked coming up on deck. 'Have you found Nicole? Is she all right?'

'No, she's not been found yet. Not as far as I know, anyway. Is Dot down in the cabin?'

'No, she went with the search party in case Nicole was hurt.'

'Damn.' Sam slammed his fist down against his leg. 'I thought we could actually do some good.'

'Why? What on earth's happened?'

Sam quickly told Zita about the sick child in Casterton. 'The question is,' he said, 'is diphtheria treatable?'

'Yes, I'm certain. We once made a video promo for a drug company. I even scripted the historical part that listed all the illnesses that killed people by the score in the past which are treatable by—'

'Do you know if we've got the drugs here to treat it?'

'We have antibiotics.' She bit her lip as if suddenly uncertain of herself. 'And I have been practising using a hypodermic on an orange. Dot thought it would be a good idea to teach me how to—'

'Great, you're our doctor, then. Grab whatever you need and meet me up at the car.'

'Sam. I've never injected a human being before. Besides I haven't a clue what dosage—'

'Zita, don't worry; we'll busk it.'

'*Sam?*'

'Please try, Zita. The boy will die anyway. At least give him one shot at kicking this bug.'

'OK. Give me two minutes.' She hurried down below.

'*Yee-ess!*' Sam felt as if a fire was sweeping through him from head to toe. It was a fusion of exultation and triumph. Perhaps in the cosmic scheme of things to save a child's life meant nothing, but perhaps just this once they could kick the grim reaper in the seat of his pants and send him packing.

By the time he returned to the car park Ryan was standing alone, feeding the rim of the bowler round and around in his hand. His eyes were large and worried-looking.

'Where's Thomas?' Sam called.

'He said he couldn't wait. So he set off on the bike.'

'Hell.' Sam wasn't going to let this slip through his fingers. The loss of Ruth in that air raid still stung him hard. He felt he was to blame.

'Wait here,' he called.

'Where are you going?'

'Tell Jud Campbell I've taken Zita into town. We're going to try and fix that sick kid.'

He ran across to the Range Rover, thumbing the remote as he ran. With a flash of lights the alarm deactivated and the door-locks clicked.

Seconds later he spun the car round the car park to the top of the steps as Zita raced up them, her long legs, tightly clad in the tiger-skin leggings, carrying her athletically. Gripped tightly in her hands was a leather briefcase containing the precious antibiotics.

He opened the door for her. Once she was in the passenger seat he accelerated ferociously across the car park.

Seconds later, the Range Rover dropped from the twentieth-century metalled roadway to the cinder track with a crunch.

'Sorry about that,' he called above the rumble of tyres.

'Don't worry about it, Sam. I guess we're on a mission of mercy.'

'You guess right. Ah, there he is.'

Toiling along the track on the heavy bicycle, his feet pumping the pedals, was the Reverend Thomas Hather.

Sam swung the car in front of him and braked hard, throwing up clouds of black dust.

'Get in!' Sam shouted to Thomas.

'Get in?' Thomas stared incredulously at the Range Rover.

Sam opened the back door to the passenger seat. 'I'll take you to where you want to go. Don't worry about the bike. I'll stick it on the roof rack.'

Thomas helped Sam lift the bike onto the roof rack where Sam lashed it in place with a piece of line.

'But why are you doing this?' Thomas asked, confused.

'You'll see.'

'But—'

'All you've got to do is give me directions to the Middletons. OK?'

'Do what?' Thomas asked dazed. Then he caught the groove of Sam's enthusiasm and he nodded sharply. 'OK.'

Moments later they were on the move again. Thomas in the back looking round in wonder at the interior of the car; Zita hugging the precious cache of antibiotics to her chest; Sam driving hard.

Chapter Thirty-Six

One

Sam made the introductions as he drove along the dirt track.

'This is Zita Prestwyck. Zita, this is the Reverend Thomas Hather.'

'Great to meet you.' It was a typical Zita greeting. Hearty, vigorous, with an almost knuckle-cracking handshake. Sam clocked Thomas's look of surprise at the firm grip. He also noticed this nineteenth-century clergyman's next expressions of surprise as he registered Zita's sassy tiger-patterned leggings and bare arms, her T-shirt, and the studs and chains in her ears and nose.

And just wait until you see the stud in the tongue, Sam thought. *That will really blow your socks off.*

In the back seat, clutching his cloth cap in both hands, Thomas gave a sharp shake of his head, obviously suspecting that this was a hallucination. He squeezed the arm-rests experimentally, looked round at the interior of the car, then stared out of the window at the meadow flying past at a dizzy rate.

'This road engine travels at a greater rate than I could have imagined,' he said a small voice.

'We're doing almost forty,' Sam called back over his shoulder. 'Just wait until we hit the road, then I can really open her up.'

'Open her up? Then it will only take a few moments to reach town?'

'If it's a clear run I can make it easily in five minutes.'

'Five minutes. Dear Lord . . . dear Lord . . . at one mile a minute that means you will be travelling at sixty miles per the hour. That's impossible.'

Zita looked back over her shoulder. 'Best wear your seat belt.'

Thomas's look of bemused innocence intensified. His mouth hung open as he looked round for the seat belt . . . whatever that might be.

'Here, let me.'

Zita knelt up on the passenger seat facing backwards; quickly she fastened the seat belt across the surprised man.

'When you want to release the seat belt, just press this button firmly. OK?'

'OK. Very OK.'

'The countryside's changed a hell of a lot,' Zita said as she strapped herself back in. 'All those crappy electricity pylons have gone.'

'And look at the fields.' Sam nodded. 'Look how small they are.'

'And all those hedgerows and trees. It looks like a different country.'

On the main road Sam took the car up to sixty. He'd expected the roads to be like rutted cart-tracks, but if this was an average example of an eighteen-sixties road, then they were pretty good. The carriageway didn't consist of blacktop. There were no white lines, or any camber to speak of. Instead the road was a broad strip of dazzling white. Probably limestone chippings rolled down until it formed a hard, flat surface. Glancing in the rear-view mirror, he noticed the wheels were kicking up a hell of a lot of dust. To anyone watching the car pass by it would look as if steam was rising in a plume from its back.

He concentrated on the road. It didn't have curves so much as sharp elbow-crook bends. It had been designed for foot and horse, not for a 1999 Range Rover that was easily capable of hitting a hundred on a good stretch of late-twentieth-century road-tar.

As with the 1940s roads there was a goodly amount of horse dung. The car's big tyres zipped through these with a slish-slash sound.

His arms and shoulders began to ache from the tension of gripping the steering wheel so tightly. He realized also that the car was turning the heads of people walking along the road. And in contrast to the twentieth-century habit of walking at the side of the road on pavements, most of these people walked in the middle, expecting to encounter nothing faster than a horse-drawn mail coach. Sam made free use of the horn, yet still he had to steer a zig-zag line to avoid flattening astonished locals, who watched open-mouthed as the metal box on wheels roared down on them.

'Good Lord,' Thomas repeated over and over in the back. 'Good Lord . . . the saints protect us . . . Oh, good Lord . . .'

'Thomas,' Sam called without taking his eyes off the road. 'Sing out which road to take when we get into Casterton.'

'Yes . . . I— oh, good Lord . . .'

Sam weaved round a horse drawing a cart piled high with cow hides. The horse reared between its shafts at the sound of the car.

'Oh, Lord, don't frighten the horses, Sam. Don't frighten them.'

'I'll try not to.' He laid off using the horn and eased down the speed a little. But the fact of the matter was that he wanted to get to the Middleton household as fast as possible.

So Carswell thinks I'm crazy, he told himself. But they could save a life here. In any day or year that was important in itself. But, again, he realized here was an opportunity to show that humankind weren't passive victims waiting for the Grim Reaper's scythe to cut them low. They could build hospitals, train doctors, develop medicines. And sometimes, God willing, they could slap Death in the face and send it on its way with its tail between its legs.

'Watch out for the geese!'

He braked at the sound of Zita's warning. There, waddling in front of the car, were a dozen fat geese being driven along the road to market.

'How far to the Middletons' place?'

'A mile, a little less.'

'Damn' geese.' He honked the horn. The geese honked back. Carefully, he eased the car forward, pushing a path through the big birds.

Beside him, Zita had taken a paperback book from the briefcase and was riffling through the pages. He noticed that her hand had begun to shake.

He guessed it was one of Dot Campbell's textbooks from the time where she'd been a nurse. 'What does that say about diphtheria?'

She read aloud: 'An acute bacterial infection primarily affecting the nose, throat and larynx. Death results from the growth of a membrane across the throat that chokes the child. And it says here it can be cured with penicillin.'

'God bless you, Sir Alexander Fleming.'

'The problem is it doesn't give any dosages.'

'So we don't know how much to inject into the boy?'

'No.'

'But is it possible to OD on penicillin? It's not as if it's a narcotic, is it?'

'Search me.'

Sam glanced at Thomas in the rear-view mirror. He was concentrating hard on the conversation, and though he probably didn't understand it completely he caught the gist. 'You think you can treat the Middleton boy?'

'We're going to try, Thomas. We're going to try.'

Thomas nodded, his expression tight with worry. 'Then we really must hurry. If I've been called he won't have much time.'

'You've got it.' Sam accelerated into town. He was concentrating almost every shred of nervous energy into getting the car through the narrowing streets in one piece.

Even so, he noticed the buildings were lower, and everywhere there were little cottages, looking like children's toys that had been gathered up in great handfuls and tossed higgledy-piggledy around the town centre.

A pall of smoke from domestic fires painted a grimy streak across an otherwise perfect blue sky.

Sam noticed Zita staring too. Women in long skirts walked briskly along the street carrying absurdly large shopping baskets. Every man in sight wore a hat of some kind. The working classes had soft brown caps while the professional classes favoured high top hats that were such a shiny black that they made him think of black licorice. The hats were complemented by frock coats from which could be glimpsed the starched cuffs and collars of shirts that were a dazzling white. These were sharp-dressed men, no doubting that.

And everyone was hurrying, too. So much for the myth of past ages being slower, less stressful, more relaxed. The town centre was hustling and bustling like any modern street in New York, London, Paris, Rome – you name it. This was like an ant heap that had been broddled with a stick.

They were hurrying busily, that was, until they saw the car. Again he was conscious of people stopping to stare at what must have appeared to them a monstrous contraption roaring through their safe little market town.

Sam had to keep the speed down to twenty now to avoid people who simply walked out into the road to stare at the car.

At that moment he wanted to yell at them to shift their butts out of the goddamn way. A mental image of the boy lying feverishly in bed, drowning in his own sputum, suddenly sizzled its way into his brain as savagely as a red-hot cattle brand. He could almost hear the hiss of air through the boy's throat as the diphtheria membrane sealed the airway shut.

'Move it, move it,' he muttered. Sweat dripped down into his eyes. Beside him Zita sat with the book open in one hand while she stared at an ampoule of penicillin in the other.

'Christ, this is going to be kill or cure,' she muttered to herself.

'Sam, turn left here. Yes! By the cooper's.'

'The cooper's? Oh, the barrel maker's?'

Sam turned into the side street. It was hellishly narrow. If a horse turned up in the other direction there'd be pandemonium.

'How far now?' Sam called.

'A hundred yards or so. It's the first one in a row of red-brick villas. You can't— There, Sam, there it is! Red door.'

Sam braked hard. The car slithered over the cobbled street, the back end fishtailing as the tyres lost their grip.

'OK, Thomas,' Sam said, slipping off his seat belt. 'Just lead the way. We'll follow.'

Already a crowd had gathered outside the house. Sam realized that this was the age when life revolved around the home. People were born in their parents' bedrooms. They died in their own homes, too. It would be another eighty years or so before it would become the custom for lives to begin as well as end in hospitals.

At first, he glared in fury at the crowd of men, women and children standing at the door, thinking that this was some ghoulish kind of spectator sport. But then he saw their expressions.

With all medical help gone, and all hope gone, friends and neighbours were mounting a silent and respectful vigil. They were offering moral support to the man and woman inside the house as their child slipped into that final coma.

The crowd parted as the vicar made his way to the front door.

Sam didn't doubt that he and Zita attracted puzzled stares, but they were focused on what they had to do now.

Inside the house it was still, gloomy, and strangely cool despite the heat of the summer's day. All the curtains were drawn.

Sam couldn't really see in front of Thomas or hear what was said, but soon they were climbing the stairs, led by a woman of around fifty in long skirts.

Already Sam's tongue had dried. He'd never seen a dying child before. And suddenly the landing in front of him when he reached the top of the stairs was filled with a kind of dark fog. He realized all this frightened him to the bone. He was frightened to see a child dying; he was frightened to see the parents, their hearts torn to little pieces by grief.

He glanced at Zita beside him. She clutched the briefcase to her chest, her eyes large in the gloom.

The walk along that landing to a closed door seemed to take forever. It was a dark and terrible journey. He'd never experienced anything like this before. Not even when the lightning bolt had flung him from that tree and killed his friends.

Then he'd been numbed by physical as well as emotional shock.

But here every nerve ending was made sensitive to a near-unbearable degree. A lavender smell flooded his nostrils; he heard the whispery rustle of feet against the polished boards; even in this gloom he could still see individual dust motes lit by what little sunlight needled its way through microscopic holes in the velvet drapes.

The woman opened the door.

Sam licked his dry lips. This was it. There was no going back now.

Two

With the curtains drawn the nursery bedroom lay deep in gloom.

The first thing Sam heard was a crackling, like brown paper being quickly scrunched in someone's hands. Then he heard the constant yet very low moan of a child in pain.

He thought he was prepared for what he'd see.

374

But the reality was still a shock.

A tiny face lay half-buried among the bedclothes while two tiny fists gripped the top of a sheet. There was some kind of exhausted desperation in that grip. It was as if the hands were trying to stop the sheets sliding up over the face and stifling what life there was left.

And, dear God, that face was so grey. So incredibly grey. The colour of wet putty. A fringe of brown hair was stuck down against the pallid forehead. Again emphasizing the pitiful grey that radiated its deathly pallor.

The boy's eyes were partly closed, with the pupils fixed on a point just above the window as if he was watching something there. The crackling in his lungs grew louder. He tried to cough out the sputum but didn't have the strength. His chest beneath the blanket merely shook slightly, interrupting the laboured breathing before it continued again in achingly shallow gasps.

Sam stopped, feeling as if he'd just taken a blow in the stomach. He heard the blood stop dead abruptly in his neck for what seemed whole moments. Then it started again with a deadly thudding sound.

Suddenly he felt their intrusion into this death was crude; fuelled by his arrogance. They had no right to be here. No right at all.

Thomas sounded in control. In a very low, very soft voice he said, 'Dr Goldman.'

The doctor looked up. A middle-aged man with dark crinkly hair and soulful eyes that expressed nothing but a tired despair.

'Ah, Reverend,' he said softly, as if not to wake the boy. 'I'm glad to see you. Very glad.' He directed those brown soulful eyes in the direction of a young man and woman who sat side by side on straight-back chairs beside the bed. Sam realized these must be the mother and father. Both leaned forward to watch their sick son with such a look of concentration on their faces that Sam realized they were willing their child to breathe. He even saw the mother take a large breath every now and again as if she could somehow breathe for both of them.

Ever so gently, with a compassion that sent a shiver down Sam's spine, Thomas rested his hands on the shoulders of the parents. Then he spoke to them in a low murmuring voice.

Zita stood statue-like beside him, watching without moving a muscle.

Oh, God. This was a tableau he'd seen in old paintings. The child's deathbed scene. The parents sitting at one side of the bed. The doctor at the other, his strained face revealing his frustration and sorrow at being able to do nothing on God's earth for the child. And the child itself, dying by inches.

Sam could almost hear the undertaker's hammer pounding nails into coffin wood, and the scraping of the grave-digger's spade opening a pitifully small slot in the ground.

Again he felt that Zita and he were ugly intruders. Blundering into a place where they simply did not belong.

He looked down again at that grey face. Impossibly grey. It was if all the grey in the world was contained there in fantastic concentration.

And the little boy's partly-open eyes still gazed at the curl of torn wallpaper above the curtain.

At that moment the father turned to Sam and Zita. He was a young man, not much more than a boy himself, yet with old eyes behind his spectacles. 'The Reverend's just told us that you've come here to try and help Harry. I'm grateful.' He spoke in a soft voice, barely above a whisper. 'Believe me when I say I am. Thank you. But—'

Sam turned cold.

'Dr Goldman here's done his very best. And the little lad's fought his hardest . . . but he's suffered so much in the last few days. We think he should be left to his peace now.'

Sam said gently, 'We won't disturb him. Or hurt him. We can give him an injection that will—'

The man shook his head. 'Thank you for your concern. But, no. We wish to let him go now . . . it's really more than our flesh and blood can stand to see him endure any more.'

Sam was going to try again, but Zita caught his eye. She gave a tiny shake of her head. *No*, she was saying, *let them be*.

He nodded at the man. For a moment he wanted to express his sympathy to him and his wife. But there was nothing he could say that wouldn't sound so crass it would jangle from those walls like the coarsest of insults.

Sam and Zita backed out of the room, leaving the doctor gazing at the dying boy's face, the parents still willing the boy to breathe. While the Reverend Thomas Hather stood behind the parents with his hands on their shoulders.

In a moment Sam and Zita were outside in the glaring brilliance of a summer's afternoon.

Sam felt chewed up and spat out by the events of the past few moments.

He'd given it his best shot.

Not good enough, Sam, old buddy. Not nearly good enough.

He followed Zita to the car. It was covered in chalky smears from the drive into town. A few people were taking a close interest in it. A boy had climbed onto the bonnet to look in through the windscreen. An old man was poking one of the tyres with his walking stick.

Zita leaned against a wall, holding the briefcase to her chest. She looked exhausted.

Sam leaned against the wall next to her.

'I screwed up,' he said in a low voice. 'I screwed up royal.'

'We did our best. But you've got to respect the parents' wishes. Besides, I don't think I could have given the boy the injection anyway.' She shrugged, looking sick with herself. 'I wouldn't have had the guts.'

Across the town came the sound of a church clock striking two. Sam allowed his gaze to range across the street with its people hurrying to and fro. He noticed a good number of them were limping. There were people with legs that were so bowed they curved outwards until they looked as if they'd exchanged legs for springy bamboo

canes. A girl of around fifteen stared at him as she walked
by, surprised at his and Zita's bizarre clothes. The girl had a
cruel squint, with one eye turned in to stare down the left
hand side of her nose.

Squints, rickets, bow legs. The kind of medical problems
that were ironed out of the human race after the Second
World War by vitamin supplements and state-of-the-art
medical care. Now he saw that perhaps one in five of all
passers-by were suffering from some visible deformity or
disability. This was the age when a glitch in your bone
structure or a cast in your eye just couldn't be fixed. So
you stayed with the limp or squint all your life. He also
noticed a couple of women with pink crinkled skin on
their necks and faces; no doubt burn scars from night-
dresses catching alight after brushing against lamps.
Hadn't he read somewhere once that in the nineteenth
century perhaps as many children were killed by their
clothes catching fire as from disease?

Despite killer viruses, homicidal psychopaths, terrorists
and speeding cars, 1999 suddenly seemed a very safe place
to be.

'Well,' Sam said at last, 'shall we be getting back to our
little patch of tomorrow at the amphitheatre?'

'Why not?' she sighed. 'I'm going to go down on my
bended knees and beg a brandy from Carswell.'

'Yeah, why not?' He walked towards the car, feeling dirty
and tired, and wishing for nothing more than to slide into a
hot bath.

Yeah, in your dreams, Sam, old buddy.

He avoided looking up at the curtained window behind
which the little boy lay dying. Shame and guilt were
working hard together in his gut and he didn't like the
sensation. He didn't like it one little bit.

He reached into his pocket for the remote to unlock the
doors. As he did so he felt a hand touch his elbow.

He turned round to see a woman of about twenty-five
looking earnestly at him through eyes that were so red

and sore-looking that it seemed as if sand had been rubbed into them.

It only took him a moment to realize that she was the dying boy's mother. She looked emotionally wrung out, her voice was a rasping whisper, but she was calm. 'Sir . . . sir.' She fixed those painfully sore eyes on him. 'You won't hurt him? You can give your word?'

He looked at Zita.

'It's just an injection.' Zita said gently. 'But we need to be as quick as we can.'

The boy's mother nodded and hurried back to the house with both following.

Sam asked Zita in a low voice, 'Are you OK?'

'I've never injected a human being. I don't know how much penicillin to use. I've never been so scared in my life before.' She shot him a tiny smile. 'But I'm going to do my level best.'

They went back into the house and up the stairs. Back across that darkened landing with dust motes hanging like silver stars in the air. Sam's mouth was dry. The fate of the child was in Zita's hands now. Maybe in God's, too.

Chapter Thirty-Seven

One

Blonde-haired Nicole Wagner, who had once aspired to a law career, sat by the stream to watch men and women eating crusts of dry bread.

She'd become a stranger in a strange land. The mouse ears twitched on the back of her shoulder, lightly tickling her skin.

It was a strange sensation but she knew she must get used to it.

There was no question of being able to cut out the mouse head, or for that matter the whole of the mouse body that had fused inside her upper torso. Even the cells were melted together, so for a few cubic inches inside her shoulder it wouldn't be possible to tell where the mouse ended and Nicole Wagner began.

'Here, you must be thirsty.' William held out to her a mug that bore the picture of a bearded man along with the words: *Edward VII. God Save The King!* This was just one of a huge haul of pots, cups and plates that these people had scrounged and salvaged from any number of periods in history. She didn't doubt for a second that here people sat side by side drinking from Roman goblets, Viking tankards, Victorian mugs and McDonald's paper cups complete with plastic lid and straw.

She thanked him and drank. It was beer, not something

she'd normally drink but this tasted good: a rich, nutty flavour and not at all gassy.

'Thanks,' she said with a tired smile. 'I needed that.'

'Oh, but if all our problems could be solved by a yard or two of ale.'

'I know mine could,' came the gruff cockney voice from William's stomach. 'Now, William, if you could see your way to putting away a cup or two of good London dry gin I'd be in boozer's heaven, so help me.'

William shook his head. 'The answer's a regretful no.'

'I bloody well knew it,' Bullwitt groaned. 'Tell me we're moving on to some other place, go on, tell me.'

'Remember, Bullwitt, it will be my feet that will be carrying your noisy head.'

Nicole watched in silent bemusement as William held a conversation with the face that bulged from his stomach. It was like watching a pair of brothers talking – a mixture of banter and argument, yet all with an undercurrent of affection.

Bullwitt's voice rumbled wistfully. 'We'd all be best going back to the seventeen hundreds. It was quieter then, no hassles; besides, the beer tastes better.'

'I don't think it is a question to which year we travel,' William said. 'We should endeavour to leave this place and put as many miles between ourselves and the amphitheatre as possible. Regardless of what time period we occupy those troublesome rogues always find us and steal our possessions, and it's as much as we can do to escape with our necks.'

'What do you suggest? Board a ship and sail away to bleedin' Tahiti?'

'No.'

'Because we'd look a pretty sight, wouldn't we? Me, you, Billy across there with a neckful of frogs, and the rest of us all marching away along the road to the seaside.'

'No, clearly we must all discuss what we should do next. Although it goes without saying that to remain here jeopardizes the safety of us all.'

At last the penny dropped. Nicole looked up suddenly.

'You mean you can choose what year you live in? So you can control this thing?'

William looked at her with surprised blue eyes. 'Why, yes. Not as accurately as some of the Liminals, but if we choose to make landfall in 1766 or 1966, then we do it.'

For the first time since they'd somehow come unstuck from the normal flow of time Nicole felt hope tingling inside of her. Maybe it was a fragile hope. But she realized that there was a chance – just an outside chance – she could somehow get all those people in the amphitheatre back home to their own date and time.

She leaned across and seized William's hand. 'You're telling me you can travel in time? How does it work, exactly?'

Two

The Reverend Thomas Hather took Sam and Zita home for a meal of ham and eggs. Bread and butter sat piled high on a plate in the centre of the table. Tea steamed in bone-china cups.

It was late in the evening and the summer sun cast a reddish glow through the tall windows. Outside on the rectory lawn a peacock fanned its feathers in a display of iridescent blues and greens.

Sam looked across at Zita. She held a cup in both hands. As she drank she stared into space, clearly still wrapped up in what had happened that afternoon.

Despite everything, he still found himself comparing 1865 to 1999, noticing the changes in even mundane domestic objects. Of course, there were no electric lights. There was an alabaster lamp on the mantelpiece with a glass tube that was scorched and sooty at the top. There were candle holders. Furniture was chunky, ornate and carved – over-carved, in fact – so there were no straight lines, only curves, bulges, corkscrew chair legs, table legs that ran from elephantine thickness down to slender points. But this

wasn't a perverse taste for bizarre furniture on the part of
Thomas: rather, it was the typical style of the time. This was
opulent 'in your face' furniture, as strong and as enduring –
and as noticeable – as the Empire that inspired it.

The meal had been served by a matronly woman of
around seventy who 'kept house' for Thomas. She'd
goggled her eyes in astonishment at Zita's leggings and
clicked her tongue, but had said nothing.

Thomas poured more tea into Zita's cup through a silver
strainer. 'What kind of chance does the Middleton boy
have?'

Zita shook her head. 'I've really no idea. If he can survive
the next twenty-four hours or so that should give the
antibiotic time to work.'

'Antibiotic? I've not heard of such a medicine.'

'It kills bacteria in the body.'

'A poison?'

'More or less, I guess. But it won't harm Harry.'

Unless he's allergic to penicillin, was the unwelcome
thought that ran through Sam's brain.

Zita sipped her tea, her hands shaking slightly. Watching
her administer the drug earlier had been like watching
someone making a record-breaking dive from a high
cliff. She'd examined the medical textbook, gazed at the
ampoules of penicillin. Then she'd simply gone for it.
Quickly filled a syringe, then injected it directly into a
vein in the little boy's leg.

A leg as grey as putty, Sam had remembered. And cold to
the touch, Zita had said later. As cold as a can from the
refrigerator.

Sam had half hoped that during the couple of hours they
were there they'd see the boy miraculously rally; see his eyes
open and that grey face break into a smile.

Of course, nothing ever happened as neatly as that. Harry
Middleton's condition had not altered. He remained all but
unconscious, the slightly parted eyes gazing dully up at the
tear in the wallpaper above the window.

After a while all they could do was promise that they'd call again later. Zita would have to administer another injection the next day.

If they were still here, that was, Sam told himself. If this weird run back through time continued like it had been doing, at any moment they could open their eyes and find themselves back in the amphitheatre.

Sam bit into a slice of bread. He found it coarse, slightly gritty as if grains of sand had found their way into the flour from the millstones, but it tasted good. The butter was good, too; in colour a very pale yellow, it was the creamiest he'd ever tasted.

Thomas was still talking about the penicillin. By now he was wanting to know why the drug wasn't widely available, mentioning about a dozen children who'd died in the last eighteen months or so.

'It's a new drug,' Sam told him. 'Still experimental. It'll be a few years before doctors will be using it. But it—'

'No, no.' Thomas gave a smile that was nervous, awkward, yet clearly determined. He wasn't a man who became angry or assertive often, but Sam saw he wasn't going to be kissed off with any platitudes this time. 'No . . . look.' With a trembling hand he made a slow-motion karate chop onto the table. 'Look. You're in my house, eating my food, I deserve the courtesy of an honest reply.'

'Thomas, penicillin is a new—'

'Please, Mr Baker, credit me with a fraction of intelligence. Clearly you are not what you say you are. Firstly, I find a group of you in most peculiar dress in the amphitheatre. And you simply appeared there with no advance warning. Surely there would have been mention of you in the local newspapers. And you, sir, were hatless.'

'I left my hat in the—'

'No, no, no. You don't normally wear a hat. Look at my face . . . no, lower down.' He pointed to his nose and cheeks. 'The lower part of my face is tanned by the sun. Above my eyebrows there's no tanning at all. Every man in this town, with the exception of yourself, has exactly the same tanning pattern. Browned face, pale forehead. Because we all wear hats whenever we are outside. You clearly never wear a hat. Your forehead is tanned.' Thomas's keen eyes studied Sam. 'It is the mark of a modern civilized man to wear a hat out of doors. Even in North America. You say you are part of an archaeological team, yet I saw no one digging at the amphitheatre. You have in your possession extraordinary vehicles that require no horses to pull them but are impelled by what you maintain is some form of explosive process that drives pistons. And this afternoon I have seen you administer a medicine that I've never heard of, which you say is experimental, but then in Heaven's name why are archaeologists – *so-called* archaeologists – in possession of it?'

Sam leaned back in his chair and sighed. 'Now that is a deduction Sherlock Holmes would shoot his own granny for.'

'And,' Thomas continued, not willing to be deflected, 'you employ phrases and words I have never encountered before. My parish might be in the provinces, but I dare say no other civilized man, at least of this nation, has heard them before.' The Reverend Thomas Hather was trembling but still in control. And without a shadow of a doubt he wanted answers – this time straight ones, not those that were so bent they couldn't stand on their own two feet.

'So,' Thomas continued firmly. 'Will you tell me *why* you are here? And just *where* are you from?'

'The truth?' Sam looked at Zita and said, 'I think it might be easier to tell Thomas everything.'

'Sam? Is that wise? And is it even necessary?'

'I think so.'

'But we could be *pffft* . . . out of here at any second.'

'And what if we aren't? We've been here a day and a night already. Remember what Rolle said? He told us that the mechanism that's dragging us back is going on the fritz.'

'We can't be sure about that.'

'I know, but what if it is? What if it dumps us here for good? We're going to need people like Thomas here to help us. We'll need a roof over our heads, for one thing. Jobs, so we can buy food.'

'But you're going to have a tough time convincing anyone what you say is true. Have you thought that it's all going to sound a bit on the crazy side?'

Sam noticed that Thomas had watched the exchange with profound puzzlement. 'What will sound crazy?' Thomas asked. 'Surely you would do me the courtesy of telling me your story?'

Sam looked at Zita. 'If you want me to keep my trap shut I'll go along with that, but we might be in for a long stopover here.'

Zita finished her drink and replaced the cup on the saucer. 'OK. You're right, Sam. We're going to start needing help before long. After all, Rolle said that there might be trouble from some of these Bluebeard characters. We're going to have to warn these people to be on their guard.'

'I am utterly lost,' Thomas shook his head. 'I don't understand a quarter of what you say. Bluebeards?'

Zita gave Sam a little smile. 'OK. Go for it, Sam.'

Sam thought for a second, looking for the most appropriate words. But the opening sentence that rose flippantly into his mind was: *Once upon a time* . . .

Instead, he rose to his feet. 'Excuse me for a moment. I'll be right back.'

Three

Sam returned from the car with a cardboard box.

When the dining room table had been cleared of the plates and cups, Sam asked Thomas to light the lamp since the daylight had all but gone.

Then, under the light of the oil lamp, which was surprisingly bright, Sam took a number of objects from the box and laid them out on the table. After that, he emptied the contents of his wallet onto the table.

He couldn't help but notice Thomas's eyes growing more and more round.

After a moment Thomas stood up and bent over the table to examine the astonishing artefacts, yet he kept his hands behind his back as if afraid of breaking – or being contaminated by – these objects that shone brightly in the light of the lamp.

'Amazing, truly amazing,' Thomas breathed.

Sam glanced at Zita as he laid out the last of his exhibits on the tablecloth. She nodded her approval.

Then, like a professor of anatomy naming body parts to curious students, he pointed at each item in turn. 'Magazines. *Cosmopolitan, SFX, Sunday Times* magazine. CD cases – REM, Rolling Stones, Mike Oldfield . . . Englebert Humperdinck?' He raised a disbelieving eyebrow at Zita.

Zita flushed. 'My mother left it there the last time I went home.'

'*Akhenaten* by Philip Glass. And a compilation entitled *Road Runners.*'

Music to cruise to ran the caption.

'Mozart's *The Magic Flute*'

'Ah,' Thomas said in recognition.

Sam continued, now listing in a dispassionate way. 'Two *A-to-Z*'s – one Birmingham, one London, and a road atlas of Great Britain. Half a dozen coins, a couple of credit cards, driver's licence. Filling-station receipts. Business cards; two postage stamps . . . US postage stamps, that is. Dollar bills and pounds sterling. And this.' He held up a dictaphone, then put it down with the rest of the exhibits.

'Good Lord,' Thomas marvelled.

'All this . . .' Sam waved his hand across the table, 'is evidence to support what I'm going to tell you next.'

Now Thomas lightly touched each piece in turn – from magazines to money to the CD cases – as if he'd pick up a psychic charge from them.

'The forms and usages of some I recognize,' he said in a whisper. 'Magazines, coins. But some not.' He touched the dictaphone, then the credit cards and CD cases. 'What on Earth are they?'

Sam picked up the dictaphone again, thumbed the rewind button then hit the play button.

Sam's voice came sharp and loud from the speaker. '. . . *support what I'm going to tell you next.*'

Thomas lurched back as if someone had touched him with an electric cattle prod. Then came Thomas's own voice. '*The forms and usages of some I recognize. Magazines, coins. But some not. What on Earth are they?*

'Good Lord,' Thomas breathed, stunned. 'My Good Lord. An echo machine?'

'Dictaphone. They're used all the time.'

'But—'

'Used all the time where we come from.'

Thomas looked at Sam, then at Zita. He looked closely, as if trying to gauge from their expressions whether this wasn't some monumental practical joke. Then he snatched one of the magazines from the table and looked at the cover, rocking it from side to side so it caught the light.

'Photographs that are coloured,' he said, examining the cover. Then he looked at the top of the magazine. '19th May, 1998.' After that he picked up the coins, reading off the years stamped on them. '1991, 1993. Another 1991. 1995. 1999. Good heavens, my word.' He put his hand to his mouth in wonder.

'I thought the easiest way was to show you, rather than tell you.'

'So you two are from . . . my word.' He looked at Zita's face as if seeing her properly for the first time. 'You are, aren't you?' Thomas picked up the dictaphone and turned it over in his hand. Then he raised it and lowered it, as if gauging the weight. When he looked at them again his face wore a look of sheer excitement; his eyes blazed behind the spectacle lenses. 'You've travelled back from the 1990s to here: 1865! My word, you must have fabulous tales to tell!'

'We have,' Sam agreed. 'And unfortunately we have a warning, too. Casterton and everyone in it are in imminent danger of attack from some extremely unpleasant characters.'

Sam realized he had a lot of talking to do. So he took a deep breath and began at the beginning.

Chapter Thirty-Eight

One

Sam Baker recalled his words to the Reverend Thomas Hather as he rowed the two priests across the river.

'And unfortunately we have a warning, too. Casterton and everyone in it are in imminent danger of attack from some extremely unpleasant characters.'

Sometimes with a prediction you can have a near miss. Now that statement missed by a mile.

The hordes of barbarian Bluebeards that he had expected to come pouring down the road into Casterton to loot and burn and kill hadn't arrived.

The summer days rolled pleasantly by.

Every morning Sam expected that with a rush of lights, like something from a psychedelic light show, the accidental time travellers would be whisked back another fifty, or a hundred, or thousand years.

But it just didn't happen.

It looked as if their time ship had run aground on the second of May, 1865. And now it wasn't going any further.

After a while he stopped anticipating the next time-leap. He stopped anticipating that the barbarians would come rushing out of the woods at them, carrying axes and swords and thirsting for blood, rapine and the whole nine yards.

The bottom line was they had to adapt to survive in the world of 1865.

Thank the Lord, as the Reverend Thomas was apt to say, that Sam had risked telling Thomas everything. He had believed. As simple as that, only adding that as a man of the cloth he believed in the literal truth of Biblical miracles. He had no problem in accepting that Jesus Christ had turned water into wine; that He had raised Lazarus from the dead. And it required from him no suspension of disbelief whatsoever to accept completely that the Son of Man had walked on water and fed the five thousand with a few fishes and loaves.

In fact, Thomas believed that Sam Baker and his colleagues had been whisked back in time for some Divine Purpose. That the Will of God Almighty was indeed present in all this. And he believed that same Hand was, in fact, responsible for curing little Harry Middleton of diphtheria through the agency of Zita and the penicillin.

Now, as Sam rowed the boat, appropriately enough, to shore with his priestly cargo, he could fast-forward through the last six months until the present day, a bright but cool fifth of October, 1865.

Nicole Wagner had disappeared without trace in May. The following day the bus driver had vanished during the search for her. Of course there was speculation about death or elopement, or that they'd been individually whisked away to another epoch. But the simple fact of the matter was that neither had returned and the rest of the accidental time travellers had to get on with their lives, coping with day-to-day survival and dealing with the fact that they'd probably never again see families they'd left behind in 1999.

Rolle appeared to them only rarely now. What he told them was always fairly impenetrable. Even Jud confessed he couldn't make much sense of it, even though the man did appear to be becoming calmer and much more lucid than before.

By mid-June Carswell had become bored of sitting in his launch. One morning he simply untied the moorings and headed off downstream without telling anyone where he was going. He'd not been seen since.

Thomas had provided the people at the amphitheatre with a home in the shape of a rambling farm, outbuildings and cottages that belonged to the church. These had been vacant for a while, and as there were no farmlands attached to it and it was some way out of town Thomas had had trouble in letting them. Now, at least, he'd found some tenants – even though they were refugees from 1999.

So, the week following that first meeting with the Reverend Thomas Hather, Sam had moved in with the forty or so surviving time travellers. Only Jud and Dot Campbell and Carswell opted to stay afloat, which in any event eased pressure on what was, after all, limited living accommodation.

To avoid any more public interest in the vehicles they moved them into the coach house and barn.

Sam had soon realized they couldn't live in 1865 for nothing. Again they pawned valuables (modern jewellery they melted down into blobs of unidentifiable gold and silver before selling them). And after buying clothes (to blend in with the local population), paying a couple of months' rent on the place and stocking the larder with enough food for forty people for a few days, they realized they'd have to find work.

So what was a TV director qualified to do in 1865?

Well, the answer was: not much – as Sam had swiftly realized.

Which was why he found himself working the ferryboat across the River Tarn, just downstream from the amphitheatre. The cost of the crossing was a penny a head. Of that, he kept back a halfpenny for himself as his fee. After working through the summer he was tanned and had developed a pair of powerful arms and a broad, hard back. There were calluses on his palms so thick he could have stubbed out a cigarette on them and not felt a thing. In the morning the old ferryman and his wife gave him breakfast (they owned the boat and were to all intents and purposes his employers; a kindly, lovable couple they were, too). Most mornings breakfast was oatmeal so solid you could stand your spoon upright in it like a flagpole. For special treats old Mrs Everton made bacon-tattie which was boiled potatoes broken into pieces then fried in bacon fat, patted down into a dish like a pie and browned in front of the kitchen fire. This was then served with bacon cooked on hooks in the coal-fired oven.

The people of Casterton went for bacon in a big way. Sometimes he was served it for breakfast, dinner and supper, either baked, fried, boiled in a soup called *cawl*, or dry-smoked. But he found he grew not only to like it but positively to relish those savoury strips of cured pigmeat. Every night he returned to the farm with a healthy workman's appetite for a meal of, if not more bacon, then bread, cheese, pickles, apple pie and an earthenware jug of ale. Then he slept like a baby in his attic room.

And, would you believe it? he told himself as he tied the boat at the landing stage, *they were putting down roots here in Casterton.*

Now Sam grew to know the townsfolk. Men would raise their hats, ladies would wish him a friendly good day. In the town's café where a huge mug of coffee was threepence, milk cake twopence and butter a penny, he could easily lose an hour or two chatting to new friends.

Within a couple of months the fraternization had deepened until Ryan Keith announced he was marrying a local girl. The daughter of a baker, she was, as Ryan told them, beaming, a good strong-boned woman of thirty. As soon as the engagement was approved of by the father Ryan found himself on the baker's payroll as an in-store assistant.

Lee Burton had found work in the local music hall as a bit-part player and general stagehand. He'd also moved into the same bedroom as Sue Royston, which had scandalized the rest of the community at Perseverance Farm. He'd moved back out, then promptly married Sue under a special licence with the Reverend Thomas officiating.

Hell, how quickly they were all absorbing the *Zeitgeist* of Victorian Casterton. That little market town which sat in the centre of Great Britain, which in turn sat in the middle of Queen Victoria's empire with dominions as far away as the Canadian Arctic in the north and New Zealand in the south. Where old soldiers sat over tankards of ale in coaching inns and reminisced about how they'd fought Old Bony at the Battle of Waterloo. And there'd probably still be an old grandma or two who could remember when they were little girls and North America was still under the thumb of King George III.

That *Zeitgeist* was slipping gradually under Sam's skin, too. In 1999 he would have called it dating, but now he was 'walking out' with Zita. On Sundays he would walk with her to Casterton's municipal park to listen to military brass bands playing to people sitting in stripy deckchairs; after that there was a cup of tea and caraway loaf in the local tea shop.

Victorian Casterton even had a substitute for television.

Every night there was a show at the music hall. This was more downmarket (and definitely more blue-collar) than the Royal Theatre with its presentations of Shakespeare and opera.

For a sixpenny ticket the music hall offered a mixed programme of entertainments (just like TV, Sam noted with a wry smile). For openers there would be ten minutes of songs and oom-pah-pah music, followed by a juggler or a magic act. Then came a half-hour play where all the players did their bit (including Lee Burton in costume and wearing white make-up that blazed dazzlingly in the limelight). Often the play was a melodrama that revolved around the theme of a drunken father who would one day get fabulously blasted on whisky and kill his wife and/or children. Then he'd be arrested and sentenced to hang. At the last moment the ghosts of his family would appear in his condemned cell to forgive him (the audience wept buckets at this, but still went out and got fabulously stinking drunk themselves after the show). A variation of the plot

would involve the hangman turning out to be the condemned man's father who'd walked out on his wife and
family because of his own drunkenness years before. Then,
by a savage twist of fate, he would find he was putting a
noose round his own son's neck. After the hanging (which
took place off stage with a scream and a thud) the remorseful
hangman would deliver an impassioned monologue on the
demon drink: marriage-wrecker and child-killer that it was.

And still the audience would hurry out of the music hall
after the show, beelining it for the nearest alehouse or wine
lodge.

But Sam saw that it was a good life in 1865 Casterton.
The town was modestly prosperous. On the whole the
people were healthy, those who survived childhood. The
women especially were statuesque and radiated health and
strength. Of course, there were those with deformities,
untreated squints, scabies and the like, but he seemed to
be noticing these unfortunates less and less. He was being
absorbed emotionally by the town. From a 1990s New
Yorker he was slowly becoming a mid-Victorian Englishman.

And he found he didn't resent the transformation one
little bit.

Before the time-slip his directorial work was the centre of
his life. He was always planning for the future, his mind
buzzing day and night about programme-making: how to
bring in some fresh element to baseball coverage; a new
twist to his *Football Diary* programme every Sunday. His
next priority had been balancing his income (pretty damn'
good even by NY standards) with his expenditure (apartment rent, taxes, rest-and-recreational bills) so he could
perhaps at last get round to making a down payment on
that new Mercedes Benz.

Now all that didn't matter.

It didn't matter a fig, a jot or a tittle, nor a sweet boogaloo.

At last he realized that a human being was the centre of his
life now. Seeing Zita made his soul light up. And in

harmony with the times he lived in he realized he was going
to ask her to marry him one day soon.

With the sun glinting in the water, and ducks somewhere
merrily quacking their heads off, he helped the pair of stout
priests (smelling of beer and onions) from the boat, raised his
cap, wished them good day, then lay down on the landing
stage with a piece of grass between his teeth, feeling the sun
warm on his face and dreaming of what the coming months
might bring.

It was a good life.

Doom seemed far away. As far away as a bitterly cold
winter's day seems in summer. Impossibly far away. But
deep down you know that one day those cold winds are
going to blow.

They're going to blow hard.

And as Sam chewed the stalk, gazing at swallows gliding
high above him, *Doom* was still a long, long way away. But
it was coming, all right. Slow but oh-so-sure as a cold and
hurtful winter gale.

Two

Nicole Wagner lived in the middle of nowhere. She didn't
know that when she first fell in with the Liminal group led
by William.

'We're the good guys. We're sort of time-gypsies,
wandering here and there, helping ourselves to a bit of
this, a bit of that,' Bullwitt would tell her from his niche in
William's stomach. 'But there's this lot called the Bluebeards: you can see how they got their name 'cos they tattoo
their chins and upper lips with blue lines, like some Red
Injun warrior markings or something. They're wretched
bastards, I can tell you, sweetie. Not only do they smash up
our gaffe but they hop over the border out of Limbo to steal
and murder poor bloody innocents. Now, if we're like
gypsies wandering through time those lousy bastards are
like pirates. Or Vikings. They launch raids across the time-

boundaries; they'll sneak into 1956, say, rob a house, cut the throats of everyone there, then leg it back here before anyone's the wiser. And it's getting worse.' Bullwitt's voice dropped to a whisper as if he was afraid of being overheard. 'I've heard there's an area of Limbo where they're gathering and they're a hundred thousand strong, maybe more; maybe two hundred thousand; a million . . .'

Nicole, with her mousy lump on her shoulder, listened, a white cotton sheet pulled up over her breasts. She hardly understood a word, but whatever Bullwitt was, and whatever the real story was of how he had become fused inside William's stomach, with just his eyes, nose and mouth protruding from a ring of skin, she was used to it now. But she remembered the absolute shock when she first saw Bullwitt's face.

Picture a lifelike mask glued to a man's stomach, just a little to the right-hand side where the appendix would be, and at a sloping angle so that one eye was higher than the other.

(Which sometimes earned him the nickname Isaiah – because one eye was higher than the other. 'Geddit, geddit' a jubilant Liminal with clusters of snail shells caking his forehead like scabs had crowed. 'We call him Isaiah because one eye's higher than the other,' he'd repeated, labouring the point over and over.)

She'd got used to the face peering lopsidedly from William's flat muscled stomach.

Pretty much as she was accustomed to the fact that she and William were lovers, and that when they were naked in bed together he wore a bandage around his waist to cover the face with its two bulging brown eyes. The effect was something like a cummerbund.

Bullwitt was a pussy cat at heart. He didn't complain.

So it seemed the least she could do was listen to him talk as William slept.

'If you ask me,' Bullwitt said, looking out from the stomach as William lay flat on his back in the double bed, breathing evenly, eyes lightly closed, his arms above his head like a sleeping baby. 'If you ask me, those barbarians are planning something big. At first only a few knew how to escape from old Limbo here. Sure, they'd knock off a traveller or two or rob a house, but there's talk that the barriers are breaking down and that soon every man Jack of them will go pouring out into who knows when. It'll be like a dam wall collapsing; the countryside will be flooded with those murdering barbarians. Poor sods on the other side won't stand a chance.'

'The other side?' Nicole asked, sleepily stroking the mouse head protruding from her shoulder. It was so sensitive. Tickling it was pleasant, sexy even.

'Yes, they'll invade the other side.'

'But I don't know what you mean by the other side.'

'Ah,' he sighed, 'sometimes I think I talk another bleedin' language for all the notice people take of me.'

'Sorry, Bullwitt, I'm new to all this, remember?'

'Indeed you are, dear. Uh, sleepy head's stirring.'

William muttered something in his sleep and turned on his side away from Nicole. Of course Bulwitt's face with the wideawake eyes looking out through the stomach turned with him.

'That's it,' Bullwitt muttered, 'turn me away from the lady so I can't see her. Now she'll say I'm nothing but a rude Cockney barrow boy.'

'No, I don't think that,' she whispered softly, cuddling into William's back. 'Now explain to me about crossing to the other side.'

'Because we're on one side of the border. Everyone else, including your old friends from that godforsaken hole in the ground, is on the other.'

Suddenly Nicole lifted herself up on one elbow. 'You mean that where we are now is outside the normal flow of time?'

'Cor blimey, my old mother. *Yes*. Nicole, my sweetie, where did you think we were all this time? The Land of Nod?'

'No, I thought it was just a few shacks in some remote part of the forest.'

'Just a few shacks to you, my girl, home to all us poor sods.'

'I'm sorry. I didn't mean to—'

'Ah, I know you didn't, sweetie.' His voice softened. 'That's why people call me a grouch; I'm touchy; quick to take offence. 'Course, that was our way down the Old Kent Road. 'You looking at me, sunshine?' Bang, wallop . . . fisticuffs every Friday night down the boozer, regular as bleedin' clockwork.' He paused for a second. 'But I'm surprised no one explained all this to you. Remember that time we took you into the wood, away from the amphitheatre and your old friends?'

'Yes.'

'Well, we took you over the boundary, back to one of our old camps. The Bluebeards had smashed up the new one. Now that was a peach with a fresh-water spring that was as sweet as honey; lotsa game and a nice pub down the road with beer that was—'

'But where are . . . I mean, *when* are we now?'

'Oh, well away from the rest of the world. It's not easy to explain but imagine that the past and present are two different places on a map. Now, if you fold the map in a certain way, putting a sort of tuck down the middle between past and present, that's where we are.'

'I don't understand.'

'Imagine this place, Limbo, is tucked out of sight in the fold of the map. Only we're tucked out of sight by a fold in time. Do you follow that?'

'Sort of.'

'Well, it's a secret place used by us and, bloody regrettably, by the Bluebeards as well. Luckily it's big enough for us to keep out of the murdering bastards' way.'

Nicole rubbed her head, dizzied by these new concepts, and dropped back onto the pillow. Above her she could see the thatch of the roof in the few rays of moonlight that filtered through a window aperture. 'I'm sorry.' She kneaded her forehead. 'I don't understand how we got here.'

'Explaining's difficult.'

'But could you show me?'

'Perhaps, if William here will taxi me there on those two legs of his.'

'Bullwitt?'

'Yes?'

'Can you take me to the year where my friends are?'

'Why?'

'I need to tell them about all this.'

'What on Earth for? Nicole, you should let sleeping dogs lie.'

'But if there's a way of moving forward as well as backward through time they should know about it.'

'Nicole, sweetie.' Bullwitt's voice was gentle. 'When I was a nipper I heard this story of what happened in the street where I lived. A toddler of about fifteen months was taken from his pram when his mother left it outside a shop. You can imagine the mother wasn't just distraught, she was torn apart by it all. Nearly went mad with grief, she did. Now, I know you're wondering where I'm going with all this, so I'll get to the point. Eight years later the truth came out. A woman whose baby had died stole the toddler. She'd loved it like her own. Brought it up. Of course, the toddler thought the kidnapper was his real mother. The police were brought in; it went to court. Now what did the judge decide? Does he return the nine-year-old boy to his natural mother, who's a complete stranger to him by now? Or does he allow the woman, who's nothing more than a kidnapper when all's said and done, to keep the boy who she genuinely loves as a son? And not forgetting this: the boy loves her as a mother.'

Nicole raised herself up on her elbows to look down at Bullwitt in the sleeping man's stomach. 'There is no easy answer,' she said.

'Exactly. Bit like the Judgement of Solomon story, isn't it? Offer to cut the child in half and see which woman loves the child enough to allow the other woman to keep it. What I'm saying is, your old friends have been living there in 1865 for, what? Around six months? They'll be putting down roots, my dear. Yes, it sounds a good idea to turn up there and say, 'All right, we're all going back home to Nineteen-ninety-whatever-it-is.' But there's some who wouldn't want to leave now. If they fall in love, do they stay with their fiancé in the 1800s or do they take them forward into the 1900s where the shock of seeing everything changed out of all recognition might send them stark, raving mad? You mark my words, dear. Let sleeping dogs lie.'

For a long time, Nicole lay there beside the sleeping William, with Bullwitt trying to reassure her how well everything would turn out if only it was left well alone.

She did realize she had new loyalties now. To her lover and to the people she lived with. She knew she'd never return to 1999. There were changes taking place in her body now. Mouse DNA had fused with human DNA. That would drive a wedge between her and the rest of humanity in any case. Nevertheless, she was uneasy about what Bullwitt had told her. If her old friends were in any kind of danger she knew she should warn them. And quickly.

Chapter Thirty-Nine

One

Ryan Keith's wedding day was a day to remember.

The bride, daughter of the wealthiest baker in Casterton, wore white, with a veil and a bouquet of peach-coloured flowers. Most of the refugees from 1999 were there, along with the bride's family, and everyone was in perfect Victorian dress, the menfolk in top hats and frock coats.

With the exception of the Reverend Thomas Hather, none of the local people knew that Sam Baker and the rest of the newcomers hailed not from some other part of the country but from, in fact, some other century – which must surely have been the best-kept secret in Casterton.

After the wedding banquet in the baker's house Sam escaped the noise and exuberance of the party games to walk through the orchard and breathe the cool evening air. Stars had begun to prick their way through the deepening blue.

The apples on the trees were fully ripe, reminding him of Ryan Keith's face duplicated over and over again. Ryan had grown plumper still, looking even more like Oliver Hardy. His cheeks were a rosy apple-red, and just as rounded.

He found Jud Campbell standing with his hand resting against a pear tree. Thoughtful-looking, he smoked a pipe as he gazed out over fields that sloped down to a railway line. A train rattled along the tracks, puffing out smoke balls.

Steam hissed from the gleaming side-rods as they turned the wheels against the rails with a pleasantly rhythmic *clickety-click* sound.

'Good party,' Sam said. 'I think they're going to make a grand couple.'

Jud pulled on the pipe. 'Grand, Sam? You're picking up the local lingo?'

'Oh, just the odd word.' Sam smiled. 'This place works its way through your skin after a while.'

'So you're turning native? But you'll be none the worse for it. It's a good place. Good people, too.' He glanced back at the house where lamps filled the windows with a golden light. There was a chanted counting coming from the big parlour as another game got under way, followed by a *whoooooow*! that rose in pitch until it disintegrated into everyone laughing.

'Aye, they'll make a good couple. Champion, as they'd say hereabouts.' Jud gave a small smile. 'But you have to remember all this could end just like . . .' He clicked his fingers.

'The Bluebeards? I've seen nothing of them, have you?'

'Not a sign. Of course, they could be away ransacking some other period in time – 1066? 1776? 2001? Who knows? No, if anything, I was referring to the time-slips. Any second we might open our eyes and find ourselves back in the amphitheatre, you sitting there alongside Zita, the reps in their fancy dress, me slipping the pin back inside my collar. Sam, all this could go. This life we're building for ourselves could vanish in a flash.'

'I guess it's possible.'

'Would you regret it if it did, Sam?'

'Yes, I would. I've grown to like it here. I like the food, the beer . . . and, as you say, this is a good town filled with good people. I don't want to lose it.'

Jud sighed. 'You might have to do just that, so don't invest all your emotions in it, will you?'

'You mean like Ryan?'

'He's in love with the girl. And have you ever seen

anyone so happy in your life? But if the time-slip comes again he'll lose his wife.'

'Maybe it won't come to that.'

'Hmm . . . have you noticed that with every time-slip we have all our personal possessions restored to us just as they were? But we've not been able to bring back souvenirs from 1978 or 1946. They just vanish into thin air.'

'Perhaps this mechanism, whatever it is, that pulled us back through time has simply gone kaput.'

'Maybe.'

'But you doubt it? Even though we've been marooned here for, let's see, six months?'

'So you think this is for keeps?' Jud pulled on the pipe. 'We're staying in 1865 for good?'

'Well, I figure we've rejoined the normal flow of time; we'll just go forward with it along with the rest of the world. If we live to a good age we'll see the new century, 1900. Not long after that we'll be reading about the first flight at Kitty Hawk, the invention of the electric light bulb, cinemas, radio.'

'You might be right,' Jud allowed in a relaxed, almost sleepy voice. The wine was working its magic. 'Still, I can't help but remember Rolle's warnings, that time was coming apart at the seams.'

'That there were barbarian hordes ready to ride out and pillage the modern world?'

'That's what the man believed.'

'Maybe he was right, but with every day that goes by it seems more and more unlikely. Unless they're raiding other time zones, as you've just mentioned.'

'In which case it's out of our hands.'

'That's right.'

'Ah, but I wonder, Sam . . . call me a superstitious nut but I do still wonder if we've been put here, in 1865, for a reason.'

'Possibly. But we've had no celestial messages written in the sky; no one saying 'Beware the ides of March' or the equivalent. So I guess we carry on with life as it's lived now.'

'And not worry about tomorrow?'

'Got it in one, Jud. Now, I think I'm going to find Zita and ask her for a dance.'

Jud's smile was warm. 'Ah, you two. Is the word on the grapevine right?'

'It depends what you've heard.'

'That I might have to wear this big top hat again before long.'

Sam grinned. 'You might have heard right there after all, Jud, old buddy.'

Jud slapped Sam on his broad back. 'I've also heard on the grapevine that our Mr Gainsbrough, the baker, keeps a fine bottle of port or two. I'm going to find out if that's true as well.'

'Then lead the way, Mr Campbell. Lead the way.'

'Have you tried the Madeira?'

'No, I stuck to red wine.'

'You must try it. It's not as sweet as I expected it would be . . . has a musty raisin flavour . . .'

They strolled back through the darkening orchard. The stars shone clear, bright as silver dust. There was singing coming from the house now; all boozy and happy, veering off every now and again into good-natured laughter. So much for misinformation about staid Victorians. In the back yard a dog barked in a rough-and-ready harmony with the music.

As they turned the corner of the house and headed for the door Sam heard the sudden shrill whistle of a policeman. It came in short urgent blasts.

Some new drama was unfolding out there in the street.

Two

Sam knew within two minutes that it would be a day to remember.

And not just because of Ryan's wedding day and all the happiness that had gone hand in glove with it.

At the sound of the whistle Sam knew instinctively that something unsavoury was hitting the fan. Stomach muscles snapping suddenly tense, he ran through the front garden to the gate. There was shouting, dogs barking.

In the street a man sat on the cobbles nursing his hand. A policeman blew his whistle. Meanwhile another couple of men were trying to steady horses jittering about in the shafts of a mail coach. One horse kicked back striking the coach timbers with a God-almighty thump.

'What's happened?' Jud called as he ran up.

The policeman stopped blowing his whistle. 'Some vagrant tried to make off with the mail coach.' He blew the whistle again while glaring down the street. 'But we'll have him . . . we'll have him good and proper.'

Sam bent down to look at the man who was nursing his hand. 'Bloody feller, knocked me one,' the mail-coach driver grunted. 'What a fucking crack. Stick or sommat. Look at that.' He held up his left hand for Sam to see. Blood gushed from a cut across the knuckles. 'Damn' bastard.'

Sam looked up as a hefty man came panting along the road from the direction in which the policeman was staring. The man held two massive bulldogs by their leashes. The dogs slobbered and panted.

'Good job you were passing, Harry,' the policeman said. 'He were an evil character. I reckon your dogs put the wind up him.'

'Good pair of brawlers, these,' the big man grunted. 'If Jug and Apollo get their teeth into yer they'll never let you go. There's the lads.' He patted the bulldogs on their huge heads.

'Did you see where the devil went?'

'Somewhere over the fields in the direction of Danby Wood.'

'He's probably got himself a camp out there.' The policeman slipped his whistle back into his pocket. 'He can't get far. I'll get some men out tomorrow. If you aren't over-busy, Harry, you'll be more than welcome with those two dogs.'

'Oh aye, Ben, they love a bit of sport, these do.'

'Right, we'll set off from the station at seven.'

'I'll be there, Ben.' With that the man allowed the dogs to pull him away down the street, their heads swinging from side to side, tongues hanging out, dripping saliva onto the cobbles.

'You all right there, coachie?' the policeman asked, shining a lamp down onto the man's bleeding hand.

'I'll mend . . . just get us up onto me feet.'

Jud and the policeman took an arm each and helped the coachman up.

As they did, Sam noticed something lying by the kerb. He picked it up. 'Is this yours?' he asked the coachman.

'Is it sod. That's what he must have clobbered me with.'

'What is it?' Jud asked as the policeman held up his lamp to shine the light onto it.

'Oh . . .' Jud breathed. 'I'll be damned . . .'

'Funny-looking thing.' The policeman scratched his chin. 'What do you make of it?'

'It's an axe,' Jud said. 'Only it has a bronze head. See how yellow it is?'

'An axe with a bronze head? It won't be much cop. Thing'll be soft as putty.'

'But it's still sharp enough to take your head clean off.'

Sam looked at Jud. 'A Bronze Age axe?'

Jud nodded, his face serious. 'That's exactly what it is.' He fixed his eyes on Sam. 'So we've a pretty good idea where it came from.'

Sam looked down at the blade that was slick with blood. 'And we know just who would have been carrying it.'

Three

A fortnight later Sam Baker was working the ferry, bringing people back and forth across the river. He and Jud had little doubt that the attack on the coachman on the night of Ryan's wedding had been the work of a Bluebeard. The man with the bulldogs had surprised him into dropping his axe as he ran.

This might have been a scouting party in advance of the main attack.

But it all went quiet again. The Bluebeard wasn't found. And pretty soon life's steady routine had regained its comfortable rhythm. Ryan had returned from a honeymoon in Brighton with his new wife and moved into the Gainsbrough family home, sharing it with the baker, his wife, her widowed sister and a clutch of children whose names Sam could never remember.

At the same moment that Sam was rowing across the river with a man and his baskets of mushrooms, Lee Burton was gathering mushrooms of his own in the fields at the back of the farmhouse. It was there that he saw the figure watching him from the woods.

Four

Lee Burton stopped dead. With the figure deep in shadow he didn't recognize who it was, but the way they stared at him was enough to make him look twice.

Carrying the wicker basket by the handle, he shielded his eyes against the bright October sun.

The figure still remained there, watching him, apparently reluctant to leave the shadows of the forest.

He walked towards the trees, curious.

Sometimes one of the lads from the music hall would come out to play one of their carefully worked out practical jokes. (He'd already fallen for going to the hardware shop for a *long weight*, only to find it was really the long *wait* – hardy ha, ha, boys. And he'd even almost – but not quite – been suckered in with the one about buying a jar of elbow grease.) Jokes could be elaborate, with fellow actors raiding the costume store for disguises. Just last week he and another actor dressed as policemen had had the stage manager believing he was being arrested for bigamy. The rest of the cast had laughed until tears had run down their faces. Stage Manager Stan hadn't seen the funny side of it. After he'd twigged, he'd chased them around backstage with a length of planking, shouting so loud his face had turned blue.

Now, was the furtive stranger another practical joke? This time one targeted at one Lee Burton?

Lee walked cautiously forward, his head tilting this way and that, trying to get a better view.

He walked faster as the figure moved backward, deeper into the wood.

In the fringes of the wood with the carpet of fallen red leaves crisp beneath his feet Lee paused. He remembered what had happened to Sam Baker well enough. How he'd confronted the axe-wielding barbarian in 1944.

He glanced back towards the farmhouse. It seemed too far away now. If someone should rush at him from the shadows he wouldn't stand a chance.

He gritted his teeth, imagining an axe head crashing down against the top of his head, the pain ringing all the way down to the tips of his toes as if he were a bell.

Far enough, he told himself with a shiver. *Don't go deeper into the wood.*

Besides, the figure had disappeared now.

Cautiously, he edged backwards, not wanting to present his own back to those shadowed depths of the wood.

His feet rustled through the leaves.

Nice and easy does it.

Don't stay here.

Suddenly danger beat from the depths of the wood in near-palpable waves. He shivered more deeply; his skin tingled. He clenched his jaw as—

'Don't turn round.'

Jesus Christ.

'Lee, please. Don't turn round.'

Shocked, he was going to protest. 'Why on earth—'

'Lee. Just listen.'

'Nicole?' he asked in wonder. 'Nicole? Good God, I thought you were dead! Are you OK?'

'Yes,' she said in such a tight, strained way that a shiver ran down his back like a cascade of icy leeches.

'Nicole—' He turned round in time to see a blonde-haired figure duck back behind a tree just a dozen paces from him. 'Nicole, what's wrong?'

'Lee, I asked you not to turn round.'

All he could see was a strand or two of hair being pulled by the light breeze from behind the tree where she hid, as coyly as if she were naked.

'Nicole. Tell me what's wrong.'

'Listen. I just came to tell you something.'

'Come down to the farmhouse . . . wait! You don't know about the farmhouse, do you?' He spoke in an excited rush. 'It's all different now. Look at the clothes I'm wearing. Genuine 1865. I'm working at the music hall. Ryan got married. *Married!* Can you believe that? He's working for his wife's father who's got—'

'Lee. *Lee*,' she spoke anxiously from behind the tree. 'Lee, please listen, there isn't much time.'

'Nicole? What's the matter? Why are you hiding behind the tree?' He took a step forward. It was as if she was afraid of being seen with him. Why? 'Can't you tell me what—'

'Lee! Don't come any closer.'

'But—'

'Please don't ask why. Just do as I ask, for my sake. Do you promise?'

'Sure. If that's what you want. But where have you been? We thought—'

'Lee. All I want you to do is please listen to me. I can't stay here long. OK?'

'OK, Nicole.'

He found himself watching the tree as she spoke, remembering the beautiful blonde-haired girl whose ambition it was to become a lawyer.

'You're too close to the amphitheatre here.'

'But we—'

'Too close. In fact, you need to get away from this whole

area. Away from Casterton. If you can, get out of the county.'

'Why?'

'There's a storm about to break. A big one. There's not going to be much standing after it hits, believe me.'

'I don't understand.'

'You don't have to understand, not entirely. Just trust me, OK?'

'But we can't uproot just like that.'

'Yes, you can. Uproot and get away from here. Look, Lee . . . you remember when Sam Baker was attacked by that man – a Bluebeard, they called him – remember?'

'Yes.'

'Well, there's thousands of men like him. Tens of thousands. They're vicious barbarians, and we know they're on the move.'

'We? Who's this *we*?'

'The people I live with now.'

'Nicole, can't you spare a few minutes to tell—'

'No. I've got to go now. I took a risk coming here.'

'Risk?'

'Yes, they – the bad ones – could have followed me across the boundary. For crying out loud, I might have even led them here. They're just waiting for such a break so they can cross over from Limbo. Once they do, whatever they can't carry away with them they'll smash or burn. No one's safe. No one can protect themself.'

'I don't understand what you mean. What boundary are you talking about? And what's this Limbo?'

At that moment he saw Nicole run away from him. She didn't look back. She just put her head down as if a heavy downpour had started and ran.

He followed, caught her by the arm, then pulled to stop her.

The momentum whipped her whole body round.

'No, Lee! You promised you wouldn't try and look at me!'

He stared into her face. It was the Nicole Wagner he knew, but her eyes were big and frightened-looking; maybe they were a little older and wiser, too.

'Why did you hide from me? You can trust me to . . . *Uh, Nicole?*' His eyes widened in shock. 'Wait. You've got something on your neck . . . *ugh, what is it!*'

She looked up at him, her eyes not flinching from his. As if he'd suddenly found her in the nude and she was challenging him not to stare down at her body.

'Don't move, Nicole. Here . . . let me knock it off.'

Her next movement was defiant. Chin held high, still meeting his eye, she put her hand over the side of her neck and gave a little shake of her head.

Then, still maintaining eye contact, she backed off into the shadows where the trees grew closer together. 'Goodbye, Lee.' A second later she turned to run lightly away into the heart of the wood.

He stood there for a moment, his arm out as if she'd left behind some phantom image of herself that he could still hold onto.

He couldn't shift from his mind what he'd seen on her neck.

It stayed there, biting deep into his memory. It shouldn't have been possible. But he'd seen something very similar before.

Nausea suddenly gripped him. He fought it for a while. Then the struggle became too much.

He dropped to his knees and vomited onto the ground.

Five

Ten minutes later he walked down to the river bank with the intention of finding Sam Baker. He had to tell him about his meeting in the wood with Nicole.

Poor Nicole . . . once she'd been so incredibly beautiful . . .

The image was still locked firmly there inside his head. He wanted it out, but it would take a long time to fade.

When he'd grabbed her and she'd swung to face him he'd looked into her face. Where her jawline reached her ear there'd been a fuzz of brown fur. It wasn't large. He could easily have covered it with the ball of his thumb. But it had been enough to make him look more closely.

At that instant he knew he would wish he hadn't.

With his eyes widening, he found himself staring at the fold of skin where the bottom of her ear joined the neck.

From a series of small puckered lumps in the skin something as long and as thin as matchsticks jutted straight out.

He'd found himself staring as they stretched out stiff, then relaxed. Then they began twitching sharply.

He thought for a moment some large (disgustingly large at that) insect with scurrying legs had landed on her neck.

But those legs that emerged from the puckered mounds of skin on her neck were, he realized, the legs of a mouse.

Delicate, grey-brown, sprinkled with fine white hairs, they each possessed tiny prehensile claws that opened and shut, sometimes catching her lovely blonde hair and holding onto it.

He wiped his mouth with the back of his hand.

That queasy sensation was rising again, filling his mouth with a bile taste.

For one mad moment he could even feel those scurrying mouse legs across his tongue.

At last he made it to the ferry crossing without vomiting again.

Sam Baker had just tied up the rowboat. His passengers, a smartly-dressed family of eight, were walking along the jetty to the banking.

With one last effort to squeeze down the hot bile rising in his throat he went down to Sam and told him everything that had happened.

Chapter Forty

One

All was quiet until Christmas. Then, when there was snow on the ground, and with the sound of the church choir singing carols drifting hauntingly through the dark and deserted streets of the town, they came at last.

Anyone watching from the top of the church tower could have been forgiven for thinking that they were seeing a dark stain spreading towards the town across the snow-covered fields.

The dark stain moved like a liquid, sometimes pausing, sometimes running faster. Sometimes drops of darkness would break away from the main body of the stain to be siphoned away to an outlying cottage or farm.

In the taverns, the bars were softly lit by lamps. Their golden light spilled through mullioned windows onto the compacted snow of the street outside. The sound of talking came loudly enough from the bars when a tavern door was opened, and the occasional gale of laughter, too. But the noise became muted when the door swung shut against the cold night air.

The black stain flowed into the town as relentlessly as flood water.

Then, for a moment, everything seemed to stop.

A hush ran through the town. For five long seconds there was a kind of preternatural silence. It was as if the

414

whole population was briefly endowed with a sixth sense; as if they had seen what approached, and then had held their breath in shock.

The clock in the town hall tower struck nine sombre chimes.

And that was when the whole town seemed to scream as one.

Two

In the neighbouring village of Ouse-Burton, four miles away, Sam Baker raised a glass of beer to Jud; the clock in the coaching inn struck nine.

Sam shivered and looked at the inn door, wondering if it had been left open to the cold night air. It was closed.

Jud took a swallow of beer. 'What's wrong, Sam?'

Sam shivered again before edging nearer to the blazing fire. 'Nothing.' He smiled. 'A goose just walked over my grave, that's all.'

'A brandy'll be the best cure for that.' Jud took a deep drink of beer. 'You know, that's the best drop of mild I've ever tasted.'

Sam didn't hear. Shivering deeply again, down to the very core of his bones, he looked out of the window.

Snowflakes whirled by outside.

'It looks as if it's blowing up a storm. Do you think we'll make it home tonight?'

Jud held up the pint and admired the firelight shining through it, turning it the colour of amber. 'I certainly hope not,' he said. 'I could sink a few more of these.'

At that moment the coachman came in, blowing into his hands. 'Five minutes, ladies and gentlemen. Five minutes, if you peer-leeeze.'

Sam smiled and shook his head. 'Looks as if you'll be home to warm your old bones in front of the fire after all.'

'Ah, and you don't get any chillier than a narrow boat in this weather. I hope Dot has kept the fire lit.'

Three

Distant shouting had brought Dot Campbell onto the deck of the narrow boat. She carried a lantern in which a single candle burned.

Holding the sheepskin coat tightly closed across her nightdress she peered into the darkness, her eyes blinking as flakes of snow were driven into them by the rising wind.

She wished Jud was home. It got so lonely out on the river when he wasn't here. The double bed was so much chillier, too.

True, she had been invited to stay up at the farmhouse. But she'd wanted to finish making the mince pies. Christmas Day, when there would be a party for all the surviving time travellers, was only five days away.

And, dear God, it was cold down here on the river bank.

Maybe those cries in the distance were nothing but cats out on the tiles.

Still, it sounded unnerving. Closer to screams than cries.

And they seemed to be coming from the cottages at the end of the track.

She held the lantern higher. The semicircle of the amphitheatre showed a flawless white in the near-darkness. Every so often the wind rushed into it, and made a sound like a gigantic seashell held to your ear.

She advanced a step or two along the gangplank towards the shore.

If she didn't see anything in the next ten seconds she'd turn back, go down into the warmth of the cabin, lock the door; then she'd sit tight and wait until she heard Jud's knock.

'And I hope he doesn't take all night to come home,' she said under her breath. A shape moved against the snow to her left. 'Jud? Is that you? Hurry up, you'll catch your death out there.' She turned the lantern towards the approaching figure. 'How did it go at the—'

Her voice died.

Coming towards her through the swirling snowflakes was an image of the devil himself.

Dot Campbell found her breath and screamed. Then she screamed again.

Four

That same fateful night Lee Burton was a clown. He stood centre stage in Rington's Music Hall Theatre before a packed house and recited a comic poem. His costume hadn't evolved yet into that of the twentieth-century clown. The trousers were tight, not baggy, and although his face was covered in white paint there was no big red nose. In fact, when he'd looked in the mirror in the dressing room (always a chaotic and noisy place, with heaps of costumes on tables and the air blue with tobacco smoke and bad language) he'd seen something that more closely resembled the Harlequin character, complete with a tight-fitting suit of black and white diamonds.

He recited the poem with enthusiastic gestures, enjoying himself enormously. The poem told the story of a stable boy's unlucky attempts to woo a dozen different ladies.

The stage lamps burning just in front of him were too dazzling for him to see whether the audience were enjoying it or not. But there was laughter (all of it in the right places); and all they were throwing were pieces of orange peel – not bottles or lumps of coal.

There's no business like show business.

He remembered the line and realized it was true. He was having a hell of a night and loving every minute of it.

Five

There was no heating in the stagecoach. The eight passengers sat facing each other on two bench-like seats. Thick rugs rested across their laps, allowing them to trade body heat with their neighbours. Ice formed on the inside of the windows. White vapour billowed from mouths and nostrils.

Sam and Jud had treated themselves to the expensive seats inside the coach. They'd had a good day in York selling pieces of jewellery and some glassware that Jud had dug out of the backs of cupboards on his boat. The money would be useful when it came to buying a few head of cattle in the spring.

Sam scraped ice away from the window. Snowflakes streamed past the window. For all the world they could be underwater and those might be bubbles shooting by. The updraught caught the snowflakes, causing them to rise rather than fall. The horses were making steady progress along the road that ran through the forest. At this rate they'd probably be in Casterton by ten o'clock.

Six

'Reverend Hather! Reverend Hather!'

The sound of a fist braying his front door startled the Reverend Thomas Hather as he dozed over a glass of port and a chunky leather-bound volume of *Don Quixote*.

'Hather! Hather! Sweet Jehovah and the angels of Christ! Hather . . .'

Clergymen, like doctors and undertakers, were not unacquainted with calls at any time of the day or night. Even a night like this, with a blizzard blowing.

As he walked through into the hall to the front door the grandfather clock chimed quarter-past nine.

'Hather!'

Crash, crash, crash!

It sounded as if a sledgehammer was being used to break in.

He slid back the bolt and hauled open the door; a flurry of snowflakes blasted in onto his hands and arms.

'Good Lord, man, what on earth's the matter?'

'Reverend Hather. Lord forgive me, I came as soon as I knew, but I'm too late! They're already here.'

The Reverend Thomas Hather rocked back on his heels, as much from the sight of the man on his doorstep as the wind driving in the flakes of snow.

He'd never spoken to the man before but he knew the locals referred to him as Gingery Joe, a wild-eyed vagrant, who dressed bizarrely in orange with long black rubber boots.

'Ahm, would you like to come in?' Hather remembered his Christian charity. 'I can offer you hot milk and bread, but I don't—'

'No, no. I don't want your food. No, Lord, no, please . . . all the angels preserve us. Sub Dominus Noster Sanctoque Benedicto.'

He'd heard the man was prone to talk in tongues. Now, his eyes blazing, he was babbling Latin.

'Incendium amoris; incendium amoris . . . a – a love that burns – *no*.' Ferociously the tramp struck his own hip. 'No. I must stay lucid – plain of speech, plain of speech.' He took a deep breath and fixed those burning eyes on Hather. 'I was coming here to warn you. The Bluebeards have broken out. They are marching on the town.'

'Bluebeards? I'm sorry, I don't quite—'

'These are barbarian men. They are here for plunder and women. Tell me, priest, is there a man called Sam Baker here?'

'Sam? You know Sam?'

'Yes, I do. The Lord sent him and his friends as protectors.'

'I hear he went to York with another man.'

'Sweet Jesus, Sweet Jesus . . . Their destiny is upon them.'

'I expect they'll be back later tonight, probably . . . Good Lord, what's that infernal racket?'

The ginger-haired tramp's head snapped round to look back across the town.

Thomas stepped through the door into the driving snow.

A huge cacophony had risen into the air. It was a mixture of wild, frightening sounds: roars of exultation, wild laughter, screams of terror and pain, hoofbeats as horses raced across the ground, dogs barking, breaking glass, deep thumping sounds like gunshots muffled by snow-covered streets.

'Dear God, what on earth is happening?' Thomas watched open-mouthed as men on horseback charged down the street towards the rectory.

A woman with long white hair ran barefoot and shrieking along the street, her hands clawing at the air in front of her as if she could tear a way through the falling snow.

'Lord . . . that's Mrs Turner . . .' Thomas's heart seemed to freeze in his chest as he saw one of the horsemen catch up with her, lean down, snatch her by the hair . . .

Thomas clenched his fists and looked quickly away. This was the night that hell rode into town.

Seven

The coach waddled like a fat old duck along the road. Enclosed in the timber cabin of the stagecoach Sam felt as if he was completely sealed off from the world.

They couldn't have been travelling any faster than walking speed. Jud sat next to him half asleep, his chin resting on a fold in the blanket. A young woman in a bonnet with ribbons tied under her chin began to sing a Christmas carol.

It was taken up by the other passengers in a sleepy, good-natured way. Already the spirit of the season was upon them.

Sam closed his eyes, looking forward to the time in about an hour or so when he'd walk through the door and find Zita waiting for him. He could already picture her smile, her big brown eyes looking up into his.

Eight

Ryan Keith walked into the wine cellar. He held the candlestick high in front of him.

Sue Burton (née Royston) had called earlier. Now it was developing into something of an early Christmas party. She was up in the parlour along with Enid, his wife, and his in-laws, singing carols around the piano.

His father-in-law had good-naturedly handed him the key to the wine cellar and asked him to bring up a couple of bottles. 'No, make it a case or two,' he'd said, beaming. 'I'll have cook rustle up some potted meats, cheeses and the like.'

The clock chimed nine-fifteen as Ryan lowered his bulk down the cellar steps, the timbers creaking under his plumply fleshed body.

The door at the top of the steps swung shut behind him. The stout wooden planks it was made from had shrunk in the dry air of the kitchen over the last two hundred or so years that it had hung there. The light from the kitchen lamp shone through those gaps, revealing itself as golden lines that ran vertically from top to bottom of the door.

Ryan reached the bottom of the steps, the last one giving almost a creak of relief as he took his seventeen stone form off it.

All around him bottles lying on racks glinted in the light of the candle.

He paused for a moment, simply enjoying being there. He'd never felt so satisfied as this. Upstairs, a happy party was in full swing; he could hear the muffled sounds of the piano and Enid's musical voice. He had a wife whom he loved and who loved him, and who was expecting their first child in the summer. He had friends, a fine home, all these wonderful bottles of wine that his father-in-law so gener-ously shared with him.

As he turned over a bottle in its rack to read the label a memory came to him. Faint, nothing more than a ghost of a distant, distant memory. He suddenly remembered buying wine for a Christmas long ago. Then the wine had stood upright beneath brilliant lights. Music had played from the ceiling. He'd paid for the wine not with the reassuring weight of solid gold sovereigns, but with an oblong card of plastic.

For a moment he paused, surprised by the memory.

That had been last year.

Only twelve months ago.

He could hardly believe it.

And for just a second his mind seemed to draw back inside his skull, unwilling to wrap itself round that old memory and actually accept it was true. It could so easily be a bizarre dream induced by a glass or two of port and a slice of that pungent Stilton cheese.

With each passing day it was easier for him to believe that he'd always lived in the nineteenth century; that his life in the 1990s had been nothing more than a hallucination. No, this was his life now. With a wife born in 1835. He had a future as owner of the biggest bakery in Casterton when his father-in-law handed over the reins.

OK. So he could muster the memory of sitting in the amphitheatre one sunny day with his three colleagues beside him – Nicole Wagner (whatever happened to her?), her blonde hair falling down over the black nylon fur of the gorilla suit; Lee Burton dressed as Dracula; Sue as Stan Laurel and himself as Oliver Hardy, complete with toothbrush tash and bowler.

But that didn't seem real any more.

No. This did. This bottle of claret in his hand: the glass was solid, heavy; the contents a dark ruby. He didn't so much wipe the dust from the bottle as caress it, stroking away cobweb strands and speckles of white.

This was life as he lived it.

And he loved it more than he could say.

Upstairs the piano player finished the Christmas carol with a flourish.

He could smell sausage cooking. The old man had a huge fondness for sausage and he guessed Mrs Gainsbrough had asked cook to roast a couple of fat pork sausages to go with the claret.

Ryan hummed to himself as he filled a wooden crate with bottles. Normally it carried a dozen but he rested two bottles of Madeira across the necks of the others.

Then he returned to the steps, humming to himself.

When he reached the top he started to push open the door with his foot while cheerfully calling out, 'Look out behind! Cellar man coming through!'

Then the inexplicable happened.

There was a shout.

And was that Mrs Gainsbrough crying out in surprise? 'My gracious . . . who are you? *What do you want?*' That was followed by a shriek.

Shaking his heavy head, puzzled, he tried again to push open the door to the kitchen.

Suddenly it was thrust back with a crash. The crate of wine, knocked from his hands, smashed at his feet.

He rocked back, nearly toppling down the cellar steps. With an effort he grabbed the stair rail before swinging himself round.

This time he shoved at the door with both hands. 'Hey! What's going on!'

The door wouldn't budge.

Now there was a whole series of crashes. Plates being broken. The clang of a pan on the stone floor.

'Hey!' He pounded on the door. 'Let me out!'

Now he heard screams and shrieks.

And there were guttural voices too, low, animal-like, with bursts of brutish laughter.

'Let me out!'

He shoved at the door.

No luck.

It wouldn't budge.

Not one flaming inch.

He stared at the door with strips of light running from top to bottom where the kitchen lamplight leaked through the cracks.

Skin turning cold, he lurched forward to wedge his face

up against the door so he could see through the gaps in the planks.

A horrible sour feeling swam around his stomach. *Dear God . . .* he knew something awful was happening. This was all wrong. The screams were terrible, like, like—

—like the people he loved were having their throats worked open with a knife.

'Let me out!' He thumped on the door.

Through the gaps in the door he could see movement.

He merely caught glimpses because of his narrow field of vision. The gaps were only just wide enough to slip a sheet of card in anyway . . .

A credit card! His mind whirled, disoriented. *A credit card and nothing more!*

You could slip that right in there.

But . . . but . . .

Dear God . . . what were they doing to them in there?

He saw the cook running this way and that as if she was bouncing from rubber walls. This was crazy.

Then she stopped still in the middle of the kitchen, covered her face with her hands and yelled.

Then he saw his mother-in-law run into the kitchen. She carried a carving knife as if to stab someone.

The next second Enid ran in. He gaped.

Her blouse was torn. One sleeve had gone entirely.

Her hair hung down.

She disappeared, then reappeared as she crossed the kitchen, calling his name.

He shouted back. 'Enid! Enid!'

The next moment the kitchen was full of dark shapes. They were burly, almost bear-like.

The shrieks grew louder.

Why can't I get out!

He pounded on the door.

But no one noticed him.

The racket from inside the house was deafening.

He crouched down to look through the gaps in the door planking once more.

A dark oblong shape lay at the foot of the door on the other side. It must be the dresser that had been toppled in front of the door, stopping it from opening.

He stood up again, forced his eye to the gap with such force it was as if he tried to push his whole body between the planks and out into the kitchen on the other side.

He had to help his wife, that was all that mattered to him now.

What were they doing to her?

Just what, Ryan? Already his imagination was supplying answers. Terrible images welled up into his brain.

'Let me out!' he yelled.

Through the gap he saw a man drag Enid away.

She was screaming Ryan's name.

Mrs Gainsbrough lunged with her knife at the man. But another was waiting for her.

With a guttural laugh the man caught her by the arms and threw her across the kitchen table as if she was nothing more than a piece of meat. Then he went to work with a carving knife.

Ryan sat on the top step in the cellar, held his head in his hands and sobbed. He was still sitting there when he saw a crimson liquid trickle under the door to join the pool of spilt wine.

He closed his eyes, put his hands over his ears, and began to rock slowly backward and forward.

Chapter Forty-One

One

What's that damn' animal doing on stage?

At that moment Lee Burton didn't think anything was amiss.

In fact, it was all going pretty damn' fine. There he was, in his diamond-pattern harlequin costume, standing in the brilliant limelights, stage centre, reciting the funny poem.

The audience weren't just laughing.

They were screaming with laughter. He couldn't see the audience, true enough, those footlights were dazzling, but he could hear them screaming louder and louder. They were loving it. He could imagine them holding their stomachs, rocking backwards and forwards in their seats, their faces purple they were laughing so long and so loud. In fact, their voices were getting shriller and shriller by the moment.

There was only one problem. The stupid pantomime horse had come galloping across the stage right in the middle of his solo act.

It was Harry and Albert playing the fool again. They were probably paying him back for smearing the inside of the horse with blue cheese. It had stunk so much that they'd come out of the horse costume gagging for air.

But Lee wouldn't let that faze him. He was a pro now. He ploughed on, delivering the funny lines that were so rich in innuendo they'd make a ship's stoker blush.

He made his hammy gestures even more extravagant.

And the audience screamed.

The brown and white panto horse lumbered back in front of him, knocking him back a step.

Hell, those two would pay for trying to screw up his act. He'd pour glue into the horse's legs next time and the two would have to be peeled out of the damn' costume.

And the audience screamed louder.

Figures ran along the space between the front row of seats and the orchestra pit. He heard a clash of cymbals, as if someone had blundered against the percussion kit.

Lee continued grimly.

It was as if the idiot behaviour of the pantomime horse had spread to the audience.

But still they yelled. Maybe they'd all got stinking drunk before they'd come into the show. He'd never seen them like this before— *Hey!*

Someone pushed by behind him. He staggered, recovered and continued reciting the poem – and he would continue to the end of the damn' thing, come hell or high water. Music-hall acts didn't quit the stage, no matter what. He'd learned that. Like a captain going down with his sinking ship you continued to the end.

Now more people seemed to be milling around the orchestra pit.

But the lights were too dazzling to see anything more than indistinct shapes. Maybe some lads were getting into a fight over a girl.

Well, let them slug it out down there, Lee thought resolutely. *I'm not going to let them throw me.*

The pantomime horse lumbered by again, but this time Lee noticed with surprise that the back legs were being dragged by the front ones as if Albert in the back half had dropped down in a dead faint (or dead drunk). And now Harry was doing all the work, the pantomime horse head twisting this way and that with the effort. The horse's bottom jaw flapped and its eyes rolled in the stuffed head.

Still reciting the lines, still performing the extravagant windmilling gestures with his arms, Lee watched the front half of the pantomime horse drag its back legs across the stage.

Lee looked once. Then looked again in astonishment.

Now that really *was* impossible.

Still reciting the poem, he stared at the back end of the horse.

It was bleeding.

But pantomime horses don't bleed, he told himself, pausing for the first time in mid-verse before continuing.

But this one did.

Blood gushed from its rear end. What was more, the brown and white costume had been torn open and—

No.

No, it hadn't been torn.

It had been cut.

Slashed in diagonal rents by what must have been a hell of a sharp knife.

For the first time Lee's delivery began to falter.

The yells in the audience were deafening now.

And why on Earth had someone tried to kill a pantomime horse?

It didn't make sense.

But so blinded by the theatre lights was he that Lee could see nothing beyond the edge of the stage.

At that moment a huge figure strode in front of him. It was dressed in something like a Viking costume and carried a large curving knife that flashed like neon in the blazing limelight. Again, Lee couldn't process the information that was rushing through his eyes into his brain.

His mindset was that this was another prank. That he was seeing Jack Shillito in the Viking costume (after all, he was the biggest actor in the troupe); that the wicked-looking knife was merely a wooden prop from the store backstage.

By now the lines had dried on Lee's lips as he stood there rigid as a statue and watched the knifeman bring the blade down in huge slashing blows. The front half of the pantomime horse tried to run.

The knife blows opened up the costume like a man gutting a fish. From the back half spilled the pantomime horse's innards which were, when all was said and done, the man in the rear half of the costume. He tumbled out at Lee's feet.

One look at Albert's bloody face and staring eyes told Lee the man was dead.

The knifeman sprang onto the front part of the horse, which struggled to escape. He slashed open the horse's throat, spilling out kapok in snowy white lumps.

The knifeman paused as if confused by the stuffing, perhaps expecting a gush of blood instead.

His confusion didn't last long. Again the knife flashed as he drove the blade deep into the horse's neck.

The jaw of the horse chewed the air with a snapping sound, then the blade passed deeply enough through the costume to find Henry's body inside. The horse jerked and dropped heavily to the stage.

The knifeman tugged ferociously at the horse's head, pulling away the costume to reveal Henry's own head.

He yelled, 'Please, don't hurt me . . . leave me alone! Leave me alone!'

The knife flashed again. '*Leave me— Ah!*' Then Henry's cries stopped as suddenly as a radio being switched off.

His face clown-white, black diamonds painted around each eye, Lee stood there in his harlequin costume and stared at the chaos erupting around him.

The shock was so great that he didn't even hear the voice in the back of his head clamouring: 'Run! Run!'

Big Jack Shillito, still in his long dress and petticoats from his pantomime-dame role, ran on stage. He'd painted his face in the caricature of a woman's: lips a luscious red; rouged cheeks glowing brilliantly in the limelight; eyelashes as thick as spider legs. He ran holding the skirt up to his knees, flashing layers of white petticoats.

He ran desperately, looking for somewhere to hide.

A pair of men followed him. They were wild, barbarian-looking. They roared with laughter, enjoying the chase. One carried a huge axe in his hands.

Jack, kicking up his skirts, tried to scramble over the bed used in one of the comic sketches earlier.

Laughing hugely, one of the barbarians punched Jack full on the jaw, knocking him back flat onto the bed. Grunting excitedly, the wild man threw himself full-length onto the panto dame and started tearing at the skirts and petticoats.

Lee carefully turned his head, hoping if he could only manage to move slowly enough he wouldn't be noticed by the men now butchering the audience and players in the music hall. He saw a man clamber up onto the stage directly in front of him. He carried a trumpet in one hand that gleamed a brassy yellow in the lights. It was smeared with blood from the mouthpiece to the finger valves.

The man was laughing as if drunk. In one hand he carried a bloodstained hammer. He paused to raise the trumpet to his lips and blow a note that, although it was monstrously discordant, still resonated with sheer triumph and sheer exultation at the slaughter.

The single thing these wild-looking men had in common was that around their mouths and on their chins were tattooed blue lines, as if they preferred artificial blue beards to the real thing.

Lee blinked. Men with their throats cut were being thrown from the theatre boxes down onto the sides of the stage. Women were being dragged by their long hair, bonnets hanging down below their chins.

The man stopped blowing the trumpet. Then he turned to bring his glittering eyes to bear on those of Lee Burton.

Now Lee understood. He looked again at the blue tattooed lines running across the bottom of the man's face. It had been a long time coming. But the Bluebeards were here at last.

Lee's muscles locked tight with shock. He couldn't move.

Not even when the Bluebeard threw aside the trumpet, then walked slowly towards him, grinning, the axe raised ready to strike.

Two

'Why have we stopped?'

Jud rubbed the icy window of the stage-coach and looked out. 'This's the junction by Borley Wood. We're still another mile from town yet.'

Sam Baker pushed away the blanket and stood up so he could open the window in the stagecoach door. 'What's the betting snow's blocked the road ahead?'

'I hope not,' said one of the female passengers. 'Our brother is meeting us in the market square at ten.'

Sam leaned out, screwing up his eyes as snowflakes immediately rushed into them. He could hear passengers riding on the outside of the coach talking in hushed voices.

Immediately he realized something was wrong.

'Oh, my God.'

'What's wrong?' Jud asked.

'Hell,' Sam breathed. 'I think you should take a look yourself.'

Sam opened the door and stepped down from the stagecoach into the deep snow. The landscape ahead had become surreal.

It was as if gigantic roses had bloomed there in the winter's night.

Yellows, oranges, yellows, pinks, reds – dark blood-reds, at that – burst out from the town that lay in front of them.

'Oh, sweet Lord have mercy,' breathed a passenger as she leaned out through the window. 'It's on fire, Mary. All the town is burning!'

Three

There was nowhere to run; nowhere to hide. That much was obvious to Lee.

The Bluebeard tearing at Jack Shillito's panto-dame skirts and petticoats was enraged to find a man beneath them. Seconds later, Jack shrieked piercingly and balled himself up onto the bed, rolling from side to side in agony. The Bluebeard grinned at a bloody lump in his hand before throwing it to one side. Then he pulled off Jack's blonde wig and slit his throat.

Meanwhile, Lee stepped back from the man coming towards him with the axe.

He could hardly breathe. His heart trip-hammered in his chest, furiously beating at his ribcage.

All he could see in his mind's eye was the axe swinging down to split his head wide open like a melon.

He took another step.

Then some instinct made him look down.

And just for a second, the next scene of the pantomime flashed into his head.

Wicked Magician Albarzar laughs and stamps his foot twice and disappears in a cloud of smoke with the words: 'I go to ground where no mortal can follow!'

Beneath Lee's feet was the blessed trapdoor.

Quickly, he stamped twice as the Bluebeard strode forward, the axe raised.

A flash, a rush of white smoke, and Lee was falling so fast his heart felt as if it would bang into the back of his throat.

He blinked in the dim light beneath the stage.

Old Billy who worked the trap paused as he raised the bottle of gin to his lips. He scowled. 'Hey, Harlequin . . . it's not you supposed to be coming down the trap . . . s' supposed to be the feckin' wizard . . . wass goin' on up thar anyways? Sounds like feckin' bedlam.'

'Billy—'

'Pissed as bleedin' newts, I expect . . . bleedin' Christmas . . .'

'Billy!' Lee grabbed the old man by the front of his jacket and shook him.

'Hey, leave me alone, yer bleedin'—'

'Billy, listen to me! You've got to get out of here!'

'What ya talking about? You drunk too, you—'

'Billy, they're killing everyone. You've got to hide.'

Loud reports sounded from somewhere above their heads.

'Feck me. Those are guns. What's happening, Harlequin?'

'Find somewhere to hide. No . . . not here. Get away from here. Oh, God. Find somewhere to hide, Billy. Don't let them catch you.'

'Where ya going, Harlequin?'

'I've got to get to the Gainsbroughs. My wife's there . . . I've got to see if she's all right.'

But already a dark suspicion was taking shape in his mind.

Four

'Where are you two going?' called the coach driver. 'You've left your bags behind. Hey!'

Sam, with Jud at his side, didn't reply. Their agreement was unspoken. As soon as they'd seen Casterton was on fire the truth had hit home. The invasion had begun. Both knew they had to get there as quickly as possible.

With the road deep in snow the coach could only move at a snail's pace. They'd be faster on foot. That was, if the snow didn't become too deep. Big feathery flakes streamed from the sky.

Sam realized running in this would be near-impossible. But at least they could take the direct route across the fields.

Ahead the town blazed brightly, casting flickering yellows and oranges across the snow.

At this distance it was still too far away to see what damage the Bluebeards had inflicted. But Sam's imagination had already begun to supply pictures that were as vivid as they were terrible.

Five

Lee knew he could have been killed a dozen times over. But by now killing had largely given way to plundering. The

433

Bluebeards were looting houses, shops, even stripping their dead victims of shoes, clothes, jewellery. Everywhere those barbaric-looking men were walking purposefully through snow-covered streets, their arms full of clothes or food. He even saw a shaggy-haired man coming towards him with a whole side of beef over his shoulder. In the light of the fires springing up from houses he saw the man's tattooed upper lip – that thick blue line that identified him as one of Bluebeards.

And he also saw something like hedgehog spines bristling from a lumpy growth beneath the man's left eye.

Lee recalled Nicole Wagner. How'd she met him in the forest. Now he not only remembered her stark warning about the Bluebeards, but the mouse legs growing from the side of her neck. Somehow she'd been fused with the creature during the last time-jump. And he remembered Sam Baker's account of an encounter with a Bluebeard in 1944; the character with snakes coiling from his face. Was Nicole one of this murdering band now? Or was she hiding alone in the woods, leading a hermit's life, ashamed to return to society because of the things growing out of her neck?

Still dazed, Lee walked on down the street. He had no answers. All he wanted to do now was to reach the baker's house, find Sue, then hold her tight in his arms.

He sidestepped a horse lying dead in the shafts of a cart, then walked on through the falling snow.

As if it came from far, far away he still heard screams, sobbing, laughter, shouting as the Bluebeard hordes consolidated their conquest.

Burning houses lit the snow in shades of flickering yellow and gold. At one point he saw his reflection in a window. He paused for a second to stare at it. It looked so bizarre and freakish against the backdrop of a burning town. There he was: a tall thin man, face powdered white, black diamonds painted over each eye, dressed in the tight-fitting Harlequin suit with its diamond pattern.

In the old harlequinade plays of hundreds of years ago the Harlequin character was supposedly invisible to the rest of the players on the stage; he'd move unobserved like a mischievous spirit.

Now he, Lee Burton, playing Harlequin in the little town that burned so fiercely it lit up the sky like an autumn sunset, felt he'd become invisible.

The barbarian army took no notice of him now they were concentrating on gathering plunder. The surviving towns-people took no notice of him either as they ran screaming through the streets. Some had their faces disfigured by beatings or knife wounds. Some had been scalped.

No one takes any notice of Harlequin, he said under his breath, his trance-like gaze fixed ahead of him as he walked.

No one notices old Harlequin. He's become invisible again.

He skirted a Bluebeard busily pulling the boots from the feet of a headless priest who lay in the snow with a crimson glory all around him.

When he reached the home of Gainsbrough, the baker, he saw it was already burning.

Roof tiles popped like champagne corks in the heat. Timbers crackled; tongues of red and purple flame lapped the sky.

Just a couple of hours ago he'd left Sue there with Ryan, Enid and the rest of the baker's family. They were eating warm mince pies and drinking sherry. While one of the Gainsbroughs played carols on the piano.

At the thought of Sue he stopped dead. Snowflakes settled on his face, melted. Water trickled down his face. Suddenly he was struck by a vision of her: she'd waved him goodbye from that very front door, standing there in her long violet dress.

With a crack, a roof joist gave way and a dozen tiles slipped out of the flames and into the snow where they hissed and steamed.

The upper storey was burning ferociously. But as yet the ground floor seemed untouched.

The image of his wife and the Gainsbroughs coughing on the smoke as they struggled to escape the burning house suddenly struck him. Snapping out of his shocked trance he ran to the door.

The moment he pushed it open a gust of searing air drove him back.

Eyes smarting, he crouched down before running inside. In less than a minute he was outside again.

Even inside the smoke-filled house he'd soon found the bodies. The Gainsbroughs were all dead. Even Ryan's wife hadn't been spared.

Outside, he coughed, wiped his streaming eyes, then picked up a handful of snow and rubbed his face with it.

He was glad the fire would cremate the bodies. He'd hate anyone else seeing what the Bluebeards had done to them for fun.

He looked round the snow-covered garden. The bodies of the family dogs lay by the hedge.

But there was no sign of Ryan Keith. Nor of Sue.

They could be lying in the blazing bedrooms.

But then again . . .

He ran round to the back of the house, calling Sue's name.

There he found more blood in the snow – from small round drops the size of pennies to great bloody swathes that covered the ground like red blankets. And everything was lit with that cruel light from the infernos that roared and crackled all across the town.

Standing there beneath shrouds of smoke, he stared up at the burning windows and called Sue's name over and over again.

Six

It took a good twenty minutes of hard running for Sam and Jud to make it through the snow to the outskirts of Casterton.

Already the heat from the burning houses had turned snow in the streets to black slush.

'My God,' Jud panted as they ran. 'Look at it. It's like the end of the world.'

Sam said nothing. All he wanted to do was find Zita.

Even so, hope was draining from him.

The desolation was shocking. Butchered men and women lay in the street. Horses ran everywhere, panicked by the commotion and the fires. More than once the two men had to throw themselves into alleyways and shop doorways to avoid being trampled by horses that galloped by, riderless, their eyes wild, foam flecking their mouths.

A dog barked shrilly. And everywhere there were cries of frightened and wounded townsfolk.

In the market square Sam saw the Reverend Hather helping the doctor bandage the wounded where they'd been laid out on market stalls.

Behind them in an awful fiery backdrop the town's church blazed. Falling masonry struck the bells to send a discordant clanging like a funeral toll across the town.

'Thomas!' Sam called. 'Did you see who attacked the town?'

'*Bastards* . . .' Reverend Hather shook his head bitterly. 'The bastards even killed the little children.'

The doctor didn't even look up from bandaging a child's head as he spoke. 'Men armed with knives and axes. They each had a tattooed mark here.' He touched his upper lip.

'Bluebeards,' Sam said.

Jud nodded grimly. 'And we were so damned complacent. We pretended we were living in nothing more than a Victorian theme park. We should have been preparing for the invasion. We were warned it was coming . . .' He shook his head sourly.

Sam gripped Thomas's arm. 'Are the men who did this still here?'

'No, at least I think not . . . the swine took what they could carry and left.'

Sam looked up. Across the market square, standing on the plinth of a statue of the angel Gabriel, was Rolle. He still wore the orange boiler suit. Firelight shone through the corkscrews of red hair, making it look like a glowing halo.

And, apparently oblivious to what was happening to the rest of the town, he stood there with one arm around the angel's stone shoulder, watching the church burning down.

The sound of the organ now joined the clang of the bell. Hot air expanding in the organ pipes threw out discordant notes that ran from high-pitched shrieks to thunderous, booming bass chords. Sam swallowed. This was music for the damned all right.

Sam felt a hand grip his arm.

He turned to see Jud's face lit a flickering yellow. 'Sam, I'm going back down to the amphitheatre. Dot is alone in the boat down there.'

'But that's miles. You'll never make it in this blizzard.'

'Don't worry about me. I'll grab a horse. Where are you going now?'

'To the Gainsbroughs'. Zita planned spending the night there.'

'Good luck, Sam.'

'And you, Jud.'

Jud turned immediately and ran away into the swirling snow flakes.

Sam turned his back on the burning church. Then he ran in the direction of the Gainsbroughs' house.

Seven

Lee had stood calling Sue's name for a good five minutes. Desperately, he willed her face to appear at one of the upstairs windows.

'Sue! Can you hear me!'

This time he paused, listening for her reply on the off chance she was somewhere nearby.

Then, above the sound of tiles cracking under the ferocious heat, he heard shouting followed by a muffled thumping like fists on a door far away.

'Sue! Sue!'

This time there was a sharper clattering. Not fists this time but a hammer or an iron bar against wood.

It was close, too.

It came again.

This time Lee realized it came from the trapdoor to the cellar which lay nearby. But for a moment he couldn't see the door. Slates had poured off the roof in an avalanche to bury the entrance.

Then he remembered. The trapdoor was set beneath the kitchen window.

Lee ran to the spot and began clawing the slates away with his bare hands.

'Sue! Is that you?'

The answering shout was male. What was more, it was familiar.

'Ryan? Ryan, hang on, I'll get you out! Just hang on!'

He tugged at the still-hot mound of slates.

Suddenly he realized that a second pair of hands had appeared to help.

'Sam? Dear God, Sam, am I pleased to see you!'

'Who's down there in the cellar?'

'As far as I can tell, Ryan Keith. I'm hoping Sue's down there, too.'

'Any sign of Zita?'

'No . . . but she isn't here anyway.'

'I thought she was stopping over with Enid tonight? They were having a party.'

Lee shook his head as he pulled away the tiles. 'She decided to stay back up at Perseverance Farm. She said she wanted to finish making a Christmas present.'

'God, I hope she's all right.' Sam's first impulse was to run home, but he knew he had to help Lee here first.

A moment later the trapdoor was clear. Sam kicked the bar that held the trapdoor shut from the outside. 'Ryan!' Sam shouted. 'We've got it clear at this side.' Almost immediately he heard bolts being slipped open on the other side. Sam bent down and heaved open the trapdoor.

An uprush of smoke gushed out, followed by Ryan who coughed and gasped as he stumbled out to fall onto the slushy snow.

'Ryan, are you OK?'

Ryan nodded, but still he coughed, his eyes streaming.

Sam said, 'I reckon he should be OK in a minute. Did you find Enid and her family?'

Lee looked Sam in the eye and gave a grim nod, then looked back at the house.

Sam didn't need to interpret that look of Lee's. 'Oh, hell . . .'

Then he crouched down beside Ryan who sat heavily in the snow, coughing so hard his chest crackled. He rested his hand on the man's shoulder.

The flames consumed the house.

Sam watched as the walls collapsed, sending gold sparks rushing into the sky. The destruction was echoed around him as dozens of houses, warehouses, shops, hotels blazed. Again the realization came to him that what they were witnessing was the beginning of the end of the world.

Eight

Later, in the borderlands that lay between yesterday and today, Nicole Wagner, William and Bullwitt saw the procession. They watched from the safety of a wooded hilltop as a thousand or so men passed beneath them in a long snaking line.

They were close enough to see the faces of the Bluebeards.

William held his cloak to one side so Bullwitt could peer through the slit in his clothes. The dark, bulging eyes missed nothing.

'Lord, there's old Snake-eye himself,' he said. 'You know, some say a battleship couldn't kill him. He's been in more battles than I know what.'

'Just look at what they're carrying.' Nicole spoke in a whisper. 'Where on earth did they get it all from?'

'They've raided the town,' William said. 'We all knew it was coming but we never thought it would be this big.'

'But we should have seen it coming, me old matey,' Bullwitt said. 'We should have seen it coming.'

'Why's that?' asked Nicole.

'Because, sweetie, their numbers have been growing apace these last few months.' Bullwitt spoke in a gruff but kindly way. 'Barbarians from all over the country, from every different century you can think of, have been flocking to them; they knew the Bluebeards were onto a good thing. I mean, just think about it, sweetie. They walk into 1535, plunder a town, then bring their loot back here. The army can't find them, so the Bluebeards get away scot-free. When they need a bit more plunder out they go again, out of Limbo here and into any bloody time they want. Take whatever catches their eye. Then they scuttle back where no one can reach them.'

'What he says is true, Nicole,' William said. 'They can raid the district around Casterton with impunity.'

'What year are they returning from?' Nicole asked with a shiver.

'They've used the time gate down by the bend in the river,' William said.

'That will give them access to the nineteenth century, won't it?'

'That's right, my old sweetie. '1865, to be precise.'

Nicole shuddered. 'Oh my, God. That's where – when – my friends are.'

Bullwitt raised his eyes to her from the slit in William's tunic. 'Then perhaps we should say a prayer for them tonight.'

Nicole shivered. She felt William's hand slip into hers and give it a reassuring squeeze. She squeezed back. But she was frightened for Sue, Ryan, Lee and the rest. The mouse claws scurried at the side of her neck, running through air as they did when her fear was transmitted to whatever remained of the mouse's brains buried inside her neck.

Absently she stroked the running legs with her free hand, soothing them.

Below in the valley the Bluebeards marched by, pulling carts piled high with food, clothes, bottles, valuables of every kind.

Then came another group. These walked with their heads hanging down.

Quickly Nicole counted thirty or more women and children.

She pointed. 'They've brought those from the town, haven't they?'

William nodded. 'As slaves.'

'Of various sorts and abilities,' Bullwitt added. 'Poor damn' fools.'

Nicole didn't need Bullwitt to elaborate. Seeing the women shuffle by in their long dresses, their hair hanging down in tangled strands, was bad enough. But then she saw a face she recognized.

'Oh God, no,' she whispered. 'I know that woman down there.'

'Then if I were you, sweetie,' Bullwitt whispered. 'I'd pray to the good Lord to strike her down dead at this very moment.'

Clutching William's hand tightly, she watched as Sue walked by. It hadn't been so long ago that Sue Royston had been the cheerful travel rep dressed in the Stan Laurel costume. Now she looked as if she'd been dragged through filth. Her hair was a messed tangle of knots.

And now she was walking along the path into the woods.

Like a lamb to the slaughter.

'I'm going to do something,' Nicole said, gripping William's hand hard.

'All we can do is hide and watch.' William spoke gently.

'And hope they leave us alone,' Bullwitt grunted. 'Which

they will do, if they've got enough rich pickings to occupy themselves for a while.'

'No.' Nicole shook her head firmly. 'I'm going to find some way of helping those people.'

Bullwitt sighed. 'I wish you could. But it's going to take a bloody miracle to help those poor devils now.'

Chapter Forty-Two

One

Tuesday evening, 21st December, 1865

Jud said to Sam, 'We're in bigger trouble than we thought.'

Sam looked up at him as he sat at the table with a mug of hot coffee in his hands. 'Bigger trouble? Christ, I thought it couldn't get any worse. Did you hear how many died in the attack? More than a thousand.'

Jud nodded as he sat in the chair opposite Sam. In the hallway of Perseverance Farm the grandfather clock chimed seven. The notes sounded sombre.

Sam continued. 'And those are only the confirmed deaths. There'll be even more bodies, or what's left of them, in the burned-out buildings. Including Ryan's wife. Did you know she was pregnant?'

'Yes, I'd heard. And I've heard about the women and children who were abducted. Did you know Sue Burton was taken, too?'

'I heard a couple of hours ago. Lee took some persuading not to throw himself in the river. He's gone to pieces over this . . . hell, what a mess. What a damn' awful mess.'

It was now almost twenty-four hours since the attack on Casterton by the Bluebeards. Buildings were still burning, although the heavily falling snow was beginning to damp down the worst of the fires.

After leaving Lee and Ryan in the town, Sam had run back to Perseverance Farm. It lay midway between Casterton and the amphitheatre and he'd expected to find the place reduced to ashes. Yet by some miracle the Bluebeards had missed it on the march into town. Zita and the rest were safe.

Meanwhile, Jud had returned to the narrow boat to find it gone. His first thought was that it had been sunk by the Bluebeards with Dot on board. But then he'd heard the familiar *chug-chug* of the motor.

The narrow boat had come gliding out of the darkness and the falling snow, his wife at the helm. She told Jud later that when she'd seen the Bluebeard armed with the axe coming on board she'd simply jumped over the side and had swum for it in the freezing water. There she trod water, well out of harm's way, while the Bluebeard had gone through the boat filling pillowcases with jewellery and bottles of whisky. After he'd left she'd climbed back onto the boat, untied the moorings and then had taken it across the river where she felt it would be safe to wait until Jud's return.

'The cold would have killed skinny folk like you,' she'd told them. 'Lucky I had some pretty good natural insulation. So, you see, cellulite does have its uses.'

Now Jud and Sam sat drinking coffee after a day helping out at the town. But it had been a Herculean task, and Sam was reminded about Humpty-Dumpty who all the king's horses and all the king's men couldn't put together again. Probably a good third of the town had been destroyed by the fires.

Sam took a deep swallow of the coffee, feeling that welcome warmth go sliding down his gullet to heat his stomach. 'You were saying that this is going to get worse before it gets better. How come?'

'For one, Casterton's cut off by the snowfalls. All the roads and railway lines are blocked. Even the telegraph lines are down.'

'So we're going to be on our own for while. But surely we'll manage?'

'Normally, yes. If it was just a case of clearing up the aftermath of what the Bluebeards have done.'

'I can hear a 'but' coming along here.'

'Yes, and a big 'but' at that. I've been talking to Rolle.'

'He's here?'

'He was in the town earlier. I managed to grab a word with him before he left. I don't know where he was going but he was in a heck of a hurry. But that's beside the point. Anyway, he told me he's seen the Bluebeards at work before – but never in such huge numbers. He says this is only the first instalment.'

'You mean they're going to come back?'

'Yes.'

'But surely they just hit and run like pirates or . . . or even muggers. They wouldn't be stupid enough to walk back into a place they've just raided?'

'But what's to stop them? They know the roads into the outside world are impassable for the next two or three days at least. Even if we could get a messenger out on foot, what could the authorities do?'

'They could send in the army.'

'What army?'

'Hell, Jud, take a look at the maps in the schoolrooms. In 1865 Britain ruled half the world. The maps are all red, showing how much you limeys actually owned. Remember the saying? The sun never sets on the British Empire? You don't conquer that much without a pretty substantial army.'

Jud gave a grim smile. 'Exactly. Today, in 1865, Her Majesty's army comprises around a million troops.'

'You see. They'll blitz these barbarians. They won't know what hit them.'

'And you're right about the huge Empire, too, Sam. And that's where most of the troops are stationed. Out there in the hot spots of China, India and Africa. Our problem is that the garrisons here on mainland Britain probably number only a few thousand men at most – and they're dotted here and there all over the country.'

'But surely they can marshal enough troops to stop those Bluebeards dead in their tracks. Our troops would be armed with rifles and artillery. For heaven's sake, those Bluebeards might be ferocious monsters but they only have axes and clubs.'

'But the cold fact of the matter is we still have to get word to the proper authorities. Then they're going to have to bring troops into barracks from Christmas leave. Put them on trains, bring them as close to Casterton as they can. Then either clear the snow off the line or somehow march them here across all those snowdrifts. All that before they can even fire a shot in anger.'

'Hell.' The penny had dropped. Sam shook his head. 'And in the meantime the Bluebeards will have come back and finished what they started.'

'Exactly.'

'So it looks as if it's down to us?'

Jud nodded.

'How much time does Rolle think we've got?'

'Anywhere between three or four days.'

'Why doesn't he think they'll return sooner?'

'Well, they'll have had a couple of hours' march through the snow to Casterton, then they'll have had to carry all the loot back with them to whatever time zone they call home. They'll have taken food and booze with them and, like any army that's won a battle, they'll want to rest.'

'And maybe party?'

'And party. Remember, they took the women back with them so . . .' There was no need for him to finish the sentence.

'Christ.'

'It sounds callous but that's going to give us a short breathing space.'

'So what next? Get everyone out of town before the Bluebeards come back and start murdering and looting all over again?'

'We could get some out. But there were a lot of people

447

hurt in the last attack. With the roads blocked, you'd have to carry the wounded out on stretchers. We also have young children and the elderly. How could you ask them to walk out across all those snowdrifts and blocked roads? The conditions out there are nothing less than Arctic. They'd drop like flies.'

'Jud, we seem to be running out of options fast here.'

'I was thinking we could fortify some of the bigger buildings in town. Perhaps we could hold them off until help does get through or they simply give up and return to wherever they came from.'

'That might work. But it's a heck of a risk. Those buildings weren't designed to withstand a siege. What if the Bluebeards simply set them on fire? They'd slaughter us the moment we ran out into the street.'

Jud sighed. 'Then we're out of options.'

'So what the hell do we do next?'

'Then, gentlemen, you ask me.'

'*Carswell?*'

Sam swivelled his head round in astonishment to see Carswell standing at the kitchen door. Immaculately dressed as a Victorian gentleman, silver-topped cane in one hand, he was smiling broadly as he slipped off his gloves.

'Carswell.' Sam repeated again, realizing his mouth must have dropped open into an astonished 'O'. 'How on Earth did you get here?'

'The river's not frozen over yet. And no, before you ask, I haven't yet quite mastered the knack of walking on water. I came by boat.'

Sam watched Carswell set down his top hat, cane and gloves on the table. Carswell looked round at the bare furnishings. 'Still hanging out with the little people, I see.'

'Carswell, did you know that Casterton was—'

'Yes, yes, dear boy. I know all about it. Quite shocking, I'm sure.'

Sam shook his head in disgust. 'Carswell, you're a son of a bitch.'

448

'Indeed I am, sir. That's why I'm rich and you're . . . well, slumming it, I see.'

'So why are you here?'

'Why am I here, dear chap?' Carswell looked from Sam to Jud, his eyes bright, a smile playing on his lips. 'What other reason could there be? I'm here to save your necks.'

Two

'Coffee?' Jud asked as Carswell sat down at the table.

'How kind. Thank you. Two sugars, please.'

Sam said, 'Carswell, did I hear you right? You're actually here to help us?'

'Your hearing is perfectly sound, Mr Baker. Ahh, now that coffee isn't completely awful.' Warming his hands around the cup he said, 'Now, forgive my eavesdropping, but I have to say straightaway that both your earlier plans were doomed to failure, as I believe you realized. You can't evacuate the town through the blocked roads – and no, Mr Baker, don't even suggest trying to get everyone out by boat. Mine is almost out of fuel, and even if fuel was plentiful and we used both boats to full capacity, we wouldn't be able to evacuate more than a small fraction of the three thousand or so souls still in the town.' He sipped his coffee, then wrinkled his nose. 'Well, a trifle bitter, but hot, which on a freezing night like this is occasionally more important than a fine flavour . . . Now, your other plan of fortifying key buildings in the town such as the town hall, the police station or whatever is quite out of the question.'

Jud began, 'But what if we were to barricade the—'

'No, no. Listen. Sam Baker here is quite right. There is far too much timber employed in the construction of the buildings. And, after all, these barbarians, the Bluebeards, are familiar enough with siege techniques. They'd roll burning barrels or carts against the timber doors. Once those were alight you'd come running out like rats smoked from a nest to be cut down in the streets.'

449

'And I suppose you have come here out of the goodness of your heart to explain how we should save ourselves?'

'Precisely. A little more coffee if you have it, please, Mr Campbell.'

Jud nodded and went to bring the pot. Sam caught Jud's eye. He would have liked to kick that arrogant son of a bitch Carswell out into the snow, but while the man dangled a solution in front of them like a sweet juicy carrot in front of a donkey all they could do was stay polite and listen.

Jud set the cup in front of Carswell.

Carswell said, 'Uhm, you wouldn't have a drop of whisky or brandy to liven that up, would you?'

Jud nodded. 'I think we have some. Will Irish do you?'

'Oh, any port in a storm, but it does have the aroma of the bog about it, don't you think?'

'OK, Carswell,' Sam said as Jud set the whiskey bottle on the table. 'Before you ask us to sit up and beg or lick the dog poop off your boots or whatever else you've got in mind, are you going to tell us this master plan of yours for stopping those murdering bastards coming back into town and killing every man, woman and child?'

'Seeing as I'm not doing this out of sweet Christian charity, I can safely ignore your impertinence.'

Jud frowned. 'But who's paying you?'

'And how much?' asked Sam.

'I don't think vulgar price-taggery is important at a time like this. Let's just say I'm here as a professional consultant.'

You mean we're paying you some kind of consultancy fee for helping us?

At that moment Ryan Keith came in. He looked like a zombie. His hair was stuck on end, and his eyes were red and sore. He saw the whiskey on the table, poured himself half a cupful and went and sat on a stool by the fire. So absorbed was he by the death of his wife just a few hours ago that he didn't even notice the three men in the room.

After giving Ryan a dismissive glance Carswell poured a small tot of whiskey into his cup. 'Well, that's injected some spirit into the coffee. Now, to action . . .' He pulled half a dozen sheets of neatly folded paper from his pocket. 'To save your lives from the next attack will require superb planning – that's my department. And a great deal of hard work and, ultimately, courage – which is your department. You'll also have to sell this scheme to the whole town and persuade every man Jack of them to work with you. In the end, they will have to fight alongside you. Fight like lions, I should add. Fight with every ounce of determination and strength they can muster. Because this isn't going to be easy . . . it's not going to be easy at all. Now, gentlemen, allow me to introduce you to Operation Rolling Vengeance.'

Carswell began to unfold the sheets of paper. As he smoothed them down onto the table top he told them what they needed to do.

Three

Carswell said, 'Today is Tuesday. My guess is that the next time the Bluebeards strike will be at dawn, probably either Friday morning, or Saturday at the latest.'

'So?'

'So, my dear Mr Baker, I suggest we should be ready to attack them the moment they exit the time gate which, Rolle informs me, is down by the river.'

'Attack the Bluebeards? Are you serious?'

'Absolutely serious,' Carswell said crisply. 'The best form of defence is attack.'

'But how? We've a town full of exhausted civilians, not a garrison full of crack marines.'

'But you'll have surprise on your side. Always a worthy ally. As you say, the Bluebeards will emerge from their lair expecting no opposition from a demoralized and beaten population with no weapons worth speaking of. What they will find – to their amazement – is an effective, well-armed fighting force with more than a few surprises up its sleeve.'

'Hell, Carswell. In the past you've accused me of coming

up with some fanciful ideas. Now this *really* takes the biscuit.'

'Hear me out, Mr Baker.' Carswell tapped a sheet of paper. 'These are the blueprints of your war machines. If you're lucky, you have around seventy-two hours – at the most – to build them.'

'What on earth are they?' Jud angled his head. 'That's a drawing of the tour bus, isn't it?'

'Spot on, Mr Campbell. And it shows just how you're going to turn it from a vehicle designed to carry trippers about the countryside into a rolling fortress on wheels.'

'A rolling fortress?' Sam looked at Jud who worriedly nipped his bottom lip between finger and thumb. 'You mean something like a tank?'

'Well, perhaps something more like a battleship – only one that moves on land rather than water.'

Sam glanced at Jud again. 'Jud, do you think it'll work?'

Jud stared back down at the plans, his lip still pinched between finger and thumb. After a while he looked up at Sam and said in a small voice, 'It's going to have to, isn't it?'

Chapter Forty-Three

One

Tuesday night, 21st December, 1865

Countdown commenced at nine o'clock that Tuesday night.

Carswell had brought the mantelpiece clock from the farmhouse and stood it on a shelf in the barn where everyone could see it. Then in firm, bold letters on the wall above the clock he chalked:-

**5 A.M. 25TH DECEMBER IS
ZERO HOUR.
ALL CONVERSIONS WORK MUST
BE COMPLETE.
FAILURE IS NOT AN OPTION!**

Through the open doors of the barn Sam could see the falling snow. Beyond that the fields lay in darkness. A darkness that was so deep and dense it was nearly tangible.

And for all anyone knows, Sam thought bleakly, *those barbarians might be moving this way again*. To finish looting the town. And to clear out the outlying houses they missed on their first raid. Houses like this one.

Sam looked back at Carswell who was striding round in his iridescent red waistcoat barking orders. In the cold air of the barn his breath came out in huge bursts of white vapour.

First, he ordered that as many oil lamps as possible should be brought into the barn. 'This is where we will work night and day,' he told them as the lamps were lit, filling the great void of the barn with a golden light. 'This is where we'll eat; this will be home until the conversion work is finished.'

Most of the people there were men and women who'd made the first time-jump back from 1999. Even so, they'd started to go native after living and working in Casterton for the last seven months of 1865. They looked at the cars, the ice-cream van, the tour bus, with surprised expressions, as if seeing them for the first time. Many were still bewildered by the plan outlined by Carswell. And there were more than a few objections.

A grey-haired man held up his hand. 'Why can't we just get out of town until all this is over?'

Carswell sighed, irritated by what he saw as flagrant stupidity. 'Do I have to explain all over again? The roads are now blocked. We are marooned here as effectively as if we'd been washed up on a desert island.'

A woman shook her head. 'But how *can* we attack these barbarians? From what we've heard, there were thousands of them.'

'Probably no more than two thousand, maximum.'

'But you were saying that we'd probably only have about two or three hundred people at most to fight them. That's suicide.'

Sam saw Carswell's hands clench as he fought down the anger growing inside of him. 'Dear lady. In 480 BC, in Greece, a force of four hundred or so Spartan warriors successfully held back the entire Persian army of several *hundred thousand* men.'

'Don't patronize me, Mr Carswell.' The woman had the bearing of a schoolteacher. 'At Thermopylae the Spartans delayed the Persian invasion of Greece by several days. However, those Spartans were highly-trained fighting men, and even so they died to a man. So how in heaven's name do you suppose a few hundred townsfolk from

Casterton are going to wipe out all those barbarians when they come marching into town?'

'I don't suppose for a moment we will kill them *all*.'

'Why on earth sacrifice our own people in what must be a futile endeavour, then?'

'Because,' Carswell said, 'my way is your only hope of survival. Also, I intend to employ the same strategy as the Spartans did at Thermopylae. You've no doubt seen the Hollywood version of this historical event? So you'll recall the Spartans didn't meet their enemy on open ground. They held them at a narrow pass between a cliff face and the sea where the ground was only a few yards wide. This meant the Persians couldn't deploy their cavalry and they could only send forward a few hundred of their troops at a time – because space was so restricted. That's why we'll launch our attack between the cliffs and the river.'

It was Jud who raised his hand this time. 'Just how do we know they'll come through the pass down by the river?'

'Oh, they will. Rolle has assured me of that. Because that's where the time-gate which they have to use to reach this year of 1865 lies.'

'But if he's wrong that means we will—'

'Then we must rely on the hope that he *won't* be wrong, Mr Campbell. Now, I must tell you we are wasting valuable time. We should have begun work on these vehicles an hour ago.'

'But what gives you the right to be in charge?' Sam asked. 'We haven't appointed you as our leader.'

'No, but that's part of the deal. This is my plan; therefore I'm in charge.'

'But who made the deal?'

'I did.'

Everyone turned to see the man who stood in the barn doorway. Snow speckled his hair and face white. His eyes blazed as bright as before.

'Rolle?'

Rolle walked into the barn, looking round at the vehicles. His eyes grew wide.

'Rolle, is it true? *You* brought Carswell here?'

Rolle nodded so sharply that snowflakes dropped from his beard. 'It is true. There are no other options now. In the past I have fought the plague with penicillin. Now the Bluebeards are the plague. We must fight them with every weapon at our disposal. All I can do is beg all of you to follow Mr Carswell. Do everything he asks, and perhaps with God's love we will come through the inferno un-harmed.' These were the most lucid words Sam had heard from Rolle. He watched as the man went to the bus and ran his fingers abstractedly over the metal sides. Already he seemed to be slipping into that interior dream-world of his. He hummed to himself while continuing to run his fingers over the metalwork as if he was drawing pictures only he could see.

Sam spoke under his breath to Jud. 'What on earth could Rolle give to a man like Carswell in exchange for his help?'

'Probably what you always give when you do a deal with the devil.'

'All right, people,' Carswell said, clapping his hands. 'You heard the man. My word is law. Get to work. Lee, I need you to go into town and bring the Reverend Thomas Hather to me – *now*. Jud, Sam. Strip the seats and the parcel shelves out of the bus. A task that will be made all the easier if you stop whispering at the back there. Oh, you'd best remove the windows from the bus first. Now, people, get busy.'

Two

And that was how it started.

With a motley range of tools collected from the cars, Sam started slackening the nuts and bolts that held the bus seats to the floor. Jud started pulling the rubber trim from the windows until—

'Mr Campbell, don't waste time taking out the glass in one piece.' Carswell's voice came from the hayloft where he'd established a kind of combined observation platform and command post. 'We don't need the glass. Smash it out, man.'

'Aye, aye, captain,' Jud muttered under his breath. He picked up a hammer. 'Cover your eyes.' Then he walked along the aisle between the bus seats and smashed each window in turn. It sounded explosive in the confines of the barn. The toughened glass burst into thousands of white crystals, scattering across the floor.

Carswell called down to the schoolteacher who'd raised the objections earlier. 'Get that broken glass swept up straight away, then find more lamps. Those men have got to be able to see what they're doing.'

Sam returned to slackening the nuts with the wrench. They were all shiny and new, without a trace of rust, but they'd been tightened with a power tool. Each one took a hell of a lot of sweated curses to turn. Fortunately, once they *had* begun to turn, it was easy enough to unscrew them. After that, Sam simply heaved the whole seat out through the side of the bus where the glass had once been.

He paused to wipe the sweat from his eyes. In the cold air he noticed that his arms had actually begun to steam from the sheer body heat he was generating. All around the bus men and women were working, each with their own special task allotted to them by Carswell. Now they knew what they were doing there was an air of determined industry. The air was full of the sounds of metal being hammered, saws cutting wood, planing, chopping, lines being tied. One of the men who Sam knew had been a garage mechanic in that faraway world of 1999 was cutting a hole right in the centre of the Range Rover's roof. Then he pushed a hefty timber fence post down into it until a good five feet of its length stuck straight up like the mast of a ship.

As Sam heaved yet another seat out through the glassless window he shook his head. Here they all were, busy as ants in a nest, but none of this activity made sense. He hadn't a clue why the mechanic was fixing a timber mast onto the

Range Rover and he didn't know why Zita was running power cables from under the dashboard to what looked like stumpy timber wings that now jutted out from the car's side.

All he did know for sure was that Carswell had told them they would transform the tour bus into some kind of battleship on wheels. But he still didn't see how.

He glanced up at Carswell who stood on the timber platform high above the barn floor. He was looking down, his hands on his hips, his feet apart, like some master architect overseeing the building of a great pyramid.

So the little workers who toiled below didn't know the grand purpose behind their labour. That didn't matter to Carswell. It didn't matter a jot. He alone possessed the vision – the great, glorious, shining vision – of the finished machine.

Sam returned to a bolt that was more stubborn than the rest. His hands had already begun to blister despite the calluses they already bore from the ferry work; but he slipped the wrench over the securing nut, braced his foot against the seat and heaved.

As he did so he realized that he, too, had at last surrendered himself to Carswell's authority.

The man might be a bastard. A high and mighty bastard at that, who had the conceit and arrogance of a Caesar, a Napoleon and a Mussolini all rolled into one.

But he was probably all that stood between Casterton and the barbarians.

Three

At a little after two in the morning Sam Baker found himself walking down to the river.

It took a good twenty minutes to cross the snow-covered meadows to the water's edge where Jud's boat lay moored.

Sam walked with his head down against the stinging cascade of snowflakes. In one hand he carried a small lantern by its iron hoop handle. Unlike an electric torch that would have blazed a cone of white light through the blizzard, it threw little more than an orangey gleam onto the snow in front of him.

After five hours cranking that wrench to loosen off the seating bolts his hands felt hot enough to burst into flame. His knuckles bled where the wrench had slipped and his fists had rapped against the inner walls of the bus. Periodically he'd move the lantern from one hand to the other, then turn his free hand so that the palm was exposed to the falling snow. The icy cool of the flakes melting on the blistered skin was sheer bliss. There was something almost erotic in the sheer intensity of the sensation.

He paused for a moment to check where he was. In that snowfall it would be too easy to wander off from the buried path and lose himself in the woods.

There was no one about.

No houses.

The only sound was the faint crunch of snow beneath his boots.

He switched the lamp to his right hand.

As far as he could tell he was on the right track. The ground was running downhill now. He was probably only three or four minutes from the amphitheatre. The river and Jud's boat would only be another thirty seconds, or so walking time beyond that.

He walked faster.

He pulled the brim of his cap lower over his eyes to try and prevent the snow from actually striking his eyeballs.

And more than once he remembered that in this weather he could walk into a Bluebeard before he realized he was there.

What then?

A brief scuffle before Sam Baker's blood stained the snow?

But there was a good enough reason for him to be here.

In 1865 electric cables were only available for the tele-graph system that sent Morse dashes and dots pulsing from town to town. They did have a bit of electric cable at the farm but they needed more.

Jud had said there were a couple of spools of cable on the narrow boat, and as far as he knew it hadn't been taken when a Blubeard had looted it the day before.

The narrow boat itself was, of course, deserted. Jud and Dot had moved into the farmhouse until the danger was over.

One way or another, Sam thought grimly.

He'd left the people at the barn still working furiously.

Already a strange clutch of vehicles were arising like mutant phoenixes from the carcasses of the original bus; van and cars that had come through the tear in time with them.

Years ago, Sam had been given a book called *Wacky Inventions*. He'd loved to sit cross-legged on his bedroom floor and slowly turn the pages, looking at each of those bizarre inventions in turn.

Of course, they weren't real inventions, not ones that would actually work, and you couldn't seriously think of operating them without being dragged away to the nuthouse. They were cartoon-like drawings of machines that allowed you to combine two completely separate activities, such as a bath tub on wheels with an engine and a steering wheel that enabled you to go shopping while still taking a bath. That drawing showed a cheerful man sitting in bubbles up to his chest and scrubbing his back with a long-handled brush while selecting products from a supermarket shelf. Another favourite was a device that allowed you to read a book while taking the dog for a walk. A pole extended out from a headband, something like a unicorn horn. From a clip at the end hung your book, comfortably at eye level. (Illustration: an unfeasibly happy young woman walking her poodle through the park as she avidly read her novel.)

The vehicles in the barn had taken on the appearance of those 'wacky inventions'. Most had stubby wings made of lightweight timber torn up from the farmhouse floors. (Did Carswell in some mad flight of fancy believe those machines would actually fly?) The only seat on the bus was the driver's seat. When Sam had left the barn, Jud and a couple of other men had been building what looked to be a large box around the seat, using the stout wooden doors from the outbuildings to form the walls.

Carswell had said he'd explain his plans fully. But that, Sam was sure, would be in his own sweet time.

Sam reached the amphitheatre car park. Falling snow still blotted out the river, but he knew he was almost there now.

He quickened his pace.

He still felt all too vulnerable and alone out here. The gateway that the barbarians had used to enter 1865 was a mile or so upstream. Even though the Bluebeards probably wouldn't attack again for another couple of days they might send out scouting patrols.

Sam crossed the car park. The snow there was flat, pristine.

When he reached the top of the amphitheatre he paused to look down into it.

Immediately he ducked back.

A dozen figures stood at the bottom.

Bluebeards.

That was his first thought.

Turning down the wick of the lamp until the speck of flame was so small it wouldn't betray his position, he cautiously looked over the edge.

If this was the start of another attack, he'd have to run as hard as he could back to the farmhouse to warn everyone.

What then, he didn't know.

He cautiously lifted his head over the rim of the amphitheatre and looked down.

Snow swirled into his face in tingling flakes.

He counted eleven figures. But they were not Bluebeards.

He recognized Rolle first of all, unmistakable with his red hair and orange overalls. He seemed to be lecturing the others.

But who the hell were they?

They didn't look like people from Casterton. And why on earth would they travel all this way out of town, anyway?

He wiped the snowflakes from his eyes and looked again.

All the figures were wrapped against the snowstorm. As his eyes adjusted to the gloom he recognized one of them.

It was the long blonde hair fluttering this way and that in the wind that did it.

Nicole Wagner. It had to be. But what on earth . . .

Then he recalled Lee's strange encounter with her in the wood. He knew that she was now Liminal – Rolle's word for those who lived in Limbo outside the normal flow of time. And that an animal had fused with her during the last time-jump.

So she's been hiding out here all along, Sam told himself in wonder. *Living like an outlaw*.

And wasn't that heavy-set man the one with a bird fused partly inside his face?

But what were they doing here?

Why were they talking to – or rather being lectured by – Rolle in the amphitheatre in this blizzard at the dead of night?

All this made as much sense to Sam as the weird and wondrous machines taking shape in the barn back at Perseverance Farm.

After Rolle wound up the meeting he stood there shaking hands with each of the Liminals as they left.

Sam left the lamp at the top of the slope and slithered down through the snow, staying well hidden behind a line of bushes.

Concealed there, he watched the heavily-clothed figures move off, following the river upstream.

He'd been right about Nicole. She walked by, her arm linked with that of a tall young man with blond hair. They leaned forward into the driving snow.

What with the darkness and the snowflakes Sam couldn't make out much detail of the other's faces, although, strangely he heard what sounded like a hive of bees as one of the men passed him – his face was bluey-dark and Sam couldn't be sure whether he was bearded or not.

Last of all came what Sam at first took to be a boy of around ten riding a cow or bullock.

He looked again, then turned quickly away, his stomach fluttering queasily.

The boy had become fused with the cow.

If anything, it resembled the mythical centaur. The half-man, half-horse of Graeco-Roman legend. The top half of the human body rose up from the neck of the cow. The cow's head was still there but was turned crookedly to the left. The bones in the neck must have locked at an awkward angle, so the head always appeared to be straining back and slightly downwards, as if trying to look back at its own hind legs.

The boy, with a mass of curly hair that had itself taken on the black and white Friesian patterning of the cow, stared impassively forward.

Sam looked back as the line headed away into darkness.

Soon all he could see was the swish of the cow's tail.

A moment later that, too, was gone.

Four

By the time Sam Baker returned with the cable to the barn at Perseverance Farm the Reverend Hather was there.

He stood in the pools of golden lamplight, his palms lightly pressed together as if in prayer, and looked round at the bustle of activity, his eyes wide.

Sam gripped the coils of cable under an arm as he pulled the barn door shut behind him to keep out the never-ending snowfall.

Hammers still clattered down against nails or sheet metal.

Sam handed the cable to Zita. 'How goes it?' he asked.

'Bizarrely,' she said. 'Carswell's now got us sawing the glass ends off light bulbs.'

'Light bulbs?'

'They're from the bus's luggage shelves that you removed earlier.'

Sam shook his head, bewildered, his face too frozen to show anything other than a blank expression.

'You know the ones? The little lights set above the passengers' heads that they could switch on to read, do wordsearches or whatever.'

'I know the ones, but hasn't Carswell even hinted why?'

'No. Like God, Mr Carswell prefers to move in a mysterious way. Anyway, must carry on, *He'll* go ballistic if he thinks I'm standing here chatting to you.' She threaded her arm through the spools of cable to carry them back to the workbenches where a couple of women were carefully cutting through the light bulbs with fine saws. 'Oh, and he goes ballistic anyway if we break a filament. Thanks for the cable; we'll talk at the next tea break.' Shooting him a dazzling smile despite her obvious exhaustion, she returned to work.

As Sam pulled off his overcoat and stamped the snow from his boots, the Reverend Thomas Hather walked across the barn floor towards him, still looking round in amazement. He could have been a kid who had somehow stumbled into Santa's workshop.

Sooty marks still mottled his face from where he'd helped pull the wounded and the dying from the burning houses.

'Lee told me something of Mr Carswell's plan.' Thomas's eyes gleamed behind the spectacles. 'But I had no idea it would involve anything like this. What has he done to your vehicles?'

'We're converting them.'

'But to what?'

'The bus is to be some kind of battleship on wheels. As for the rest?' Sam shrugged. 'Search me.'

'And he thinks he can really defeat the barbarians with these machines?'

'No, not defeat them. But, hopefully, inflict enough

casualties among them to dissuade them from ever coming back here again.'

'But I still don't understand where those men came from. Those Bluebeards.'

'It's not exactly a case of where they come from, Thomas, but *when*.'

'You mean to say they have travelled through time like yourselves?'

'Yes.'

'Good Lord.'

'Only they've come from the past, not the future.'

'But why? Why attack a law-abiding town? What harm have we ever done to them?'

'None. These Bluebeards are nothing but bandits. What they're looking for are easy pickings. So they travel through time looking for a vulnerable period to raid.'

'But why now? Why this moment in 1865?'

'We were just unlucky. And, like I said, we are vulnerable and comparatively wealthy. They probably wouldn't bother raiding this place five thousand years ago when there'd be nothing more than a couple of daub and wattle huts here. And they wouldn't have raided the town 1700 years ago when there was a Roman legion garrisoned here.'

'I see your point; the Roman troops would have given them a sound thrashing.'

'Got it in one, Thomas.'

'Now Mr Carswell's summoned me here, and I gather that, during the term of this emergency, he is in charge.'

'You gather right. And if you ask me he's getting a kick out of being our lord and master.'

'Getting a kick?' Thomas gave an understanding smile. 'Oh, I see, you mean he's rather enjoying himself?'

'And that's putting it mildly.'

'But why in heaven does Carswell need me? I'm a man of God, not a fighting man.'

'Well, Thomas, old buddy. Speak of the devil. I think we're just about to find out: here he comes.'

Five

Carswell had been dishing out instructions. Jud nodded and began cutting letter box like slots out of the doors that formed the walls of the container around the driver's seat in the bus.

Now, briskly rolling one of his plans into a tube, Carswell tucked it under one arm like a sergeant-major's swagger stick and strolled across to join Sam and Thomas.

'Ah, Reverend Hather. We've never met before.' He held out his hand which Thomas shook. 'My name is Carswell. You're well acquainted with Mr Baker here, I see.'

'To all intents and purposes, the Reverend Hather is our landlord,' Sam explained. 'The farm here is church property. We took—'

'Excellent,' Carswell said with no interest in the explanation whatsoever. 'Now, to business, and why I asked you to come here to see me.'

On the shelf the clock chimed three a.m.

'Yes, I – I did wonder,' Thomas said in his shy, stammering way (a mannerism that Jimmy Stewart would make famous one day). 'Is there anything I can do?'

'Yes, Reverend, there is.' Carswell gripped Thomas by the elbow and moved him away from the people working on the vehicles, as if he wished to share a secret with him. Sam was determined not to be excluded and followed.

Carswell said, 'The truth of the matter is, Reverend, I need your help. Rather, *we* need your help.'

'Help?' Thomas looked back at the frenzy of activity behind him as something resembling a ship's mast was hoisted above the roof of the bus. 'How can I help? This machinery is beyond my understanding.'

'No, the technical side of this operation is my province. But I understand that there is a military barracks outside town. I need you to persuade the commanding officer there to supply me with men and arms.'

Sam's thumb scars prickled as a mixture of surprise and shock hit him. 'A barracks? Why the hell didn't they help us when the town was attacked?'

Thomas pushed the glasses up the bridge of his nose with a trembling finger. 'Ah, they are some way out of town on the York road. Firstly, they wouldn't have been aware of the trouble until several hours later. Secondly, as far as I know the barracks is deserted, with all men on Christmas leave.'

'That's not entirely correct,' Carswell said. 'Most of the troops are on leave, true. However, there are still some forty cavalry-men of the Queen's Own Lancers on station and some seventy or so foot soldiers of the Yorkshire Light Infantry.'

'Recent recruits still undergoing training, I understand, which means—'

'Which means the makings of a fighting force. Therefore, Reverend, at first light you will visit the barracks, taking a delegation of senior townsfolk with you – a solicitor, a magistrate . . . I understand Mayor Woodhouse was killed in the attack last night, which is unfortunate. Nevertheless, if you can take enough people of high civic standing with you you will be able to convince the commander we need his men to give our fighting force backbone.'

Thomas stammered. 'Really, I – I don't know, it's quite a – a—'

'Reverend Hather, our salvation here depends on you being persuasive enough.'

'But—'

'And you will also need to persuade the townspeople of Casterton to accept me as their leader for the duration of this emergency. I repeat, I am their only salvation.'

'Their physical salvation, maybe, Mr Carswell. As for their spiritual salvation, that's in another – and altogether mightier – pair of hands entirely.'

Sam recognized what the clergyman had seen. Carswell wasn't only taking charge. He saw himself in a Messianic role as saviour of the town. The man's egotism knew no bounds.

Meanwhile, Carswell began to describe his plans in more detail.

'See the bus?' he said. Thomas watched as Jud and half a dozen other men clambered over it, securing with ropes the mast structure that protruded through the roof. 'Well, that will be our gunship on wheels. I'm going to fix four cannon to where the seats once where. Two at each side. They will fire straight out through the windows.'

'You mean something like the pirate ships of old where the cannon fired directly out from the flanks?'

'If you like. Fortunately, the artillery pieces of today are breech-loaders so it will increase the rate of fire.'

Sam jumped in. 'And I take it those extensions at the sides of the bus and the Range Rover aren't actually wings?'

'No, although they do resemble wings, don't they, Sam old boy? Why, you didn't think I believed these vehicles would actually fly, did you?'

Sam shook his head and feigned a smile.

Carswell gave a cold laugh. 'No, we won't be flying into the attack against the barbarians even though it is a charming idea. No, Mr Baker, those wing-like protrusions will carry the rocket pods.'

'You mean we're actually going to fire rockets from them?'

'Of course. Rockets have been used by the British army since they were badly mauled by them in India in 1799. Naturally, they developed their own war rocket. One Sir William Congreve successfully developed a missile that had an explosive warhead and a range of several thousand yards.'

'But they were something like firework rockets, weren't they? Lit by a match? How do you propose to fire them from rocket tubes outside the bus?'

'Ah, I'll give you all a practical demonstration of that in a little while. But now you have an idea of how our gunship on wheels will actually work. The artillery guns mounted inside will deliver a heavyweight broadside with their eighteen-pound shells. Firing forward from the wing-assemblies – for want of a better description – will be sixteen three-inch-diameter rockets, tipped with high-explosive warheads. The Range Rover will carry eight rockets. I also plan to pack the bus to the gunwales with soldiers wielding rifles and throwing grenades. Devastating firepower, hmm, gentleman?'

Sam rubbed his jaw. 'But once the rockets are fired aren't we going to have to withdraw to a safe place to reload?'

'Yes, absolutely. We hit the barbarians hard as they come through the narrow pass between the cliff face and the river. Then we withdraw, reload, attack again. Those barbarian Bluebeards won't know what hit them.'

'I see,' Thomas said, 'that you have it all thought out.'

As Carswell painted a verbal picture of victory over the Bluebeards more and more people stopped work to listen to him.

'Now for a practical demonstration,' he said. 'Sam, you're quite right. The rockets are little more than larger versions of the sort of firework rockets used by you on the Fourth of July and here in Britain on Guy Fawkes Night: the fuses are normally lit by a match. That won't be possible in the field. These rockets may actually be fired when the bus is moving forward, so . . .' He waved his hand over a workbench on which was a metal dish. From the dish a pair of wires trailed to a battery. One of the wires lay loose on the workbench, still awaiting connection to its terminal.

'Some people have been questioning why I have asked them to remove the glass casing from light bulbs. Well, here's the reason.' People formed a semicircle in front of the bench like students watching their lecturer perform an experiment.

Carswell smiled, enjoying the moment.

'The light bulb makes light when an electric current is passed through a fine filament, causing it to glow white-hot. Reverend Hather, I take it you won't be familiar with light bulbs since they won't be invented for several more decades.'

Again the patronizing tone, but Thomas merely gave a diplomatic nod.

Carswell continued, 'Expressed simply, my idea is to remove the glass case from around the filament and insert the remainder of the bulb into the fuse end of the rocket with a small quantity of gunpowder. A cable connected to the bus's battery via a switching arrangement on the bus itself runs out to the rocket. When the switch is pressed the electric current turns the filament incandescent, which in turn ignites the gunpowder, which in turn ignites the rocket propellant. A second later the rocket screeches from its firing tube to the target.'

There was an appreciative murmur from some parts of Carswell's audience; already they were falling for the image of saviour-genius the man was projecting.

'Now pay attention, please,' Carswell said, waving his hand above the workbench. 'Here is a battery. The wires are connected to one of the bulbs with the glass removed. I have placed the bulb into a small quantity of gunpowder in the metal dish. See what happens when I connect the wire to the battery terminal and send a charge of electricity down into the bulb's filament.'

Carswell picked up the wire and brought the end into contact with the battery terminal.

People leaned forward to watch what happened in the bowl. The Reverend Thomas Hather shielded his eyes against the expected flash.

Someone put their hands over their ears.

Nothing happened.

Carswell brushed the bare end of the wire against the terminal. There was a clicking sound and Sam clearly saw the blue-white spark of the contact.

But no flash and no puff of smoke from the metal dish.

'Let's see there must be some . . . ahm . . .' Carswell lifted the bulb assembly from the bowl, blew it, checked that the wires were connected, then rested it on the small mound of gunpowder and brushed the wire against the battery contact again.

And again nothing happened.

Sam expected Carswell to make some excuse about a loose connection or a lack of charge in the battery, but suddenly he locked up as if every muscle in his body had gone into spasm. His face turned white, a sweaty dangerous-looking white; his eyes locked onto the dish of gunpowder with his light-bulb rocket trigger; for all the world he could have been a snake, its eyes transfixing a victim, ready to strike.

The silence became uncomfortable.

At last Jud cleared his throat. 'Perhaps one of the wires inside the casing has cracked?'

Carswell didn't appear to hear. The only thing that existed in his universe right now was the light bulb that had treacherously betrayed his great scheme. Veins stood out in his temples and neck, a tracery of purple cables beneath his skin that seemed to pulsate with pure boiling rage.

Without a word he marched out of the doorway into the yard.

A moment later someone said, 'Well, they do say there's a thin line between genius and madness.'

That was enough to break the tension. A couple of women even laughed, but it was high and scared-sounding. People drifted away to sit around the barn. No one resumed their work.

'What now?' Jud asked. 'Carry on without him?'

'Or forget the whole stupid thing,' a man said. 'We could still just get out of town until all this is over.'

'Through those blocked roads?'

'Why not?'

'One reason "why not" is that we'd have to leave the old, the very young and the sick behind. They'd never make it through the hills on foot. It's like the Arctic out there.'

'Well, what's the alternative?'

'There's only one course of action,' Thomas said thought-fully, while gazing at the open door through which Carswell had exited. 'Someone has to go to Mr Carswell, eat humble pie, and persuade him to come back so he can complete what he started.'

Sam looked at Thomas. 'You think Carswell's plan will work?'

A grey-haired man laughed. 'Did you see the man? He's off his head.'

Thomas said, 'There's a saying: *Come the hour, come the man.*'

'You have to admit he's a bit . . . brittle.'

'You are right, of course.' Thomas returned to the workbench and experimentally flexed one of the cables that connected the battery terminal with Carswell's im-promptu rocket triggers. 'But although my name might be Thomas, I am no doubter. I believe that, when Man is in crisis, the Lord God *does* send help. Even if at times it is in a perplexing form.' He picked up the loose cable and looked at it thoughtfully for a moment. 'And I do believe that, however difficult and challenging Mr Carswell's personality might be, he is heaven-sent.'

'Heaven-sent?'

Thomas lightly brushed the frayed end of the wire against the terminal. Instantly there was a loud *pffft*. With a brilliant flash a perfect smoke ring rose from the bowl towards the ceiling of the barn.

'You're right, Jud,' Thomas said. 'The wire was cracked in the casing, after all.'

Jud gave a wry smile. 'Come on, Sam, it's time we cultivated an appetite for humble pie.'

Chapter Forty-Four

One

Wednesday morning, 22nd December, 1865.

Jud and Sam worked on the king post. This was the vertical pole that protruded through the centre of the bus's roof. Rigging cables ran down to the stumpy 'wings' at either side of the bus that carried the rocket-launcher tubes. Each 'wing' was probably around ten feet long, four feet wide and consisted of wooden spars held together with glue and nails. Lashed by cord to the wing spars were the rocket-launcher tubes themselves. They looked like lengths of drainpipe around five feet long, and they pointed forward in line with the body of the bus. If anything, the criss-cross effect of spars resembled what lay beneath the canvas skin of an old-time aeroplane. A skeleton of wood that, to Jud, looked far too fragile.

Sam and Jud slithered across the slippery roof of the bus, tying rigging cables to the king post.

'Get them good and tight,' Carswell called from his platform in the hayloft. 'The rocket tubes must be in alignment when they're fired.'

Jud gave a kind of salute and smiled.

Then, under his breath, he said, 'If I keep sweet-talking him much longer it's going to send me barking mad.'

'Just keep smiling as you work; it was a miracle we got

him back here again . . . Jud, catch hold of the rope. It's slipping from the post. Damn.'

The line already tied to the tip of the wing assembly slipped off the bus's roof and onto the barn floor.

'I'll get it,' Jud sighed. 'I need a sharper knife to trim these lines anyway.'

Sam watched the others at work for a moment.

His description of the activity he saw would have been that it was a kind of symphony of endeavour. Every one of those accidental time travellers was working. Sometimes there were quieter periods when there was hardly any noise as people attended to small-scale detailed jobs: plaiting string, threading wiring through the wings, fixing small screws, or just talking in whispers. Then, as if they were in some kind of mystical harmony with each other, they turned to work of a larger scale: hammering metal plates, furiously sawing timber while workers whistled and people shouted for more tools. The sounds would rise to a crescendo, becoming the *fortissimo* movement of that symphony of endeavour. Then the whole barn would be a swarm of movement as a hundred different sounds rose to a near-deafening, teeth-vibrating climax.

And above it all, Carswell worked at his pieces of paper, calculating, sketching, pondering, occasionally breaking off to watch his people labouring.

'Sam . . . Sam. Catch the line.' Jud threw the line back up onto the bus's roof.

Sam caught it deftly enough and began feeding it through one of the iron rings set into the top of the king post. The post itself ran down through a hole in the bus's metal roof, down again through into the floor of the passenger compartment, then on down further into the luggage hold beneath where it was secured to a hefty baulk of timber bolted to the chassis of the bus.

Good God, at least we're making progress.

What they didn't need now was to hit some fundamental flaw in Carswell's plans. Not for the first time it occurred to

Sam that it would be touch and go whether they could even get the king post under the frame of the barn door, high though it was.

Jud's brain worked in a similar direction. 'Not that I want to pour cold water on Carswell's plans at this stage, but . . .'

'Go on.'

'But he's been making some basic practical errors.'

'I know. I still wouldn't like to bet my life on those light-bulb fuses firing the rockets.'

'And he had me box in the bus driver's compartment with the wooden doors before he told me I had to cut slots so the driver could see out. It seems obvious now, but at the time he was keeping us in the dark.'

'That's deliberate,' Sam said. 'He likes to keep us ignorant of his master plan so it shows him up as some kind of genius.'

'Which will cause problems. It might not seem a major difficulty, but if I could have chiselled those view-slots while I had the doors out there on the ground it would have taken me half the time that it did after they were in place.' He held up a hand with three fingers bound in sticking plaster. 'Cost me a drop or two of blood, trying to chop the wood out at a difficult angle. If only he'd explained what he wanted earlier it would have saved time as well as blood and effort.'

'He sees himself as the grand architect.' Sam heaved the line tight through the iron ring on the king post. 'He's not going to welcome us suggesting we form a committee to oversee his plans.'

'I know, but I wish he'd have the sense to agree to some kind of consultation before we actually begin the next job. I was a carpenter for twenty-five years, surely that experience counts for something?'

'Not in his eyes, Jud. If you grab that end of the line I'll cut it . . . there, got it. No, if anything the human element is going to be the weak link. After all, he's expecting nine-teenth-century soldiers to man the guns on this bus – a machine they've never seen before – and perhaps fire the

guns as the damn thing charges across a field at maybe forty
miles an hour. Rather than loading and firing they're going
to be hanging on for dear life.'

'Then maybe we should be talking our concerns through
with Carswell?'

'Yeah,' Sam said doubtfully. 'But who's going to break it
to him that he's going to have stop playing the dictator and
start accepting advice from others?'

'Well, it certainly won't be now. Here come the cavalry.'

At that moment troops arrived on horseback. They were
dressed in bright red coats and wore brass helmets from which
crests of green feathers caught the still-falling snowflakes. A
moment later field guns, hauled by sturdy ponies, arrived in the
farmyard. The gun barrels were a silvery-gold in colour and
perhaps seven inches in diameter and five feet in length.

Sam grinned. 'It looks as if the Reverend Thomas Hather
has a silver tongue after all. He's persuaded the military to
join us.'

'Hell. Take a look at those cannon. They're solid-looking
brutes, aren't they? It's going to take some sweat hauling
them on board here.'

'As Carswell might say, there's no time like the present.'

Two

Carswell, after gentle persuasion by Jud and Sam, agreed to
introduce a shift system of working to allow the exhausted
men and women to sleep. Even so, Carswell stipulated that
these rest periods would be limited to five hours.

However, with the arrival of the troops the conversion
work did become easier – once the men had overcome their
surprise at the bizarre machines taking shape there in the
barn. Strange devices like the bus, with its mast, rigging lines
and stumpy wings. Then there was the Range Rover with
its own wing-like rocket launchers sprouting either side at its
roof level. And there also were the other motley vehicles,
from the ice-cream van (still garishly painted with pictures

of cornets and lollies) to the domestic cars. The cars would be used as support vehicles for the bus and Range Rover gunships.

Jud called across to Sam as he helped Zita wire the rocket launchers to the Range Rover, 'Sam, it's time for your rest break.'

Back muscles aching, his hands still throbbing and painful from unbolting the seats on the bus, Sam headed across the snowy yard to the farmhouse. It was midday; he'd not slept in more than thirty hours.

He did wonder if he would sleep at all, what with the tension of the impending confrontation with the Blue-beards, but the moment his head touched the pillow his eyes closed and he slept without dreaming.

Three

'These are the grenades,' Carswell told Sam. He was sitting at the table in the hayloft. 'I don't expect you'll have the opportunity to use them; they'll be in the hands of the professional soldiers, but you might as well see what they look like and how they work.'

Carswell handed Sam what appeared to be a section of iron piping about the same size as a beer can. It was a discoloured bluey-black and looked pretty roughly made; it was far heavier than Sam had expected, too.

Carswell said, 'You'll see that it's basically a section of iron piping sealed at both ends by welded discs of iron plate. Then it's filled with blasting powder, and this is the fuse. If you should ever need to use one of these beauties light the end of the fuse with a match, then throw the grenade at the enemy. The fuse will detonate the powder five seconds later and anyone close enough will be sliced to pieces by the red-hot chunks of iron pipe hurled outwards by the blast. So make sure you throw it far enough away from you. Got that?'

Sam nodded. 'Have you decided where we – the civilians – will be during the battle?'

'I have, and I was just coming to that. Most will be stationed at the amphitheatre car park. The plan being that the bus and cars drive close enough to the barbarians as they emerge through the time-gate. They fire a volley of rockets and artillery shells at the enemy, then return to the car park to reload. Of course, the artillery men can keep reloading and firing their guns several times before we need to return.'

'But you will need some of us to drive the vehicles.'

'That's true. Lee Burton will drive the bus . . . he's had some experience of it in the past.'

'He has a PSV licence?'

'Ah, no, he used to move the bus from the car park to the front of hotels.'

'So he's had no real experience driving the bus on roads? Never mind on the kind of open terrain where we'll be fighting this battle?'

'No, but he'll be able to practise before we attack.'

Sam felt his face tighten. A little practice in the road between here and the amphitheatre wouldn't be nearly enough. It would demand all an experienced driver's expertise to throw that coach around snow-covered fields as though it was an army tank while the artillery fired broadsides or rockets whistled from their firing tubes.

Carswell moved on crisply. 'Needless to say, we need a relief driver.'

'Who, Jud?'

'No, I've chosen Zita.'

'Zita? Why?'

'She drove tractors and an assortment of farm vehicles when she was in her teens.'

'But—'

'She'll do a good job, Mr Baker.'

Sam swallowed his doubts. Zita *was* extremely capable. Indeed, every man and woman there had worked minor miracles, but it seemed as if Carswell was expecting positively superhuman performances from them. All Lee had to do was to catch one of the rocket-tube 'wings' on the barn-door frame as he backed the bus out and that would be twenty hours of work down the drain. Again Sam had the nagging suspicion that Carswell's battle plan was too complex for it to work – especially without the time to practise.

'You, Sam. You'll drive the Range Rover. Jud Campbell will be in the passenger seat. He'll operate the switches that will fire the rockets. You'll have a couple of soldiers in the rear seats armed with rifles. I suggest you stuff your ears with cotton wool; it'll get very noisy. Any questions?'

Yes . . . loads.

The light-bulb igniters haven't been properly tested. What if the rockets don't fire?

What if the rocket-tube wings are too flimsy after all and simply drop off when the car goes over a bump?

What if the cars become stuck in snowdrifts?

Can four or five hundred men and women stop three thousand battle-hardened barbarian warriors?

That was just the start of the questions. Sam could think of hundreds more. But it was all too late in the day now.

What he heard next came as something of a shock. He should have anticipated it, but somehow in the white heat of the conversion work he'd pushed the eventuality to the back of his mind.

Carswell said, 'It's been four days since the Bluebeards attacked Casterton. I don't envisage them delaying any longer on the off chance the town could call on help from outside; therefore, I'm going to have the vehicles moved up to the amphitheatre car park tonight.'

'Tonight?'

Carswell gave a curt nod. 'If they come at first light tomorrow we need to be ready.'

Sam forced a smile. 'So this is it. The eve of battle. Hell of a Christmas present, isn't it?'

Chapter Forty-Five

One

Dawn. Saturday, 25th December, 1865 – Christmas Day.

'God rest ye, merry gentlemen, let nothing you dismay . . .
for Jesus Christ our Saviour was born this Christmas day . . .'

The words came from Ryan Keith. He'd hardly spoken
more than a word since the death of his wife. Now the Christmas
carol wasn't sung so much as grunted syllable by syllable.

They were at the amphitheatre. It was eight in the
morning. From the grey sky only the occasional flake of
snow spiralled down with a luxurious laziness as if enjoying
the slow glide to earth.

Sam watched Ryan. The man had armed himself with a
double-barrelled shotgun. He didn't say why he was here,
but Sam hoped it was to inflict some damage on the
Bluebeards. Not on himself. Nor on any of the other
townsfolk and soldiers now preparing the vehicles that
were dotted around the car park.

For a moment Sam actually regretted that the conversion
on the vehicles was finished. While they'd been hammering,
sawing, splicing away there in the brightly-lit barn they
could make believe that the eventuality they were preparing
for would never come.

But here it was.

Crunch time.

This was Casterton's only line of defence against the Bluebeards. A fragile line at that. One that looked insignificant there on the car park that was surrounded by several hundred acres of snowbound meadows.

Sam allowed his gaze to travel to the huddle of vehicles. He saw the bus with its stumpy 'wings' housing the rocket launcher tubes that gleamed a brassy yellow in the daylight; Carswell had decided the bus should be named and he'd ordered Zita to paint *Thunder Child* on the side in chunky black letters. There too was the Range Rover with its own small 'wings'.

Mounted on the roof of the ice-cream van was a muzzle-loading cannon, which as weapons went was already pretty much of an antique in 1865. Parked in a line by the visitors' centre were half a dozen cars. All this formed Carswell's army for his Operation Rolling Vengeance (named tongue-in-cheek, Sam guessed).

Sam turned his attention to the strip of land between the river and the rock face, along which the barbarians would come. It was nothing more than a grassy bank now buried beneath five or six inches of snow. Although here and there were deeper drifts that threatened to bog down an unwary driver. At the top of the cliff Sam could see the edge of the forest. From here, with its dark, leafless branches, it looked like a heavy black fringe of hair running along the cliff. Half a dozen crows circled high above the trees themselves, their mournful cries filling the air.

Just at that moment Sam could picture the Bluebeards' surprise at seeing the approach of this motley bunch of vehicles.

Somehow he couldn't believe their reaction would be one of fear.

They were more likely to burst out laughing.

Along the track that led to the main road came the cavalrymen with their long steel-tipped lances held vertical. Behind them came horse-drawn carts that carried the foot soldiers, together with barrels of wood alcohol that would serve as a Victorian equivalent of napalm.

'Ah, good.' Carswell walked briskly up to Sam. He was dressed in a long tweed coat and riding boots. 'You're ready with the Range Rover?'

'All the rockets are in the tubes, ready to fire.'

'You will remember that the light-bulb triggers will only work once, then the whole trigger assembly has to be replaced when you come back to reload?'

Sam nodded. 'We're ready to go when Bluebeard shows himself.'

'Good man. Ah, here are the foot soldiers. Now, I don't intend to deploy these fellows in the battle unless I have to. They're our insurance if Johnny Bluebeard should happen to break through.'

Sam saw Jud catch his eye. Carswell's plan sounded so slick. As if nothing could go wrong. But Sam remembered clearly enough his first demonstration of the electric rocket-trigger he'd devised. It hadn't fired.

Nevertheless, they'd all agreed to put their lives in Carswell's hands. His plan seemed plausible; certainly it was the only one with any chance of success. Love it or hate it, they were stuck with the thing now.

Carswell pulled on his leather gloves. 'I'll see about having fires lit. This cold's going to be a devil of a problem if we have to wait long. At least it's no longer snowing to speak of.'

He walked away to where the soldiers were unloading their equipment from the carts.

'Well,' Sam said with a grim smile. 'December the twenty-fifth. Merry Christmas, Jud.'

'And a Merry Christmas to you, Mr Baker.' Jud's smile failed on his face. He looked a worried man. 'Maybe we should have fortified some of the buildings in town after all; just in case . . .'

'Don't you think those vehicles are going to do the job?'

'On paper they should.'

'So Carswell was fond of repeating. But we're not fighting this battle on paper. It will be on fifty acres of snow and ice.'

'You know, Sam, if the Bluebeards do attack and it goes badly for us, there might come a time when we have decide it's every man for himself.'

'Don't let Carswell hear you say that. He'll accuse you of defeatism.'

'That he might. But the bottom line is we might have to concentrate on saving our own skins and the skins of individuals who are closest to us.'

Sam looked at him. 'You're serious, aren't you?'

'Too bloody right I am. If Carswell's Operation Rolling Vengeance goes up Shit Creek I'm going to get Dot and myself away from here on the river.' He nodded to his boat, moored down by the jetty. 'You, Zita, Lee and Ryan are welcome to join us.'

Sam nodded, thinking hard about Jud's offer. For a lucky few a boat would be a means of escape. But what about the rest?

Jud glanced across the car park. 'Rolle's arrived with the Reverend Hather. Maybe that means we'll have God on our side.'

After speaking to Rolle, Carswell walked briskly across the car park towards Jud and Sam. He shouted something to the commanding officer of the lancers. Sam didn't catch the words. Maybe it was something about lighting fires to warm themselves as they waited.

Carswell walked up; a high red colour had flushed through his cheeks. The tremor had started again under his left eyebrow.

He spoke just two words.

'They're here.'

For a moment Sam thought the man was referring to the soldiers. Then, with a pricking of those two extra fingers that served as his thumbs, the penny dropped. *They're here.*

He twisted to look back along the river where the strip of ground ran between water and rock face.

They're here.

Like a solid wall of darkness he saw the figures. There was no flash of light, no pyrotechnics, no fuss, as the Bluebeards came through the time-gate. They were just there.

And they were marching this way.

Thousands upon thousands of them.

This was the beginning of the end.

Two

Carswell took his position in the visitors' centre that now served as the battlefield command post.

Sam watched Zita join Lee Burton on the bus as the soldiers clambered on board to assume their positions at the four artillery pieces: the big gun barrels jutted out from the sides of the bus where the windows had been.

Everywhere else there was a buzz of activity as people readied themselves.

'D-Day,' Jud said as he climbed into the passenger seat of the Range Rover.

Sam nodded. He opened the door, taking care not to knock his head on the 'wings' that held the rocket launchers out at either side of the car. The thing quirkily resembled a helicopter gunship without the rotors.

He belted himself into the driving seat, then turned the key in the ignition. Into the seat behind him climbed two apprentice infantrymen. Although they'd been deliberately 'exposed' to twentieth-century technology, even being taken for a short ride in the cars to acclimatize them, they still looked round the interior of the car with a mixture of astonishment and suspicion.

Sam glanced back as they sat with their rifles upright between their feet. 'Everyone ready?'

They nodded, their round eyes still scanning the interior of the car.

'You OK, Jud?'

'Yes, touch wood.' He tapped a finger on the short section of plank that had been fixed to the dashboard in front of him.

Nailed to that were eight switches, rudimentary things made from strips of metal cut from food cans. When a metal strip was pressed, the circuit was completed and a jolt of electricity would run from the car battery to the rockets set in the wings.

Carswell appeared at the doorway of the visitor's centre and made a windmilling motion with one arm. 'He's waving us out . . . damn.'

'Sam, what's wrong?'

'Back in a minute.' Sam opened his door. 'One of the wires has come adrift from the rocket tube.'

'Leave it.'

'It won't fire unless it's connected. It won't take long.'

Fixing the wire back to the light-bulb terminal only took a moment, but then Sam spotted something else.

'Jud, there's something wrong with the van. They're not moving.'

Sam ran across the car park, his feet making a soft padding sound on the snow. 'Why aren't you moving out?' he called to the man driving the ice-cream van.

'It won't start . . . the battery's flat.'

God Almighty. Carswell's perfect Operation Rolling Vengeance was showing cracks already.

'Pop the hood,' Sam called. 'I'll bring up the Range Rover and we'll jump-start her.'

Sam drove the Range Rover across the car-park to the ice-cream van. While Jud lifted the bonnet Sam brought the jump leads from the boot. In the back seat the Victorian soldier sat and watched, mystified.

'At least the rest are waiting for us.'

The bus had stopped at the edge of the car park. But now people were running from vehicle to vehicle to find out the reason for the delay.

Down there on the river bank the Bluebeards were approaching, slowly but surely. Sam guessed it would take them another ten minutes to reach the car park.

Carswell hurried towards them. His barely suppressed rage was quivering to the surface.

'What's the hold-up? Why aren't you moving!'

'Engine trouble,' Sam replied.

'Jesus wept. The thing ran perfectly well last night.'

'It's no one's fault.' Sam snapped the big crocodile clips onto the battery terminals of the Range Rover. 'The van's battery's on its last legs.'

'Get a move on, man! The whole strategy will fall apart unless you hit the enemy at the narrowest part of the pass!'

'I know. Just give me thirty seconds. Right!' He called to the van driver. 'Try it now.'

The van's starter motor turned. It was a weary sound, like rusty metal plates grating together.

Sam ran back to the Range Rover, swung himself behind the wheel, stamped on the accelerator pedal. Then, revving the car engine until it howled, he nodded to the van driver. *Try again.*

The van driver twisted the key once more. A moment later his face brightened and he gave a thumbs-up.

Carswell shouted, 'Now, for crying out loud, *move it!*'

Vibrating with rage, Carswell marched back to the building.

After Sam had stowed the jump leads in the boot, he climbed back into the driver's seat and said in a low voice, 'Here goes.'

Three

They left the car park in line.

Ahead was the snowy strip of land between the river and the rock face.

First in the line of vehicles rumbling at little more than walking speed was the bus.

Sam could see the heads of the soldiers on board as they manned their positions at the field guns. At the front of the bus he recognized Zita by her thick ponytail that swished from side to side as she scanned the road ahead. Lee Burton would be sitting in the driver's seat inside his armoured compartment. Surprisingly, there were also the red cork-screw curls of Rolle.

The stubby 'wings' of the bus's rocket launchers waggled at each bump in the ground, however slight, as if the bus were some huge ungainly box-shaped bird flapping its wings ready for take-off.

It occurred to Sam once more that if one of those flimsy 'wings' hit so much as a branch or even a mound of snow it would shear off, reducing the bus's firepower.

Again Sam couldn't decide if the bus resembled a pirate ship, with its guns mounted on what was after all the passenger deck of the bus and with the timber mast that served as the king post. Or perhaps it was more like one of the old wartime B-17 Flying Fortress bombers that bristled guns from every direction.

Sam wiped his forehead. Despite the cold he was sweating.

Between his vehicle and the bus was the ice-cream van. It still had its garish paintings. Surreally, the plastic ice-cream cones hadn't been removed and sat at either side of the cannon that was lashed to the roof.

The heavy cannon of foundry-cast iron made the vehicle look top-heavy. Taking a sharp bend at anything more than a crawl would probably turn the van over.

Sam shot a glance at the 'wings' on his own car, the rocket tubes shining a dull yellow. They too flapped up and down over the tiniest of bumps. He could even hear the creak of the supporting cables over the roof of the car.

Jud looked at him. 'You know, Sam, this reminds me of the day when I walked out onto a frozen lake in the middle of winter. There I was, slap in the middle. Ten years old and feeling bloody good about how clever I was. Then I heard all these little cracking sounds. Like hundreds of pencils being snapped in half all at once. I couldn't see anything. The ice looked perfect. But all the time this snapping sound went on and on, and then . . . Yes, you guessed it. The ice just gave way under me.'

'And that's how you feel now?'

'Yes, I'm standing on thin ice. I can hear it cracking. It's just a question of *when* it gives way.'

'Sir,' one of the men barked from the back. 'When are we going to get a shot at them bastards – sir!'

'It won't be long now, corporal,' Sam said. 'We're going to fan out. Then we're going to let them have it.'

'Sir – then what?'

'We turn one way, pause. You fire at the enemy. Then, as we turn round, the private takes his shot.'

'Sir!'

Sam took the barked 'Sir' to be army-ese for 'OK, I understand.'

Jud groaned. 'It all sounds more like choreography than military strategy.'

'I know . . . we perform a damn' Busby Berkeley number with the cars, while the soldiers fire their guns. Then we dash back to the amphitheatre to reload.'

'Oh, well, here's where we find out if Carswell's plan works.'

With the Bluebeards about three hundred yards away, moving in a great amorphous mob, the vehicles fanned out so that they were travelling side by side. Still, the speed was low, no more than ten miles an hour. Beneath the snow the turf was as hard as concrete.

'I'm remembering this right?' Sam asked, his voice rising as tension gripped hard. 'At a distance of two hundred yards Lee sounds the bus's horn.'

'And we fire.'

'Then we stop, allowing the bus to move forward, turn to the left so it can deliver a broadside.'

'You've got it, Sam.'

Right on cue came the sound of the horn.

A long, booming note, like the war cry of some warrior tribe of long ago.

The Bluebeards were still too far away for Sam to actually see individual faces, but the leading edge of the mob painted a thick black line from the river to the rock face.

'Here goes.' Jud pressed the strips of tin to close the contacts.

Sam stared in fascination at the rocket pods, imagining electricity spurting along the wire to the light-bulb igniters. In his mind's eye he could see the filaments glow white-hot against the wads of gun cotton.

With a gush of smoke and a kind of *zwish-sh* sound the first rocket left the tube to flash like a shooting star into the faces of the mob in front.

'One away,' Jud shouted.

Seven left.

He keyed another strip of tin.

Zwish-sh . . .

The rocket sped from the tube, trailing smoke and sparks.

Six left.

Jud hit the next switch.

Nothing.

He tried again.

'It's a dud,' Sam said quickly. 'Go on to the next.'

Then, one after another in quick succession, Jud fired the rockets.

Five, four, three . . .

Rocket number three, no good. Another dud.

One more away in a flash of red.

Then there was only one rocket left. It left the tube with a *whoosh*.

Sam shot a glance to his right. Rockets were streaming one after another from the 'wings' of the bus.

He couldn't tell if there were any duds. From the sixteen rocket tubes there seemed to be a never-ending stream of blazing rockets.

To his left he heard the brittle thump of the cannon firing from the top of the ice-cream van.

Now he allowed the bus to pull forward and then turn so it could fire an artillery broadside at the still-advancing Bluebeards. Soon a cloud of blue smoke hung over the snow. And two hundred yards away more smoke billowed as the shells exploded in the midst of the Bluebeards.

Sam couldn't tell what effect the rockets and artillery fire were having on the barbarian hordes. But it must have been pretty devastating.

He pictured them reeling back in surprise – some in agony as hot metal buzzed through the air slicing faces, arms, puncturing chests, stomachs. Blood would be steaming there in the snow.

Payback time.

The next part of Carswell's plan went smoothly. The bus did a U-turn so that it presented its left flank to the Bluebeards. The two artillery guns poured a dozen or more shells into the barbarians' advancing line.

Then, as the bus headed back to the amphitheatre to reload, the cars formed a line as if waiting in turn at a car wash. The troops sitting in the backs of the cars took it in turn to pepper the barbarians with well-aimed rifle fire.

Sam swung open the car door and stood on the bonnet, the engine idling beneath his feet.

From the line of cars spurts of smoke blasted as rifles discharged. The gunfire sounded like a crackling inferno.

Sam watched the slaughter. He could even see the red-hot bullets moving like sparks across the snow and into the crowds of Bluebeards.

By now, at little over a hundred yards, he could see individual figures, not just a mob. And the flying red sparks that were the bullets disappeared into individual bodies. Men pitched face forward into the snow, limbs twitching.

And one bullet might strike down more than just one man. Sometimes it passed through body after body.

The slaughter was immense.

Carswell's men were cheering from the cars.

But then, as the firing stopped and the smoke cleared, Sam's blood ran cold. Because he saw that they had, in fact, been wasting their time.

Four

In the borderlands William, Nicole and a dozen or so others levered open the doors of cages built from timber. Inside women and children whimpered in terror.

'It's all right,' Nicole whispered. 'We're here to help.'

'Here to help us all get killed,' came Bullwitt's voice from the slot in the side of William's jacket.

'Hush, dear fellow.'

'No, I won't hush. This will get us killed. You've just gone and cut open a couple of Bluebeards' throats, we're making off with their prisoners – they won't rest until they've hunted us up hill and down dale.'

'Bullwitt, shh.'

'I hope your legs are stronger than your wits, William, because you're going to need them to carry you and me both out of here and far away.'

'Bullwitt, not now . . . ah, there.' With a snap the door gave way. He pulled it open, helped by the boy whose upper torso and head grew out from the cow.

Nicole looked into the gloomy cage at the Bluebeards' prisoners where they cowered beneath blankets.

'Don't worry,' Nicole whispered. 'We're here to help you.'

'Go away,' hissed a middle-aged woman dressed in nothing but a long white petticoat. 'If they hear you they'll come back and punish us, too.'

'They've gone out on a raid. We can get you away to safety.'

'Nicole?' came a tentative voice from the back. 'Is that you?'

A figure came out from the shadows at the back of the cage. 'Nicole. It's me, Sue. Sue Burton.'

'Sue, thank God. Are you all right?'

Sue's voice dropped. 'We're alive.'

'Come on,' Nicole said, as calmly as she could. 'We're going to get you out of here.'

For a moment she thought she'd hear Bullwitt's bitter nasal voice adding, 'And we're all going to get ourselves killed.'

But he'd seen what state the women were in. This time he stayed quiet.

Five

'We were right all along,' Sam said as they drove back to the amphitheatre car park. 'It's not going to work.'

'But we saw the carnage; Bluebeards were dropping like flies.'

'Carswell's plan's failing, believe me.'

Jud said, 'I thought I was the pessimist, Sam. But now I think we're actually going to win this battle.'

'Not a hope in hell. We killed and wounded only a couple of hundred at most.'

'*Only* a couple of hundred?'

'Only a couple of hundred,' he repeated. 'Jud, when I stood on the bonnet of the car I could see maybe three thousand of them still feeding through the time-gate. They're like a plague of hyenas. Killing a few of their number won't stop them.'

'But if we reload and go back we can—'

'What, Jud? Kill another two hundred? Another three hundred?'

'Yes.'

'We'd have to repeat the operation another half a dozen times before we made a sizeable enough dent in their numbers. And I figure we've another two runs back there at the most before they reach the open ground. Then they'll either attack us or go round us. If it's the latter, they'll fan out across the open countryside before regrouping in Casterton.'

'But—'

'No, Jud. No buts. Carswell's plan won't work.'

'You mean we've had it?'

'No . . . there might be a chance after all'

Jud raised a questioning eyebrow.

'Our only chance,' Sam told him, 'is if we tear up Carswell's Operation Rolling Vengeance plan and start all over again.'

'I hope you've got a heck of a good idea, Sam.'

'I've got the idea. Whether it's good, bad or indifferent . . .' He shrugged.

Jud nodded forward through the window. 'I've seen something that just might prove you right, Sam.'

Sam looked ahead.

There, lying in the snow, in front of the entrance to the amphitheatre car park, was one of the bus's 'wings'. Lee must have clipped one of the now-redundant visitors' signs. The wing lay in a twisted mess of wooden spars, wire, and launching tubes.

Half a dozen people, including Zita and Ryan Keith, had reached the ruined wing and were even now dragging it back towards the bus as if, with some fabulous burst of energy (as well as an equally fabulous amount of good luck), they could repair the damage in the next four minutes.

Carswell was striding across the car park. Gripping his hat by the brim he flung it aside in frustration. Sam pulled up alongside the wreckage and climbed out.

'Hell's teeth! You clumsy idiots!' Carswell barked. 'The launcher's ruined. Leave it . . . *leave it*. Reload the other tubes and be ready to leave here in five minutes.'

'Carswell—'

'We must attack again while we have the advantage of surprise.'

'Carswell,' Sam began again. 'It's no good.'

'Never mind, we'll reload and press on with the attack.' A look of triumph flashed over the man's face. 'Did you hear, we took out nearly three hundred men during the last attack?'

'Carswell, it's not enough. They're going to break out of the pass.'

'Don't worry about that. We'll hold them there.'

'We won't.' Sam grabbed Carswell's arm. The muscles were hard; they quivered as if an electric current crackled through them. 'Carswell. There are thousands of men pouring along that pass. We can't hold them.'

'Of course we can.' Carswell shrugged Sam's hand away, then clapped his hands. 'Everyone listen. Reload your vehicles. Then get ready to go back in again.'

'No,' Sam told him. 'It's not enough. OK, if we were facing a thousand, perhaps it would be. But there are too many of them. We need a change in tactics.'

'You mean you need a change in leadership,' Carswell said with a sneer.

'No, but if you saw the numbers of Bluebeards coming through the pass down there you'd understand.'

'Well, Mr Baker, what do you suggest?'

'I think he's right, Carswell,' Jud said cautiously. 'We seemed to be hitting them hard, but they kept on coming. Seeing their own kind being killed doesn't faze them.'

'He's right,' Lee said, coming across the car park. 'From the bus I could see them running forward over the bodies of their own people.'

'So this is mutiny, then? I'm being deposed to make way for who? Mr Campbell here? . . . No, I don't think so. Not his style. I think the one person who hankers for the role of leader is none other than our American friend, Mr Baker, here.'

Sam shook his head. 'Carswell. It's not a question of taking over. But I've seen them. I've seen the numbers coming through down there. They aren't just running towards us. They're stampeding like a herd of cattle.'

Now Rolle came through the growing knot of people. 'I've seen the number of Bluebeards, too. They are far more numerous than I anticipated.'

Carswell considered, then he said to Rolle, 'Whatever happens now the terms of our agreement remain the same?'

Rolle nodded. 'Indeed they do, Mr Carswell.'

'Very well, Mr Baker. The ball's very much in your court. You're in command now.' He gave a tight smile. 'So what do we do?'

Six

Sam looked at the expectant faces around him. They were a mixture of the time travellers who'd made the journey back from 1999, and the men and women of Casterton who were now fighting for their very lives.

A flurry of snow came on a gust of cold air.

Perhaps this was Carswell's revenge against him for daring to suggest a change in tactics. He'd handed him control of this tiny fighting force of three hundred or so. If he failed, then it would be all the fault of Sam Baker, the interfering know-it-all who didn't know squat.

Now they waited expectantly for him give the orders. Thomas Hather watched intently. Jud gave a reassuring nod. Zita shot him a faint smile. Lee stood expectantly and Sam sensed the man's faith in him. Even Ryan Keith with his red-rimmed eyes and gunsmoke-blackened face waited, burning to exact whatever revenge he could against the men who had murdered his pregnant wife.

Just for a second Sam felt as if a tiny part of him was being whirled outside time. Once more he sat in the director's chair at the studio. The seconds were ticking down to zero. Transmission time. Then the red light would glare on the panel in front of him.

But, by heaven, when that red light came on you hit the transmission button – and you just went ahead and did it.

This situation demanded infinitely more guts to give orders and get the show on the road.

This is it, Sam, old buddy, he told himself. *Showtime*.

'All right,' he said. 'We're pulling out in . . .' he checked his watch, '. . . four minutes.'

'It will take at least eight to reload the rocket tubes,'

Carswell said, already slipping into the role of the intelligent objector who would subtly undermine Sam's decisions.

'It doesn't matter,' Sam said. A buzz of adrenalin ran through his body; his fingers tingled. 'We'll go back into battle with only a few of the tubes loaded. Besides, the bus has already lost half its rocket launchers.'

'You're going back into battle with only a few rockets? They won't do much damage to the enemy, will they?'

'They won't have to, Carswell.'

'So you have a secret weapon up your sleeve? How remarkable.'

'As a matter of fact, I have.'

'And that is?'

Sam walked across to a parked car and patted the roof.

'This,' he said. 'And all those.' He nodded at the cars parked around the car park.

'Cars?' Now Carswell looked uncertain of himself.

'Yes, cars. Forget tanks and jet fighters. This is the most devastating killing machine ever invented.'

'You can't be serious.'

'Oh, but I am, Carswell. The car has killed more than twenty million people since it was invented. Twenty million. That's more than the combined populations of Australia and New Zealand.'

'My God, how do you suggest using them as weapons?'

'Form a line, side by side, where the pass is narrowest. When the Bluebeards reach the bottleneck between the rock face and the river we drive straight forward into them. They'll be hit by a sold wall of steel travelling at forty miles an hour.'

Carswell rubbed his jaw, considering. 'Well . . . I wish you Godspeed.' With that he turned and walked smartly back to the visitors' centre.

Well, if that's the way he wants to play it . . . Sam turned to the rest of the people and told them what they needed to do.

After they had returned to the vehicles Sam checked his watch again. Two minutes and counting.

Seven

On impulse Sam went into the visitors' centre.

Carswell had returned to his desk. In his waspish way he was briskly gathering papers and neatly slotting them into a briefcase.

'Mr Baker. I thought you'd be directing your troops,' Carswell said without looking up.

'You're going to sit out the battle here?'

'I intend to leave, Mr Baker.'

'You're not interested in the outcome?'

'I've fulfilled my obligations.'

'Your contractual obligations? Those you entered into with Rolle?'

'Yes. The poor man was so desperate to save all you innocents he offered me a . . . a handsome fee, for want of a better phrase, to come here and give you the means of saving your necks.' He gave one of his cold smiles. 'I think I've played my part to the letter, don't you?'

'The battle's not over yet.'

'No, but my role here is finished.'

'What did Rolle offer you?'

'Ah, that would be telling.'

'It must be more than money?'

'That's very astute of you, Mr Baker.'

'He's taught you how to use the time-gates, hasn't he?'

'See, you are brighter than I thought. You constantly surprise me, Mr Baker.'

'So you're going home? Back to 1999?'

'Now you're disappointing me again. The ability to travel in time is an exploitable commodity. Like discovering gold at the bottom of one's garden.'

'You're going to exploit time travel?'

'Why not? Think of the potential.'

'I can think of the potential disaster.'

'Mr Baker, Rolle exploited time travel for humanitarian purposes. He took twentieth-century drugs back to his rabble in the thirteenth century with their disgusting diseases. I haven't a humanitarian bone in my body, Mr Baker. I'm a businessman.'

'So you're running out on us?'

'I thought I'd been sacked, deposed, compulsorily retired – call it what you will.'

'We still need you, Carswell.'

'No, you don't.'

'You know we do.'

'Now, if you will excuse me, I've got to be moving on . . . or back as the case may be . . .'

'Carswell.' Sam caught him by the arm as he walked past. Again Sam felt the muscles taut as guitar strings beneath the sleeve of his jacket.

Carswell looked down at the hand on his arm, then back at Sam. His face was tight, holding back all that repressed rage. The look was clear enough: *Take your damn' hands off me.*

'Carswell, wait a moment. Months ago you told Jud and myself a story. You told us that when you were a little kid your father used to get drunk every weekend, get into fights, come home in a mess and your mother covered up for him, telling you that it was his job to stop a huge serpent from eating up London. Is that right?'

'There's nothing wrong with your memory, unlike your manners.' He glanced down at Sam's hand gripping his forearm. 'Now, if you will—'

'And you were told that you'd inherit the duty of fighting the snake . . . that huge snake that used to come out of the River Thames every Friday night. Remember?'

Carswell's eyes burned into Sam's.

'Mr Baker. Your own foe approaches. Don't forget them, will you?'

'Listen, Carswell. Remember when I told you I fought one of these Bluebeards? The man with the snakes growing from his head? Well, there are plenty more monsters like him on their way here. They're going to destroy the town and everyone in it. Can't you interpret what your mother told you as some kind of omen?'

'That snake came out of my mother's troubled brain, not the Thames. Now if—'

'Carswell, humour me then. Pretend the serpent is sliding out of the river. Come kill it with me.'

The man pulled a gold watch from his waistcoat pocket and held it up in front of Sam's face by the chain. 'Tick-tick-tick-tick, Mr Baker. Time's running out.'

'Carswell, please, we need you.'

'Go launch your attack on the Bluebeards or it will be too late. Far too late.'

'Carswell, we need you because you are a mean son of a bitch.'

'Flatterer.'

'You know what I mean. I need someone as ruthless as you to take charge of the bus . . . the fighting machine you created.'

'What, Mr Baker? Me as captain of the good ship *Thunder Child*?'

'Yes. What do you say?'

'Tick-tick-tick . . . ding, ding, ding. Ooops, there goes your wake-up call. It's time to smell the coffee, or rather the sweat and the bloodlust of your enemy. Now, you can almost taste it on your lips, can't you, Mr Baker?' Carswell smiled icily, his eyes never leaving Sam's face.

Sam sighed. Without another glance at Carswell he left the visitors' centre and ran across the car park to where the Range Rover sat, engine idling, with two infantrymen armed with rifles in the back seat. This time he assigned Jud to the bus.

Sam sounded the horn twice, then accelerated to the head of the vehicle column.

Ahead the cavalry and the foot soldiers had already set off for the pass, making as much speed as they could in the snow. Ahead lay the river, worming its way black as ink between the white banks. More flakes of snow spiralled from the sky.

As he pulled away from the car park Sam heard the sound of the bus horn.

He braked.

For some reason the bus had stopped. It sat there looking lopsided in the snow with just one 'wing' remaining.

Sam frowned. There could be no hold-ups now. They had to hit the Bluebeards at the narrowest part of the pass. Any other place would be too wide and the barbarians would flood past at either side of the forty-yard-wide battering ram of vehicles.

He looked back at the bus. There was no obvious reason for the hold-up. He could see Lee's eyes behind the slot of the boxed-in driver's compartment.

He looked back along the line of vehicles.

Then he saw Carswell walking briskly towards the front passenger door. He jumped lightly onto the first step. Then, holding onto the edge of the door with one hand, he leaned out and gave Sam a relaxed-looking salute.

Sam nodded to himself. *Thunder Child* now had her captain.

As Sam engaged the gear and pulled slowly away, big tyres crunching through the snow, he suddenly recalled where he'd seen the name *Thunder Child* before. Years ago he'd read H. G. Wells's *The War Of The Worlds*. When the Martian fighting machines had been laying waste the countryside with their death rays the human armies could do nothing to stop them. But humanity did claim one small victory. As a Martian fighting machine walked out into the sea, sinking ships, there was one warship, the ironclad HMS *Thunder Child*, that had steamed out of the smoke and wreckage to charge at the seemingly indestructible alien invader. *Thunder Child* rammed the fighting machine's legs, toppling it into the sea and destroying it.

But the *Thunder Child's* brave charge had been a suicide mission. Sam, driving along the track to face his own destiny, hoped that Carswell's choice of name for his 'warship' hadn't been some kind of dark omen.

Sam looked up at the foreboding gathering of storm clouds. Then he switched on the wipers as the snow began to fall heavily once more.

Chapter Forty-Six

One

Mid-morning, Christmas Day, 1865

The vehicles formed a line in the snow.

Each a yard from its neighbour, they stood side by side, engines idling, the noses of the cars, bus and van facing forward. It was like the starting line of a cross-country race.

Waiting.

The snow blew in flurries. Sometimes the bottleneck of the pass between river and cliff was clear, the next obliterated in swirling white flakes.

Sam's hands tightened around the steering wheel. A bitter flavour like aspirin not swallowed quickly enough flooded his mouth.

Behind him sat the two soldiers, rifles at the ready. The engine purred, catlike.

Sam could smell the exhaust fumes.

The Bluebeards were perhaps still a couple of minutes away from the bottleneck. They were undisciplined, little more than a mob of bandits and murderers, but they were smart enough not to exhaust themselves running towards their adversaries yet. They slogged through the snow at a steady pace, their axes, swords, spears at the ready.

They had numerical superiority. But Sam Baker's people

had guns, and motorized vehicles that were fast – and lethal weapons in their own right.

And somewhere behind the line of vehicles the forty or so cavalrymen were forming up. And behind them were the ninety foot soldiers, already fixing bayonets to rifles, checking grenade fuses.

No one spoke.

They were waiting for the Bluebeards to become a compact mass of men as they entered the bottleneck.

Sam glanced at his watch. The second hand swept by with agonizing slowness.

Waiting.

His jaw muscles ached as he clenched his teeth.

What if that dizzying swirl of the fall through time came at that moment? What if he found himself sitting next to Zita with the rest of the surviving time travellers, watching Jud slip the pin into his collar, with the vehicles just as they had been in the car park?

It could happen at any moment.

Surely it was long overdue.

Then the remaining natives of 1865 Casterton would have to fight this battle alone.

Once more Sam thought about his theory – that strange theory, as it had seemed at the time. That perhaps all this was part of a greater plan by some third party. Maybe those scientists of a distant future had deliberately plucked a mixed group of civilians from the amphitheatre of 1999 and transported them back to fight this battle. A desperate act by desperate human beings.

At that moment the snowfall eased off to nothing more than a few individual flakes. And that was the instant the Bluebeards reached the bottleneck some two hundred yards ahead of the line of waiting cars.

Sam sounded the Range Rover's horn in one long blast.

At either side of him the engines revved, exhaust smoke billowing.

Slowly the steel cavalry of cars, van and bus moved forward.

Slowly, slowly does it.

A unified line of cars. A single unbroken line.

Moving slowly across the snow.

All along the line drivers hit light switches. Headlamps blazed dazzlingly against the snow.

Sam sounded the horn again.

Then he reached across and hit the strips of metal that formed the triggers of the rocket launchers.

With a loud swishing sound the rockets flashed from their pods at either side of the car, engulfing it in smoke.

Sam watched the exhaust flames of the rockets shoot like red sparks towards the enemy line in front of him.

He counted the rockets.

One, two away.

Three, four, five, six.

Not bad, Mr Carswell. Only two duds.

He glanced to his right.

Thunder Child fired the rockets from her remaining 'wing'.

Streaks of smoke drew the trajectory line of the rockets. Somewhere ahead they were exploding in the faces of the barbarians. More blood would be speckling the snow.

To his left, the roof-mounted cannon of the ice-cream van fired its single shot. The sound of the explosion rolled along the cliff wall like thunder.

Sam sounded the horn again in a long blast.

The Bluebeards were perhaps a hundred yards away, a dark raggedy line spiky with spears.

Now Sam accelerated, taking the car up to forty miles an hour.

Beside him the other cars, matching his speed, stayed in formation.

A tight line rushing across the snow to hit the flesh-and-bone mass of Barbarians head on.

Two

Ahead of the group of men and women lay the time-gate. Nicole put her arm round Sue as they rested before entering the world of 1865. It was a gesture of reassurance as well as affection. They'd gone through a lot together over the last few months. Nicole was determined to see her safely back with Lee.

Here there was no snow. It was a cool, damp place, with trees and grass and sluggish streams.

All around her the women and children they'd released not an hour or so before sat exhaustedly on the ground. They'd have had precious little sleep in the last three days. The women especially.

William stood at Nicole's side.

From the slot in his jacket Bullwitt looked out with his brown bulging eyes. 'There it is,' he said in his nasal voice. 'The doorway back to 1865.'

'The way to home and safety,' William said, pleased.

'Unless we happen to run into the Bluebeards face to face.'

'The Bluebeards have embarked on another of their raids.'

'I know, but what if something makes them turn round and come back bleeding home. Have you thought of that?'

Three

The speedometer needle hovered on forty. Snow spurted from either side of the tyres like the V-shaped spray of a speedboat.

At either side of Sam the vehicles held their line. A near-as-dammit solid wall of steel rolling along the pass towards the line of barbarians.

Sam gritted his teeth. 'Hold on,' he said to the men in the back. 'We're going to hit them any second now.'

The windscreen wipers batted away the snow.

Headlamps blazed.

The drivers began laying into their horns, sending an automotive battle cry before them – from the high bleating of the Fiat's horn down to the bull-like bellow of the bus.

Suddenly the blurred dark line ahead resolved itself into sharp focus as the speed annihilated the open ground between the vehicles and the Bluebeards.

Now Sam could see faces.

He could see the whites of their eyes, as the saying went.

He stared into the faces of brutalized and brutal men. Their ferocious glares raked the oncoming vehicles.

Then the cars slammed into the oncoming line of warriors.

Sam wasn't prepared for what happened next.

Bodies crashed over the bonnet and up over the roof.

The sound was incredible.

He could hear the screams and shouting of the Bluebeards above the roar of the engines.

As well as screams of pain there were screams of bloodlust and fury too.

The wipers slashed at the snow on the now-cracked windscreen.

The snow had turned pink.

A face slammed against the glass, leaving a great sunburst of red. The wipers slashed at it, the whispery sound of the blades giving way to a wet slip-slop sound.

Sam hit the screen-wash.

Still the momentum of the car carried them on deeper into the pack of men in front of them.

The 'wings' at either side of the car were sheared off the moment they hit the solid bodies.

And still the car moved on.

But now it was slowing.

Thirty. Twenty-five.

Twenty.

Slowing fast as bodies compacted against the front of the car.

The tyres rolled over more bodies, throwing the car from side to side like a boat on a storm-riven sea.

'We're stopping,' Sam shouted. 'Get ready to fire!'

Pushing the muzzles through the open windows of the rear doors, the men cocked the rifles.

Ten miles an hour.

The vehicles had pushed the barbarians back like a snowplough heaping snow in front of it. Now the weight was so great it defeated the forward motion of the car. Probably the bus was doing better than him. Its huge bulk would charge on for another hundred yards or so yet.

But as for the lighter cars at either side, they'd probably been stopped dead in their tracks by now, their bonnets and body panels mangled by the impact of so many hard warrior bodies.

'Fire!' Sam yelled as the speedo needle kissed zero.

The reports of the rifles crashed against his ears, deafening him.

Now he pushed the gear leaver into reverse, then stamped the pedal to the floor.

With a buzz-saw sound the car lurched, tyres spinning, not gripping.

Plumes of blood-drenched snow turned the air red above the mound of bodies.

The car's tyres at last bit; they began moving back.

A couple of cars weren't so lucky. They'd either become stuck under the bull-dozed mound of bodies or the tyres' treads simply couldn't bite deeply enough into the snow, slush and blood.

Instantly a wave of Bluebeards clambered over the bodies of their fallen dead to leap onto the cars, hammering at them with their axes and swords.

He watched in horror as car windows shattered under the blows. Drivers and soldiers were dragged out to be hacked to death in the snow.

A face appeared at the side window. Sam saw for a moment the blue tattoos across the upper lip. The man raised his axe ready to smash it through the open side-window of the Range Rover.

A blast of sound smacked him in the side of the head. One of the soldiers in the rear seat had fired a pistol.

SIMON CLARK

The barbarian clutched his mouth. With blood squirting between his fingers he fell back onto the tangle of bodies behind him.

Sam reversed hard now, not waiting to be overrun.

He reversed until he was well clear of the wall of broken bodies, then he spun the car until it faced forward.

A second later he drove away, leaving the mayhem behind him.

Four

What remained of Sam's fighting force regrouped.

Three of the cars were missing. The remaining 'wing' on the bus was a tangled mess being dragged alongside by one of the supporting cables from the king post. A soldier hung dead and bleeding through one of the glassless windows. One of his comrades pulled the body back.

This was going to be no easy victory. Sam knew that now.

And with the Bluebeards still surging strongly towards the exit of the pass that led out to the relative safety of open ground and woodland there was no option but to go back in again.

And just hope the remaining vehicles could knock the fight out of the barbarians. Even so, Sam knew that they couldn't possibly have killed more than a couple of hundred in the last charge. There would still be more than two thousand of them.

And now those bastards had a score to settle.

Sam swung open the car door. It crunched against the remains of the wooden framework of the wing that held the rocket tubes.

And that framework held more now. There was a severed head, skewered onto one of the timber spars, and elsewhere a couple of bloody hands were trapped in the mess of cables and twisted tubes.

Swallowing, Sam stood on the driving seat and leaned out so the cavalry and soldiers could see him. The car itself was awash with blood.

He waved the cavalry and soldiers into the next attack. They needed every man now.

Sitting down heavily, he slammed the door shut and accelerated once more towards the enemy line.

The other vehicles did their best to keep up with him. But now, with the pass wider and with fewer autos, the line was more widely spaced. Some of the Bluebeards would dodge the oncoming cars and pass through the gaps.

That, Sam hoped, was where the troops following behind would join the fray: picking off the enemy before they made it away from the pass.

He looked from left to right. The bus and the cars, their bodies dented and crumpled, smeared with barbarian blood, raced through the snow.

A group of Blubeards in front of him parted before the Range Rover could plunge like a torpedo into their bodies.

A series of bangs sounded along the car.

He glanced down. From the door panel arrow heads and shafts pointed at his leg and hip.

Hell, he thought in amazement, *those brutes can fire arrows with such force they pierce steel doors.*

Behind him the soldiers fired from the back seats. One of the bowmen slumped onto the snow.

Sam looked ahead to see the dense main pack of Bluebeards emerging from a flurry of snowflakes.

A second later the vehicles once more smacked into them.

Five

The battle had become a dream. Or at least it seemed like that.

In an unearthly way it had actually become quiet. Sam spun the car round, aiming it at individual groups of Bluebeards. Behind him the rifles fired.

He glanced back. One soldier lay back in the seat, head twisted at what would have been an uncomfortable angle if the man had been alive. An arrow jutted from his face just below the cheekbone.

Sam saw cars looking like hedgehogs as arrows bristled from their bodywork.

There, a car had been turned over, the occupants spilled out in a bloody jumble. Flames erupted from the back of the vehicle. Seconds later its store of grenades exploded and a ball of orange rose into the sky like a sunrise.

All around him, bodies looking like crushed strawberries were scattered across the snow.

To his left, the bus moved slowly. Its field guns roared every few seconds or so, blasting explosive shells into the mass of the Bluebeards as they pressed towards the vehicle in a huge tightening noose of men.

Sam realized they were trying to box the bus in so it would eventually become bogged down in the snow.

Arrows cascaded onto it, piercing its flimsy sides of steel sheeting.

Sam looked round. There was precious little in the way of reinforcements. There were perhaps two dozen cavalrymen riding furiously to and fro, killing the enemy with lances and swords.

The bus stopped. Instantly the Bluebeards rushed forward.

Lee flung the bus into reverse, backing it towards the cliff wall as fast as he could, catching and crushing a few of the barbarians in the process. Then the vehicle lumbered forward again, but it was all too slow.

If Lee stopped once more the Bluebeards could probably rush the bus and hold it fast with their own body strength. Once they'd stopped it, even for a moment, they could flood on board and finish off the crew with knives.

Sam edged the car forward, watchful lest any Bluebeards should rush him. But most seemed to be interested in the bus now. Its flanks were so streaked with blood that even its name, *Thunder Child*, was obliterated.

Sam laid heavily into the horn, attracting the attention of the cavalrymen.

He pointed at the Bluebeards circling the bus, then he let out the clutch. The Range Rover fishtailed as he aimed the car like a missile. 'Brace yourself!' he called back at the surviving soldier in the back. 'I'm going to hit them as hard as I can!'

The slipstream whipping by the window tore at his face, plastered his hair against his forehead, then pulled it away again.

The car had reached sixty when he hit the barbarians at their densest point.

Most wouldn't even know what killed them: they were pushing towards the bus, their backs to the car.

The concussion was terrific.

Sam threw his arms in front of his face to protect his eyes, But he still saw enough.

Bodies exploded across the bonnet, turning the windscreen crimson, then smashing it.

In front of the car more bodies fell. The first ones went under the front tyres. But then, as the bodies were bulldozed into a mound, the front end of the car lifted.

Sam glimpsed the speedo.

Forty.

The engine still roared.

The falling men formed a ramp of blood and bone, lifting the nose of the car even higher. A split second later it took off and flew.

The car screamed clear above the heads of yet more men. Then, rolling to the right, it fell on its side.

Dazed, hanging by the seat belt, Sam looked to his right and down. A carpet of dying men, crushed by the car, lay on the other side of the driver's window.

He felt a hand push at his shoulder.

The surviving soldier was signalling him to get out.

He nodded.

Unbuckling the seat belt, he wriggled from under the steering wheel that had collapsed into a figure-eight shape.

More bodies were pressed against the windscreen that was now a crazy frost-pattern of cracks.

As far as Sam could tell the car had come to rest on the driver's side. That meant he had to climb out of the passenger door.

His whole body ached.

Gritting his teeth, he scrambled over the seats. Deciding not to even try and lift the heavy passenger door up and open, he worked his body out through the shattered window.

The soldier's rifle barked.

Sam saw that the soldier was standing on the passenger side of the car that now faced the sky.

Sam stood there too, his legs shaking badly.

All around him, Bluebeards pressed towards them, ready to tear the two men limb from limb.

'Sir. Take this.' The soldier handed him a revolver. He had one of his own. Sam took the gun, cocked it, then aimed at the face of a Bluebeard standing on the ground below. The barbarian was just about to swing a sword at Sam's legs.

Sam squeezed the trigger.

The gun recoiled in his hand.

And the Bluebeard rolled back onto the snow, arms flung out, blood pumping from a hole in his forehead.

Sam chose another target, fired again.

Then again.

Three rounds left.

When they were gone he'd be dead.

Already a spear jab had punctured the soldier's leg just above the knee. With one hand holding the wound closed, the man carried on firing.

Then came a sound like the bellow of an angry bull.

Dazed, Sam looked up to see a wonderful sight.

Slowly, foot by foot, the bus was pushing through the crush of barbarians.

Lee was pumping the horn, sending out that bellowing note.

Seconds later the bus was alongside the Range Rover. At this height, standing on the side of the car, the bus windows were almost level with Sam and the soldier.

Straightaway a crop of hands appeared. Sam saw Jud's and Zita's anxious faces. Even Rolle and Thomas Hather reached out their hands.

Sam grabbed at them and was pulled on board.

He collapsed into a sitting position as the bus powered across the snow to break out of the Bluebeards' line that Sam had smashed through earlier.

Sam glanced across at the soldier who'd saved his life.

The man had been less lucky. The swipe of a barbarian axe had taken away his hand.

Another soldier bound the wound as the bus bucked and heaved across the snow-covered meadow.

He noticed that Jud's leg was bandaged at the knee where an arrow had perhaps found a target. Although limping badly, he managed to light the fuses of some grenades and hurl them out at the Bluebeards.

His face dripping with sweat, Sam waved people away so he could stand.

He saw they were heading back to the amphitheatre.

'No!' Sam hung onto the wooden king post that ran through the bus like a pin through the thorax of a butterfly. 'Lee! No, we can't stop now. Turn back! We've got to hit them again!'

Chapter Forty-Seven

One

Noon, Christmas Day, 1865

Even in the bloody mire of the battle there was a weird grace and harmony to it all.

From the height of the bus's passenger deck Sam witnessed it.

The movements of the fighting men were like that of a basketball match. There was an ebb and flow of motion. One moment they were fighting down by the river. Then the focus of the action moved smoothly away to the middle of the pass. Clumps of men formed into intense clamouring knots, battling with absolute passion. Then these groups dissolved, moved away, reformed, fought again, before dissolving once more.

Sam watched as the bus drove backward and forward. Artillery guns thundered. Soldiers fired rifles, muskets, pistols. They threw grenades.

Explosions formed a surreal pattern of orange, yellow and gold blooms above the surface of the snow. They were like huge roses, abruptly flowering before vanishing into nothingness again. Everywhere, barbarians and Casterton's defenders alike lay dead in the snow. Most of the cars were reduced to wrecks now, some upside down, wheels still turning. One burned with a furious intensity, a black smoke-column rising from it into the air.

And everywhere, the landscape was flecked red with blood.

At the front of the bus Carswell gripped the door strut and, leaning forward like a carved figure on the prow of a ship, fired his handgun down at the barbarians. Miraculously he was unharmed. He didn't seem to tire, either. His eyes still blazed icily as he fired, reloaded, fired, reloaded.

Ryan Keith fired the shotgun, swearing, laughing, crying, all at the same time. 'This is yours!' *Bang*. 'Come and get it!' *Bang*.

Zita and Jud stood behind the boxed-in driver's compartment where they lit the fuses of hand grenades from a lamp before pitching them over the side of the bus. The explosions tore holes in the air with a God-almighty *CRACK!* Red-hot pieces of the grenades' casings tore radiating lines in the snow. More tore holes in the bodies of the attacking barbarian warriors.

And there was a gleaming intensity to the way they – everyone – worked on the bus. If the bus had been destroyed there and then Sam could have believed the spirits of those on board would still continue as before – loading, firing, reloading, firing again.

Sam hung onto the king post as the snow-covered ground blurred by. He felt a hand on his arm.

'*Sam*.' He looked up into the face of Rolle. The corkscrews of red hair fluttered and his eyes blazed. 'Sam Baker . . . have you seen what's happening?'

Sam looked round the landscape of the dead and dying.

He shook his head puzzled. 'What's happened to Bluebeards? Where have they gone?'

Two

Here goes, Nicole told herself as the group of freed captives and Liminals approached the barrier between Limbo and 1865.

There wouldn't be time to run away if they met the Bluebeards returning from their latest raid.

Ahead, the boy who was fused into the cow, so creating a kind of bovine centaur, was first through, moving at a slow gallop.

Quickly, Nicole did a head count. There were perhaps a hundred or more of Casterton's people there. Many of the women simply hadn't survived the last three days. There were also perhaps one hundred and fifty Liminals. They were armed with anything from clubs to shotguns. Not nearly enough if they should meet a returning army of barbarians.

William smiled at her. 'It is just one short step, Nicole.'

She was going to hold her breath and grit her teeth ready for the transition. But then it had happened as quickly and as easily as stepping through a doorway from one room to another.

The England of 1865 was full of snow.

The cold rushed at her; she shivered.

And coming towards them through the falling snow were figures.

'What did I tell you?' came Bullwitt's croak. 'Bluebeards. Bloody Blubeards!'

Three

'Stop the bus! Lee, stop!' Sam shouted the words as soon as he noticed something about the battle had changed.

Lee braked hard, bringing the bus to a sliding halt.

He killed the engine.

Instant silence.

No gunshots.

No sounds of battle.

Only a silence that seemed so devoid of anything it cast a ghostly spell over the landscape.

Sam leaned out through one of the glassless windows.

Snowflakes drifted down from the sky.

Here and there riderless horses stood, not knowing where to go next.

Bodies littered the snow. Everywhere there were either black smudges left by exploding shells and grenades, or pools of bloody red that stood glaring out from the white.

But there was no movement.

Casterton's surviving soldiers stood looking around, baffled.

'Dear Lord,' Thomas said in a hushed voice as he took off his glasses. 'Where have they all gone?'

'They've run for it,' shouted one of the soldiers. 'They've only gone and bloody run for it.'

'We've won!'

Rolle held up a hand. His piercing gaze swept the landscape.

'No,' he said. 'It's not over yet.'

Four

Nicole saw there were Bluebeards walking towards them.

That was, *moving* towards them. Those that could actually walk were either bent double or limping. Many, crawled on hands and knees.

'Something tells me they've taken a rather severe beating,' William observed.

'About bleeding time. If they've had a bloody good hiding it serves the bastards right. Go on, William.' Bullwitt gave a delighted chuckle. 'That one over there. Give him a good kicking while he's down.'

William glanced down at one of the Bluebeards. A huge man in a grey cloak with a clutch of starling chicks springing from his face was dragging himself along the ground. He left a red smear that ran across the snow and into the distance, as if he'd been dipped in red paint.

'What're you waiting for, William? Stick the boot into the ugly sod!'

William shook his head. 'There's been a battle fought here. And undoubtedly the Bluebeards have met formidable opponents.'

Nicole gazed down at the dying warrior as he struggled back in the direction of his home. 'But Rolle told us that Casterton was defenceless?'

'No doubt we will find out more presently,' William said softly. 'But in the meantime we should devote our attention to these poor souls from Casterton, and see them safely back home.'

Five

Sam shook his head, then said to Rolle, 'You're telling me that the Bluebeards aren't in retreat?'

'Retreat? No, far from it. They have only fallen back to regroup.'

'Damn. We were that close to stopping him.' Sam placed a forefinger and a twin-jointed 'thumb' together as if about to pluck an invisible flower stem from out of the air in front of his face. 'That close. We'd nearly finished the Bluebeards for good.'

'What a pity,' Carswell said drily. 'I was rather beginning to enjoy this. So, what are your orders now, Sam, old boy?'

'We don't quit. We hunt them down. Every last one of the sons of bitches.' He called across to Jud who was pulling arrow shafts out of the flanks of the bus. 'Jud . . . Jud! Get all the foot soldiers and cavalry together . . . tell them to follow the bus.'

'Oh, goodie.' Carswell snapped a fresh clip of ammo into his automatic. 'The fun isn't over yet.'

'Right,' Sam called out to the people on the bus. 'Reload the guns.'

Zita shook Sam by the arm. 'I think we're going to need them sooner than we thought. Look what's coming this way.'

Sam looked along the pass. A straggling line of people approached through the falling snow. 'Damn,' Sam hissed under his breath. 'OK, everyone. More Bluebeards are coming this way. We're going have to deal with those before we go after the others.'

Rolle looked too. 'Not more enemy.' He turned back to Sam and smiled. 'These are our allies.'

'Our allies?' Sam looked again. Approaching the bus were what appeared to be two or three hundred men and women. Some of the women he recognized as having been taken from Casterton on the night of the raid. Others were strange-looking figures. One he immediately recognized: the creature that was part cow, part boy. It moved quickly across the snow, the thick bovine legs eating the distance easily. The boy carried a bow with the arrow notched lightly against the string, ready to shoot the moment he needed it.

'These are our reinforcements, Sam Baker.'

'Dear God,' Thomas breathed in astonishment as he saw what kind of people were approaching. He couldn't take his eyes from the man with the mass of bees squirming on his face. A blond haired man held up a hand to halt his people. Meanwhile a pair of bulging brown eyes peered from a slot in his jacket. 'My dear God,' Thomas whispered. 'Who are these people? Where are they from?'

Sam smiled grimly. 'I think we should consider them as heaven-sent and leave it at that, don't you?'

Introductions, and reunions when Nicole and Sue came on board, were, of necessity, brief. Half a dozen Liminals continued walking on towards town, accompanying the rescued women and children.

The rest of the Liminals, armed with swords, axes, spears and shotguns, would follow the bus, together with what were left of the cavalry and foot soldiers.

'Is everyone ready?' Sam shouted from the front of the bus.

This time he was greeted by a cheer. Everyone there had got the bit between their teeth. They wanted to finish the job.

Six

It didn't take long to find the Bluebeards. Rolle had stood beside the timber box where Lee sat at the steering wheel. Like a maritime pilot he pointed ahead, talking to Lee constantly.

The bus lurched across the snow-covered meadow.

Hanging on tightly to the king post Sam watched as hundreds of figures emerged through the mist of the falling snowflakes.

Already the Bluebeards had regrouped and were ready to fight once more.

He thought: *If it's a fight the barbarians want, then they've got it. They're going to get themselves the mother and father of all battles.*

The bus must have appeared as a great roaring dragon to them.

One that spat fire.

The artillery thundered from the sides of the bus, tearing the barbarians apart.

Soldiers fired their rifles. More barbarians fell dead.

Meanwhile, the surviving Bluebeards charged the bus.

They ran straight into a blizzard of bullets and grenades.

Dozens fell, kicking and screaming, clutching their stomachs, chests, faces.

Now there was pandemonium.

Even though there must still have been two thousand or more of the barbarian warriors they'd had enough. Turning their backs on the advancing soldiers who followed the bus, they scattered back along the pass and into the woods.

Rolle shouted, 'Don't let them use the time-gates here. Drive them into the gorge further along the pass.'

Sam leaned through the window and shouted to the soldiers to follow the retreating Bluebeards.

Rolle hung onto the king post and called to Sam. 'Have the bus cut them off from going back through the pass.

You've got to make sure you drive them up into the gorge. There's no way out of there.'

No way out? Sam licked his dry lips.

Was Rolle, the Christian mystic, suggesting that they trap the two thousand Bluebeards in the gorge, then kill them one by one?

Sam watched, feeling cold inside now, as the soldiers from Casterton barracks, helped by the Liminals, sealed the trap.

In less than an hour a cavalry officer rode up alongside the bus as it stood in the mouth of the gorge. 'We have them locked up in there, sir. There's no way out unless they grow wings and fly up the cliff faces. What are your orders now?'

Sam paused, thinking hard. The gorge held the two thousand or so men, that was true. But it was perhaps half a mile long by almost a quarter wide. Deeper into the gorge the trees grew densely in the spaces between the walls of sheer rock. If he sent the soldiers in there the Bluebeards would still cut them to pieces.

If anything, they'd reached a Mexican stand-off. Going into the gorge and massacring the Bluebeards would be nigh impossible, irrespective of the morality of butchering the trapped enemy.

The mouth of the gorge was narrow, and largely open ground, so the Bluebeards would have a hard time of it, trying to break out.

Sam rubbed his jaw. This was a stalemate. They couldn't kill the Bluebeards without losing most of their own people. And, for sure, they couldn't stand here at the mouth of the gorge forever, holding the Bluebeards prisoner in there.

He told the cavalry officer to wait. Then he found Rolle.

'What now?' Sam asked. 'We can't just sit here and keep the prisoners in the gorge forever.'

'No, I had no intention of doing that,' Rolle replied. 'There is a time-gate there, just a little way inside the gorge.'

'But do the Bluebeards know that?'

'They do,' Rolle nodded.

'Then why aren't they disappearing through it like rats into a hole?'

'Because it leads further back than they've ever gone before. Also it is the only entrance – and the only exit – to that particular time.'

'You mean, they're afraid that if they go there they'll never be able to come back?'

'Yes. And that's what I intend.'

'But how do we get them to leave the woodland and go through the time-gate?'

'There's the knot of the problem.' Rolle scratched his beard. 'How do we do just that?'

Sam looked back at the soldiers standing in a line across the mouth of the gorge with their rifles ready. They looked as if they could hold the Bluebeards there for an hour or so. But soon the barbarians would probably recover their senses, and their strength, and rush the line. If they broke through it they'd scatter into the woods upstream. It would be only a matter of time before they regrouped, rearmed, then raided Casterton again.

Sam realized he must nip this in the bud once and for all. He looked back at Rolle. 'Can you stay here and make sure the soldiers hold the Bluebeards until I get back?'

'Where are you going?'

'There's something I need from the amphitheatre.'

Seven

That 'something' was the twenty or so barrels of wood alcohol.

Before taking the coach back to the amphitheatre Sam had the cannon unceremoniously dumped over the side of the bus and into the snow. They'd done their work well enough, but they'd be dead weight when it came to the bus making its last short journey.

'OK, what's the plan, Sam?' Lee called as he drove the bus back to the amphitheatre.

'After loading all these barrels of what to all intents and purposes is Victorian napalm? I reckon you can guess for yourself.'

'That's what I was afraid you were thinking.'

'Don't worry, Lee, I'll drive the bus for this one.'

'We're talking crash-and-burn here, aren't we?'

'Got it in one, Lee. Got it in one.'

Eight

Carswell laughed with disbelief when he heard Sam's plan.

The bus stood facing the entrance of the gorge where the remaining Bluebeard forces had taken refuge. On the bus Carswell, Zita, Lee, Jud and Sam were holding a council of war.

Every so often Sam would glance out at the line of soldiers and Liminals who stood at the entrance of the gorge, ready to try and prevent any breakout. Not that their chances would be over-favourable now. They were running low on ammunition. Many of the soldiers were wounded; all were exhausted. As Zita observed, this was the Last Chance Saloon. A flurry of snowflakes dimmed the line. If it fell any heavier visibility would be reduced to virtually nil.

Meanwhile, Carswell was still making the most of his dry humourless laugh.

'Mr Baker, you mean to say,' he said, 'that you intend getting onto that bus and driving it alone into the narrowest part of the pass, where you will then set it alight?'

'I am, Carswell.'

'What then?'

'Then either the Bluebeards roast in there or they make use of what, after all, is a temporal fire exit back into the dim and distant past.'

'No, Mr Baker. I mean what do *you* do then?'

'I run back here as fast as these two legs can carry me.'

'Your optimism is astonishing. From where I'm standing your plan is nothing less than a suicide mission.'

'It's a chance I'm going to have to take.'

'Oh, I see . . . playing the little people's champion again, are we?'

'Carswell—'

'If you're not killed by the fire, those barbarians are going to rip you limb from limb.'

Sam acknowledged the statement with a grim shrug. 'You're welcome to ride shotgun with me, Carswell.'

'Ah, no. I'm going to decline. I think I've done more than enough for the little people. It's time for me to leave now and enjoy the fruits of my labours.'

Lee said, 'Sam, I'll drive.'

'No, Lee. This is my idea. If anyone's going to stick their neck out it's—'

'No, Sam. I know how to handle the bus. You don't. You've got to let me drive.'

Sam considered for a moment. 'OK. Thanks, Lee. I appreciate it . . . wait, Lee.'

Lee had opened the door way to the timbered driver's compartment.

'You're not going alone,' Sam told him. 'Those devils will probably rush the bus the moment you enter the gorge. I'll ride up front with a couple of rifles.

'Those will be pretty cumbersome,' Carswell said. 'You'd best take these.' He handed Sam a pair of automatics, then gave one of his characteristic dry smiles. 'Happy Christmas, Sam.'

'They're loaded?'

'They are. Eight rounds apiece. Also I've used Glazier Safety Slugs. Basically they explode inside the target's body. One slug can bring down a charging bull.'

'Thanks, Carswell, I appreciate . . . wait. Where are you going?'

'Oh, Mr Baker, I've been here more than long enough and now I have some more fish to fry. Good luck and goodbye.'

With that he climbed down from the bus, pulled his collar up against the falling snow and walked steadily away in the direction of Casterton.

Jud sighed. 'It was too much to expect him to await the outcome of this, I expect.'

'We don't need him any more,' Sam said briskly. 'Right, let's finish this once and for all. Jud, what're you doing?'

'You'll need someone to chuck a grenade or two.'

'Maybe, but not you, Jud.'

'But—'

'But nothing. When that bus starts to burn we're going to have to run like hell. How are you going to run with that injured leg?'

'But you still need more people to ride shotgun. Those Bluebeards are going to be swarming aboard like rats the first chance they get.'

'He's right.' The voice came from behind Sam and he turned.

'Ryan?'

Ryan Keith stood with his double-barrelled shotgun over one arm. 'I want to help.'

Sam looked Ryan up and down. All signs of the chubby kid who had played the Oliver Hardy role were long gone now. He looked calm, cool, collected.

Sam gave a nod. 'Lee drives. Ryan and I are going to repel boarders. OK, let's do it.'

Nine

Zita and Thomas Hather also offered to ride along. Sam firmly refused their offers.

Deep down he knew why. Carswell was probably right, damn him. This might well turn out to be a suicide mission after all.

Sam intended taking the bus that, to all intents and purposes, was now nothing more than a huge firebomb on wheels into the narrowest part of the gorge.

Somehow they had to get clear of the thing as it began to burn, then run back to their own lines at the mouth of the gorge.

And that would be with some mightily pissed-off Bluebeards hard on their heels.

'Ryan, are you OK?'

Ryan nodded and took up his position at the right-hand side of the bus. He pulled the hammers back on the shotgun. Behind him, wedged the full length and width of the bus's deck, were the barrels of wood alcohol. Sprinkled liberally over those were fifty or so grenades.

Quite a nice little firework cocktail it all makes, Sam told himself as he pushed the automatics into his belt.

'See you in ten minutes,' he said to Zita, touching her cheek.

'Make it five, you big lummox.' She tried to force a smile, but only managed to make her lips twitch.

'God go with you, Sam,' Hather said and shook his hand.

Sam nodded. Behind him, Lee fired the bus's big diesel motor into life.

Quickly he climbed onto the bus and slapped the driver's timbered compartment twice. *Move it on out.*

The engine bellowed and they were moving forward through the line of soldiers, and then between the cliff walls of the gorge itself.

Sam was aware of Zita, Hather, Rolle, Jud and the rest watching them go. He didn't look back now.

Ahead the gorge was nothing more than a narrow channel cut by a million years of rainwater. Snow covered the ground.

Here there were only a few bushes and saplings. But deeper into the gorge he knew it became thickly wooded.

Sam had told Lee to drive as far as he could before the trees stopped the bus. In theory the Bluebeards would be penned there in front of him in the couple of hundred yards or so of gorge that remained.

What would happen then God alone knew.

'Take it nice and steady,' he shouted to Lee as the bus flattened saplings. 'I think we've got company.'

Ten

'Dear Lord, help them,' Thomas said under his breath.

'I'll second that,' Zita said. She put her arm round him. The man was trembling like a frightened child.

She watched as the bus disappeared into the swirling blizzard. Now all she could hear was the growl of the motor.

She stared into the snow, willing her vision to penetrate that wall of white. But she could see nothing.

Seconds later the sound of gunshots reached her.

Eleven

A dozen or so Bluebeards ran at the bus and began hurling rocks.

One glanced off Sam's shoulder as he hung onto the window frame.

Behind him he heard the deep thuds of Ryan's shotgun.

Two of the attackers fell back onto the snow.

Now Sam drew one of the automatics from his belt as a giant of a man armed with a spear ran in front of the bus.

Sam aimed. Fired.

The man dropped to his knees, clutching his stomach.

The bus rolled steadily forward. Sam heard the thump of flesh against metal. Then he felt a jolt as the front wheel of the bus passed over an object in the snow.

More Bluebeards appeared at the sides of the bus. He hoped this wasn't the main force, only a picket line protecting the rest deeper in the gorge.

If those two thousand or so did break out, he didn't give much for the chances of Zita, Jud and the rest back there.

'Step on the gas, Lee, old buddy,' he called. 'Let's kick these bastards' asses once and for all.'

Through one of the slots in the timbered driver's compartment, Sam saw Lee nod. The engine roared and the bus's tyres slipped in the snow.

But the weight of the vehicle kept the tyres biting.

The machine lurched. Vibrations ran from end to end.

It took a moment or so for Sam to gauge it was picking up speed.

But when he looked out of the windows he saw the saplings had started to blur.

Pushing the automatic back into his belt he shouted back to Ryan, 'Hang on tight. This is it!'

The bus must have been hitting the forty mark.

Snow sprayed up at either side. Bushes, saplings, men were smashed against the front of the bus.

The rock faces of the gorge began to close in.

Behind him the barrels of wood alcohol bounced. One broke free from the lines, rolled forward and crashed against the timber sides of the driver's compartment. Instantly it cracked open to flood the floor of the bus. Sam's nostrils tingled and his eyes watered at the intense aroma of the stuff. It smelled pungent, lethal.

Hell, Sam thought, *one spark and this bus becomes a shooting star*.

He looked ahead. That was when he gritted his teeth. Just yards ahead was a line of mature oaks.

'Lee! Hit the brakes!'

Lee braked.

But on that snow no way was the bus going to stop in a hurry.

Without losing speed it slid on, throwing up gouts of snow like whale plumes.

The line of trees seemed to hurtle towards them, as if eager to meet the charging steel and rubber of the bus.

Sam heard the crash. Then he was flying.

Twelve

After she heard the gunshots Zita froze. They only lasted for a moment, then stopped.

For a second she thought all had gone silent. She stared into the falling snow in the direction of the gorge.

Then she heard the sound of the bus's motor. It grew louder and then abruptly stopped.

Before she even knew it, Thomas had grabbed her arm in his two hands.

'Don't go in there,' he told her. 'We must wait.'

'We can't just stand here.'

'Yes, we must and we will. They're in God's hands now.'

Every fibre of Zita's body strained to carry her into the gorge to find out what had happened. Her gut instincts told her something had gone badly wrong.

Thirteen

It came from far, far away. A distant calling. The sound was indistinct. It seemed to shimmer. But there was something about it. Something important.

For a while Sam Baker didn't know what it was.

He opened his eyes.

'Sam . . . Sam . . . *Sam?*'

Floating above him was the man in the moon. A big round disc with dark smudgy eyes and down-turned mouth.

'Sam? Can you hear me?'

The man in the moon's voice was muffled.

Then it did a peculiar thing. The face turned away. A moment later came a loud bang.

The face turned back to Sam, the smudgy eyes looking down into his. 'Sam . . . *Sam!*' More explosions.

'Sam, snap out of it! They're going to kill us!'

Sam did his best to speak. Only his mouth didn't work. What was more, he felt like a broken doll lying there.

His shoulder throbbed. His ribs radiated pure agony every time he breathed. He was sure his arm was broken at the elbow. And from the exciting new way his tongue could roam about the inside his mouth he figured that most of his teeth were smashed, too.

'Sam . . .'

He hoisted himself up painfully onto one elbow.

SIMON CLARK

The moment he looked round, his mind snapped into focus. They were in deep, deep shit. Lee and Ryan were firing their rifles at the Bluebeards who were coming at them through the woodland, whooping like Red Indians.

He turned his head. A flash of pain cracked up through his neck and into his head where it seemed to bounce around the inside of his skull for a while – clearly in no hurry to leave.

He took a deep breath, blinked.

Twenty paces from him was the tour bus.

Carswell's *Thunder Child* had made its last valiant charge.

It lay on its side. The barrels of wood alcohol lay all around it in a tumbled heap. Some had shattered; pools of violet liquid lay in the snow.

Sam sneezed. To his astonishment a crimson spray filled the air.

He touched his nose. It had a flattened, rounded feel to it, like a mushroom.

'Sam!' Lee shouted. 'We'd appreciate a hand if you're up to it.'

Lee fired a rifle at one of the attackers who ran from the trees, an axe gripped in his two hands.

The man's face disappeared in a splash of crimson.

Sam felt at least half the bones in his body were broken. His teeth were gone. One eye was nearly closed.

He must have been thrown clean out of the bus when it hit one of the trees.

Nevertheless, he heaved himself to his knees, then from his knees to his feet.

Pains shot from head to toe.

Only one arm worked; the other hung limply, terminating in a bloody cluster of fingers.

With his single functioning hand he pulled a handgun from his pocket and blasted a pair of Bluebeards. Carswell was right about the killing power of the ammunition. The two went down in midstride.

'Thank God you're back with us,' Lee shouted. 'They're swarming out of the woods like ants!'

'Lee . . . you've got to . . . set fire to the bus.' Sam had to work the words through his broken mouth. 'We'll hold them back here.' He nodded at Ryan who'd just decapitated another axeman with a single shotgun blast.

'OK, then I'll come back here and help.'

'No, you won't, Lee. Once it's burning get out of here.'

The smell of neat wood alcohol filled the gorge. Although it was evaporating slowly, the rock faces were containing the vapour as if it were a liquid. If anything, the cold air brought by the snowfall pressed it down from above, too.

A Bluebeard ran from the trees at Sam.

Sam dropped him with a single shot in the stomach.

He glanced back to see Lee light the fuse of a grenade, then toss the miniature bomb into the bus.

Lee clearly hoped he would have chance to escape the blast before the grenade exploded.

But the burning fuse was enough by itself to ignite those hundreds of gallons of spilt alcohol.

That didn't so much burn as explode.

One moment the world was white with snow.

The next it was a shimmering blue.

A fireball ripped from the bus.

And it did not stop.

It just kept on coming. Like a moving wall of flame.

Sam glimpsed Lee running out of the fireball, his hair on fire.

'Run!' Sam yelled to Ryan.

Instinct kicked in.

Sam turned and ran away from the bus, deeper into the gorge.

He didn't feel the pain any more.

He flung himself under the cover of the trees. Ahead of him he saw the Bluebeards running too. They were throwing away their swords, spears, axes.

Sam looked back. That wall of flame wasn't stopping.

It advanced remorselessly through the undergrowth, popping, snapping, firing out sparks like machine-gun bullets.

Sam's smashed ribs barely allowed him to breathe; even so, he ran faster.

Now he heard the explosions of detonating grenades.

He jumped over a stream.

A rainbow sheen on the water told him that more wood alcohol floated there.

A second later the blue flames rushed along that, too.

Now it seemed as if the whole wood was ablaze.

A man ran towards him. Sam didn't notice the face, only the wickedly curving knife. Sam fired point-blank into the chest. The man went down like a sack of potatoes, eyes bulging.

Just for a moment he glimpsed Ryan Keith. He was using the shotgun as a club and was trading blows with a massive man in an iron helmet.

Ryan's forehead had been split open by a sword blow. Blood streamed down his face, but still his two eyes blazed like twin silver balls. Sheer rage drove him on.

Sam turned, intending to help. But with another tremendous roar like thunder, a wall of fire ran between him and Ryan, obliterating the two men as they fought.

Now the flames seemed to be all around him. The heat was so intense that snow melted in seconds to reveal black earth. Sap bubbled from tree trunks. Then they, too, flashed into flame until the wood became a mass of pillars of fire.

He backtracked until the heat grew too intense, then he cut along a different path. Fires raged on either side. The blood that soaked his shoulder began to steam. His skin smarted; his eyes watered. Sparks landed on his clothes and hair.

Brushing them off with his one good hand, he ran again towards the mouth of the gorge.

Ahead was a mound about as high as his shoulder. He ran up it in order to get a better idea of the lie of the land.

From there he saw he was surrounded by a sea of fire.

He screwed his eyes against the incandescent flare. With difficulty, he could just see over the burning scrub to where the mouth of the gorge lay, perhaps a hundred paces away.

The heat had driven Casterton's defenders back but they were still holding a steady line, preventing the Bluebeards' escape.

And now Sam could see the Bluebeards. Rather than burn in the gorge or be gunned down by the soldiers they were running into the time-gate.

For a moment Sam watched them being funnelled from this world of 1865 back to God knew when.

So it really was over. The last of the surviving Bluebeards ran with their hands over their burning hair into the gate.

Sam held up a hand to protect his own face from the stinging heat as the flames crept closer to him.

In theory, once the fires had died down the Bluebeards would be able to return, but he knew that somehow Rolle would seal the gate shut for ever. Maybe the soldiers could . . .

But, no. That didn't matter now. That was a problem for someone else to solve.

Now the flames were like a rising tide that encircled the mound. His cool island in a burning sea.

Sam realized he could stay put and slowly roast.

Or he could make one last dash through the burning bushes to the mouth of the gorge.

You never know, he told himself, *I might make it. The miracles have been coming thick and fast today.*

Strangely, he felt a grin come to his face as he took a deep breath.

So this was it. All the roads of his lifetime converged on this single moment. Maybe this was why he'd survived that lightning strike after all.

He pushed his face into the crook of his raised arm.

And ran.

The flames enveloped him. He'd entered a world full of light . . .

There was no pain.

Epilogue: Time and tide . . .

Sam Baker opened his eyes to find himself in the amphitheatre.

Sitting beside him on the wooden bench was Zita, dressed once more in tiger-skin leggings.

At the other side of him Sue and Lee were back in their old Stan Laurel and Dracula costumes. Lee ran his fingers through his hair as if unable to bring himself to believe that not only was it still there, it wasn't blazing like a Roman candle.

Nicole had vanished. Sam knew she was with the Liminals now and off the time-travel trail. Ryan Keith was gone, too. The last Sam had seen of him he'd been slugging it out with a big guy in an iron helmet. Clearly he hadn't made it.

For a moment or two, the accidental time travellers sat dazed after the sudden time-jump.

Below them, at the bottom of the amphitheatre, Jud Campbell slipped the pin into his shirt collar, while his gold waistcoat looked as pristine as the first time Sam had set eyes on it.

Meanwhile, Sam was still a good few seconds away from actually being able to frame the question: *which year is this now?*

For the time being he was content to run his tongue over his restored complete set of teeth, and to feel that his bones were magically intact once more.

Despite the dizziness, he realized *it* had gone and done it all over again. Whatever process had hauled them back through the years had also restored perfectly the bodies and possessions of those who'd been alive before the time-jump.

Although their numbers were dwindling. He saw that there were perhaps only a dozen or so left out of the original fifty-two who had made the first time-leap that sunny afternoon in 1999.

After a while, he felt Zita's hand on his forearm. She gave a small smile. Without a word she stood up, walked to the steps, then climbed to the top of the amphitheatre.

Sam followed. That woolly dreamlike sensation was leaving him now.

As his mind gradually focused itself he began to notice the changes. Big changes.

At the top of the steps he stood and looked around him.

Of course the car park appeared as it always had done: bathed in clear sunlight, the bus and the cars and the ice-cream van looked pristine. There was the visitors' centre, and the church just inside the boundary.

Zita stood there, gazing at the new landscape. 'Well, Sam,' she said. 'I guess this is the big one.'

Sam looked back at the river. It flowed along a different channel now. Jud's narrow boat and Carswell's launch floated on the still waters of a crescent-shaped pond, which was all that remained of the twentieth-century river.

A moment later Jud came up the steps to join them. 'I've just seen Carswell and he's mad as hell. I think Rolle's advice to him about travelling in time hasn't worked as well as he hoped. Clearly Rolle pulled a fast one, to stop Carswell playing havoc with . . .' Jud's voice faded mid-sentence. He stood with his hands on his hips and surveyed the landscape in astonishment. 'Good God . . . whatever year this is I think we've gone way, *way* back.'

'Or forward,' Sam said.

'But look at the hills. They're a different shape now. Instead of oak and chestnut they're covered in pine. And can't you just feel the difference in the air? The climate's changed.' Jud smiled. 'You know, if I didn't know any better I'd say we're going to end up being our own ancestors.'

Despite everything, Sam felt inwardly calm.

'So you say we've gone back into the past, Jud?'

'I do.'

'What about you, Zita? What do you say?'

'I'd have said the same. Until I noticed that building across there.'

Sam followed her gaze. On a hill in the distance stood a large white building. From here it was impossible to say whether it was a Roman villa built of limestone or something that belonged to a future where buildings were extruded from some fabulous synthetic material. All he could tell for sure was that it gleamed a pure white in the sun. And that there was something tantalizing about it that seemed to invite closer inspection.

Jud spoke softly. 'What do *you* say, Sam? Past or future?'

'There's only one way to find out.' He nodded at the car. 'I think it's time we took a little drive. But first I could do with a drink.'

He crossed the car park in the direction of the vending machine that stood by the visitors' centre, its contents miraculously replenished once more.

Only when that devil of a thirst was well and truly quenched would he go out and find what this new destination had to offer.

Besides, there's no rush, he told himself with a wry smile. *After all, don't we have all the time in the world?*

THE END

SIMON CLARK

VAMPYRRHIC

Not far from the coastal town of Whitby, nestling in the purple hills of the North Yorkshire Moors, is Leppington. Quiet. Unassuming. A forgotten backwater.

Yet beneath Leppington's streets terrifying creatures stir. Driven by an ancient passion that has become an obsession. United in their burning hunger. They share an unending craving. They are *Nosferatu*. And they have the power to drain your will to resist. To drain it so utterly that you will cheerfully, gladly, eagerly surrender yourself to their sharp, brutal teeth.

IN LEPPINGTON DEATH ISN'T ALWAYS FOREVER.

'One of the best contemporary British horror writers'
            DEATHREALM

'Horror fiction as it should be written . . . Absolutely bare-bollocked terrifying'
            SFX on King Blood

HODDER AND STOUGHTON PAPERBACKS